THE TALISMAN OF

UNIFICATION

Sam,

Enjoy Harrison's continuing adventure.

THE TALISMAN OF UNIFICATION

¤

The Overlords

A Novel

J. Michael Squatrito, Jr.

The Talisman of Unification
The Overlords

The Overlords books may be ordered through Internet booksellers or by contacting:

J. Michael Squatrito, Jr.
www.the-overlords.com

Because of the dynamic nature of the Internet, any Web addresses or links contained in this book may have changed since publication and may no longer be valid. This is a work of fiction. All of the characters, names, incidents, organizations, and dialogue in this novel are either the products of the author's imagination or are used fictitiously.

Edited by Laura Vadney
Cover design by Colby Cook

ISBN: 978-1480118270 (pbk)
Printed in the United States of America

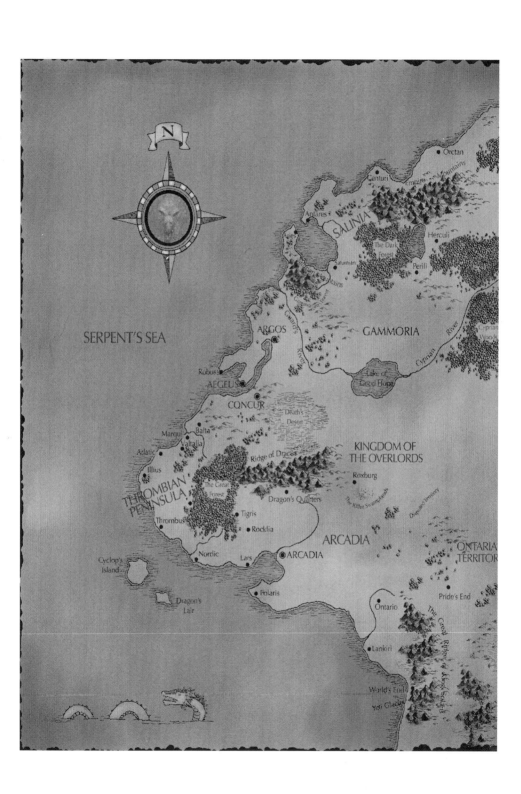

Prologue

The morning brought another cool, misty day to the island of Dragon's Lair. The isle itself consisted of myriads of rocky hills, with only a few open pastures. Many times throughout the centuries, mercenaries had brought caravans of treasure to one of the countless small ports along the shore. From these docks, soldiers would cart the riches up one of the interconnecting paths leading to the entrance of King Holleris's castle. They would then bring the caches to their leader himself so that he could display them in one of his glorious showcases. Today, however, the king was about to send forth his men to gather the treasure he had sought for an eternity.

From the balcony off his royal bedroom, King Holleris sensed the removal of the sacred book from its resting place. Looking at the mainland on the cloudy horizon, he exclaimed, "After all these years of waiting, I can finally put my plan into action!

"They thought they could banish me — the fools. Allowing me to stay immortal as long as I remained on the isle of Dragon's Lair has turned out to be their final mistake. They have underestimated the power of greed. As soon as my men post the ransom for the book, it will quickly be in my possession. And after it is destroyed, my fellow lords can never return!"

Though banished from the mainland for almost a thousand years, King Holleris maintained the appearance of a man just past middle age. Wearing black clothes as a constant reminder of his exile, he vowed never to sport any colors that symbolized his royalty until the completion of his plan. Only his hatred toward his old adversaries had kept him from going insane.

The king raced through his bedroom and dashed into the corridor. "Troy!" he bellowed, making a swift approach to the spiral staircase that led down to the entrance of the castle. He cried out again for his general-at-arms.

"Troy! Our time has come at last!"

A soldier dressed in full chain-mail armor appeared at the stairwell and gazed up in concern. "What is it, my king? Are you all right?" The man then began to climb the stairs in haste.

Though young, General Troy Harkin was a very seasoned fighter. Many an enemy had perished due to the inflictions he made with his long sword, and his talents had become well known throughout the mainland. On more than one occasion, he had set out for his king's desired treasure and returned with more than expected.

Troy had remained loyal to King Holleris his entire life and his mentor had given him all the necessary tools to prepare for his life's journey. His ascent up the staircase ceased when he stood by his leader's side.

In obvious concern, he asked, "What is the matter, my lord?"

"I am fine." The king motioned to Troy, indicating that he was not in any immediate danger, before staring into his general's blue eyes.

"Many generations of Harkin men have prepared for this battle, only to grow old and die without seeing the true enemy. You are the chosen son of your family, for it is during your lifetime that someone has taken the book. Follow me."

King Holleris then began to lead Troy back down the staircase. Across from the base of the stairs loomed a set of double doors that led to an adjacent room. Troy had seen this chamber before and a sense of awe overcame him every time he entered.

"All those journeys to the mainland you made," continued the king, as he approached the doorway, "all the riches you brought back to me, mean nothing compared to the treasure you will return with." The king pulled open the large, wooden doors revealing a showcase of wealth.

Troy panned the chamber, taking in all of the riches. On the wall to his left rested the best weapons ever forged by the Salinian Dwarves, a race now extinct. Seven battle-axes comprised the set of arms, and a different ancestor of the Harkin family had collected each one. Renowned for being the best engineers by far, the diminutive weaponsmiths took years to finish every axe. Placed in the hilt of each weapon nestled a different jewel, one for each god of their beliefs.

Taking his gaze downward, Troy looked upon a decorated carpet with ornate markings. Wizards had flown the magical item over 500 years ago, in order to track down the last of the knights who comprised the Legion of Knighthood.

Behind the enchanted rug sat the sturdy, hand carved wooden table that the knights had used for their emergency meetings, which Troy himself helped heist from Roxburg.

Looking to his right, behind a golden glass case hung various pieces of chain-mail body armor. Mages throughout the land had enhanced all of the body protection with magic. Only on rare occasions did the king allow his wearing this type of covering, but Troy had a feeling that he would be using some pieces today.

King Holleris motioned for Troy to sit. "I want you to go to the mainland and offer 10,000 gold pieces in exchange for the book." The king started to pace in front of his soldier.

"I don't care what you do to get the scripture; all I ask is one thing." The king stopped and locked his gaze on Troy. "Bring the lucky souls to me." King Holleris began pacing again. "The beings that possess the book now must be capable warriors. They could prove to be useful to me someday."

Troy crinkled his brow in puzzlement. "But sir, how will I know what the book looks like?"

The king scowled. "I don't know what inscriptions it contains, nor do I know how to use the book, but I do know the skin of a red dragon binds the scripture. If you scrape the cover, it will bleed."

Concern swirled inside the young general's head, unsure at how to begin his new quest. "And where should I start to look for this book?"

"Take your ship to Polaris, the closest port on the mainland from this island. Create signs with a description of the manuscript and the ransom I mentioned to you, then post them from town to town. Make yourself readily available." The king stopped pacing, placed his hands on the table, leaned forward, and met Troy's gaze. "You are the *only* one I want handling the scripture and I want you to return it to me personally."

King Holleris paused before gawking at his stolen collection of riches. "Look around you, Troy, at all these treasures — the rare weapons, armor, artifacts, sculptures. This is but one room."

Turning to his pupil, he continued, "You know of all the gold, precious gems, and jewelry that I have throughout this castle. If I cannot go to my kingdom," the king pounded his fist on the table, "my kingdom shall come to me!

"That is why I sent your father, and his father, and his father before that to the mainland to gather treasures. For a thousand years I have retrieved what is rightfully mine!"

The king paused, then stood tall, interlocking his hands behind his back. "Now, as for you, gather your best soldiers and tell them to prepare for their journey. Tell them I will pay ten times their usual allowance. I want you ready by the morning. Now go!"

"Yes, sir!" said Troy, rising from his seat. Rounding the table, he walked by the king, but before he reached the entranceway, the general-at-arms stopped and spun around.

"I am honored to be the one from my family to bring you your ultimate treasure. I will not let you down, my king." With that, he turned away from King Holleris and departed from the room.

After Troy left, King Holleris remained standing in the middle of his showcase gallery. A wry smile stretched across his face, before he said aloud, "Ballesteros, your time is all but over."

CHAPTER 1

◻

"I'm moving as fast as I can!" yelled Harrison at Swinkle.

The young warrior slashed through the thick underbrush as his frustrations started to get the better of him. Murdock and Pondle had ventured off somewhere in front of them, but neither man could see their friends.

Exasperated, Harrison asked, "Swinkle, have you seen Lance?"

The young cleric stopped his trek for a moment to answer his friend. "No, but I can hear his footsteps to my left," he said, in reference to the little dog.

"This is ridiculous," muttered Harrison under his breath.

The men had wandered lost in the wilderness for the past three days, ever since they secured the Treasure of the Land. To their surprise, after getting the ancient Four King's hoard of treasure in their possession, a magical staircase led them into the middle of a forest. Nobody in the group had any idea where in the countryside the stairwell had deposited them. Furthermore, the task of hiding their newfound riches every time they needed to investigate the landscape proved more tiresome than anyone could have expected. Harrison knew Murdock and Pondle possessed excellent tracking skills, but he could not believe their current predicament.

Suddenly, Lance popped out from behind a bush and appeared in front of Harrison. With a sigh and a smile, the young warrior said, "I'm glad to see you."

Harrison bent to one knee and scratched the dog behind his ears, using the time to rest his tired muscles in the process. He then wiped the sweat from his brow before standing up again.

Swinkle approached Harrison, his breathing heavy from trudging through the thickets. "Has it really been three days since we left the catacombs?"

"Believe it or not, yes." Harrison's brow quickly cringed in anger. "How many times do I have to tell those two to slow down?"

Swinkle looked into the thick woodlands. There was no sign of Murdock or Pondle anywhere. "I'm sure they are fine."

"That's not the point." Harrison's demeanor displayed his disapproval. "They've done nothing but lead us around in circles for the past three days. There's no pattern to their tracking and they don't tell us what they're planning. I'm getting tired of this!"

Swinkle tried to calm his friend. "Harrison, in the past week we have lost two dear friends. Murdock and Pondle are doing what they do best, trying to find a way out of this place."

Harrison attempted to control his anger. "I understand that, Swinkle, but this isn't going the way I would've liked. We have in our possession an incredible treasure that has become very difficult to hide. Instead of heading back to our hometown of Aegeus, we're lost. We've made no progress since leaving those catacombs."

"I'm just as frustrated as you." The young cleric sighed. "You'll see. We'll be on the right path soon enough."

"I hope so." Just then, a familiar face emerged from the forest.

"There's nothing out there," said Pondle in exasperation, returning from his search. "No trace of any activity, only woods." The thief then looked around in concern. "Where's Murdock?"

"We thought he was with you," answered Harrison, the worry in his voice rising.

"Here we go again." Pondle readied his short sword. "He went in that direction." The thief pointed to the right of Harrison and Swinkle.

"Swinkle, try to keep up." Harrison and Lance ventured into the surrounding woods after Pondle, with the young cleric following close behind.

Murdock momentarily halted his search for a way out of the thickets. After heading deeper into the brush, he found that the woods thinned out and led to a small, enclosed meadow. The clearing appeared no more than a hundred yards long, but contained a valuable prize.

The ranger readied his longbow. "Ahhh! Dinner!" Murdock pulled the string back with an expert touch, then fired a fatal arrow into the side of an unsuspecting sheep.

With a blat, the sheep fell to the ground, causing all the other animals in the herd to run away in a panic. An anxious head turned toward the pasture, noticing the sudden activity.

Murdock walked up to the sheep and hoisted it onto his shoulders. "We'll be eating good tonight," he said to himself as he reentered the woods.

Trekking back in the direction of his party, he ran into Harrison, who did not hold back his look of anger.

Harrison pointed to the animal that lay across Murdock's shoulders. "You were supposed to be securing the area, not collecting dinner!"

"Look, nothing's around here," answered the ranger as he walked past the young warrior. "I didn't see anything unusual."

Harrison followed his friend. "Don't you think unattended sheep are a little bit unusual?" Just then, Pondle, Swinkle, and Lance emerged from the underbrush.

Murdock dropped the carcass onto the ground after seeing the rest of his friends. "Pondle, a fire would be nice right about now, don't you think?"

Before the thief could answer, the sounds of heavy footsteps more than startled the bunch. For coming through the trees appeared the keeper of the fallen animal.

Harrison's eyes opened wide in shock. "By the gods! A cyclops!" The young warrior quickly went for his battle-axe, while Lance began to bark with a feverish pitch at the unwanted intruder.

"You will pay dearly for stealing from my sacred herd!" the cyclops bellowed.

The beast's shadow covered Harrison's entire body. Advancing on the young warrior, the creature swung its sickle-like weapon in Harrison's direction with all its might.

"We didn't know the animal belonged to you!" The young warrior ducked to avoid the cyclops's fatal blow. "We'll pay you for your trouble!"

The creature was in no mood to bargain. "The cost shall be your lives!" The beast then hit Harrison with the butt of his weapon, knocking him over.

"So be it!" Harrison said to himself, as he quickly rolled out of the way of another blow.

With Harrison battling the cyclops, Murdock scurried to position himself away from the two combatants. From where he stood, he now had a clear avenue in which to fire an arrow. In one swift motion, he released the tension from his bow, allowing the projectile to hurtle toward the monster. As luck would have it, the beast swung at Harrison again, maneuvering just enough out of the way to cause the arrow to whiz by harmlessly into the woods.

"Damn!" Murdock loaded his longbow with another arrow. "I won't miss again."

Meanwhile, Pondle took the opportunity to stealthily maneuver through the underbrush. "If Lance can distract the beast with his barking, I should be able to do what I need to do," he mumbled, as he set himself in a perfect attack position behind the cyclops.

"The creature's wearing only clothing and not armor. I just hope I'm strong enough."

The cyclops stared down Harrison. "You shall be the first to die, human!" The beast then slashed the young warrior with its blade, cutting him above his bicep. Harrison fell to the ground bleeding, but managed to get to one knee.

The young warrior began to worry. "Where is everybody?" Glancing around in a controlled panic, Lance alone remained in the immediate area, and his barking only added to the ensuing confusion. The cyclops swung again, but Harrison blocked its blow with his battle-axe.

Glaring with its single eye, the beast bellowed, "I shall have revenge for my sheep!"

Holding its weapon with both hands, the creature raised it overhead one more time. Harrison looked up and saw an arrow penetrate the upper arm of the creature.

"Arrrrghhh!" groaned the beast, as it buckled to its knees.

Harrison took the opportunity to scurry away from the cyclops. Why was the one-eyed giant in that much pain from one arrow, the young warrior wondered while regaining his composure.

Harrison raised his battle-axe in a strike position, only to see Pondle jump on the cyclops's back. With chilling precision, the thief inflicted a fatal slice to the beast's neck, severing its jugular vein, blood squirting everywhere. The cyclops clutched its throat before crashing to the ground. A large gash ran down its back, ending with another of Pondle's daggers. With a final gasp, the beast lay dead.

"A creature like this has very poor peripheral vision." Pondle removed the daggers from the fresh corpse. "A backstab seemed to be the best method of defeating it."

Murdock returned from his position in the woods. "Good work, Pondle."

"The toughest part was jumping high enough to get the dagger into his back." Pondle wiped the blood from his blade. "Once I managed that, I just hung on. Cutting his throat was the easy part."

The thief then noticed a tankard hanging off the cyclops's belt. He removed the flask and tied it to his own.

"Yeah, good job, Pondle." Harrison brushed the dirt off his clothes, then touched his open wound.

"Ouch! This cut is deeper than I thought." The young warrior panned the area. "Where's Swinkle?"

"I'm over here." The young cleric emerged from behind a large tree. "I saw everything. Give me a second to gather myself."

"As for you," barked Harrison at Murdock, "you really want to get us killed? Once again you're more worried about yourself than the rest of the group!"

Murdock gave Harrison a look of astonishment. "Listen, I investigated the area. I didn't see or hear any cyclops when I shot the sheep. As far as I'm concerned, I did my job."

"Did your job?" Harrison's anger began to elevate. "You should've come back and told us about the sheep, then we all could've checked the meadow. Who knows, maybe one of us would've thought that someone might've been shepherding the animal!"

"Maybe you just lost your hunger for battle." Murdock took a step towards Harrison. "Always wanting to think everything out, never wanting to take on a good fight." The two now stood face to face.

"How dare you say I lost my hunger for battle?" Harrison snarled, staring into Murdock's eyes. "Is not my battle-axe stained with the blood of Scynthians, while your quiver of arrows is all but full?"

"All right, that's enough, you two!" Pondle separated the fighters. "And people wonder why thieves like me choose to venture in solitude. This bickering is more than enough proof."

Pondle looked at Harrison. "Let Swinkle examine your arm. No matter the consequences of Murdock's actions, we do finally have something good to eat."

The thief then turned his attention to Murdock. "Why don't you help me start setting up camp? I think we'll be staying here for the night."

"That sounds like a good idea to me." Murdock kept his stare fixed on Harrison. Swinkle gently took hold of the young warrior's arm, pulling him in the opposite direction, causing the two fighters to part.

Harrison, peeking over his shoulder, watched Murdock walk away before turning his attention to the young cleric. "Sometimes I don't know about him," he mumbled.

"I'm going to pray over you. My works won't completely heal your wound, but you should be feeling much better come the morning."

"Your mission'll be successful as long as you don't pick up any bad habits from Murdock." Harrison kept his eye on the ranger while Swinkle placed his hands on his friend's injured arm. As he prayed, a light aura formed around the wound, almost closing the entire cut.

A moment later, the soft white glow ceased. "Like I said, you should feel better in the morning."

Harrison kept his voice low. "You don't think I was out of line with Murdock, do you?"

Swinkle glanced in the ranger's direction. "No, not exactly. Murdock does like to do things for himself, but he has never left us in the hands of an enemy. You might not think so now, but I feel he'd die fighting for us."

"Maybe so, but he takes too many chances." Harrison swung his battle-axe over his shoulder. "We might as well help them with the camp duties."

"That's a good idea." Swinkle and Lance then followed the young warrior to the campsite.

While Pondle built the fire, Murdock began setting up a campground for the party. When he finished that chore, he walked over to the dead body of the cyclops. Grabbing it by the legs, he started pulling the corpse towards the woods, then gave a look of disgust as a foul odor wafted over him.

"Not only are these creatures heavy, they never bathe!"

"I'll help you in a few minutes," Pondle said in Murdock's direction. "It's going to take some time to bury that thing."

"Bury?" Murdock gave his friend a quizzical look. "I'm not digging a grave for a creature that almost destroyed our party!" The ranger grinned, as he stopped dragging the body and proceeded toward the fire. "But I will have some of that ale you took from its belt."

Pondle raised an eyebrow. "Oh, you saw that." The thief pointed a finger at his friend. "First, get that corpse away from the camp. When you're done with that, you can help me quarter the sheep. I'll give you some ale after all of our chores are finished. Fair enough?"

Murdock shook his head, reluctantly obliging. "Just like a thief. Always making a deal that benefits himself."

A short time later, Harrison, Swinkle, and Lance entered the campsite. With the onset of twilight, the fire became the sole source of light in the area.

"Do you need any help?" Harrison placed his belongings on the ground.

"How's your arm?" Murdock did not bother to look up at Harrison; instead, he continued to quarter the sheep.

"My injury feels better since Swinkle looked at it." The young warrior sighed. "Look, I'm sorry if I got angry with you, but it has been a long three days. We've been through so much between the battles and lost men. I just need to rest."

"I understand. I'm just as upset about losing our friends as you." Murdock paused, recalling the loss of their leader Marcus Braxton and his fellow adventurers Jason Sands and Aidan Hunter on their way to finding the land's ultimate treasure.

"Maybe I took on that battle out of frustration."

"Let's just eat and get a good night's sleep." Harrison lay back against his backpack. "We'll set out in the morning again to try and get our bearings straight. How long until we eat?"

"As soon as the meat gets done cooking." Murdock finished quartering the sheep and began to roast it over the fire. "Oh, Pondle? I've carved up the animal. I think you owe me something." The ranger flashed his friend a wide grin.

"At last, I think I found a way to motivate you to help with our camp duties." Pondle tossed the leather tankard of ale to Murdock.

The thief then sat next to Harrison. "The ale these beings produce is well fermented," he whispered as the ranger put the tankard to his lips. "Extremely well fermented! Vinegar would quench your thirst better!"

Murdock took one taste of the liquid before spitting out the sour ale. "What kind of brew is this?" The ranger threw the tankard at Pondle. "And to think, I slaved over a fire for this garbage!"

"I kept my end of the bargain! I had no idea what it tasted like!" lied Pondle as he laughed, along with Swinkle and Harrison, for the first time in days.

"I hope you all think this is very funny." Murdock spit again.

Harrison waited a moment before changing subjects. "Do you two think we'll find a village any time soon?"

Murdock looked at Pondle, who shrugged, before answering. "I don't know, but finding that meadow might prove to be very important. That cyclops wouldn't tend sheep in a thick forest. There must be some thinning out of the underbrush beyond the clearing."

"I planned on leading us off in that direction tomorrow," added Pondle. "Murdock's right. I believe the woods will thin out, too."

"We can only hope." Harrison sighed. "We need to get our bearings straight. The sooner we find a village, the better off we'll be." Everyone nodded in agreement.

Harrison paused before speaking again. "What do we do with the treasure once we find a town?"

Murdock looked over to Pondle, knowing that the two had discussed the very same subject together. "We keep it hidden in the outskirts of the city."

"There's too much to tote around and still go unnoticed," added Pondle.

Harrison nodded. "Well, you've certainly done a good job so far." The young warrior gazed toward the underbrush on the outer edge of camp. "Is it over there?"

Pondle and Murdock peered in the same direction. "Yes," said Pondle. "Being a former thief, I know how to hide things from view. Especially items of extreme value."

Harrison kept his gaze fixed on the spot where his friend had hidden the treasure. "I know the hoard is over there, but I still couldn't begin to tell you where it actually lies."

Pondle smiled. "Good. Then I did my job well."

Murdock poked at the cooking food. "The meat's done. Let's worry about eating for now. Hand me your plates."

The ranger then gave everyone a healthy portion of food. Swinkle mumbled a prayer and, when he finished, flipped a piece of meat over his shoulder as an offering to his god of compromise and diplomacy, Pious.

"You know, I'm really getting tired of that." Murdock pointed at the tossed food. Lance scurried over to the discarded vitals, sniffed it, then gobbled it up in one bite.

"It's part of —" started Swinkle before Murdock interrupted him.

"Yeah, we know," said the ranger, nodding, "it's your sacrifice to your god. It's a waste of good food if you ask me."

"I'm starting to feel that you will never understand my beliefs." Swinkle took a moment, then looked at the other men before speaking.

"I believe that the treasure we have found will help people for years to come and I want to reaffirm to all of you that I will remain with the party until we deliver this prize. Making sure that all people benefit from what we have uncovered will be the focal point of my two year mission."

"Isn't that noble of you." Murdock's voice was thick with sarcasm. Using his thumb to point at Swinkle, he said, "Pondle, it looks like we'll be covering his back for two more years." The ranger grinned, then took a big bite of food.

Murdock's comment agitated Swinkle. "Am I that much of a bother?"

"Let's just say I would respect you more if you wielded a weapon," said the ranger, speaking through a mouthful of food.

"I'm sorry you feel that way, but you know I cannot."

"You know he helps us in other ways." Harrison placed his dish down. "He's healed all of us before."

Pondle extended his arms wide. "Let's stop right there. We all have our strong points and weaknesses." He then looked at Swinkle. "I'm glad you'll be with us. Deep inside Murdock does, too." The ranger rolled his eyes.

Pondle continued. "Let's all get some rest after everyone's finished eating. I'll keep watch tonight. We're in for a big day tomorrow."

"That sounds like a good idea." Murdock then took his food, backpack, and longbow and walked in the opposite direction of the fire. Settling down away from the others, he continued to eat his meal.

Pondle grabbed his food and stood up. "I'm going to survey the perimeter. I'll be back later." Harrison, Swinkle, and Lance watched the thief leave the campsite.

Swinkle looked over in Murdock's direction. "What is wrong with him?"

"Murdock has always done things his way." Harrison tore at another piece of the fresh meat. "That's also his biggest problem."

"I hope he changes his ways. For our sake."

Harrison shook his head. "Don't count on it. Just don't let him get under your skin."

Swinkle sighed. "I'll try, but it won't be easy."

After they finished their meal, Harrison gave Lance a healthy portion of bones and fatty pieces of mutton. The little dog graciously accepted the food from his master.

Harrison and Swinkle then prepared themselves for the evening. The young warrior lay on his back and gazed at the stars overhead.

I wish my parents were here to see what we have accomplished, he thought before Swinkle interrupted him.

"I have a good feeling about that meadow." Swinkle patted his backpack, readying himself for sleep. "I think we'll be out of this forest before too long."

"I hope you're right." Harrison pulled a blanket over his body. "It's time for a well-deserved rest."

Lance curled up next to his master, while Swinkle searched for his own blanket. Harrison looked up at the stars above him again, and a short time thereafter, he closed his eyes and fell into a deep sleep.

C H A P T E R 2

✿

A light rain fell from the early morning sky, waking Harrison out of a sound sleep. "Wonderful. Just what we needed, a rainy day in the middle of nowhere," the young warrior muttered as he sat up and looked around for the rest of the group. Scanning the area, he saw no one. Even Lance had vanished.

"Where is everybody?" Harrison hastily stood up and reached for his weapon.

A voice came from behind him. "Good morning." The young warrior turned to see Swinkle walking toward him swinging a pouch.

"Not the best of days, is it?" The young cleric extended the bag to his friend. "Would you like some wild berries? They're very tasty."

Harrison put down his battle-axe and approached Swinkle. "Sure, I'm a little hungry. Where are Murdock and Pondle?"

"They went to make a more thorough survey of the land." Swinkle handed the pouch to Harrison. "They will be back within the hour."

"Did they take Lance?"

The young cleric panned the area for the dog. "I think so."

"Why didn't they wake me? I would've helped." The young warrior took a handful of berries from the small bag.

"They told me to let you sleep. They believed that your arm could use more rest and felt secure enough to leave you with me. I'm going to pack this away for our journey." Swinkle took the pouch from Harrison and placed it in his pack. "I hope that Pondle and Murdock find a safe way to get out of here."

"I'm sure that they will." Harrison pointed to a huge oak with many overhanging branches. "Let's go over there so we can get out of this rain."

The two moved to the shelter of the tree. With nothing else to do but wait for their friends, the two men went about their own tasks. Swinkle took out his holy book of prayers and began to study them. Harrison took the time to sharpen his battle-axe and put on his armor. When he completed that task, he moved a comfortable distance away from the young cleric and began to practice wielding his axe against imaginary enemies.

After Harrison's practice session, he placed his weapon down and took a seat near his backpack. Reaching for his tankard of water, he noticed Swinkle gazing at an old scripture.

"What do you have there?"

Swinkle maintained his fix on the book. "We found this manuscript in the chamber along with the other treasures." The young cleric paused, then shook his head. "I can't put my finger on it, but I have the feeling that this book has a deeper meaning."

Harrison strolled over to his friend. "What do you mean?"

"Well, I know the text is definitely magical because I said a prayer and noticed an aura around the book. But more than that, it is the feeling I get just holding the scripture."

"You can't read magic?" Harrison peered over his friend's shoulder to get a better look at the item.

"No, I cannot." Swinkle turned and gazed up at the young warrior. "I'd like to find a mage to decipher this text. I'll use my own gold to pay for his services."

Harrison laughed, recalling the wealth of treasure that they had with them. "I'm sure that will be fine with the others."

Just then, Pondle and Murdock returned to the camp, with Lance scooting behind them from the underbrush.

"Good morning, Harrison," said Pondle as he and Murdock arrived under the tree. Lance rushed to his master's side. "I'm glad to see that your arm's doing better."

"It still feels a little stiff." Harrison stretched out his limb, trying to loosen the area around his wound. "It's a good thing Swinkle healed me after the battle with the cyclops." He then bent down on one knee to pet Lance, still gazing at his friends.

"What did you two find out there?"

Murdock placed his gear on the ground. "We found a well-traveled path several hundred yards to the west. There are tracks of men, horses, and carts that are no more than a day old. They seem to be heading west, so I believe there must be a town close by."

"The visibility with the rain and all makes it pretty tough to see," added Pondle, "but if we stick to the path we shouldn't have much of a problem. With that many tracks I find it hard to believe that it would be dangerous."

Harrison secured his backpack. "Then let's get going. Swinkle and I are ready to continue." The young warrior gazed into the underbrush. "Shall we begin our tedious task of moving the treasure?"

Murdock frowned. "I never thought I'd say this, but carting all that stuff around is getting old."

The young warrior nodded. "Everything will be fine once we get our bearings straight. I just know it."

Pondle then led the men to the hidden treasures and, as they had done so many times in the past few days, they gathered up as much of the sacred hoard as they could.

"You know the drill," said Murdock. "Pondle and I will lead, then we'll stop fifty yards from here —"

"Yeah, I know," interrupted Harrison. "Then Swinkle and I'll guard the riches until you return with the rest of the bounty."

The ranger nodded his head matter-of-factly. "It's what we must do."

"I don't disagree."

Murdock looked over to Pondle, the thief indicating his readiness to start journeying again. Satisfied, the ranger said, "Harrison, you keep an eye out for our backside. Like I said, there shouldn't be anything to worry about, but you never know."

With everyone set to continue their journey, the party began heading west through the wet woods.

The waves crashed along the rocky coast of Dragon's Lair. The storm that had besieged the island over the night began to subside. Troy Harkin had gathered thirty of his loyal soldiers the evening before and informed them of their next journey.

"The troops seem very eager to collect their extra wages, Teleios," he said to his longtime advisor.

Teleios was a rather dark character, being part human and part elf, but with a hint of Scynthian, something he never would admit. His elven heritage limited his height and weight, making him smaller than a human or Scynthian. His size deceived many though, and he slayed scores of adversaries who had taken him too lightly. Teleios had the strength of a Scynthian, but the mind of a halfling. Having the intelligence of the latter allowed him to possess magical ability. Because of this trait, the king had elevated him to second in command behind Troy. For many years, Teleios had helped Troy plan his battles and had advised him in certain situations.

"Good, then they will fight harder," said Teleios. "How do you feel about my suggestion for our battle route?" The two men walked down a long corridor that led to the outside of the castle.

"I concur with your thoughts. We can discuss the finer points of our plan after we set sail." The soldiers passed through a guarded doorway and exited the castle.

Troy looked toward the sky and felt the rain beat onto his face. Outside, two soldiers waited on horseback, with two more steeds awaiting Troy and Teleios.

"We'll escort you to the dock, sir," said one soldier as he dismounted to help his leaders to their horses.

"The ship is supplied to its full capacity, and all the men are on board," said the other. "They're ready to leave as soon as you arrive."

The men left the castle and started their trek down a muddy path that headed to the coast. The rain continued to fall, heavily at times, as the soldiers led their horses in a cautious procession down the slippery landscape.

It's going to be nice to leave this desolate place for a while, Troy thought as the rain and wind lashed out against them.

Twenty minutes later, the group reached the shores of the coast where they found a large wooden dock. Anchored alongside the pier rocked a large ship with two masts. The inscription on the front, port side of the vessel read *VENTURE 3*, and two red flags with white crosses waved from the masts.

"The storm's heading towards the mainland," yelled one of the soldiers into the heavy downpour. "There'll be enough wind along with it to get you there a half day early. We brought your armor and weapons on board this morning as you requested. Have a safe trip, sir."

Troy nodded to the soldier, then he and Teleios dismounted and proceeded up the plank that led to the ship.

"Welcome, General," bellowed Portheus, the captain of the ship. "Have no fear. We have sailed in much worse weather than this."

"I know you won't let me down." Troy rested a hand on the large man's soggy shoulder. "Set our course for the town of Polaris and let me know when the mainland is in sight. Teleios and I will be in your quarters. Remember, captain, there is a big reward for success on this journey." Troy and Teleios left Portheus and headed to the captain's cabin.

"Yes, sir!" answered the heavyset, bearded man. "Up with the anchor! We're leaving the island!" Portheus's men cheered at the command.

After securing the anchor, the crew raised the sails. The ship creaked as the sails grabbed the gusts of wind, filling them to their full capacity. Within minutes, the ship moved away from the island's rocky coast and headed for Polaris.

After several hours of uneventful travel, the group finally found themselves on the outskirts of a small town. Before allowing anyone to see them, Pondle had meticulously hidden their bounty several hundred yards away from the town's outer limits.

With the task of hiding the treasure completed, Harrison and his friends departed the wooded area and began to trek toward the town. The young warrior looked down the center of the village. "This isn't much of a city."

Pondle agreed. "City? I'd say it looks more like a stopping point than anything else."

Harrison took a closer look. From where he stood, he could see that only one major road ran through the heart of town, and only a few shops and houses lined either side.

"There aren't many stores here."

"They must be farmers." Pondle took his gaze to his left. "There's an abundance of livestock over there." Sheep, goats, and horses grazed in an open pasture, and on the right, the land resembled a jousting area.

Murdock scanned the vicinity with a careful eye. "Good. That means there's less of a chance of someone finding our treasures."

Pondle nodded. "True, but no one would find them anyway. I've hidden them quite well."

The ranger shook his head, unhappy with the sequence of steps that they had to follow in order to hide their fortune. "I don't like taking chances with those riches. We fought long and hard to get them and I don't want any farm boy to stumble onto them."

The thief brushed off his friend's worrisome attitude. "Don't worry, they won't."

Harrison had faith in Pondle's skills, but still had reservations about leaving their sacred prize unguarded.

"Still, we should be careful. There are a lot of people milling about the area."

Pondle nodded. "I agree."

Harrison addressed his friends one last time before they began to enter the town. "All we need to do is find out where we are in this land, then we can try to find a place where we can inquire about a mage."

Murdock gave his friend a look of surprise. "A mage? What do we need a magician for?"

Harrison used his thumb to point to his friend. "Swinkle wants to have someone read one of the books we found in the underground chamber. I didn't think there'd be any harm in that."

Murdock glanced at Pondle, who shrugged. "I guess not. Let's go."

As the men began their trek down the main road, they noticed several townspeople, tradesmen, and farmers showing off their wares. Many of the people gave them curious stares as they walked past.

"All right, let's try to find a place where we can gather information," said Harrison.

Murdock gazed at the sparse, old buildings. "I'd be surprised if we found anything of worth in this place."

Changing the subject, he said, "All this adventuring has made me thirsty. Why don't you and Swinkle look for a mage? Pondle and I will look for some supplies and we'll meet over there." The ranger pointed to a building with a sign reading "Johannsen's Pub."

Harrison pointed toward his friend. "The only supplies you'd return with would be arrows and ale! We'll all accompany you if you need a drink that bad. Let's just try to be a little subtle. I don't want everyone alerted to our presence."

Pondle scanned his surroundings, trying to get a fix on their location as the group headed for the pub. "Does anyone recognize this village?"

Murdock shook his head. "Nothing looks familiar." The ranger then smiled. "I kind of like it that way. This gives me the chance to show you that I can figure out where we are in this land just by the way they brew their ale."

The men then approached the entrance to the building and proceeded to walk in. When the large man sitting at a table near the doorway saw Lance, he jumped from his seat.

"We don't serve animals in here!" He then pointed at Pondle. "And as for him, he wears the tools of a thief!" The man reached for a club that leaned against the wall.

The person's actions surprised Murdock. "Is that any way to welcome customers?"

The bouncer, standing a good six and a half feet tall and with a girth that obscured their view of the bar, started to approach the group.

Rethinking his last statement, Murdock said, "I see what you mean, good man. Pondle, why don't you take Lance and go get some supplies." The ranger nodded at Pondle, hoping he would comply.

"That's fine with me. We'll wait outside when we're finished. Let's go, Lance."

Murdock watched the two leave before turning his attention to the large man in front of him. "Halflings! They don't appreciate good ale anyway!"

Unimpressed with the ranger's joke, the bouncer stepped aside nevertheless, allowing the rest of the group to quickly enter the establishment and approach the bar.

Harrison scanned the tavern for possible trouble. "Keep an eye out, Swinkle." His friend nodded as the young warrior made subtle glances from side to side.

Harrison remembered his days at the Fighter's Guild. One test he had learned had to do with recognizing everything in the general vicinity by scanning the area once with his eyes. His quick examination told him that the pub consisted of a large bar with many long tables. A balding, middle-aged man wearing an apron stood behind the counter. To the left, several townspeople played darts in the back of the room, and to the right, a couple of tradesmen conversed at a table.

Murdock, speaking in a low voice, interrupted Harrison's investigation. "Let me do the talking. I fit in a little better than you two." The two men nodded in agreement.

Just then, the bartender approached the group. "Can I help you?"

"Two ales for my friend and I." Murdock motioned toward Harrison.

The man pointed at Swinkle. "What about him?"

The young cleric waved his hands. "Nothing for me, sir. I had a bad experience with alcohol once and I don't wish to have it happen again."

The bartender shrugged, poured two mugs of ale, and placed them in front of Murdock and Harrison. "So, where are you men coming from?"

"We started our journey from Aegeus, but we seemed to have gotten lost." Murdock fumbled with a sack on his belt. "How much do we owe you?"

"That will be six gold pieces. So, do you know where you are now?"

"I'll tell you in a minute!" Murdock took two quick gulps of ale before making a face and setting the flagon back on the bar.

"We must be near the Great Forest. They always seem to brew their ale longer around those parts, giving it that stale taste."

The bartender glared at Murdock. "Are you trying to say that my brew is stale?"

"No, he's not." Harrison placed a stack of coins on the bar, trying to diffuse the situation. "Here are ten gold pieces. My friend here thinks he can tell where he is in the land by the way they brew their ale."

The bartender collected the tribute. "Well, he's right about his location. This is Tigris and the road you came in on makes a direct connection to Dragon's Quarters. Many of the tradesmen hunt in the Great Forest and sell their wares between the two villages."

Murdock beamed. "See, I told you!" The ranger looked toward the back of the room. "I'll let you two chat. I'm going to join that dart game over there. But before I go, one more ale!" The ranger took a final gulp and placed his empty mug on the bar.

Harrison gave his friend a worried look. "Just take it easy, Murdock. We don't want any trouble," he said as the bartender handed the ranger another ale.

"Trouble?" Murdock smiled at Harrison. "It's me, remember? You can take care of this for me, right?" The ranger then took his drink and headed toward the back of the tavern.

While he started to clean a few dirty mugs, the bartender kept his eye on Murdock. "Your friend is some character."

"Yes, he certainly is." Harrison watched Murdock approach the group of three men before turning his attention to the barkeep.

"Maybe you can help us. As we traveled through the forest, we stumbled across a pouch containing a few vials of colored liquids. We didn't want to open them ourselves, but wanted a mage to look at them first. Do you know of any in the town?" Harrison took a sip of his drink.

"A mage, huh?"

Just then, a young woman approached the bar. "Johannsen, the man in the back of the bar wants another ale. He said these two would pay for it." Harrison rolled his eyes.

"Sure. That all right with you?" The bartender looked at Harrison.

"Yes, but that's his last one. We haven't been here more than ten minutes and that's his third drink." Harrison handed the barmaid five gold pieces. "Keep one for yourself."

"Thank you." The young girl smiled at Harrison, then left to take the goblet to Murdock.

"As I was saying," continued the bartender, "the only mage I know of is Gelderand. He lives at the end of the town.

Take a right out of these doors, then go down ten buildings on your right. His home is set back a bit from the road. He likes to keep to himself." The man squinted, peering past Harrison and to the barmaid, who returned to the bar in a hurry.

"I think you better get your friend," she said, poking Harrison's shoulder in anger. "He pinched me!"

Harrison looked down and sighed. "I'm sorry, miss. Swinkle, let's go."

The two men went in haste to join Murdock. As they approached him, they found their friend in a heated discussion with one of the three townsmen.

"What do you mean it's not on the '3?'" Murdock and the patron stood nose to nose, staring at one of the darts on the board.

"See, it's under the wire." The slightly intoxicated man pointed at the tip of the dart. "It's not on the '3!'"

Murdock shrugged and shook his head, incredulous. "It's close enough! Where I'm from, that's a legal throw!"

"Well it's not here! Pay up!" The man held out his empty hand.

"I will not! You never told me of these rules!"

The man glanced back at his friends. "Did you hear that, men? He's not going to pay!"

In one swift motion, one of the townsman's friends grabbed Murdock, holding his arms by his sides. The first person then took a swing at the ranger, striking him in the face.

"Hey! Hold on here!" Harrison tried to intervene, but the third townsman pushed him into a table.

Murdock then kicked the man in front of him in the midsection, sending him flying over a couple of chairs. Harrison quickly regained his footing and punched the person who pushed him, sending the patron careening into Murdock and the other townsman.

"Cyrus, break that up!" yelled the bartender. The bouncer grabbed his club and advanced towards the melee.

Harrison rushed over to Murdock and helped him up. "Let's get out of here!" As he grabbed his friend's arm, he felt a large hand grab him.

"I didn't care for the likes of you as soon as I saw you with that halfling!" The bouncer lifted Harrison clear off the floor and tossed him over a table, sending him crashing into a wall in the process. The young warrior winced in pain.

To his surprise, Harrison heard a familiar voice. "I'm going to get Pondle." Swinkle, who had been hiding where the young warrior had landed, then made a quick dash to the exit.

"Good idea," said Harrison, still groggy from hitting the wall.

While trying to get up, Harrison saw the bouncer grab Murdock by his shirt, jerking him off the ground. Repositioning the ranger by the seat of his pants, the bouncer, with one heave, tossed Murdock out of the pub and into the street. He then turned his attention to Harrison.

The young warrior realized he was alone. This doesn't look too promising, he thought, scanning the room for another way out.

The bouncer pointed at Harrison. "You're next!"

Harrison raised his hands, gesturing that he had had enough. "I'm leaving, I'm leaving."

Cyrus grabbed the young warrior by his chain-mail armor. "I'm helping you!" The large man used only one hand to lift Harrison off his feet. Carrying him to the exit, he stared into the young warrior's eyes.

"Have a nice day!" The bouncer then threw Harrison out of the establishment, where he landed beside Murdock in the road.

Both fighters lay on the ground, dazed and confused. Several townspeople took time from their daily chores to witness all the commotion.

The two men attempted to lift themselves from the ground. Harrison, in a sarcastic tone, said, "Good going, Murdock! Let *me* do the talking!"

"Great, my mouth is bleeding." Murdock touched his lip with two fingers. Just then, Swinkle, Pondle, and Lance came running over.

Pondle helped Murdock from the ground. "What kind of trouble have you two gotten yourselves into now?"

"Just a little misunderstanding." Murdock used his sleeve to wipe the blood from his mouth. "They don't call it a legal throw in a game of darts if you don't hit the number cleanly in this town. What a charming place!"

"I'm glad you at least had the decency not to draw your weapon." Harrison shook his head in disgust. "All we wanted to do was get some information, but you had to make a scene."

"I'm sorry," said Murdock, in a not-so-convincing tone. "Pondle, what did you get for us?"

"Since I didn't have the honor to witness the blessed event, I managed to find food, torches, and water. We have more than enough weapons associated with our treasure, so I didn't go to the weaponsmith."

Pondle directed his next question towards Harrison and Swinkle. "Did you find out where we are?"

Harrison continued to brush himself off. "It appears we've stumbled into the town of Tigris."

"And we found the name of a mage," added Swinkle. "The bartender said he lives ten buildings down on the right."

Pondle crinkled his brow. "Tigris? How did we get all the way over here?" The thief stood in amazement, wondering what kind of magic could transport them from the Dark Forest to the outskirts of Tigris, some one hundred miles away.

Swinkle shrugged. "Magic can yield strange results."

"Oh, by the way, Swinkle," said Murdock, "thanks for running to get Pondle. I enjoy being outnumbered in a fight."

"I am not a good fighter." Swinkle raised his voice just a bit. "Besides, it was not a life or death situation. I'm not allowed to fight unless otherwise."

Harrison came to the young cleric's aid. "Leave him alone, Murdock! You know he's not allowed to fight!" The young warrior noticed that the townspeople continued to stare at them. "Let's get moving. I don't like attracting all this attention in a strange town."

Murdock shrugged. "Fine with me. Where does this wizard live again?"

Swinkle pointed down the road. "Up this way. Follow me."

The group then began their trek towards Gelderand's residence. After a few minutes, they found themselves in front of a small house.

Swinkle placed his hands on his hips. "This is Gelderand's home. We should try not to startle him."

Murdock gave the young cleric a perplexed look. "What makes you think he'll be startled by us?"

"I'm sure he doesn't have strangers knocking on his door every day." The young cleric took a closer look at the mage's dwelling and noticed the meticulously maintained landscape. "Look at this place."

Pondle gazed about the residence. "Is it me, or is everything a little too perfect?"

The men could see that someone had landscaped all of the bushes and plants to perfection, the area appeared debris free, and the upkeep on the house was excellent.

"I feel the same way," said Murdock. "My senses tell me that he won't like battle-hardened warriors in his precious little home."

Without warning, an orange tabby cat came bounding out of the bushes, with a loud meow. Lance saw the animal and began to bark at a feverish clip.

Harrison scolded the dog. "Lance! Stop that barking. It's only a cat!" Lance tried his best to control himself, but he still growled under his breath.

Showing no fear of Lance, the feline cautiously walked over to the men and began to rub against the party members' legs.

Murdock peered down at the animal. "Just what I love, cats." Lance began to bark again.

Harrison gave the dog a look of exasperation. "Lance, stop!" Again, the dog obeyed his master.

The young warrior then looked back at his friends. "Just let the cat be. The animal belongs to this Gelderand in all likelihood." Turning his attention to the matter at hand, he said, "Now, let *me* do the talking."

"Go ahead." Murdock gestured toward the closed door. "But I don't like the looks of this."

Harrison ignored Murdock's last comment and knocked on the door. He could hear someone approach the entranceway, then heard the latch unlock. The door swung open and a very attractive young girl stood in the doorway.

"Can I help you?"

Harrison stood speechless as he gazed into her beautiful, blue eyes. "I, I, I, uh, we're …" he stuttered as he turned an embarrassing shade of red.

"Yes?" The girl crinkled her brow, appearing confused.

Swinkle stepped forward. "We have come to see Gelderand. Is he home?"

"Yes he is. Please wait here while I get him," she said as the cat ran through the open doorway.

After the girl disappeared from view, Murdock let out a laugh. "Real smooth, Harrison!"

Harrison could still feel his embarrassment. "I didn't expect a girl!" Just then, a bearded, middle-aged man came to the doorway, the young lady following close behind.

The man offered a curious stare. "I am Gelderand. Who might you be?"

Gelderand wore a green, hooded robe with a thin, gold belt tied around his midsection. His eyes were a shade darker than his cloak, and they gazed back at the group of men before him with anticipation.

"My name is Harrison, and these are my friends Murdock, Pondle, and Swinkle. We would like you to look at something that we stumbled across."

The mage remained skeptical. "Why should I let a bunch of strangers into my home?" Gelderand motioned for the girl to step back, then took a closer look at Harrison and Murdock.

"You two wear the armor of warriors. I'm not comfortable with your kind near my residence."

"Didn't I tell you," said Murdock under his breath in Harrison's direction.

Harrison acknowledged Gelderand's apprehension. "We need a mage to read some text, that's all. We'll gladly pay you for your service."

Gelderand squinted, never removing his stare from the strangers. "What makes you believe that I can read magic?"

"The bartender at Johanssen's Pub told us you were a mage." Swinkle tried to put the man at ease. "I am a cleric. I will assist you in any way, sir."

Gelderand let out a heavy sigh. "I only wish to be left alone. People should not be talking about my business."

Swinkle pressed on. "Sir, if I might. If you are indeed a mage, all that we ask is for you to help us with this scripture. After you have read it, we will be on our way. That I promise you."

Gelderand deliberated over the situation. As he thought, he looked down at Lance. "Who might he be?"

The young cleric gazed down at their canine friend. "This is Lance. We befriended him during our adventure. I assure you, he is harmless."

After a moment of thought, he looked back at the girl, who shrugged. "Against my better judgment, I will allow you in."

Before he let Harrison and his friends enter his home, he pointed a finger at them all. "What you heard is true — I am a mage. I won't hesitate to use my powers if I'm threatened. That is your only warning." The men all looked at Gelderand and nodded in compliance.

Gelderand then waved them in. "This is my niece and sometimes apprentice, Tara. Please, have a seat." The mage motioned towards a table in the middle of the room.

The men looked about Gelderand's home. Harrison found the house had a basic design, consisting of one main living room with a kitchen off to the side. Two closed doorways led out of the room, besides the one that they had just passed through.

The men sat down, with Lance lying on the floor next to his master. Harrison admired Tara's beauty again. The girl appeared to be a couple of years younger than Harrison and had golden blonde hair. She wore a pure white blouse and a long brown skirt. A simple necklace adorned her neck and she had a single sapphire ring on her right hand. Gelderand's voice interrupted his gaze.

"Tara, can you bring our guests something to drink?" The girl honored her uncle's request, traversing the room and entering the kitchen area.

Harrison once again found himself admiring Tara's golden locks. She's gorgeous, he thought, gazing at her petite frame.

The young girl elegantly poured wine into four goblets, then brought two of them to the men, placing one in front of Swinkle and the other in front of Harrison.

"Thank you." Tara's smile warmed Harrison. As she went back to the kitchen to retrieve the remaining goblets, he turned his attention to Gelderand, who had a firm gaze on the young warrior.

"I hope you find everything to your liking," he said in a stern tone, not removing his stare from Harrison. Tara then delivered wine to Pondle and Murdock.

"The wine is delicious." Murdock, noticing the older man's stare, tried the best he could to break the uncomfortable moment. "Let's get down to business."

"Let's." The mage finally removed his glare off Harrison.

Before they could get started, the orange cat appeared out of nowhere and began pawing at Harrison's arm as it reached from the floor.

"Hey!" yelled the young warrior, prompting Lance to spring to his feet and bark. "Easy, boy!" The dog sat back down and stared at the cat.

Gelderand glared at the feline. "Rufus, get down! Is that any way to treat our guests?" The cat scurried toward Tara.

Turning his attention back to his visitors, Gelderand said, "I'm sorry, he's just curious. Now, what do you have for me to read?"

Swinkle retrieved the magical scripture from his pack. "Just a book we stumbled across in our travels."

"A book? You don't just *stumble* over a book." Gelderand accepted the scripture from Swinkle. "You didn't steal it, did you?"

"No, we didn't. We discovered it in a chamber while adventuring."

Gelderand made a close examination of the book, then opened its cover and methodically leafed through the pages of magical text. "I'm positive that someone used magic on this book."

The mage closed the scripture and looked at Swinkle. "Two hundred gold pieces."

Swinkle's eyes widened in shock. "Two hundred gold pieces! Isn't that a bit steep?"

Gelderand gave the men a look of skepticism. "I'm not sure that I believe your story that you simply stumbled upon this book on some adventure. Furthermore, if an evil wizard performed this magic, I might disintegrate before your eyes. Two hundred is low if you ask me."

Swinkle sighed, then looked toward his friends. "He is right. I once witnessed a good cleric friend become insane because he read evil scriptures by mistake."

Murdock smirked at the young cleric. "You really know how to help your own cause, Swinkle."

The young cleric mulled over Gelderand's offer. Swinkle knew that the money was a non-issue since they had more than enough with their newfound hoard. Furthermore, his mind kept returning to the ancient scripture and he knew that if he did not take this opportunity now, it would continue to haunt him.

"I suppose I have no choice. I accept your price."

Gelderand smiled. "Good, but in order to read this material I'll need to perform a spell." The mage turned to his niece. "Tara, can you please get me some of the magical powder that I made along with a vial of snake's venom. Be careful of the —"

"I know, I know, the snake's venom is deadly." Tara turned and proceeded through the doorway that led to Gelderand's work area.

A few moments later, the girl reappeared. "I mixed it the way you've showed me a thousand times before." She handed her uncle a small bowl containing a fine black powder.

"Thank you, Tara. Now, let us see what this book is all about."

Gelderand began to sprinkle the powder on the book. As he did so, he mumbled, turning the pages of the manuscript at the same time. When Gelderand finished the spell, he closed the book. A second later, a soft red glow encompassed the scripture, before returning to its normal self.

"If the spell worked, I should be able to read the magical text after I reopen the scripture." Gelderand took care in opening the book's cover. "Let's hope that my magic is stronger than the one that possessed it."

The wizard proceeded to the first sheet of magical text. "By the gods! The spell worked!"

"What does it say?" Murdock, along with the rest of the group, waited in anticipation.

Gelderand read the first few lines to himself, then brought a shock-filled gaze to the men. "This scripture speaks of the Treasure of the Land."

Harrison made eye contact with the rest of his friends, reluctant to say anything just yet. "Please read the contents out loud."

Gelderand took a deep breath, then began. *"Fortunate are the souls who possess this scripture, for the Treasure of the Land is surely with them. The bounty of the ancient kings is not to be taken lightly and must be protected at all times. Hide your hoard away and tell no one of your accomplishment until your new quest is complete. For all the riches in the world will be nothing but a burden unless your mission is a success. Continue with your next test and prove your worth once again."*

Gelderand wrinkled his brow. "It seems that we have ourselves a little riddle." The mage leafed through the pages again. "The rest of the book seems to be in some kind of code."

Swinkle shook his head, perplexed by the mage's comment. "What does the riddle say?"

Gelderand continued reading the passage on the first page. *"Unlucky is the letter to start with. This letter becomes the end and the end becomes unlucky. From here, we go left to right, right to left, expanding to the end, one becoming the other, the other becoming the one."*

Swinkle frowned. "May I have a look at the text?"

"By all means." Gelderand handed the book to Swinkle. "But I don't think you will be able to read it. Only a mage is capable of reading the magic. You may look nonetheless."

Swinkle's eyes widened in surprise. "I can clearly understand this passage. I can see the exact words that you just spoke." The young cleric leafed through the pages. "The rest of the book is unreadable. You seem to be right, it looks more like a code than magic."

Gelderand stared at the young cleric in amazement. "What do you mean that you can read this passage?"

"Like I said, I can read the text. The spell must have made a permanent change to the composition of this book."

Gelderand looked around, stunned. "That cannot be. A spell like the one I just cast is only useful for a brief period, and only the caster can read the magic."

Harrison peered over Swinkle's shoulder. "I understand it, too!"

Swinkle thought back to the chamber where he found the scripture, aware that the manuscript was part of the Kings' hoard. "Whoever wrote this book knows what we have."

"And they're sending us on another quest," added Harrison.

Murdock held up his hands. "Wait just a second! We need to get back to Aegeus! The elders can decide what they want to do from there."

Pondle gazed over to his friend. "Do you really want them to tell you what to do? I say we decipher this riddle, embark on this new quest, and find whatever is next."

Murdock had known Pondle the better part of his life and respected his opinions more than anyone else. "I suppose the elders can't reprimand us if they don't know what we're up to."

Harrison smirked at the ranger. "Look what we found already. Imagine what more there's to come."

Murdock smiled, his mind churning with the thoughts of more riches. "Yeah, you're right. Those kings were very powerful indeed."

"But the kings also intended to have someone interpret the riddle and use it to decode this book." Swinkle did not care so much about the riches; instead he wondered about the final outcome.

"I guess they figured that once someone removed the scripture from its resting place, anyone who could figure out its meaning would be fair game to whatever it yields."

"And whoever lost the book allowed someone else a chance to decode it," added Murdock. "I don't think that's something we want to happen."

Harrison nodded in agreement. "Murdock's right. If this book is ever stolen from us, the thieves could decode it themselves."

"And that could lead them back to us." Murdock raised an eyebrow.

Gelderand waited for his chance to speak. "Is there something you gentlemen want to tell me?"

Harrison panned the room; no one said a word. "What is it you wish to know?"

"Do you possess the Treasure of the Land?"

Harrison took a deep breath as everyone fixed their eyes on him. "What if I told you that we did?"

Gelderand's eyes widened. "There are many myths about the treasure, but this book states that it is part of the bounty of the ancient kings. A hoard of that magnitude would be impressive indeed."

"And a burden." Harrison chose his words carefully. "The rigors we went through were incredible. We lost friends along the way, too."

"I can imagine." The wizard nodded, understanding the pains the group must have gone through to acquire such a prize. "Where is the treasure now?"

"Harrison, don't." Murdock glared at his friend.

The young warrior raised a hand to the ranger. "It's in a safe place tucked away where no one can find it."

"You are that confident?" Gelderand sat back in his seat. "I notice it is not with you as we speak, meaning it is somewhere unguarded." The mage folded his arms, raising an eyebrow.

Pondle leaned forward. "No one will find it. That I assure you."

The older man slowly moved forward, squinting at the thief. "You are a young fool! Your skills may be good, but your overconfidence will be your downfall. The longer your treasure is unguarded, the better the chance it will get stolen."

Harrison could feel his apprehension rise. Gelderand reminded him of his old mentor Marcus Braxton, and the young warrior knew what his teacher would say.

"What do you propose?"

Gelderand stroked his beard. "Stash the treasure here. We can decode the book and begin the next adventure."

Murdock gave the mage an incredulous look. "We? First of all, who said anything about you being part of the group, and second, why in the world would we leave the treasure here?"

"I have an underground cellar on my premises that has not been disturbed in years." Gelderand watched the group for a response; none came.

"Furthermore, Tigris has not seen any significant activity for as long as I've lived here, some thirty years. This village is the most obscure in the land, and no one will come here looking for riches."

Harrison nodded. "That might be true, but why would we want you to join us?"

Gelderand did not hesitate. "Because you lack a mage. If this manuscript has anything to do with the Treasure of the Land, you can bet that magic goes along with it. Have you not encountered magical phenomena on your journey?"

The wizard could read the positive expressions on the men's faces. "Just what I thought. You will need me, or a person like me, eventually. The decision is yours, but remember, I now know your secret."

Harrison knew what Gelderand stated made sense, but any decision would have to come from the group. With that in mind, he said to the wizard, "My friends and I need to speak in private. Is that all right with you?"

"By all means. I'm not going anywhere."

The four men rose from the table and exited the house. Murdock waited for Swinkle to close the door before launching into a tirade.

"We are not letting this stranger join our group!"

"Let's discuss this rationally," said Harrison. "How many of us feel there will be more magic along the way?"

Murdock shook his head. "We ran into plenty of magical situations on our last journey and we survived. I'm sure we can handle whatever comes next."

Swinkle did not share Murdock's confidence. "I'm not saying we got lucky, but many things did break our way in the past. What if we encounter more scriptures that we cannot read, or magically sealed doorways and the like? Only a wizard can help us at those times. I can only detect magic, not manipulate it."

"I agree, that might be true," added Pondle. "But do you believe we can hide the treasure here like Gelderand suggests?"

Harrison nodded. "I think so. Let's face it, we can't keep doing what we've been doing. Chances are someone is going to find the hoard as we try to transport it to Aegeus. Keeping it hidden while we venture for more treasure makes sense."

Pondle pondered Harrison's last statement with a frown. "I suppose you're right. We can't keep carrying this treasure around with us."

The young warrior pointed at his friends as he spoke. "And if Gelderand is with us, we won't have to worry about him running off with the treasure when we're away."

Murdock shook his head. "You mean to tell me that you trust this person enough to want him to join our group? We don't even know this man! He could be evil, or worse."

"Murdock, look around you." Pondle gestured toward Gelderand's dwelling. "Does this look like the home of an evil being?"

Murdock looked around at the manicured landscape, the flower gardens, and the wildlife that played about Gelderand's home.

"He even has his niece as an apprentice," continued the thief. "You know as well as I do that he's not evil. I'm a thief. I make a living by being sure about people I can and cannot trust. Gelderand is no threat to us."

Murdock looked at his close friend, then shook his head from side to side. "Fine, but I'm not taking the blame for this one. I remember the last mage that journeyed with me. When he got nervous, his fireballs turned into puffs of smoke!"

Harrison could sense the tide turning. "Then it's agreed. We have Gelderand help us decode the book; we stash the treasure here; then he joins us on our new quest." The young warrior's friends nodded, albeit with reluctance.

"All right. Let's go and tell him the good news." The front door had remained open a crack when Harrison reached it. With a knock, the young warrior pushed the portal open and shouted, "Gelderand, we've reached an agreement."

The wizard motioned for the men to reenter his home and joined them sitting at the table again with Tara standing behind him.

"What have you agreed to?" asked Gelderand.

Harrison leaned forward. "We would like you to help decode the scripture, then join us for our next adventure. I believe you're right when you said that we'd need a mage sooner or later.

"And we want to hide the treasures in your basement, since we cannot conceal them for much longer, especially if we embark on another long journey."

Gelderand played with his beard, taking in Harrison's offer. On the one hand, he felt he owed staying in Tigris to Tara, to help continue with her studies and to train her to become a wizard as himself. However, he also understood that if he let this opportunity slip by now, he would live to regret it for the rest of his life.

"I was once like you, adventuring in search of magical artifacts and scriptures," started the older man. "Many times I had wished to achieve the level of a supreme wizard, only to realize that the more powerful I became, the more people would want me to do deeds for them. Finding this treasure is something that I could have only dreamed about.

"We will be in for many battles against unimaginable enemies. The question is, are you ready for what lies ahead?" Gelderand leafed through the pages of the book once again.

Harrison did not waver, staring down the older man. "Yes, we are. Does this mean you'll join us?"

"I graciously accept your offer. But, if what you have told me is true, that you have uncovered the Treasure of the Land and this book is part of the bounty, then I think we all realize what we must do. This book must never leave our possession and no one else must ever know what we have found."

"Then it's a deal. Welcome to the group." Harrison extended his hand to Gelderand.

"Let's get to work," answered the mage, as he shook Harrison's hand. "I suggest you bring your treasure here under the cover of darkness. Until then, I will need a couple of days to get my home situated and to pack my belongings for our journey. I suggest that we get supplies here in town."

"Hold on a minute! Did you say a couple of days?" interrupted Murdock. "What are we going to do while you're getting ready?"

Gelderand shrugged. "Get supplies, help me pack, and learn some magic."

"Learn magic?" Murdock wrinkled his brow. "You can count me out. I don't want to have anything to do with that hocus pocus stuff."

"That is up to you. Tara is a very good teacher." Gelderand moved away from the table.

Harrison's interest in learning magic peaked after hearing Gelderand's statement. "Tara? She's going to teach us?"

Tara had kept quiet up until now, waiting to see how the situation with her uncle would unfold. Feeling that she had bided her time long enough, she said, "What do you mean you're going with them? You just can't leave!"

"Now don't worry." Gelderand rested his hands on Tara's shoulders. "This is not any little treasure chest of gold. What we seek is part of a larger puzzle, one that might bring incredible wealth to all. Kings had sent countless armies out to find the Treasure of the Land, only for them to come home empty-handed. With that bounty already discovered, fulfilling this quest is of utmost importance."

"What about the house and your shop? What's my mother going to think?" Tara's worrisome voice trailed off and she shook her head in bewilderment.

"You can stay here until I return if you like. You have been doing very well with your studies and everything you

need is here. As for your mother, she will think I'm crazy."
Gelderand laughed.

"You're not a young man anymore." Tara hoped to
change her uncle's mind. "It's been a long time since you
ventured away from Tigris."

Gelderand hugged his niece. "Now that is what my
sister would say."

Tara looked into her uncle's eyes. By the way he
looked back at her, she knew any efforts to change his mind
would be fruitless.

"I'm going to miss you," she said as she hugged her
uncle back.

"I need you to help me now, though. We have work to
do."

Harrison heartily agreed. "Let's start figuring out this
riddle!"

"Harrison, why don't Swinkle and I take a closer look
at the book? Five people will only make things more
difficult." Gelderand then turned to face his niece.

Pointing in the direction of his workbench, he said,
"Tara, take care in placing the necessary ingredients for all of
my spells in the pouches near my work area. Fetch my spell
book, special robe, and cloak, too."

"Yes, Uncle. I'll make sure that you will be able to find
anything you need with ease."

Before she could leave, Gelderand continued. "There
is more, Tara. Place the vials of potions on my workbench in
an easily transportable container. And, as always, be careful."

"Of course I will." Tara dashed from the room in order
to start gathering her uncle's belongings.

"Why don't the rest of you help her?" Gelderand
looked in Harrison, Pondle, and Murdock's direction.

Murdock flashed his friend a sly grin. "Harrison, you
help the girl. Pondle and I will get more supplies." Then
turning to the mage, he said, "By the way, Gelderand, after
you decode this book, where do you think we'll be heading?"

"I suggest that we head north. My old mentor lives in the town of Valkala. He was a very powerful wizard in his day, and knows much more than I about the treasure you have found. He also possesses a crystal ball that he might be able to use that could help us with our quest."

"Crystal ball?" questioned Harrison. "What good will that do?"

"After he has the book in his possession, there is a chance that he might be able to see the course of events that led to the placing of the book in its resting place. However, I stress, it's only a slight chance. This book is ancient and my teacher is now quite old."

"We might be able to help you with that," said Swinkle. "Before we left on our journey, Harrison met with an old man named Philius."

Murdock waved the young cleric off. "We can fill him in on that part later, Swinkle. That story can take all night to tell."

"Do you mean that we will be traveling through the Great Forest?" asked Pondle.

Gelderand shifted his focus from Swinkle to Pondle. "That would be the quickest route. There haven't been too many stories of strange happenings there, but you should get adequate supplies. It's a good ten-day journey to Valkala."

"Pondle and I have enough gold to buy food, torches, and oil," said Murdock. "Let's go, Pondle. Maybe we can find a little more excitement, too." The two men got up from the table and exited the house.

After Murdock and Pondle left, Gelderand looked over to Swinkle. "I would like to hear that story some time."

Swinkle smiled. "With pleasure. Let's work on this riddle first."

Harrison, sensing that they would not need his assistance, said, "I'll help Tara with her chores," and hastily left the table. "If you need anything, just call. Lance, come with me." The dog followed his master and the two entered Gelderand's workshop.

"Just be careful!" Gelderand watched Harrison go into the work area, then looked over to Swinkle. "Why do I have the feeling I'm going to have to keep an eye on them?"

Swinkle shook his head. "It's just the way he is. I wouldn't worry about his intentions." Changing the subject, he said, "I really want to start figuring out this mystery."

Gelderand let out a laugh. "You're right. We have a lot of work to do."

The two men then hovered over the sacred book, each one secretly hoping to be the one to decipher the clues.

CHAPTER 3

Q

Troy and Teleios sat in the captain's quarters where they had sprawled out a detailed map of the mainland over a large wooden table. The Gammorians, a humanoid race now extinct, were the original owners of the map. Everyone had appreciated the stocky beings for their artistry, but their cultural brilliance ceased to exist on one memorable day.

The Gammorians had controlled most of the land north of the Lake of Good Hope, but the ever-expanding Scynthian civilization had begun to squeeze them southward. The two races detested one another and fought vicious battles for decades.

On a blustery winter day, the entire Gammorian race disappeared. No one ever determined how this happened, but all civilized beings accepted one general hypothesis. A wicked warlock had conjured an ancient evil scripture known only as the Genocide Scroll. The scroll, when read aloud, would eradicate the race named while reciting its malevolent text. Though the scripture remained lost for years, the consensus believed that the Scynthians recovered the scroll and wiped out the Gammorians. The Scynthians vehemently denied those allegations, and to this day claim they simply outlasted the Gammorians in their war.

Troy took care in spreading the detailed drawing over the table. "I love this map," he said, as he gazed at the many brilliant colors that marked various ancient towns and villages. "This is one of my favorite treasures."

The young general took a moment to peer at the soft colors that separated the diverse landscape. Gazing at the upper left hand corner, he admired a brilliant drawing of a sea creature with the label "Serpent's Sea" scripted underneath it.

The artist had drawn all of the mountain ranges in a stunning purple hue and had colored the seas a majestic royal blue.

After he had finished admiring the map, Troy turned his attention to Teleios. "Explain our route so I can prepare the soldiers."

"We will land here in the morning hours tomorrow." Teleios pointed to the port of Polaris with an unusual, clawed finger, different in appearance to Troy's and more like that of a cat. "From there we will travel to Arcadia, then to Lars."

Troy's advisor paused a second before continuing. "Next we head inland to Rocklia, then to Tigris and finally over to Dragon's Quarters. We can evaluate our progress when we reach there."

Troy raised an eyebrow. "And the rationale for going inland instead of along the coast?"

"Many adventurers and tradesmen use the villages of Rocklia, Tigris, and Dragon's Quarters as outposts to sell their wares.

"But most important of all is that Arcadia is the main hub in this part of the land. If someone found an item of great worth, it would be brought there."

Troy nodded in understanding. "Meaning if someone discovered the book in the Great Forest, it would be brought to Arcadia to attain the maximum value for the treasure."

"Exactly."

Troy ran a hand through his blonde hair and thought for a moment. "That suffices with me. Do we have enough horses for the men?"

"No. We will need to purchase several more steeds after we dock in Polaris." Just then, both men heard a knock at the door.

"Enter!" yelled Troy. The door swung open and one of the young general's men came into the room.

"I'm sorry to bother you, sir, but the captain has said that we'll be arriving earlier than expected. The storm has pushed us along much faster than anticipated. We'll be docking around sunrise."

Troy waited for the soldier to finish his report. "Thank you. You're relieved." The fighter turned and exited the room, closing the door behind him.

"We'll be finding our treasure sooner than expected, Teleios." Troy smiled at his advisor.

"Let's get something to eat now," he continued, taking care in rolling up the map and placing it in an ivory container. "We'll need rest later. This could be the last quiet night we have for a long time."

Harrison and Lance entered Gelderand's workshop. The young warrior gazed longingly at Tara and, again, found himself smitten. The lass turned to face the young man, drying her hands on a cloth in the process.

Harrison just stared at Tara, overwhelmed by her gorgeous appearance. "I'm here to help you," he said softly.

"You can help me gather these ingredients." Tara motioned to a shelf full of magical items. "Watch what I do."

The girl picked up a small mixing bowl from the workbench, then reached for a jar of orange grains.

"First, fill the bowl half way." Tara filled the container to its midpoint. "There, that should be enough.

"Next, take care in placing the ingredients in the pouch," she said, filling a small sack with the grains. "When you're done, hand it to me and I'll mark it so my uncle will know the contents of each one."

Moving her gaze over to Harrison, she noticed him staring at her with a blank expression. With a crinkle of her brow, she asked, "Are you listening?"

Harrison snapped out of his trance. "Yes! Yes, I am. I was just thinking about the book," he said in a most unconvincing way.

Tara gave him a wry look. "Yes, the book," she said, raising an eyebrow. "You must be very proud to be the one to find the Treasure." The girl then turned away to mark the pouch.

Harrison took a second to regain his composure. "Yes, it took a long time to reach our goal. But we have many more obstacles ahead of us."

Tara spun around, her lip quivering as she spoke. "This journey will be dangerous, won't it?"

"Any time you venture through the wilderness, there's a chance of danger." The young warrior took a step toward the girl. "I'm confident that the group and I are more than adequately prepared."

Tara nodded, taking in what Harrison had said. She stared intensely at the young warrior, her crystal blue eyes melting him further.

"Please take special care in watching Gelderand. He's not a warrior like you and he hasn't used his magic against anyone in years. I'm afraid he'll get hurt."

"I'll make sure he's all right. I won't let anyone harm him." Harrison did his best to comfort the girl before gazing deeper into her indigo pools of beauty.

"You have the most beautiful eyes I've ever seen."

Tara rested her hands on her hips, shooting him a look. "You're not the first person to say that to me."

Harrison fumbled for words. "No, I'm being honest. I've never seen such a stunning shade of blue before."

The young girl rolled her eyes. "Thank you." Tara then turned, faced the wall of ingredients, and reached for another jar from the shelf.

"I think we better continue with our packing."

Harrison smiled behind her back. "Of course," he answered, as he reached for a jar of his own.

Swinkle repeatedly ran the riddle through his mind. The young cleric knew Gelderand had more experience in dealing with magical text and the like, but a riddle was different.

Many times a child can see the obvious when others over think matters, thought the younger man. "Unlucky is the letter to start with," Swinkle mumbled to himself as he and Gelderand began their attempt at deciphering the riddle.

I have to concentrate, the young cleric thought. What do people consider unlucky? Just then, an answer popped into his head.

"Thirteen!"

"Thirteen?" Gelderand gave the lad a look of bewilderment. "What are you talking about?"

"Thirteen is considered an unlucky number! Look —" Swinkle pointed to the first passage in the book.

"If thirteen is considered unlucky, then the thirteenth letter would be the one to start with." The young cleric paused, counting the letters in his head. "'M'! 'M' is the letter to start with!"

The mage nodded, agreeing with Swinkle's rationale. "I think you have uncovered the first clue to this riddle." Gelderand wrote the letter 'M' on a scroll of paper.

Well, it is worth trying his idea, the mage thought. The boy seems to be more of a student than a fighter. Maybe I am not giving him the credit he deserves.

Gelderand peered toward the ceiling as he spoke. "It becomes the end, and the end becomes unlucky."

"That would mean 'M' would become the end. The end of what?" Swinkle's anxiety level rose.

"The end, the end," muttered Gelderand, "the end of the alphabet, maybe?"

Swinkle's eyes grew large as he took in the new information. "If what you say is true, then that would make an 'M' a 'Z', and 'Z' unlucky — meaning 'M'! I think that sounds reasonable," said the young cleric with excitement, as Gelderand wrote a 'Z' beneath the 'M'.

Swinkle read the next passage aloud, as he tried to piece the puzzle together. *"From here, we go left to right, expanding to the end, one becoming the other, the other becoming the one."*

The young cleric placed an elbow on the table, using it to hold his head in his hand. "How do you feel about this? We go left to right like it says. That means we go to the left of 'M', which would be 'L'. To the right of 'M' would be 'N'." Swinkle hurried to scribble his idea on his own scroll of paper.

"The next clue says one becoming the other, and the other becoming the one. That would mean that an 'L' becomes an 'N', and an 'N' would be an 'L'."

"And expanding to the end means we continue until we reach 'Z'," concluded Gelderand as he, too, began to work with Swinkle's idea.

"No, we expand to 'Y' since 'Z' has already become 'M'. See?" Swinkle hastily handed his scribbling to Gelderand, hoping that he could be the one to say he solved the riddle.

"Well, it's worth a try." Gelderand looked at Swinkle's writings, then to the book, turning at the next page to reveal the first page of coded text.

"The first group of letters is 'JYGGYSU 1'. Using your code, that would be —" The mage paused as he wrote down the letters 'P', 'A', 'S', 'S', 'A', 'G', 'E', and '1'.

Swinkle's eyes widened. "'Passage 1'! It works! That's the code! We've figured out the riddle!" The young cleric shouted in the direction of Gelderand's work area.

"Congratulations, Swinkle." Gelderand handed the young cleric the book. "I'll let you finish deciphering the rest of the text since you determined its code."

A wide toothy grin overtook Swinkle's face. "This is the happiest day of my life! I'll let you know as soon as I'm finished!"

Gelderand walked over to a small desk to open a drawer. Returning, the mage waved a metallic case in Swinkle's direction.

"Take your time. We are not going anywhere for a couple of days." Gelderand handed the young cleric the container. "Write as neat as possible, then place the scroll in this case when you are finished."

"I will." Swinkle accepted the tube from Gelderand. "I'll make sure no one but our group will ever lay their hands on our finding."

Suddenly, Harrison bolted into the room with Tara and Lance close behind. "Did someone say they figured out the riddle?"

"Swinkle's idea seems to be correct." Gelderand headed to the front door. "We should let him be so he can finish decoding the passages."

Harrison stared at his friend with a look of astonishment. "Good job, Swinkle!"

The young cleric could not contain his happiness, his smile never leaving his face.

Gelderand glanced around the doorway, appearing to look for something just out of view. Raising his brow, he asked, "Tara, have you seen Rufus?"

"No. I think he's still outside. It's starting to get dark, you better let him back in for the night." She then noticed the absence of the other men.

Turning to Harrison, she said, "By the way, where are your other two friends?"

The young warrior shrugged. "They're probably in some kind of trouble. The two of them are always looking for adventure."

"Do you think we should go and look for them?" Swinkle's question was more in the manner of being polite, rather than actual concern.

Harrison shook his head. "No. They can handle themselves." Looking in Tara's direction, he said, "We still have more pouches to fill."

"I'll help you two now that Swinkle is decoding the book himself," added Gelderand, much to Harrison's dismay.

Tara looked at the young warrior and noticed his look of disappointment. "We can finish the pouches, Uncle. Why don't you gather your other magical items?" Harrison looked at the girl, who gave him a smile.

"Well, all right. Just make sure you're careful in there." Gelderand directed his words more towards his niece than to the placement of ingredients in bags.

Tara motioned to Harrison. "Let's get to work." The two abruptly left the room, with Lance scooting behind them.

"Come on, Rufus." Gelderand shuffled to the front door as the cat came meowing into the house. "It looks like it's just me and you."

The wizard began to light strategically placed candles in an effort to combat the ensuing nightfall. When he approached the lamp nearest his workshop, he peeked inside, knowing that his niece was alone with Harrison.

"Just another problem to deal with," Gelderand mumbled to himself as he continued the mundane process of lighting the candles. Just then, Murdock and Pondle arrived from purchasing more supplies for the group.

"Good evening!" slurred Murdock as he entered the room. "You have to love a small town with *two* taverns!"

"And we didn't get thrown out of either one," added Pondle. Changing the subject, he asked, "Have you made any progress with the book?"

"We have determined the code and I'm deciphering the text as we speak," answered Swinkle, full of pride. "I should be done later tonight."

"You've figured out the code so soon?" Murdock appeared genuinely surprised at how fast Swinkle and Gelderand cracked a code invented to protect the scripture from brute warriors. "Maybe we can leave tomorrow."

Gelderand shrugged. "That is a possibility. If I can collect all my belongings, we should be able to leave sooner."

Pondle peered about the room, noticing the absence of an important member of the group. "Where's Harrison?"

"He's helping Tara," answered Gelderand, his tone synonymous to that of a concerned father.

"Helping?" Murdock laughed. "I'd check up on the two from time to time. I've seen that look on his face before."

"I know. I saw it, too." Gelderand shook his head. "I was young once you know. I hope they realize we are only here for a short time. I don't want Harrison to be thinking about Tara when he should be concentrating on this treasure."

"Let me tell you this." Murdock placed his pack on the floor, then shook a finger in the older man's direction. "It's a good thing we're leaving soon. The last time this happened we had to rescue him from a prison cell. Then in order to elude the soldiers searching for us, we had to be carted out of the town in coffin-like boxes along with the city's garbage."

The ranger shook his head, recalling the incident. "A good battle will set him straight again." With a frown, he asked, "When should we go out and bring back the treasure?"

"Not until the middle of the night," said Gelderand, waving a hand at the two adventurers. "The carousing settles down in a few hours and no one should be left lingering around."

Murdock nodded. "Fine by me. I'm going to bed now, so that I can be fresh for later on tonight."

"Me, too," added Pondle. "I better get some sleep as well."

Swinkle added to the conversation. "I'll inform Harrison of our decision when he's done helping Tara."

"Good," said Gelderand. "I'll help arrange the hoard in the basement as you bring it from its hiding place." With everyone in agreement for the course of their nighttime maneuvers, he added, "I'll try to be quiet while you settle in for the evening."

The mage started to head to his room, but stopped when he saw Rufus sitting in front of him. Picking up the animal, he gazed into its eyes.

"Rufus, go and watch over Tara."

Gelderand put the cat down and patted the animal on its head before the feline scurried off toward the work area. The wizard watched Rufus enter the other room, then continued to his bedroom for the remainder of the evening.

Harrison handed Tara the last of the pouches, as Rufus came bounding into the room, jumping from the floor to the workbench. Lance, upon seeing the cat, began to bark.

"Well, look who has come to help us." Tara gave Rufus a big hug. "And who sent you in here?" she asked, knowing very well who did.

"Lance!" Harrison used the tone of a father chastising a small child, causing the dog to stop his barking. The young warrior examined Gelderand's shelves and realized that they had finished collecting all the magical ingredients.

"What else do we need to pack?"

Tara gazed about the general area, cradling her pet. "My uncle can take care of the rest. Many of his belongings can be dangerous if handled improperly." The young girl rubbed the cat's head. "Does Rufus want to go and sit outside with me?"

The feline jumped out of her hands and scurried to the back door. Tara followed the cat to the portal on the other side of the room. With a flirtatious glance back to the young warrior, she said, "Would you like to join us?"

Harrison did not hesitate to answer. "Sure."

The young warrior watched Tara stroll over to a rather large tree, some fifty feet away from the house. The cloudy weather had finally given way to clear skies, and a crescent moon shed just enough light for Harrison to see the outline of the young girl's body.

Tara sat down under the tree with Rufus in her arms and began to gaze at the stars. Lance trotted around the perimeter of Gelderand's land, his nose close to the ground. Harrison casually proceeded to join Tara.

Sensing Harrison's approach, she said, "I like coming out here on nights like this." She continued to gaze upward. "Rufus is always nearby to protect me from the evil spirits."

Harrison took a seat under the tree. "Evil spirits?"

"When I was a little girl, my uncle would tell me never to wander too far from our home because the evil spirits might get me." Tara stared in the direction of the vast plains. "He would always point toward the open country and tell me that they will come from there.

"Then one day he came home with this little orange fur ball and told me that I better take care of Rufus, because when he grew up, he'd watch over me." The girl scratched the cat behind its ears.

Taking her gaze to Harrison, she said, "Weren't you afraid of anything when you were younger?"

"Me? No." Harrison looked out at the open land. "As long as I can remember, I have always wanted to be a warrior. I used to have a wooden sword that I made when I was a child." He laughed. "It was just a flat piece of wood, but I sharpened the end to a point and kept it by my side when I slept."

"Was your father a warrior?"

Harrison squirmed, uncomfortable with the girl's question. "No, he never became a warrior. Scynthians murdered my parents when I was twelve."

Tara ducked her head to gaze into his eyes. "I'm so sorry. I had no idea."

"It's all right. Their deaths happened a long time ago and I've dealt with my loss." The young warrior stared into the openness, watching the light breeze sway the branches on the trees and bushes.

"I'm a warrior today because of that incident," Harrison continued. "My parents instilled in me the passion to do good. I'll always be a just fighter and bring righteousness to everyone I meet. That's why I feel we must succeed on our quest."

Tara could see the pride Harrison felt talking about his parents, and could sense the pain he tried so desperately to hide.

"I feel that you will." Tara let Rufus go and reached down to hold the young warrior's hand. "You must succeed, for all of us."

"There's a lot you don't know." Harrison spoke reluctantly.

"Tell me." Tara stroked the young warrior's hand.

"We've been through so much." Harrison shook his head. "Lord Nigel Hammer of Concur killed our leader, Marcus Braxton." Harrison lifted his head and gazed into the girl's eyes.

"Our friends Aidan Hunter and Jason Sands also died during our journey to obtain the Treasure of the Land. They were such good men." The young warrior was overcome with emotion.

"Continue, please," Tara pressed. "I need to know what to expect. For my uncle's sake."

Harrison took care in choosing his words, not wanting to upset the young girl. He watched her closely. "We might not look like it, but all of us are experienced fighters. The Scynthians captured and tortured us, but we survived. Lord Hammer's soldiers imprisoned us, but we escaped. We even successfully navigated the catacombs that led to the Seven Rooms."

The young warrior paused, trying to gauge Tara's reaction. She did not waver and waited in anticipation for Harrison's next words.

"Your uncle is taking on a monumental task. I know he realizes this. You must be strong for him."

Tara's expression did not change. "My uncle used to be a very formidable wizard in his day. He's older now and his skills might need rekindling, but he will never let you down." She kept her eyes fixed on Harrison. "Never."

Harrison returned Tara's stare. The moonlight seemed to cast a glow around her small frame. In that instant, she appeared absolutely beautiful. Against his better judgment, he leaned toward her, his lips dangerously close to hers.

"I shouldn't do this," he said.

"I want you to." The two exchanged a passionate kiss. After a moment, Tara pulled away and stared at Harrison. Without saying a word, she leaned forward and their lips met again.

After their long kiss, Tara pulled away a second time. "This isn't a good idea. You're leaving in two days," she said, a tear glistening in one eye.

"You're right," Harrison agreed, but his tone did not. "I've known you less than a day, but I can't keep my eyes off you."

"Can't keep your eyes off me?" Tara let out a little laugh. "You've ventured throughout the countryside with men for who knows how long! I'm probably the first girl you've seen in months!"

Harrison laughed, too. The last woman he recalled seeing was Meredith, Lord Hammer's lady. He also remembered the promise he made to her.

"You're right, I haven't seen many women for quite some time. But, there is someone I made a pledge to."

Tara wiggled away from Harrison. "You already have a woman and yet you still feel you can kiss me!" She then tried to move further away.

"No, it's not like that at all!" Harrison lightly took Tara's arm in an effort to keep her still. "Meredith's held captive in Concur. She's Lord Hammer's woman."

Tara gave the young warrior a skeptical look. "What do you mean she's held captive?"

"She's neither his wife, nor his queen. When Nigel and his army overtook the city, he claimed Meredith as his prize. She's treated like royalty, but the truth is, she's a prisoner."

Tara remained unconvinced. "I don't see where you come into the picture."

Harrison nodded, understanding her apprehension. "Our party ventured to Concur to find a clue to the Treasure. I met Meredith then and learned of her fate. She pleaded for me to help her, but I couldn't at the time. That's when I made my promise to rescue her after we secured the Treasure." Harrison let out a laugh. "I know this all sounds ridiculous, but it's true."

Tara raised an eyebrow. "So, this woman is not *your* woman?"

The young warrior shook his head. "I can't say that she is, but I do know I must honor my pledge. I will see her again."

Tara studied Harrison and knew without a doubt that he had told her the truth. She also knew that Harrison would not be in town long enough to start a romance, but she found it hard to say no to him — perhaps because she did not want to.

Harrison did not act like other adventurers who had wandered into town and taken notice of her. Many a man had come courting Tara, only to experience her rejection in the end. Harrison was different. He seemed more sincere and trustworthy, not to mention his very handsome features. Maybe she needed a couple of days of fun, she tried to convince herself.

No matter the reason, she found herself saying, "I believe you, Harrison." She wiggled closer to him again and their lips met for yet another kiss.

Rufus, appearing out of nowhere, reached up with his paw and began to lightly sink his claws into Harrison's cheek, causing the couple to separate.

"If I didn't know better, I'd say that your uncle could see through his eyes!" said Harrison with a laugh.

Tara reached over and picked up the cat. "He's just jealous, aren't you?" The girl held Rufus up to her face, gazing with purpose at the animal.

You better not be looking through his eyes, she thought. Tara then placed the cat gently on the ground and

Rufus scooted back towards the house. Lance watched the feline scurry away and growled under his breath.

"Where were we?" Harrison moved closer to Tara.

"I think you were going to kiss me again." Tara leaned over to Harrison, their lips meeting. Before too long, Tara heard Rufus meowing as he stood near the door of the house, waiting to go inside.

"We better stop." Tara pushed Harrison away and stood up. "I have to let the cat in and it's getting late."

"Hey! Wait a second! Can't the cat stay outside a little longer?" Harrison pleaded, but to no avail.

"I don't think so," Tara said, peering through her lashes. Smiling, she added, "There'll be other times."

Harrison cocked his head, raising an eyebrow. "Really?"

"We'll see." Tara flashed him another flirtatious smile as she walked away from the tree and started toward the house. In the same instant, Lance sprung to his feet and teleported to the doorway.

Tara stared at Harrison with her eyes wide in amazement. "Did you see that?"

Harrison peered at Lance. The dog wagged his tail, then sniffed the startled cat. "Like I said, there're still a lot of things I haven't told you."

Tara remained in a mild state of shock. "He just reappeared out of thin air."

"Lance can teleport a short distance in any direction," said the young warrior with a blank expression to hide his amusement, reaching the doorway in the process.

"He can?"

"Yes." Without missing a beat, the young warrior added, "And I can understand his barks and he can understand my verbal commands."

"What?"

Harrison shrugged. "I have the ability to communicate with animals."

Tara opened the door, allowing both critters to enter. She continued to stare straight ahead, not sure what to make of Harrison's last comment.

"Good night, Tara." Harrison kissed the girl on the cheek as he passed through the doorway.

"Yes, good night," she said, watching the young warrior pass her by.

Tara shook her head in disbelief. "Why didn't I see this coming?" she whispered before closing the door behind her and settling in for the night.

CHAPTER 4

○

What had been a difficult day at sea turned into a peaceful voyage at night. The rays of the rising sun touched the not so distant mainland, with the docks along the coastline of Polaris coming into view at last. The ocean had calmed so much by daybreak that one of the young general's soldiers was sent to awaken Troy and Teleios out of a sound sleep.

The young fighter knocked on his superior's door before entering. "Sir, I'm sorry to disturb you, but it's sunrise and we'll be on shore soon. Shall I round up the men?"

Troy wiped the sleep from his eyes. "Yes. Have them ready for me on deck. I'll go over our plan one last time before we disembark."

"Yes, sir." The sentry nodded, closed the door, and exited the room.

"In due time, the greatest treasure this world has ever known will finally be in our possession," said Troy's advisor.

"I agree, Teleios." Troy rose from his bed and began to gather his belongings.

"There are thousands of books in this land. Finding one in particular will be a daunting task," continued the young general, "but, as the king has said many times, a man desires riches more than anything else. Someone's greed will lead us to the book."

Teleios went over to the captain's desk and reached for his backpack, which he had placed there the night before.

"This journey might be a dangerous one, Troy." Teleios opened the pack and peered in. "After the townspeople learn about this treasure, they may be reluctant to part with it, even for the large ransom. I will need all of my powers to help convince people to accept our gift."

Troy's advisor then removed an ancient book from the bag. An obvious relic, many of the pages barely remained attached to the binding. Teleios held the manuscript in front of his face, scanning its cover with his cat-like eyes.

Troy gazed over at Teleios with a look of astonishment. "Did the king allow you to take that book from the castle?"

"I didn't ask him." The halfling leafed through the pages. "But we will need it, that I am sure of. Indeed, a very powerful shaman used this scripture centuries ago."

Troy continued to stare at Teleios in disbelief. He never doubted his advisor's intelligence, and he appreciated Teleios's trustworthiness. Nevertheless, asking to use one of the king's spell books was one thing, but to simply take it was another. Looking at Teleios as he focused on a page of text gave Troy an uncomfortable feeling.

Could he be planning something on his own, the young general wondered. Teleios might be odd at times, but he has never double-crossed me. All of his strategies have worked in the past, so why wouldn't they work now? Troy felt himself ease. I'm just overreacting.

Teleios removed his gaze from the book and noticed his superior's look of apprehension. He understood Troy's complete loyalty to the king and could sense his leader's concern.

"Troy, the king would have allowed me to take the book. Looking back, I should have asked him personally, but he was unavailable and we were ready to disembark. I assure you, my intentions are just."

Troy took in his advisor's words and felt his anxiety wane. "I'm sorry, Teleios, I'm making too much of this. I'm sure that anything you do will get us closer to finding the king's sacred prize."

Dismissing the conversation with his advisor from his mind, the young general looked about the room for his gear and weaponry. "I'm about ready to address the men. Are you?"

"Yes." Teleios closed the book and placed it back into his pack. "The men are waiting."

On deck, the sun began its ascent from the horizon, while the cool morning air breezed through Troy's men. Troy and Teleios advanced with a firm forceful stride toward the awaiting platoon. The young general took his time to scan each soldier, checking to see if they were indeed ready to begin their search. One of Troy's captains, sensing satisfaction from his commanding officer's inspection, stepped forward.

Looking straight ahead and making sure not to make eye contact with his superior, he said, "General Harkin, the men are ready for any obstacle that might come their way. They eagerly await your orders."

"Thank you, Captain." The soldier nodded before scurrying back into the ranks. Troy continued, "In a few short hours you will embark on a journey that will make you richer than you could have ever imagined."

Troy then began to traverse in front of the soldiers. "After we land in Polaris, we will purchase the finest horses the town has to offer. When every man is equipped with a steed, your first responsibility will be to post the ransom signs. If *anyone* finds information that seems to have the *slightest* bit of significance, I want it reported to me immediately. Is that clear?"

"Yes, sir!" responded the men in unison upon hearing their general's command.

"Good." Troy continued scanning the men from left to right. "You are to leave no stone unturned as you search for the book. We'll venture to several villages and will evaluate our progress after we reach the town of Dragon's Quarters." The young general stopped his speech and stared at his men.

"Under *no* circumstance will you take it upon yourselves to return the book to the king without going through me. Is that understood?"

"Yes, sir!" shouted the men again.

Troy paused, the only audible sound being the gentle splashes of the waves against the ship's hull. "If any of you feel the reward will be greater by returning the book to the king himself, you're wrong!"

The young general again began to pace before his men. "I will not be embarrassed in front of the man who has given my family and me all we could ask for. I assure you, the person who finds the book and hands it to me shall be given a most generous reward." Troy stopped marching and looked toward his soldiers.

"Remember, the sacred book will bleed when you scratch its cover. Good luck. You may return to you duties." With that, the men quickly scrambled back to their respective posts.

Teleios approached General Harkin. "Impressive, Troy. The king would be most proud."

"I know that he would." Troy turned and looked out at the sea. "The king has bestowed on me a great burden. I won't let him down."

"I'm sure that we will recover the book in no time."

The young general maintained his gaze on the approaching shoreline. "I hope you're right."

Swinkle awoke to the sounds of birds chirping, finding himself still at the table with the book open and the scroll of decoded text in front of him. Murdock, Pondle, and Harrison remained sleeping on the floor as the young cleric gazed around the room. Lance, noticing Swinkle stirring, came over to him.

"I don't even remember falling asleep," the young cleric said as he straightened out his back. As he stretched, he felt the effects of sleeping the whole night in a hard wooden chair.

"At least I finished decoding this book. I can't wait to tell the rest."

Without warning, the front door opened to admit Tara and Rufus inside the house. Lance darted over to greet the young girl.

"Good morning," whispered Tara, trying to make as little noise as possible. She patted Lance on the head, then said, "I gathered some apples to go along with our breakfast. I'll try to be quiet."

"I was about to awaken them anyway," answered Swinkle, still eager to let everyone know the secrets he had uncovered. "Is Gelderand up? I've finished decoding the book."

"You decoded the book? That's fantastic!"

"Thanks." Swinkle left the table and headed toward his sleeping friends.

Tara started to take the apples out of her basket. "Gelderand woke up early to get a head start on his packing. Harrison and I didn't get to all of the items."

While Tara prepared breakfast, Swinkle went about waking up the group. The young cleric lightly shook Harrison, causing the young warrior to open his eyes.

"What's wrong?" Harrison's fighter training kicked in, instantly trying to get a fix on the situation.

"It's morning and I have important news to tell everyone." Swinkle then went about waking Murdock and Pondle.

The ranger rubbed his eyes, his body still sluggish from gathering their treasures a few hours ago. "Is everything all right?"

"Better than you could imagine," said the young cleric. "And Tara is preparing breakfast for us to boot."

"I have freshly baked breads, eggs, fruits, and apples for us all." The girl caught Harrison's gaze, giving him a wink.

The young warrior flashed Tara a wide smile. "Good morning," he said, taking a seat at the table.

After several minutes of organizing themselves, Murdock and Pondle also joined Swinkle and Harrison at the dining area. Tara had begun serving the meal, when she noticed Swinkle praying. A moment later, the young cleric finished his prayer, then tossed a slice of apple over his shoulder. The young girl stared in disbelief while Lance gobbled up the food.

"Why on earth would you do that?" she said in Swinkle's direction.

"It's just my way of thanking Pious for the food I am about to eat."

"Oh." Tara frowned. "Who's Pious?"

"Pious is my god of worship."

Tara then looked at the dog who continued to chew the apple. "Is it right for Lance to eat your sacrifice?"

At that point, Murdock let out a laugh. "That stupid dog has eaten every sacrifice Swinkle has made since he joined our group!"

Swinkle tried his best to brush off Murdock's comment. "Lance is part of the natural order in this world and I'm sure Pious does not mind his actions."

Tara seemed to understand. "I suppose you're right, but it does seem a bit odd to me." Just then, Gelderand entered the room.

"Tara, that smells delicious." The mage approached his niece and gave her a kiss on the cheek.

"Sit down, Uncle," she said. "Everything's ready."

Gelderand looked over the rest of the men who had started eating their breakfast. "I take it that everyone had a good night's rest after our early morning chores," he said as he took a seat at the table.

The night before Murdock, Pondle, and Gelderand made a successful transfer of the land's greatest riches from the thief's hiding place in the woods to the safety of Gelderand's basement. The three men spared Harrison and Swinkle from helping with the hoard, the rationale being with less people involved in the transfer, the smaller the odds at being seen.

The mage also declined in casting a spell to hide the loot from plain view in fear of leaving a magical signature that could be detected by others who possessed magical capabilities. To the chagrin of all the group members, the priceless trove of treasures rested below a trap door covered by a worthless piece of carpet.

"Eat well," said Gelderand. "This will probably be the best meal we will have for days." After serving her uncle, Tara prepared a plate of her own and sat next to Harrison.

"You're a very good cook," said the young warrior, biting into an apple.

"I'm glad you like your breakfast." Tara ate a spoonful of food, keeping her gaze fixed on the young man.

Harrison took a long look at the young girl. All had seemed to go well the night before, but today would be different. The young warrior knew they had to obtain the Talisman and that would always be his first priority. Finding Tara had become just a pleasant surprise, though he still thought of her all night long. Now with her by his side, it became more difficult to concentrate on the matters at hand.

"All right, Swinkle, let's hear what our treasure has to offer." Harrison tried to put Tara out of his mind for the time being.

Swinkle finished his mouthful of food before starting. "Well, let me begin by saying that we have many more riches to find. This book contains the clues to a number of precious jewels, an artifact, and a lantern of some sort." The young cleric then unrolled his scroll and began to read.

"The text starts like this. *Passage 1. As you read this page, disturbances of trivial happenings have significant meaning. All occurred at the same time; the time that you removed the book from its resting place. You, the reader, have proven that you are worthy of decoding and reading these passages, but now your patience and intelligence must prevail.*

"*Found throughout this great land are the jewels of the Talisman, though no one knows of them. Those who might have stumbled across them know nothing of their powers, for alone they are just ordinary gems. However, when placed in the correct order in the Talisman, they will allow the gateway of all gateways.*"

Harrison interrupted Swinkle. "How many jewels do we need to find?"

"I'm getting to that." Swinkle began reading again. *"You must now use these clues to help you on your quest.*

"The light of knowledge will be turned off in the town of Ballesteros. Here is where the red jewel resides. Down you must travel, where those who are eternally asleep lie. You must dig for your treasure, but where you might say? It is where a treasure should be found; there are no tricks here."

"Ballesteros?" A funny look overtook Murdock's face. "Where in the world is that?"

Pondle shook his head. "I've never heard of the place either."

"We can discuss this later," said Swinkle. "There is much more." The young cleric then continued reading.

"A beautiful, majestic explosion has taken place; its traces can be seen from great distances. Here is where the green jewel resides. Get by the heat and wear on your feet, and the prize will be yours."

Swinkle paused again. "This clue I don't care for. *It knows you have this book — it has the diamond."*

Swinkle stopped reading and looked at his friends. They all reflected on the words he had just spoken.

"Who or what is 'it'?" asked Harrison.

Gelderand waved a hand in the young warrior's direction. "We'll worry about that after, too. Swinkle, continue."

The young cleric nodded. "There are a few more passages. *Passage 2. The artifact is of crude design, no need to alarm the commoners with some majestic piece. The relic is comprised of a stand to hold this book, three places to hold the jewels, and a place for Dracus's lantern of blood. No one knows the artifact to exist at all, except for Sir Jacob, for someone must know."*

"Sir Jacob!" exclaimed Harrison. "I knew we'd hear his name again!"

Gelderand gave his new friends a confused look. "Who is Sir Jacob?"

"He was a loyal knight to King Ballesteros who helped design and distribute the Treasure of the Land."

Murdock had another disturbing thought. "Who's Dracus?"

"Dracus," mumbled Gelderand aloud. "Now that's a name I haven't heard in a long time."

The ranger gave the wizard a skeptical look. "What do you mean? Do you know of the person?"

"Person?" Gelderand answered with a slight laugh. "He's no person. He's a dragon." The men all stared at the mage. "We'll need to gather some additional information on him."

After a short pause, Swinkle said, "We can discuss these topics in greater detail later. Let me finish the scripture."

Continuing, he said, "*Passage 3. Place the jewels thusly.*"

Swinkle held up the scroll and showed his friends a triangular image with a diamond at the point of the triangle, and a ruby and emerald securing the base vertices. A lantern sat in the center of the picture, and a small stand that held the book protruded off to the left side.

He then read, "*Make no mistakes, for death can be a painful experience.*" After pausing briefly, he continued once again.

"*Passage 4. Take your treasures and find a secluded place, then light the lantern to open the gateway. Only then will you understand your true destiny.*"

Swinkle placed his scroll down, still in awe of the task ahead, even though he had read the passages repeatedly the night before. "That's it. What do you make of this, Gelderand?"

The mage still seemed a little unsure at how to handle the situation. "From the way it sounds, this Sir Jacob is an integral part of this whole puzzle. If he knew of this artifact, then it seems reasonable to believe that he would also know of all the other clues. The only problem is that he has been dead for centuries."

"I might be able to help with that," said Harrison, while everyone listened intently.

"Remember when I said someone named Philius gave me a manuscript? When I read his scripture, an entrancing feeling overtook my body and I felt as if I was present when certain events took place.

"I saw Sir Jacob and a very powerful mage named Maligor the Red in those writings. They constructed everything for the Treasure of the Land — the metal plates, the jewels, the Seven Rooms — everything. And, I believe that their handiwork will be evident when we go searching for the Talisman."

"Interesting," said Gelderand, stroking his beard.

Harrison's face changed to one of apprehension. "I'm also concerned about the statement that says we'll learn our true destiny. What does anyone make of that?"

The mage raised his hands. "I think we need to concentrate on finding the pieces to the Talisman before we worry about the bigger picture. I'm sure our fate is very significant, but we must take one step at a time." Gelderand panned the room, and everyone's actions led him to believe that they agreed. "Perhaps we should focus on the clues to this mystery."

"The first clue says something of this town of Ballesteros," intervened Pondle. "Maybe we should begin there. After we get to this town we can inquire about the works of Sir Jacob, as well as to look for the red jewel."

Harrison remained confused about the information he had just heard. "Like Murdock said before, I've never heard of a town named Ballesteros. Where do we even go to look —"

Murdock interrupted his friend's question. "I think that you've forgotten another major issue here. Some *thing* knows we've taken this book. That happened almost a week ago. I have to believe that it'll come looking for us, if it hasn't already."

"He's right." Pondle knew with his thief's mind that whenever others believed that a treasure existed, many would come searching for it.

"We have to be on guard at all times from here on out. We can take nothing for granted. Consider anyone you meet an adversary — anyone. Remember, a dragon can transform itself into many things, even that of a harmless child."

"As I stated yesterday," remarked Gelderand. "I feel we should venture to Valkala and talk with Martinaeous, my old mentor. His crystal ball might be able to help us see where Sir Jacob laid the jewels to rest. That, coupled with Harrison's knowledge of the land, could be enough to decipher these clues. I know Martinaeous can help us more than if we just sat around this table."

"I agree," said Murdock, the thrill of adventure in his voice. "When can we get started on our journey?"

"Later this morning." Gelderand looked over to Tara with a somber face. "All I have to do is pack some belongings for Rufus and to make sure Tara will have everything she needs while I'm away."

"This morning?" Harrison came to the realization that this would definitely be his last few hours with Tara. "I thought last night you said we'd need two days!"

"I didn't think we would finish decoding the book so soon. Swinkle did an outstanding job deciphering the text and I think that the rest of you don't really appreciate the fact that he managed to do it so fast.

"The creators of this code intended for clever beings to solve it, not brute warriors. The beings that performed this magic want intelligent people to succeed, not battle-scarred veterans."

Harrison sighed, looking down to the floor. "You're right, Gelderand." The young warrior turned to face his friend.

"Swinkle, we're sorry if we all got caught up in what the book states instead of letting you know how much we appreciate your efforts."

The young cleric smiled. "I'm just trying to do my part. Hearing your words validates all of my actions."

"Swinkle, you did a fine job, but it's time to get moving." Murdock got up from the table. "Let's gather our backpacks and check all our supplies one last time, while Gelderand finishes his chores."

"I'll double-check the hoard we stashed away last night, too," said Pondle, leaving with his friend.

"I will let you know when I am done." Gelderand then headed to his room.

Tara looked at the young warrior. "I'm going to help my uncle, but I want to see you one more time before you leave, Harrison."

The girl gazed at the young warrior with sadness in her eyes. All night long she tried to put him out of her mind, but she could not. She had finally found someone she could care for, and he was about to leave.

"I'm going to really miss you," Harrison said. "I'll be outside. Come look for me there." The young warrior left the table, not hiding his disappointment.

Tara waited a moment, allowing Harrison to gather his armor and weaponry before leaving the house. The girl flashed Swinkle a tearful smile, then left him alone at the table, joining her uncle in the other room.

Outside, Harrison let Lance roam free while he proceeded to the tree that he and Tara had sat under the night before. Lance went his own way, keeping his nose glued to the ground.

"I need to stay focused on our quest," the young warrior said to himself as he started to put on his armor. As he did, Murdock, who had finished gathering his belongings, came up from behind.

"Harrison, I've seen you looking at the girl in that way of yours." The ranger's words startled the young warrior.

"Look, we need you focused on this quest. If you let your guard down, you'll be killed, plain and simple. The passage said that some being knows we have this book. This creature might send something out after us, or worse. All I know is that we have to be alert at all times. Do you understand?"

Harrison had never heard Murdock use such a serious tone of voice. His friend's sincerity towards the common goal of finding the Talisman impressed the young warrior.

"You're right, Murdock. Tara has consumed most of my thoughts since we arrived in Tigris." Harrison shook his head before trying to offer an explanation. "I don't know why, but she just has. I know how important our task is. I'll regain my focus. I just want to say good-bye to her and we'll be off."

Murdock maintained his stare at his friend, while Harrison continued to secure his armor. The young warrior peeked over to see the ranger's constant glare. With a sigh, Harrison said, "You won't have to worry about me. I'll be fully prepared for any battle."

"Good. We're counting on you." Murdock sensed someone approaching from behind, and turned to find Tara coming toward the two of them.

"I'll be inside with the rest of the group. I want to make sure Pondle's all set with the Treasure." The ranger turned and headed back towards the house. As he passed Tara, he gave her a look of concern.

Tara watched Murdock walk by her, before approaching Harrison. "Is everything all right?"

"Yes, everything's fine," he said, fastening the last of his armor.

Tara gazed into the young warrior's eyes. "I guess you'll be leaving soon."

"Yes. We might not return for quite some time." Harrison knew that he had no idea when he would see her again. "I'll be sure to take special care of your uncle."

Tara hugged the young warrior. "You take care of yourself," she said with sadness. "I wanted you to know that I enjoyed our time together. Even if it didn't last very long."

Harrison looked down at the girl. "I enjoyed our time, too. Tara, I will see you again."

Though unhappiness filled the young maiden's heart, she felt the same way. "I know you will, too." Trying not to cry, she said, "Be careful. This trip sounds very dangerous."

Harrison nodded. "I'm sure it will be. But I'm ready. I've made a pact with my friends that we'll find this treasure, and I extend that pledge to Gelderand."

"I'm still so afraid. Gelderand's like a father to me. I love him so much."

"I'll watch over him. I promise." The young warrior placed his right hand under the girl's chin and raised it, both sets of blue eyes locking their gaze on each other. Harrison then leaned forward and gave Tara a passionate kiss.

Separating after a moment, he said, "Like I said before, I don't know how long I'll be away, but I'm coming back."

Tara gazed at the young warrior with teary eyes. "You're a good man, Harrison. Come home soon."

"I hope to do just that." The two kissed again for the last time. "Now, I must go."

"I know," said Tara somberly. "Your friends are waiting."

Harrison grabbed his pack and weaponry, then led Tara back to the house, with Lance following close behind. Inside, the rest of the group waited for the young warrior to return in order to begin their new journey.

"Well it's about time!" exclaimed Murdock as the party members picked up their belongings.

Gelderand went over to his niece and gave her a hug. "You take care of yourself. Everything you need is here for you. I don't know how long I'll be away, but I will return." The mage tried his best to hide his emotions.

Tara embraced her uncle, sniffling. "I'm going to miss you. Just take care of yourself." Regaining her composure, she asked, "Are you taking Rufus, too?"

The mage gave his niece a reluctant nod. "Yes. You know he always accompanies me on my journeys." Gelderand swung his pack around, revealing Rufus's scrunched orange face. "I'll take good care of him for you."

Tara patted the cat on the head. "Good-bye, Rufus. Stay out of trouble." Tears began to roll down the girl's face.

"Don't cry, Tara." Gelderand gave his niece a kiss on the cheek. "I'll see you soon." Tara nodded, not saying a word.

Gelderand knew his niece would be fine and did not want to have a long, drawn out farewell. Turning to his new friends, he said, "It's time to go!" The mage then motioned for the group to depart.

As the rest of the party proceeded outside, Harrison came over to Tara, wiped the tears from her face, and kissed her once again.

"I'll be back before you can forget about me."

"I'm sure that you will," she said, sniffling again. "Take care, please."

Harrison took one last look at Tara before turning and leaving her behind. The young warrior joined the other party members and headed down the main road of the town.

As the men left the confines of Gelderand's property, Tara could hear Rufus's meows as she gazed at his little face sticking out of her uncle's pack.

"Oh, please be careful," she said softly, as the adventurers left her view and headed toward the Great Forest.

CHAPTER 5

◻

People described the town of Polaris as being a place where a man's net would always yield an abundance of fish. Many of the townspeople were fishermen by trade who would look towards the sea for their adventures. Today, a man would ask them to turn inland to search for a treasure worth more than many of them could earn in a lifetime.

Troy's ship dropped anchor in the harbor of Polaris in the early morning hours. After his men gathered their belongings, the young general addressed them on the vessel's deck one last time. All the soldiers lined up and waited for their commander's instructions.

"I want every major establishment to post our ransom," barked Troy. "Tell the shop owners that General Troy Harkin will answer any questions that they might have. By the time you're finished, you'll be fully equipped with horses, armor, and weaponry. Now carry out your duties!" His men gathered the ransom signs in haste, then proceeded to leave the ship and enter the town.

Teleios smiled. "The news of this prize will spread like wildfire, Troy." Thinking ahead, he said, "Arcadia is a day's ride by horseback. We will have to camp out in the wilderness for a night."

Troy watched his men disembark the boat and wander into town. "That's not a problem. The men are more than seasoned enough for our trip. I wonder if people in the town of Arcadia will know of our quest before we even get there."

Teleios nodded. "They will. Most of the human civilizations reside in these coastal towns. I wouldn't be surprised if even a band of bounty hunters sets out for the book right after we leave."

Troy looked back at his advisor with a curious gaze. "What makes you believe that bounty hunters will bring us the book?"

"Because they will kill for it." A cold stare followed Teleios's answer. "There are many men out there who spend their lives adventuring. The thrill of hunting down another band of intelligent beings to return a prize for a ransom is more than enough incentive."

Troy's advisor squinted before speaking again. "Use caution when you accept the king's sacred book. Bounty hunters are known to receive payment with a smile, then stab you in the back as you turn away."

Troy raised an eyebrow. "I'll keep that in mind."

"I'm just trying to be completely honest with you." Noticing the apprehension on his superior's face, Teleios changed the subject.

"I think our presence has already stirred some interest in the townspeople." Two fishermen stood at the end of the pier, gawking at them.

Troy turned his gaze away from his advisor and peered at the men. "This is just the beginning, Teleios. I'll handle this." The young general then proceeded down the dock and approached the townsmen.

Teleios watched his commander converse with the townsfolk, knowing that Troy wanted nothing more than to please his king. The halfling also realized that his leader was commanding his first true adventure.

When King Holleris announced that Troy would be the next general-at-arms, Teleios took it upon himself to take the young lad under his wing. Troy was sixteen at the time, and though he had fought in many battles, veteran soldiers still viewed him as inexperienced.

Teleios could have made a strong case to be the king's lead soldier, especially with his successful battle record. Instead of resenting his placement of second in command, the halfling chose a nobler route.

Since the king chose Troy to be his heir apparent, Teleios knew there would be no changing his mind. Instead, he vowed to see that the boy would succeed. Teleios would make detailed battle plans and explained them to his leader the way a mentor taught his prize student. He would advise Troy on all probable outcomes of key battle decisions, and he always made himself accessible to his superior for consultation whenever the young man needed him. Because of these traits, Teleios more than gained his commander's trust.

Teleios knew his place in the military pecking order and allowed Troy to make first contact with the townspeople. After a few moments, he muttered, "You will find this book, Troy. I will make sure you succeed." Feeling that he had waited long enough, he approached Troy and allowed his friend to introduce him to the fishermen.

Several hours had passed since Harrison and his friends left Tigris behind. Pondle and Murdock led the men through the forest, followed by Harrison, Swinkle, and Gelderand. Lance spent his time scurrying between the lead men and his master, occasionally stopping to investigate scents on his own.

With no pending danger, Harrison continued to talk with Gelderand about their quest as they trudged through the muddy underbrush. "Does this town of Ballesteros really exist?"

"I don't know." Gelderand had trouble keeping pace with the younger men and began to grow weary from the extended traveling. To make matters worse, his breath had started to become very deep and ragged.

"I've never heard of a town with that name, but if it is in the book, then it must exist."

Harrison continued to think aloud. "What does 'the light of knowledge has gone out in this town' mean?"

The mage shrugged. "I am not sure of that either."

"I've been thinking about that, too." Swinkle had kept quiet while the two men conversed. "Does it mean that the people suddenly have become incompetent?"

"That is a possible explanation." Gelderand staggered to an abrupt stop. "Can we rest?"

The poor mage was not accustomed to journeying for such long stretches at a time. Looking around, he found a tree to lean against in order to catch his breath.

"Rest again?" retorted Murdock from up ahead. His agitation toward Gelderand had already started to rise, and today was only the first day of their journey.

"We've left behind so many tracks that a child could follow us to Valkala. We have to keep moving or something's going to be upon us soon." The ranger knew the forest had many eyes, more so at nighttime, which loomed only a couple of hours away.

"Murdock, you can't expect Gelderand to travel for so long the first day," defended Harrison. "We'll stop here for just a little while."

Pondle agreed with the young warrior. "I'll check out the area up ahead." The thief whistled for Lance, and the two darted away from the group and advanced deeper into the forest.

Gelderand gently placed his pack on the ground, allowing Rufus to wriggle out of the bag. The cat meowed as it stretched its legs. The group had traveled for only a short time, yet the older man already could feel the effects of the journey. The mage knew this type of adventuring suited the other members of the party much better than him and could not help but feel that he slowed down the progress of the other men. Murdock had told him they would break only twice a day, once for food and again to camp for the night. Already they had to stop and rest for him two times.

Murdock sat down on a nearby log. "You have three days to get yourself into shape," said the ranger, using a terse tone to convey his message. "The terrain hasn't even begun to get rough yet. I don't want to spend too long in this forest."

"I'll be better in a few days." Gelderand took a seat on the ground. "Just bear with me."

In an effort to change the subject, Harrison said, "We should get a better understanding of these clues when we meet with your old friend, right?"

Gelderand wiped the sweat from his brow. "I hope so. If not, we'll have to take another course of action."

"You know we'll be entering Lord Hammer's territory on the way to Valkala." Murdock directed his words at Harrison.

Harrison glanced down at the ground. "I've thought about that."

The ranger shook his head. "We can't be spotted by his men or we're dead."

"I don't want to go anywhere near Concur." Swinkle felt his apprehension rise at the sound of Lord Hammer's name. "At least not until we are ready."

Gelderand listened to the men, but their conversation further confused him. "What's so bad about Concur?"

Harrison stepped around the question. "Let's just say we had a little misunderstanding in that city."

"A little misunderstanding? Is that what you call it?" chided Murdock. "Gelderand, remember the story about rescuing these two from a prison?" The ranger pointed a thumb at Swinkle and Harrison. "That happened in Concur, and not too long ago."

Murdock then began to fiddle with his longbow. "Our faces are still fresh in people's minds there."

Gelderand furrowed his brow. "Then, by all means, let's avoid that place."

Harrison thought about his time in Concur. The vision of Meredith's blue eyes and radiant smile remained clear in his mind. The young warrior looked down at his right hand and gazed at the ruby-set ring that she had given to him.

"I have unfinished business to settle there."

Murdock spoke in a stern tone and pointed a finger at his friend. "That's for another time. We must secure the Talisman first."

"I agree." The young warrior continued to stare at his hand, recalling the powers associated with the ring.

Without warning, Pondle reappeared from the woods with Lance right on his heels. By the look on his face, he had apparently found something quite disturbing.

"You have to come and take a look at this." Pondle's words trembled as much as his hands as he gestured toward the forest.

Murdock stared at his friend with concern, knowing something was very wrong. "What is it, Pondle?" he asked, rising from his seat on the log.

"You have to see for yourself." The thief motioned for his friends to follow him through the underbrush. The men raced after Pondle, as Lance hurried past the group and joined the thief.

Harrison caught up to Murdock. "What do you think's out there?"

"I don't know. It takes a lot to move Pondle like this," he said, as he ducked under a low branch.

Up ahead they could see four short bushes that gave way to a small open area. Pondle and Lance reached the clearing first, followed by Murdock and Harrison. The three looked on in horror as Gelderand and Swinkle reached their position. There in front of them stood what Pondle had seen.

"May the gods have mercy!" cried Gelderand, as a blank expression overtook his face upon seeing the gruesome sight.

Before them rested two overturned carts, ripped bags that contained some kind of seeds, pelts of small animals, and the bloody, dismembered corpses of three humans. Lance went about sniffing around the carnage.

Murdock stared in disbelief. "Pondle, look at the bodies!"

"Scynthians," answered the thief. The group immediately felt the chill of what lay ahead of them. The

Scynthains were an evil humanoid race, and well documented accounts of their atrocities abounded.

"The beasts even killed the child!" Harrison's anger boiled deep inside, seething that not even a young boy could escape the wrath of hatred from these creatures. Further away from the little body lay the remains of a middle-aged man and that of a young male.

"They ransacked the whole family." Pondle's eyes remained fixed on the shocking sight. "These bodies aren't even two days old. These are fresh kills, Harrison."

The young warrior maintained his gaze on the corpses. Puzzled, he said, "The Scynthians are supposed to be north of here." Harrison shook his head, disbelieving. "Way north of here."

"It gets worse." Murdock pointed to the tracks on the ground. "These markings over here suggest they dragged something, perhaps the mother. They head north, too."

Gelderand looked at the scene in shock. "Why didn't they kill her with the rest of them?"

"They probably raped her and will sacrifice her later, if she's not dead already." Murdock turned his head away in disgust.

"I can't even anoint them." Swinkle knew that one of his clerical duties was to insure that every being receive a proper burial. "They have been dead too long. The least we could do is to lay them to rest."

"I'll help." Murdock took out a small shovel from his backpack, as did Pondle. "The faster we dig the graves, the sooner we can get out of here."

The ranger then looked over to Gelderand. "Help Swinkle prepare the bodies."

The mage gave Murdock a blank stare. "Of course," he said, snapping out of his trance.

Harrison came over and began to dig with a shovel of his own. Lance followed his master and watched over the men.

"Murdock, you don't think the Scynthians would be heading south?" the young warrior asked in a concerned, low voice. Constant images of Tara, defenseless in her quaint home, had flashed through his mind the moment they discovered the gruesome scene.

The ranger looked toward Gelderand before answering Harrison. "I don't know," he whispered. "They certainly don't belong here."

Murdock looked at the young warrior while he continued digging. "Let's just assume this renegade band of warriors got lost. I don't want Gelderand to worry about the Scynthians heading towards Tigris. I think you know what I mean."

The Scynthians wouldn't travel south, Harrison thought. If they did, they would have to bring an army to defeat the many humans in towns and villages south of the Great Forest. Tara would be perfectly safe in Tigris. The young warrior knew deep down that Murdock was right about this being some lost group of beasts that this poor family intercepted.

Even so, the tracks did seem to head in the same general direction that they traveled. The only good thing about this disgusting encounter was that the men would be on the alert for this ragtag band of creatures. No way could the likes of a Scynthian surprise them now.

"Let's just finish burying these bodies, then find a place to camp for the night," said Harrison. "We'll need to be extra careful. I don't plan to end up like these people."

"Not with me around," answered Murdock. "No Scynthian is going to do me in."

"Me either," added Pondle.

After some time, the three men finished their digging, then placed the dead bodies in the fresh graves. After they buried the corpses, Harrison summoned Swinkle.

The young cleric removed a holy book from his backpack, opened it to a page, then looked over the makeshift graves. The other men, as well as Lance, stood by Swinkle's side.

"Dear Pious," started the young cleric, "please find room in your heart for these unlucky souls. Though we did not know them, we know all too well the horrors they must have endured."

The young cleric turned to another page in his book. "Please accept our humble sacrifice, as we pray for their eternal well-being." Swinkle mumbled the words from a passage, then sprinkled holy water onto the graves.

"This family is now in your hands. Please, watch over your children." After a moment of silence, the young cleric said, "That's the best I can do."

Harrison peered at his friend. "You did a fine job, Swinkle." Turning his attention to the rest of the group, he said, "It's time to gather our things and continue onward." Everyone nodded in agreement.

Gelderand rounded up Rufus and positioned him in his backpack, while Swinkle put away his holy book and water and readied himself to venture again. The other men secured their belongings, too, and when they appeared ready to travel, Harrison summoned Murdock and Pondle.

"Get us out of this desolate place." The two men assumed their role as the front men for the group and led the party away from the area.

Harrison drew his weapon and kept a careful eye out for Swinkle and Gelderand. Lance came to his master's side.

Harrison gazed down at the dog. "You let us know if something's out there."

"Yes," barked Lance, who then scurried off to be with Murdock and Pondle.

Harrison scanned the forest with an intense eye. The sun began to sink in the afternoon sky, casting scattered sunbeams through the branches of the trees. The young warrior knew better than to allow the otherwise pleasant scenery to fool him. Danger was close by; he could feel it.

Harrison raised his blade to his face — its steel edge glistened in the waning light. His thoughts shifted to

Tara and he hoped his instincts were right, that the Scynthians would not travel further south. A fleeting thought of Meredith also entered his mind and he prayed for her safety, too.

The young warrior stepped on a twig, the snap jerked him out of his trance. His focus then went back to his battle-axe. More than a week had passed since he used his weapon in battle. Something inside told him that it would not be much longer until he used it again. Harrison continued onward, ready for whatever might lie ahead.

CHAPTER 6

○

The terrain of the Great Forest had changed from flat woodlands to a series of small wooded hills and valleys. Just as Murdock had said, the trek through the landscape increased in toughness, much to Gelderand's dismay. After a restless night of sleep, the poor mage could feel the effects of the journey taking a toll on his body.

"Can we please rest again?" Panting, Gelderand stopped and leaned against a tree.

"I suppose we have no choice, now do we," snapped Murdock, as he stared at the older man from up ahead.

"Just a few minutes to catch my breath. Rufus needs to roam about a bit, too." Gelderand let the cat climb out of his pack to stretch its legs.

Harrison knew the wizard was doing his best to keep up with the younger men. "Gelderand, we really shouldn't be stopping so often. I know you're not used to this type of journeying, but the Scynthians could be anywhere around here. We have to get out of this forest as fast as possible. You have to push yourself."

Gelderand closed his eyes and nodded. "I know. All I need is another day and I will be able to travel like the rest of you."

"We might as well camp here for the night." Murdock glared at the two in disgust, then removed his backpack and began to set up the site for the evening.

"Pondle has secured the area and it's starting to get late. If my calculations are correct, we should be able to reach the end of the forest by sundown tomorrow. Make that we *will* reach the end of the forest by tomorrow night."

"We should be safe from the Scynthians for now," added Pondle as he helped Murdock. "All of their tracks lead north. I haven't seen any that headed in our direction."

The party had traveled the entire afternoon without any hint of Scynthian activity. Now they rested by the warm glow of a campfire. Besides the horrifying encounter of the slain family, they had hardly come across any perils through the rather large forest. The area seemed uninhabited, but that would all change.

After a few hours of discussion about their quest at hand, Pondle rose from his seat on the ground in a slow, deliberate motion.

Murdock noticed his friend's sudden apprehension. "Pondle? What's the matter?"

"Do you hear that?" The thief stared with intent into the dark woods. Lance immediately sprung to his feet and began to whimper.

"Hear what?" Harrison, too, stood up and stared in the same direction.

"Listen," answered Pondle in a hushed tone, as he seemed to focus in on an inaudible target. "In the distance."

"Pondle, I don't hear a thing. All I hear is —" started Murdock until he also heard a low rumbling sound.

"Drums!" intervened Harrison.

Swinkle and Gelderand joined the rest of the group as they peered into the depths of the forest. "What could it be?" asked Gelderand with concern.

"I hope it's not what I think." Pondle began to gather his weaponry. "Murdock, Harrison, light your torches. Let's have a look."

Murdock and Harrison grabbed their torches and rounded up their weapons, as Gelderand and Swinkle nervously looked on.

Swinkle stared at the three fighters as they prepared themselves for what seemed to be a battle. "What about us? You can't just leave us here!"

"You're right," said Harrison. "Gather your belongings. It's too dangerous to leave you both here in the middle of the night."

"Hold on a minute!" Gelderand's exclamation managed to get everyone's attention. "Will you all please stop and tell me what is going on here?"

Harrison approached the mage. "The drums you hear are probably the beginning of some tribal ritual. They might symbolize the beginning of a battle and we could be standing in the middle of some enemy territory. We need to investigate. At least we'll be able to know what to expect instead of waiting for something to happen."

"Do you think it could be the same Scynthians that slaughtered that family?" Gelderand swallowed hard with fear.

"We don't know. That's why we have to look into this," said the young warrior, knowing in all likelihood that it would be the same barbarians.

Murdock waited for his chance to speak. "If everyone's ready, I suggest that Pondle and I lead the way. Let Gelderand and Swinkle follow us next, with you bringing up the rear." The young warrior nodded in approval.

"What do you expect from us?" Swinkle felt a little more than apprehensive about following the faint sounds of drums in the darkness.

Harrison gave both cloaked men a lit torch. "Just listen for Pondle and Murdock's orders and follow them as quietly as possible."

The young warrior held his gaze on the worried men. "You two stick close together. Gelderand, we may need you to perform a spell. I hope you realize that."

"I feared you would say that," said the wizard, nodding. "I have not used my more intense spells in quite some time."

Harrison gave the mage an incredulous stare. "You knew the perils of this journey before you agreed to join our group. If we only wanted the book decoded, we would've paid you by now."

"I understand. I just want you to realize that I have not performed magic against living beings for a long time. I just hope my spells still work."

"Well, they better," intervened Murdock, pointing at the mage with intent. "I'm not jeopardizing my life only to have you crack under the pressure of battle."

Looking at the rest of the group, the ranger asked, "Are we ready? The faster we investigate these sounds, the sooner we can evaluate our situation."

"Give me another minute." Harrison bent to one knee. "Lance, I need you to stay with Swinkle and Gelderand. You need to protect them. Do you understand?"

"Yes." Lance scurried to Swinkle's side.

"Good, boy." Harrison looked over to Murdock. "Let's go."

Murdock motioned for his friend to lead the way, and with a nod, the thief guided the men into the dark forest. Pondle, being a halfling, benefited from his infravision instead of needing the light of a torch. Just as the men could see in daylight, Pondle could survey a good forty feet into the darkness with ease. Although they did not know the beings responsible for making the drumming sounds, his instincts told him they would be in for a horrifying scene.

To his right, some thirty feet away, he could see the glow of Murdock's torch as he stealthily headed in the same direction. From behind, he could see the dancing lights of two anxious torchbearers, as well as a faint shimmer farther away. Everyone seemed to have things under control as the terrain began to take a gradual slope upwards.

Murdock watched Pondle begin to scale the hill. From his viewpoint, they would be facing trouble — not so much from the enemy, but perhaps from his own party. Gelderand was no fighter, nor was Swinkle, which he had expressed many times before. If any fighting broke out, he would have to defend them instead of being the one on the attack.

The forest continued upward for some two hundred yards with the trees thinning out at the top of a small hill. The drumming had increased in intensity, and they could see a faint glow ahead in the distance.

"Swinkle, look over there," Gelderand whispered as the two continued up the slight grade. "Is that some kind of light?"

The looming glow symbolized the first sign of battle Gelderand had witnessed in almost fifteen years, since the time he helped on a quest to find the Ancient Scrolls of Arcadia. The Scrolls detailed the founders of Arcadia and how they built their ancient civilization. All people throughout the land respected the ancient Arcadians for their art and culture, but barbarians had overrun their empire. Today, the city prospered, but at a fraction of the sophistication of the past.

Gelderand had enjoyed researching the Arcadian people and gladly accepted a role in helping discover their past. To his dismay, they never found the hidden artifacts.

The mage felt the same joy when he had agreed to join the group to search for the Talisman of Unification. Now, the reality of what might lie ahead replaced the thrill of adventure that he had sensed earlier.

Swinkle squinted into the distance. "It seems to be —" At that moment, both men heard a faint scream over the constant pounding of the ever-deafening drums.

The young cleric's head swiveled to meet the frozen gaze of the older man. "What was that?"

"I think someone screamed." Gelderand peered into the nothingness in shock. "I'm not getting a good feeling about this! What do you think is going on?"

Before Swinkle could respond, the mysterious drumming came to a halt. They both heard a definite scream for help, and it came from a woman. Harrison had also heard the cry and knew he must acknowledge that plea.

"Gelderand, Swinkle! Stop!" The young warrior spoke just loud enough to catch them both off guard, with

Gelderand almost dropping his torch. Lance turned and went to his master.

"Don't sneak up like that!" The wizard felt his heart begin to race faster.

"Put out your torches and follow me. Try to be as quiet as possible as well." Gelderand and Swinkle did as Harrison ordered.

Turning to Lance, the young warrior admonished, "No barking, boy."

Harrison knew that Pondle and Murdock had heard the scream too and had probably positioned themselves close to the top of the small hill already. The young warrior could not see anything that resembled Murdock's torch, which he took as a good sign. This meant that his friends had teamed up and were using the thief's infravision to lead them.

As the three men climbed closer to the summit, the light brightened and the sounds of other beings became clearer. The low, guttural voices they heard could only be that of a Scynthian chieftain barking commands. Up ahead, they could see the silhouette of two figures peering over the hill. Harrison put out his torch as they approached Pondle and Murdock. The ranger motioned for them to get down as they reached the crest of the rise.

"They're Scynthians all right," informed Murdock as Harrison cautiously peeked his head over the hilltop. "We're just in time for a sacrifice."

What Harrison saw astounded him. The Scynthians had started construction on a small outpost with several makeshift huts in the distance. Unfinished buildings and lookout posts sat at the base of the hill, while a large campfire burned in the middle of the encampment, its flames climbing high into the dark sky.

The mere fact that the Scynthians had started establishing an outpost this deep into human territory was bad enough, but what Harrison saw to the right of the blaze was far worse. Two bodies, one of a man and the other of a woman, lay tied on raised wooden platforms. The horizontal stagings stood a mere three feet off the ground, just high enough to allow the poor souls' feet to dangle over the edge. The man's body appeared lifeless, but the woman was definitely alive and trying in vain to free herself.

The leader of the outpost stood in front of the raging inferno; standing close by was a Scynthian shaman, who began to mutter something as he hovered around the man's body.

"We have to save the woman!" Harrison continued to stare at her sorry state of affairs.

Pondle's answer came in a somber tone. "We counted seventeen total Scynthians, Harrison. I feel it's in our best interest to continue around this camp and save ourselves before they see us. The woman's as good as dead."

Harrison's paladin instincts could not allow him to accept his friend's rationale. "Since when have we backed down from helping another human being?"

The young warrior reflected back to his training at the Fighter's Guild and recalled a very important rule – always attempt to save those in a dire position. This scenario more than adhered to the adage.

Even Murdock, not one to avert confrontations, did not anticipate success with the current predicament. "The odds are heavily stacked against us, Harrison. This would be suicide."

The young warrior did not feel ready to give up just yet. "There must be some way we can help. Let's have a look around."

Pondle shook his head in disbelief. "Fine," he responded with reluctance in his voice. "The hill has a more gradual slope to the left. Murdock and I'll scale around the camp that way. You stay here with Gelderand and Swinkle until we get back."

Harrison nodded. "Make it quick. She doesn't have much time."

Murdock and Pondle commenced with their trek down the left side of the hill. Fortunately for the two, all the

Scynthians they had counted now faced the platform, which left them with their backs to the adventurers.

Gelderand continued to stare at the scene in front of him. "What do you think they are going to do to her?"

"They will kill her," answered Swinkle, saddened at the thought.

Just then, a rather large Scynthian stepped onto the platform and approached the motionless man. The executioner waited patiently while the shaman chanted over the body. When the shaman finished his task, the savage raised the sharp edge of his one-sided battle-axe. In one smooth stroke, the blade came crashing down, slicing the right arm off the body.

"No!" exclaimed Harrison, in obvious shock.

The woman, watching the entire scene, screamed in terror, then began to sob uncontrollably. The man's limb dangled from his rope. The men could now see that the Scynthian had sliced the man's other arm in the same fashion. With both limbs severed, the body no longer had anything to support itself and came tumbling off the platform, falling to the ground.

The Scynthian put down his bloodied axe and stepped away from the structure. The shaman then began to wave his hands before mumbling an evil prayer over the body. As he did, the savage took a dagger-like object and began carving a symbol on the dead man's chest. When the shaman had completed that task, the executioner picked the fresh corpse up over his head and walked to the fire. With a heave, the body went hurdling into the flames, causing them to crackle and pop.

Harrison felt the rage boil inside him, knowing that he could not stand to watch another Scynthian murder. "You two stay here." The young warrior pointed to the right. "I'm going to scale down this side of the hill."

"Pondle and Murdock told you to wait here with us!" Gelderand pleaded, but to no avail.

"It'll be too late by then! Just stay here and wait for them." Turning to Lance, Harrison said, "You watch Swinkle and Gelderand. Do you understand?"

Lance gazed at his master with a most worrisome look on his furry face. "Stay."

Harrison sensed the feeling of uneasiness coming from the dog. "I'll be all right. Keep them safe."

Swinkle gazed at his friend with concern. "Harrison, don't try to be a hero. You are greatly outnumbered." The young cleric had seen that same look in his friend's eyes before and it had almost killed him on more than one occasion.

"Don't worry about me. Just stay out of sight." The young warrior drew his battle-axe and began to scale down the hill.

The slope itself appeared steeper than the one Pondle and Murdock had descended, but Harrison felt determined to make the best possible attempt to save the poor woman. His strong point was fighting enemies in hand-to-hand combat, not to quietly investigate.

The young warrior made a rather fast descent to the bottom of the hill. His burning desire to do good caused him to be noisier than he would have liked. Many times, he stepped on twigs that snapped under his foot.

I wish I could be more like Pondle in times like these, he thought, rustling through the leaves. Harrison stealthily positioned himself behind a tree and peeked around it, seeing his dire enemy up close.

"A hut and, one, two, three, four, five beasts between me and the platform," he muttered as he began to formulate a plan in his head.

"If Murdock could take out three from a distance, then Pondle and I could —" but before he could finish his thought, the young warrior felt the smack of a wooden club against the side of his head.

Harrison fell to the ground, dizzy and in pain. Rolling over, he gazed upon the sinister grin of a Scynthian sentry hovering above him. Trying to regain his senses, he attempted to get up, only to have his body relieve him of his pain by falling unconscious. The guardian grabbed Harrison's weapon and dragged the limp fighter by his feet, ending his intense desire for goodwill.

"Pondle, over there." Murdock pointed to another Scynthian sentry some fifty feet in front of them. Oblivious to Harrison's own plan, they continued down to the base of the hill.

Pondle nodded. "I'm going to sneak around behind him and continue to the other side of the camp. Why don't you —" The roaring of an overjoyed guard caused the thief to stop in mid-sentence.

"Oh, no!" Pondle watched helplessly as the Scynthian dragged Harrison from the other side of the woods to the campfire area.

Murdock shook his head in disbelief. "I told him to stay put! Let's get back to Swinkle and Gelderand before it's too late!"

The two men began scaling back up the hill as fast as they could, trying their best not to attract attention to themselves. As they did, they could hear the Scynthians cheer, for they would have another sacrifice tonight. Two savages went into the hut closest to Harrison's former position and dragged out a smaller platform. The young warrior remained unconscious as they tied his arms away from his body. All this took place in full view of Swinkle and Gelderand.

"They're going to kill him!" Gelderand came to the realization that the group would be short one person if they did not do something soon.

Lance sprang to his feet and growled. The little dog could see his master's sorry state and knew something was terribly wrong.

Swinkle knew they had precious little time, sensing that Harrison's sacrifice was close at hand. "We have to do something!"

The young cleric knew firsthand that the Scynthians were evil, but consistent. They did not take humans as prisoners for very long — they killed them. Swinkle realized that they had to rescue their friend from that platform at that very moment.

"What kind of spells do you know?"

"Let me think!" Gelderand tried to gather his thoughts. The mage understood he had to have a clear mind to perform any spell, and the pressure he felt now would cause his magic to fail. As spell after spell crossed his mind, Pondle and Murdock finally reached the top of the hill.

"We need a plan. Now!" Murdock knew that every wasted second could cost Harrison his life.

Pondle wrung his hands, worried. "Gelderand, we need a distraction of some kind in order for us to get Harrison off that platform."

"I could try a fireball. If I cast it into the campfire, it should react with more than double the explosion." Pondle and Murdock nodded with approval.

The mage continued. "Harrison seems to be far enough away from any potential danger that it might cause."

"Pondle, I'll scale back to our last position." Murdock turned to leave. "I can take out that one myself." The ranger pointed to the guard that had joined his fellow warriors.

"You and Swinkle will have to get down the other side. The Scynthian that spotted Harrison hasn't returned to his post."

"What are you going to do?" Pondle gave his friend an incredulous stare. "You can't take on ten warriors yourself!"

"I know." Murdock took a moment to explain his strategy. "After Gelderand casts the fireball, I'll try to shoot down as many of those beasts as I can. With the explosion, they won't know where everything's coming from. I should be able to sneak around to the other side of the camp and from there, I'll start lighting their huts on fire.

"I hope that when they see this, they'll forget about Harrison and try to put out the fires. That's when you and Swinkle will have to untie Harrison and bring him back."

"That will never work!" Swinkle threw up his hands. "You will never be able to do everything on your own. Plus, they won't all leave Harrison unattended."

"I have to agree with Swinkle, Murdock," added Pondle. "I find it hard to believe that you could manage to do everything you said and not be seen."

"Do you have a better idea?" snapped the ranger. "We're out of time!"

Gelderand appeared ready to proceed with Murdock's plan. "Where do I go after I cast the spell?"

"Back to the camp where we started from." The ranger pointed to the little dog. "Lance'll be able to lead you to that location. The Scynthians won't come looking for us in that direction. I'll lead them the other way."

Murdock then looked at his friend. "Pondle, you and Swinkle will have to drag Harrison back quite a ways. Can you handle it?"

"We'll have to." The thief still felt very unsure of their makeshift plan.

Murdock drew a heavy sigh. "All right. Gelderand, wait a few minutes to allow us to get into position, then cast the spell. Are we ready?"

"Wait." Gelderand grabbed his backpack. Rufus, who had patiently remained in the pack, could sense the imminent danger. The feline stepped aside to allow the mage to pull out a black velvet sack. Loosening its ties, a gold ring with a garnet stone dropped into Gelderand's hand.

"You might need this later." The mage handed the ring and pouch to Murdock. "You will turn invisible as soon as you put it on. But, anytime you draw your weapon, including bows and arrows, your enemy will see you."

"Thanks." Murdock took the ring, placed it inside the small bag, then secured it to his belt. "Let's get moving. Harrison needs us."

With that Murdock, Swinkle, and Pondle went their separate ways leaving Gelderand, Lance, and Rufus at the top of the hill.

"Lance, we cannot fail now. Harrison's life depends on it," Gelderand said, with the dog appearing to understand.

The mage then went into his pack again to find an ingredient for the spell. During that time, Lance peered over the hill and barked.

"What is it, Lance?" Gelderand peeked over the hilltop to see the shaman approaching the woman, who continued her hysterical screaming.

"The woman! What are we to do about her?"

Pondle and Swinkle followed Harrison's footprints from tree to tree, as they scaled down the hill. Pondle realized with relative ease that his friend had exposed himself too many times on his mission to save the woman. Knowing this, the halfling led Swinkle deeper into the woods. Reaching the base of the hill, they positioned themselves behind a rather large tree. As Pondle bent down to one knee, he looked back at the young cleric.

"Swinkle, listen," he said, peering at the hut near the edge of the encampment. "We'll have to wait until the fireball explodes before we can maneuver behind that hut over there." Swinkle nodded in approval.

"This is a good place to wait." Pondle motioned to the Scynthian near Harrison's platform. "Lucky for us, the sentry that must've captured Harrison's over there."

"I feel Gelderand will come through for us." The anxiety of not knowing what would happen next had started to become unbearable for Swinkle.

"You have more faith than I." Pondle then saw the shaman advance toward the woman. "Not the female! Don't these creatures have any decency?"

"What are we to do?" exclaimed Swinkle, not knowing what the beasts had in store for the wretched soul.

"Our goal is to save Harrison, not the woman. If we can save both, we will."

Swinkle stared in horror at the unfolding scene. "We have to make an attempt if the situation arises! We have to!"

Pondle's mood turned sullen. "Only if the situation arises."

Murdock finally reached the point where he and Pondle had stood before the Scynthians spotted Harrison. The sentry they had seen remained there, facing in the direction of the platforms.

"This will be easy," Murdock said to himself.

Being as quiet as possible, the ranger withdrew a dagger from his belt and maneuvered from tree to tree, feeling the adrenalin take over his body. Without even the sound of a twig snapping, Murdock made a quick advancement upon the unsuspecting Scynthian and, with chilling precision, slit his throat.

The sentry put his hands to his neck, while the ranger pulled the beast towards himself, making haste in hiding the dying Scynthian from anyone's view. With the savage tucked away, Murdock returned to the spot where the guardian last stood. Unbeknownst to him, another situation had arisen. As the ranger readied his bow towards the unsuspecting creatures near the campfire, he heard the screams of a terrified woman.

"Stick to the plan, men. Stick to the plan," he said softly to himself as he lined up an arrow with the head of a Scynthian.

"Anytime you're ready, Gelderand."

Gelderand and Lance watched the shaman chant over the screaming woman. All the time, Harrison laid motionless on the platform. The mage knew that the Scynthians thrived on seeing the terror-stricken faces of their victims as they killed them, thus the reasoning in sacrificing the fully aware woman first, just as they had sacrificed her companion as she watched in horror.

As the shaman chanted, he took out his dagger-like object and cut through her clothing, exposing the left side of her body. While she screamed in horror, the savage began to cut into her skin, forming a bloody circle around the woman's small arm, just above her bicep. When finished, the shaman summoned his executioner, who made a rapid advance to the platform with his battle-axe.

Gelderand stared at the horrible scene. "They are going to kill a defenseless woman!"

Lance began to whimper, sensing something awful would happen soon. As Gelderand stared in amazement, he heard Rufus meowing from behind. The mage looked back to see the cat gazing at him, then to his pack.

"The spell! What have I been thinking?" Gelderand exclaimed to himself, realizing that he had wasted precious time watching the disturbing scene instead of concentrating on his spell.

As the wizard collected his thoughts, the executioner raised his blade. Gelderand held out his hands containing the crushed remains of red fire ants, as an orange glow formed around them. As the blade fell toward the helpless victim, the radiance ceased.

Anyone in a one-mile radius might have heard the blood-curdling scream. The executioner pried his battle-axe from the wooden platform, while the woman's petite arm dangled from its tied position.

"What is he waiting for?" exclaimed Murdock in exasperation, lowering his bow in the process and glaring at the summit. The ranger stood alone in stunned amazement as the brutes cheered for more.

The woman ceased screaming, but remained alive. From his vantage point, Murdock could see blood pouring out of her body at an alarming rate and knew that there would be almost no way to save her now. The only good thing for the poor soul was the fact that her body would go into a state of shock, allowing her to fall unconscious before dying.

"My patience runs thin, wizard." Murdock raised his bow once again. "Don't make me come after you!"

"Am I not the elder of the group?" Gelderand lamented as he watched the Scynthian shaman untie the woman's other arm, causing her to fall to the ground.

"Is it not I that these young fighters should be looking to in times like these? My failure will cause that poor woman to perish! I must pull myself together before Harrison is dead as well!"

Apparently satisfied to watch the woman bleed to death, the shaman turned his attention to a more formidable enemy, a male fighter. As the Scynthian advanced towards Harrison's platform, the executioner grabbed the woman, who had tried to scurry away. Carrying the poor soul to the campfire, as he had done with the man earlier, the beast tossed the hysterical woman into the roaring flames.

Harrison mumbled. "My head." The young warrior still felt dazed and his head throbbed with pain, but he began to regain his senses. "Murdock? Pondle? Where am I?"

Peering upward, Harrison stared into the shaman's sickly green eyes. Realizing that the young warrior was alive, the savage yelled back to the other beasts, who roared in delight, knowing another sacrifice would soon be at hand.

Harrison tried to lift himself up, but came to the realization that someone had tied down his arms. "Oh, no."

Again, the shaman yelled back in the direction of the Scynthian fighters. Their chieftain then summoned two of his warriors to assist their medicine man; both dropped their weapons and quickly ran over to hold Harrison down. The shaman then began to remove the young warrior's chain-mail armor.

"I need more fire ants!" Gelderand fumbled through his pack, searching for more of the vital ingredients for the spell.

"I will not fail again." The mage grabbed another handful of the spell's components, then proceeded to the hill. Peering over again, Gelderand noticed that the shaman had removed Harrison's armor and had taken out his dagger-like blade.

"I must concentrate." The wizard positioned his outstretched hands toward the campfire.

"Put that thing away!" yelled Harrison in vain, as the shaman stared at the young warrior with a demonic grin. Using his weapon, the savage began to cut into Harrison's skin in the same way he did to the woman.

"I have to hold on! I know they have a plan to save me — they must," Harrison said to himself as he felt the jagged blade pierce his skin.

The shaman continued making his incision until he completed the bloody circle. "Now, wretched human, you will understand the meaning of pain," he said in a vaguely understandable tongue.

The executioner advanced to Harrison's platform. Upon seeing this, Murdock repositioned his bow. Pulling the arrow back to its maximum tension, he let the arrow fly just as the beast lowered his blade.

"The bastards! It will not end like this!" Murdock exclaimed as he spun to his right and with the accuracy of an expert marksman, fired arrows into the backs of three unsuspecting Scynthians.

Harrison could feel the cold, steel blade cut through his skin, severing his left arm. Looking over in horror, he saw his limb dangling free from his body. Just as he let out a scream, he saw an orange blur hurtle through the air. An arrow intercepted the fireball and made its mark in the executioner's back, igniting him. The savage wailed in pain, then fell forward and landed face first into the platform, just as a massive explosion engulfed the area.

With the glow ceasing from his hands, Gelderand fell to the ground. Many years had passed since he had used a spell of such magnitude. Near mental exhaustion, the mage crawled over to his pack and fumbled for a round object. Upon taking hold of it, the orb began to produce a soft white glow, radiating just enough light for him to see.

"Lance, Rufus, our part is complete. We must go now," he said motioning for the animals to leave. Rufus climbed back into the backpack and Lance began heading away from the hill.

Gelderand slowly made it to his feet. The wizard took care in picking up his pack, before peering one last time over the hill and into the ensuing confusion.

"May the gods have mercy tonight," he said in a quiet whisper as the small party departed for the rendezvous point.

Murdock, sticking to his part of the plan, ran to one of the huts on the other side of the encampment and hurriedly fumbled with his flash and tinder. "Come on, light up! Light up!" he lamented, but to no avail.

"Forget it!" The ranger threw down his lighting materials and began waving his arms and screaming.

"Over here!" Murdock yelled at the top of his lungs, in a desperate attempt to get the attention on him and away from Harrison. "I'm over here!"

As fate would have it, one of the Scynthians noticed his antics and pointed in the ranger's direction. Within seconds, six of the savages headed towards Murdock at full steam with their weapons drawn.

"Here goes nothing." Murdock made a dash from the encampment, heading into the darkness of the forest.

I must stay conscious! If I pass out I'll die! Harrison felt the tingling sensations of his exposed nerves as the thoughts passed through his mind.

The blood poured out of his body at such an alarming rate that he began to feel very lightheaded. Closing his eyes, he could see a vision of his parents, then envisioned leafing through the pages of the sacred book with his friends. Though he could sense that something was tugging at him on the platform, in his mind he could see Tara's beautiful face as their lips met in a passionate kiss.

"Harrison! Can you hear me?" Swinkle yelled frantically as he began to untie the young warrior from his bonds.

Harrison opened his eyes. "Swinkle?" was all he could muster as he peered at his friend's worried face. Closing his eyes again, he heard Swinkle's voice.

"He's alive! We have to hurry!" yelled the young cleric to Pondle, who had begun to remove the charred body of the executioner from the platform.

From their vantage point they had seen the fireball hit near the bottom of the blazing fire, causing the explosion to occur lower to the ground. Still, the force of the blast had engulfed five Scynthians, including the chieftain. To their surprise, the remaining beasts had heard Murdock's screams and had proceeded to run after him. Amidst all the confusion, Pondle and Swinkle had managed to scamper from the woods to the hut, then to Harrison's platform without incidence.

Pondle motioned for Swinkle to move out of the way. Taking his dagger, the thief sliced the rope that had kept Harrison secured to the staging. Swinkle caught the young warrior's body before it fell to the ground.

"Swinkle, can we save him?"

Swinkle nodded, more out of hope than certainty. "We have to stop the bleeding now." Pondle helped the young cleric lower Harrison to the ground. "If we can stabilize that, we might be able to save his arm, too."

The thief then returned to the platform and retrieved the bloody, severed arm, placing it gently into his pack.

Swinkle applied pressure around the main artery in Harrison's limb, causing a dramatic slowdown of the bleeding. "I can't recite a healing prayer or it will close the wound to the point where we couldn't reattach his arm."

The young cleric turned his focus back to Pondle. "We will have to apply a tourniquet." The thief nodded in understanding.

"Pondle, dump my backpack out," continued Swinkle. The thief did what the young cleric asked of him. Looking at the pack's contents on the ground, Swinkle realized he could not use any of the items in his efforts to save Harrison.

"Pondle, do you have some kind of rope?"

"Yes." The thief quickly retrieved the twine from his bag.

Swinkle pointed to a specific spot on Harrison's arm. "Place your finger here." Pondle, a little unsure of himself, obliged.

The thief pressed on Harrison's artery, while his friend's blood spilled onto his hand. Swinkle reached over, took a dagger off Pondle's belt, and started to cut his burlap pack.

Pondle shook his head in confusion. "What are you doing?"

"I am going to cover the wound with this material, then tie the rope around it. By tying it tight enough, the bleeding should stop."

In no time, Swinkle managed to create a makeshift dressing out of the burlap. Next the young cleric successfully tied the rope around Harrison's arm, causing the bleeding to all but stop. After he finished that, he gathered his belongings as fast as he could and placed them in Pondle's magical sack.

"This knapsack really comes in handy," said the young cleric, motioning to the item Pondle took from a dark ranger in the underground catacombs while they had ventured for the Treasure of the Land.

"The capacity of that thing's amazing, and it's as light as a feather." Pondle, noticing Harrison's battle-axe nearby, used the swiftness associated with his halfling heritage to retrieve the blade and slung it over his shoulder.

Swinkle gazed over to his friend. "It's the best we can do. Let's get out of here."

The young cleric grabbed Harrison by the legs while Pondle awkwardly took hold of his friend's upper body. Unbeknownst to them, a figure silhouetted by the campfire peered in their direction as they reached the confines of the woods.

CHAPTER 7

Ö

The darkness of the forest made it difficult for Murdock to continue. With little light from the moon, low hanging branches and hidden bushes constantly impeded his progress. Peering back, he could see six bobbing torches advancing behind him. The ranger knew that the only hope for him now was Gelderand's ring. Looking over his shoulder one last time, Murdock estimated that the Scynthians meandered about three hundred feet away.

This had better work, the ranger thought as he maneuvered behind a large tree.

Murdock untied the pouch attached to his belt, then took the ring out of the sack and gave it a closer look. The item looked like nothing more than a cheap piece of jewelry. With the Scynthians closing in behind him and having no other options at the time, he made haste in placing the object on the ring finger of his left hand. At first, it appeared too big, but then the ring magically resized to fit his finger. Holding his hand to the faint moonlight, Murdock could still see the outline of his body.

"Great! I can see myself, but can they see me?" he contemplated, his nerves getting the better of him as the beasts closed in on his position.

"I can't even draw a weapon!" Murdock whispered to himself in a soft murmur. "Gelderand, your magic had better work."

The ranger took a deep breath, then peeked his head around the tree trunk. Scanning from side to side, he noticed that the Scynthians had halted their charge and began to survey the area around them in earnest.

Murdock's heart began to race faster. Though he was a capable fighter in one-on-one situations, he knew that six Scynthian fighters would overmatch him with ease. As time dragged on, the ranger heard the grunting creatures advancing ever so close, even though they tried their best to be as quiet as possible.

Murdock closed his eyes, swallowed hard, then drew a long shallow breath. When he opened them again, the flickering of a torch shed a faint, but ever stronger, light some fifty feet to his left. After several excruciating seconds of debate, the nervous ranger again peered around the tree. To his right, the outline of a torch-bearing Scynthian continued to close in on his location some thirty feet away, but worse yet lumbered a beast that headed straight for his position. The gentle rustling of leaves and the soft cracking of twigs filled the immediate area as the savage came ever so close. The dim light of the soft flame increased in brightness with each step the beast made. The Scynthian was so near that Murdock could now *hear* his enemy's deep breaths with its every movement.

The ranger stood motionless in front of his tree, too scared to look back and too worried that the ring's magic would fail. With one final step, the Scynthian tiptoed by the nervous human. Murdock held his breath, as the beast passed no more than five feet away from him. The savage continued his stealthy search, scanning in every direction for his enemy.

Murdock knew he was not out of his predicament just yet. The apprehensive ranger figured the beast had wandered about fifteen feet ahead of him when, all of a sudden, the Scynthian stopped.

The savage took his time in turning back around, holding his torch in front of himself while he gazed right at Murdock. The Scynthian tilted his head slightly to the left and seemed to focus on something that the ranger could only hope was not he.

Is the ring working or not, Murdock wondered, his lungs yearning for more air as the stress of the situation rose. The ranger anxiously stared at his adversary. Can he see my body's outline? Why isn't he leaving?

Murdock did not know if the creature could hear his shallow breaths. Either way, he knew the Scynthian sensed something amiss, but the ranger refused to make the first move. The beast began to take a step in Murdock's direction when the ranger heard the sound of footsteps advancing from behind the tree.

Another beast? I only count four; where are the other two, lamented Murdock as another Scynthian grunted to his fellow warrior, walking past the invisible human in the process.

The first savage, distracted by the sudden advance of his comrade, took his gaze away from the ranger, then both Scynthians began muttering to each other.

Murdock noticed that the torches in the distance started to make a rapid dance to his right, leading away from him. One of the beasts pointed in the direction of the fleeing lights and the two savages began to follow their new avenue of search.

The ranger remained motionless until the Scynthians scurried a good hundred feet away. Murdock counted six faint lights in the distance ahead of him and only then did he begin to feel at ease with his situation. The ranger waited a few more minutes until he was convinced that the savages would not hear him if he began to move again. Seeing no one as he peeked around the tree, Murdock began his long trip back to the rendezvous point.

"What is taking so long, Rufus?" muttered Gelderand, his nerves getting the better of him as he waited for the rest of the party. "I hope they all make it back alive."

Gelderand, Lance, and Rufus had returned to the old camp, but decided not to set a fire for fear of the Scynthians seeing it. Gelderand sat against a tree, holding the orb in his hand, while Lance stared in the direction of the enemy outpost.

A few moments later, the mage heard the rustling of leaves in the distance. Lance heard the sounds, too. The small dog let out a nervous whimper as he turned and looked at Gelderand. The mage quickly put the orb by his side, extinguishing its light.

"Lance, come here." The dog scampered to the older man's side at once. "We all need to stick together." After a few moments of hiding in the dark, Gelderand heard the sounds of a familiar voice.

"Swinkle, I think we've reached our meeting place, but I don't see any sign of Gelderand," said Pondle, scanning the area with his infravision. Lance saw his friends and darted over to greet them.

"Lance!" exclaimed Swinkle, overjoyed at seeing their canine friend. The young cleric then looked around in concern. "Where's Gelderand?"

"Pondle, Swinkle, I'm over here." The mage picked up his orb, providing a soft white glow to the area.

Pondle gave the older man a look of relief. "Gelderand, we need your help."

The wizard could see the fatigue on his friends' faces and the sweat that soaked their clothing. By the looks of Swinkle and Pondle, he could tell that they had had a rather rough time carrying Harrison back to the camp.

As for the young warrior, he appeared semiconscious and what noises he did make sounded unintelligible. Lance saw his master and came over to greet him, licking his face with the hope of getting a positive response, but the dog received no reply.

Gelderand rushed to their side. "Will he live?" asked the mage, looking over the young warrior in concern.

"The beasts severed his arm and he has lost a lot of blood," said Swinkle, while he and Pondle took care in laying Harrison on the ground.

"I didn't pray over him because it would have closed his wound. If that had happened, there would be no chance of reattaching his arm. Do you know of any spell that can help him?"

Gelderand thought for a moment. "I could perform a regeneration spell on his arm, but I am so tired from the last spell that I'm afraid it might not work." The mage removed his cloak and used it to cover Harrison's body.

"You'll have to try," answered Pondle. "It's his only hope." The thief then began in haste to put together a campfire in order to provide illumination for Gelderand and Swinkle. Pondle knew that any source of light might draw unwanted attention, but regarding the circumstances, he had no choice.

Swinkle knew that every second wasted could mean permanent loss of Harrison's arm. "What if I recited a healing prayer at the same time you performed your regeneration spell?"

Gelderand shrugged, shaking his head. "I don't know. I think it's worth trying, considering the situation."

The mage withdrew from the three in order to retrieve the necessary ingredients for the spell. Looking into his backpack, he found a small brass case marked with ornate engravings. Pulling it out, he opened it to find three vials of colored liquids.

"I knew you wouldn't let me down, Tara," he mumbled as he retrieved the vial containing a light blue liquid before returning to the awaiting men.

Gelderand showed the men the tube. "First he needs to drink this." The mage removed the container's stopper.

"What is that?" asked Swinkle as he propped Harrison in an upright position.

"This liquid will help to heal his wounds." Gelderand started to pour the elixir into the young warrior's mouth. "His injury is far worse than what the potion can handle, but it will help him to recover faster, nonetheless."

Still dazed, Harrison took two gulps before he started to cough, causing quite a bit of the liquid to end up on the ground.

Swinkle tried to keep the wounded fighter at ease. "Harrison, if you can understand me, try to drink the potion. You are going to need all the help you can get."

Gelderand then emptied the rest of the vial into Harrison's mouth as the young warrior swallowed the liquid down. The mage turned to Pondle.

"Can you bring me his severed arm?" The thief quickly retrieved Harrison's bloodied limb.

The mage gazed over at the young cleric. "All right, Swinkle, the time has come to help our friend."

"Pondle, I need you to hold his arm here." Gelderand motioned for the thief to position the limb no more than a quarter of an inch away from the severed point.

With Pondle placing the arm in the appropriate place, Gelderand continued. "Good. Now, Swinkle, you must gather your thoughts and be prepared to recite your prayer as soon as you untie his tourniquet." Swinkle nodded in acknowledgment.

After several seconds of meditation, Swinkle took a deep breath and closed his eyes, then slowly undid the dressing. Blood began to spill out of the wound after he released the pressure from the major artery. The young cleric then laid his hands on the separated body parts and mumbled a prayer, causing a white glow to form around the wound.

Gelderand took hold of Harrison's limb in the same fashion. Mumbling the words of his spell, in an instant, a blue glow intercepted the wounded area.

Pondle, still holding the severed arm, watched in amazement as skin from Harrison's upper body began to gradually bridge over to the injured limb. The blood flow also began to subside as the young warrior's arm started the reattachment process. After several minutes of intense concentration, Gelderand and Swinkle both let go of Harrison and slumped to the ground.

Pondle made a closer inspection of Harrison's injury. "It worked!" he shouted, staring at Harrison's limb in total amazement. "The bleeding has stopped! The arm's reattached!" Lance licked his master's face, sensing, too, the success of the operation.

"Only time will tell if his body will accept the arm again," whispered Gelderand in near exhaustion.

"Pondle, we need to rest." Fatigue had overtaken Swinkle from his intense concentration, as well as from the journey of carrying Harrison through the dark woods.

Pondle understood their dire predicament. "I'll secure the area. Both of you take it easy."

Before he could start his task, the thief felt a sharp pain in the back of his thigh. Pondle instinctively looked back and saw a blade lodged in his leg. Lance stared beyond the injured halfling and began to bark in a fury.

Pondle turned around and saw an unwanted familiar face. The Scynthian shaman had followed the two back to their camp and watched as they performed their delicate operation on their friend. Waiting patiently in the cover of the woods while two of the three capable fighters exhausted themselves, the savage enhanced his odds of defeating the group. Now, with Pondle incapacitated, he showed his hideous face to the adventurers.

"Did you really believe that you could get away so easily?" said the shaman in the low guttural sounds of the Scynthian language.

Carrying a large wooden staff, the beast advanced past the exhausted party members and headed for Pondle. Lance teleported closer to the intruder, barking all the while. The shaman, surprised at the dog's sudden actions, raised his staff at Lance, causing him to cower back.

"You should leave while you have the chance!" shouted Pondle. The thief hobbled away from the savage, trying to avoid driving the blade deeper into his leg. Withdrawing one of the last daggers from his belt, Pondle pointed it at the shaman.

The beast laughed. "No halfling can match the strength of a Scynthian! Such pathetic creatures you are indeed!"

The savage took a mighty swing at Pondle, hitting his outstretched hand, and the dagger hurtled into the darkness. Lance barked at a feverish pitch, then teleported closer to the beast again in an effort to stop him from reaching Pondle. The Scynthian poked his weapon at the dog, grazing him on the side and forcing him to move back.

"I will have my vengeance for the disruption of our sacred ceremony!" the beast snarled, his face showing the hatred the Scynthians had to the lesser beings.

Pondle looked over to the other members of his group in hope of some kind of support, only to see Swinkle and Gelderand barely able to sit up due to their fatigue.

The shaman took another step in Pondle's direction. "Payment for your foolish actions is now due!"

Suddenly, out of the corner of his eye the beast saw the brief image of a man releasing the tension of a long bow. Before the shaman could react, an arrow's steel tip pierced his flesh and entered his heart. The savage fell backwards, his body lifeless before hitting the ground.

Murdock removed the ring from his finger, allowing the rest of the group to see him. "What's going on here?" The ranger rushed to Pondle's side in an effort to help his friend.

A wide grin overtook the thief's face. "Am I glad to see you!" Pondle strained to see the full extent of his injury. The blade had entered his leg, but not as deep as he first anticipated.

Murdock took a closer look at Pondle's wound. "This looks bad. Good thing I arrived when I did or I might be searching for this treasure alone."

The ranger took his time removing the blade from his friend's leg, allowing Pondle's clothing to soak up any excess blood.

"I'll be fine." Pondle applied pressure to his wound. "Help me to the campfire so that Swinkle can look at me."

Murdock put his arm around his friend and led him to the blaze. The ranger gazed about the makeshift camp and found everyone incapacitated to some extent. A look of disgust overtook his face.

"Seventeen Scynthians!" said Murdock, using a loud voice in Harrison's direction. "I told him trying to save that woman would be suicide and it almost was, but no one ever listens to me."

"You are going to have to discuss that with him later." Gelderand struggled to keep himself in an upright position. "He is going to need a lot of rest."

"Look at all of you!" Murdock stared at the injured and exhausted men. "How are we going to get out of this forest with everyone in this condition?"

"We might have to remain here for a few days," said Swinkle in a soft tone. "We are in no shape to journey."

"A few days!" snapped Murdock. "I think not. We'll rest tonight and start again first thing in the morning!" The ranger glared at the young cleric. "Who are you to be making decisions regarding the group anyway?"

Pondle, sensing hostilities brewing inside his friend, put an end to the ranger's comments before a full-blown argument commenced. "Murdock, look at us. Do you really believe we'll be ready in the morning?"

Murdock gazed back at his friend. "We've spent too much time in this forest. You should know as well as any of us that these woods have eyes." The ranger scanned the surrounding darkness.

"We'll evaluate our status in the morning," continued the ranger as he settled in to keep watch. "And be prepared to travel at that time. We'll be leaving this place a lot sooner than you think."

The rest of the group did likewise in order to get some much-needed rest. Seeing Gelderand and Swinkle near exhaustion was something Murdock had figured on, but he never expected having Harrison and Pondle hurt at the same time as well. The ranger grabbed his tankard of water and took a sip, then whistled for Lance to come to him. The dog hesitated before obliging.

"I'll need you to help watch the camp tonight." Murdock scratched the dog behind his ears. "It's just you and me, Lance."

The two of them then heard Rufus meow. Shaking his head, the ranger muttered, "What good can there be in bringing a cat on this journey?"

Rufus walked over to Lance and rubbed against him, being careful to leave Murdock alone. The ranger took out portions of dried meat and handed one to Lance who quickly devoured the food.

Our first real test of battle and this is the outcome, he thought, shaking his head.

Murdock then secured his backpack, removed his short sword, and readied himself for a long night of sentry duty, all the while scanning the area for the eyes that he felt watched over their group.

C H A P T E R   8

⬡

The morning sun glistened on Serpent's Sea, while sea gulls flocked to the shores of Polaris. Troy and his men had spent all of their time in the small fishing town searching for information about the sacred book. Even though they posted ransom signs and interviewed many townsfolk concerning the treasure, they came away with nothing.

With their first day of investigating behind them, Troy's men readied themselves to embark on the next leg of their journey. The small army assembled near the pier with their anchored ship and waited patiently for their general's orders.

Troy appeared from the ship along with Teleios and Portheus. After giving the captain his final orders, Troy and Teleios walked down the gangplank and over to their awaiting steeds. Though Troy viewed the first leg of their journey as a failure, his advisor had other thoughts.

"We made quite an impression on the townspeople of Polaris, Troy." Teleios secured his belongings to his horse.

Troy, on the other hand frowned, showing his displeasure with the situation. "We alerted them to the existence of some sacred book. That's all we accomplished."

The young general lowered his head in dejection. With a huff, he continued, "I admit they appeared very interested in the ransom, but we didn't receive a shred of information about the scripture." Troy secured his belongings to his horse as well, then mounted the animal.

Teleios positioned his horse next to Troy's steed. "You cannot expect to find the book overnight. Discovering the scripture will take time."

"I understand that, but I know how much the king wants this book. The faster we recover it, the happier he'll be." The young general then brought his gaze to his men. "It's time to give them their orders."

Troy pulled away from Teleios and moved his steed to stand before his men. "The time has come to advance to our next destination," he started, glaring down at the rank of soldiers.

"Though we did not receive any pertinent information about the book, I still want to commend you for a job well done. This town is in full awareness of our intentions and it's because all of you performed your tasks efficiently. Let's hope we have better luck in Arcadia." After a pause, Troy waved his men forward. "Positions, everyone!"

His men fell into their ranks with his advanced scouts, fighters, and bowmen arranged in accordance to Troy's pre-approved plan. The platoon then proceeded out of the small town by horseback and set their sites on the larger city of Arcadia.

After the squad left the outskirts of the town, Troy maneuvered his horse alongside Teleios. Though he knew it would take some time to find the book in all probability, he already entertained thoughts about alternate plans.

"Teleios, I've been thinking that it might be wise to seek the consul of a sorcerer, someone that could help lead us in the right direction."

Troy's advisor gazed cautiously at his commander. "We should continue as we are. By the time we get to Lars, we should have some solid information we can go on."

"I'm sure you're right." After a moment, Troy asked, "Do you think a wizard would be helpful, though?"

Teleios paused before answering. "Not yet. We must consider anyone who is well versed in magic a threat. A powerful mage could destroy our group, take the book, and use its powers for himself.

"The king must understand our situation. He knows it will be some time before he has his sacred prize."

General Harkin nodded in agreement. "You're right. We'll keep to our plan and evaluate our progress in Lars."

With that, Troy led his platoon of men deeper into the countryside, leaving Polaris behind them.

The long night gave way to a bright sunny day. Gelderand and Swinkle managed to take advantage of the surprisingly quiet evening to get the much-needed rest they deserved. Pondle, though his leg remained tender, managed to walk about with tolerable pain. Harrison, on the other hand, remained days, if not weeks, away from any normal activity.

The men had positioned themselves around the young warrior, who they had situated near the campfire in an effort to keep him warm throughout the night. Lance continued to lay next to his master, only leaving his side to survey the surrounding area with Murdock. With everyone settling in for breakfast, the ranger spoke first.

"Good morning, *hero*," he said, addressing Harrison for the first time since he and Pondle left him at the top of the fateful hill. "And you call me reckless."

"Just what happened exactly?" asked Harrison. "I remember a hideous face and then —"

The young warrior stopped speaking and glared at his arm. The last thing he remembered from the previous night was seeing his detached limb dangling from a rope. Staring at it now, he could clearly see that it was attached to his body.

"You had to play the noble character and save the maiden in distress," snapped Murdock. "You almost had yourself and the rest of us killed!"

Harrison's expression went blank, oblivious to Murdock's remarks. "I have no feeling in my arm." The young warrior attempted to lift his injured limb, but no matter how hard he tried, it would not budge.

"Give it some time, Harrison." Gelderand knew all along that a good possibility existed that the young warrior might never use his arm again. "Your body has gone through a very traumatic experience."

"Then those beasts really did sever my arm! I wasn't dreaming!" exclaimed Harrison, trying to piece together the events of the previous night. "If the Scynthians cut it off, how did it get reattached?"

Gelderand leaned forward to address the young warrior. "Swinkle and I used a combination of prayer and spells to heal you. I hope you understand how fortunate you truly are."

Harrison looked at his two friends. "I can't begin to thank you enough." Gazing at his surroundings, he said, "How did I get back to the camp?"

"You were knocked unconscious, dragged from the woods, placed on a platform, and lay next in line for a sacrifice," answered Murdock, his voice thick with sarcasm.

"That's the usual outcome when you're outnumbered three to one against Scynthians. Of course we saved you, carried you back, and now we're ready to clean you up so that we can continue with our quest."

"Enough, Murdock," snapped Gelderand. "You cannot take back what has happened. We need to band together and journey as a unit. Bickering will only separate us. Be thankful we found a way to save him and all still be alive."

Murdock knew Gelderand was right, but he had grown tired of being the scapegoat whenever something he did went awry. This time Harrison had made a glaring error in judgment and he was just trying to get his point across the best way he knew how.

"Let Swinkle and I care for Harrison," continued the mage. "You can tend to Pondle and in a little while we will be able to evaluate our well being."

Gelderand looked at the ranger with conviction. "Murdock, you must realize that you are the strongest member of the group now. With Harrison and Pondle hurting, we need you to guide us to safety."

"I know," said Murdock, taking in what Gelderand said. "We'll leave tomorrow morning. Pondle will be ready by then. As for Harrison, we'll have to help him take every step."

"I'll be ready," responded Pondle, in reassurance. "I'll be able to take my point position as usual."

Swinkle gestured in the thief's direction. "I'd like to take another look at your injury, too. There might be more I can do to help you."

"That would be fine." Pondle then stood up and grabbed his small sword. "But first, I'm going to have a look around. I'm surprised we didn't hear from the remaining Scynthians last night."

Murdock reached for his longbow. "I'll go with you."

The thief raised his hand in protest. "No, you stay here. You need to protect the others while I'm away." Pondle then looked over to Lance. "I'll take the dog."

"Great," cursed Murdock under his breath. Pondle whistled for Lance, who sprung to his feet and followed the thief away from the camp.

Gelderand heard what Pondle said about the Scynthians. "Do you think those beasts are gone?"

"Those savages are idiots," said Murdock, not holding back his disdain for the barbaric race. "We were completely vulnerable last night, yet they couldn't track us down." The ranger began to fumble with his pack. "We're lucky they didn't find us."

The rest of the men let Murdock's last words sink in. Harrison, reflecting again on his actions, said, "I want to tell you all how sorry I am for last night. I guess my good intentions clouded my judgment."

Murdock glared at the young warrior. "You could say that again. Harrison, we're out trying to find another treasure, not to save the world."

"Maybe not yet." Harrison sat up and cradled his injured right arm. "But we will some day."

The ranger, continuing to fumble with his pack, lifted his eyes. "There's a long way to go. Look at how last night concluded."

"And yet we are all still alive," said Gelderand. "Tired, hurt, but still alive. That has to tell you something."

Murdock pulled dried meats from his bag for their meal. "It tells me we're lucky."

Gelderand gazed at the ranger. "It tells *me* that we can come together as a team." The mage looked at Harrison, Swinkle, and Murdock as he spoke.

"We all used our combined strengths to overcome great obstacles yesterday. That is why I say, as long as we band together, anything is possible."

Harrison nodded. "I agree. We'll find this Talisman and whatever else comes with it."

Just then, Pondle and Lance returned to the camp. "The Scynthians are gone," he said. "Their tracks head off in the opposite direction."

Murdock nodded, relieved. "That's a good sign. We need to steer clear of them."

Pondle stuck his sword in the ground. "We will. I'll make sure we're nowhere near them."

Murdock gestured to his friends. "Like I said before, let's rest and be ready to journey again tomorrow." The men all continued with their breakfast, knowing that the momentary pause in their quest would be over the next day.

CHAPTER 9

◘

The large, busy port of Arcadia was the center of cultural diversity in the southern part of the land. Famous for its artistry, many talented painters, sculptors, and craftsmen showed off their wares in the city's main streets. Since it rested at the end of a large bay, countless captains would welcome its calmer waters to dock their ships. This combination of seaport and culture center allowed Arcadia to be one of the busiest villages of trade in the land.

Adventurers from the north would travel to Arcadia to sell what they had found in the Great Forest. Journeymen from the south would bring artifacts discovered from the Great Ridge of King Solaris, and trappers would cart furs and pelts into the city from the Arcadian countryside. Still, with all of its strong points, Arcadia brought more frustration to Troy.

"Teleios, how can it be that no one has heard of our ransom yet?" asked the young general with an incredulous look on his face. Troy and his men had diligently posted their signs, but still they could not find one person who had heard of the proposed payments from Polaris.

Teleios remained unwearied. "Troy, we have only been here one day," he said, trying to put his leader at ease. "Time is our ally, not our enemy. We must be patient."

Troy nodded, knowing Teleios was right. "I understand that. I'm being too hasty again."

"That you are." Teleios gestured to the streets littered with people. "Come, let us enjoy this fine city. We will be journeying through dense woods and rugged countryside before too long." The halfling looked over to Troy and found him staring down one of the city's busy roads.

"Might I suggest that we stay an additional day in Arcadia? Remaining here a little longer will give us time to receive any news from Polaris."

The young general wrinkled his brow. "What about our schedule?"

"We dictate our own schedule, Troy. We can amend it as we see fit."

Troy thought for a moment. "You're right again, Teleios. Let's relax and allow the townspeople to come to us."

Teleios let out a sigh of relief. "Let's alert the troops. They will be pleased to learn of our new departure date."

Troy nodded in agreement, then looked down the street again, taking in the sight of the bustling town. Shops and buildings lined the road, people congregated around tradesmen, and children played next to their parents. Troy could see his men blend in with the townsfolk, posting their signs and speaking to curious onlookers.

The young general smiled. At that instant, he realized what Teleios had said was true; time was on their side and information about the book would surface at the appropriate moment. Finally convinced of that fact, he and Teleios dismounted their horses and joined the throngs of Arcadians in the streets.

Two more days had passed and, with it, the last shreds of Troy's patience. Upset over the lack of information about the book, the young general abruptly summoned his troops and left Arcadia.

Teleios again preached to him that Arcadia would prove fruitful in the end, but Troy had just about lost all hope. After yet another day's journey through the coastal woodlands, off in the distance the outline of the small town of Lars came into view.

"Lars at last," said Troy, using his hand to shade his eyes from the setting sun. "I hope someone in this town can lead us to the scripture," he continued as the army advanced toward the town.

"Troy, you are taking this lack of information too personally," remarked Teleios. "I don't know how many times I have to explain to you that finding a book that bleeds when scratched is a monumental task. Especially when that is our only clue."

Teleios could understand the young general's desire to please the king, but he began to lose patience when it came to Troy's whining about not finding information.

"When will we meet someone who even knows what we're talking about?" asked Troy, trying to reason his way through the situation. "Maybe we should consult some of the town's elders or wizards, or someone with any link to events of the past."

"No," answered Teleios with emphasis. "I am sure that there will be a lead after we have reached Dragon's Quarters. We will have posted ransoms in six cities. You must give our system time to come to fruition.

"Everyone in the southern portion of the land will know of our quest and someone will lead us in the right direction. Arcadia is full of adventurers. Every day they come in and out of that city in droves. Someone will learn of this book. That I am sure of."

Teleios knew that they had given the townspeople their proposed travel route. If all went well, they would certainly receive some pertinent information.

"I've always trusted your judgment, Teleios." The young general fixed his eyes on his advisor. "I hope you're right this time as well."

Lars resembled a smaller version of Polaris. If not for its rocky coast, the small fishing village would rival its sister city as the intermediate stop to Arcadia. Instead, fishing and trade between itself and Nordic, another small town to the west, generated much of the village's income. The sight of over thirty men on horseback entering their little community caused many of the townspeople to scurry off the streets into nearby shops and buildings, with many curious heads peeking out of half closed doorways.

"Let's find a place to settle in for the night," said Troy. "We'll allow the men to get supplies tonight and we'll post the signs in the morning."

Teleios nodded. "That is a good idea. The men could use a night of rest." Troy's advisor waited a moment before bringing up a sensitive issue to his leader again. "I think it might be wise to entertain the idea of hiring bounty hunters to help aid in our search."

Troy glared at his advisor, a look of surprise and shock overtaking his face. "Absolutely not! Did you not just spurn my idea to bring wizards into the fold?"

Shaking his head, the young general continued his rant, "Bounty hunters cannot be trusted — you even alluded to that yourself! The likelihood of one of them finding the book and returning it to the king is far greater than for them to bring it to us. Besides, a person of that trade might try to use the book for himself."

Teleios knew it would be difficult to change Troy's mind, but he tried nonetheless. "As if a magician would not? I told you before; sorcerers are too dangerous and powerful. Bounty hunters are more predictable. They will take the extra steps necessary to find the book."

"What extra steps?"

"Whatever it takes to uncover the scripture."

A look of exasperation overtook Troy's face. "Like murdering innocent people?"

Teleios shrugged. "If that's what it takes? Yes."

"I don't agree with that plan," said Troy pointedly. "There's no need in harming people who are trying to help us with our task. I understand that many evil people will read the signs and try to use the book themselves. We'll deal with them once we find them. I consider bounty hunters evil people. If we don't hire them, then we'll have no obligations to them."

Troy's advisor did not hide his agitation. "I understand your concern. If you want, I can handle the treasure seekers myself."

A frozen gaze met Teleios's green eyes. Troy, equally upset, pointed a finger at his advisor and said, "My decision is final. You are not to hire bounty hunters! Do you understand me, Teleios?"

The loyal halfling paused before answering, knowing that Troy was too angry to deal with now. "Yes. I just had an idea that I thought might help us. I'm sorry if I upset you."

Troy looked at Teleios and gave him a look of remorse. "This journey's starting to get the better of me." The young general drew a heavy sigh. "I'm sorry to have yelled at you like that. I just don't trust scum like bounty hunters."

Teleios nodded. "I understand. There is no need to apologize."

The young general then proposed a deal. "I say we forget about entertaining the thought of bringing anyone from outside our platoon into our search until a much later time."

"Fine with me." Teleios peered over at the contingent of soldiers and noticed that they had witnessed their altercation. "I think we should allow the men to disperse into town."

Troy looked over to his soldiers and recognized the same thing. "Good idea." He turned his horse to face the armed men.

"I want you all to resupply yourselves," Troy started. "When you're finished, you may enjoy the comforts of the village tonight. I expect all of you to be ready to perform your duties tomorrow. You're dismissed."

Troy and Teleios watched the soldiers scatter into the streets. "Let's find ourselves lodging for the evening," said Troy. "There's still work to be done." With that, the two men began searching for a place to rest for the night.

Troy and Teleios had barely settled into their room at the inn when they heard a knock at the door. "Enter," barked Troy.

The door opened and one of his younger soldiers entered the room. Troy noticed a rather strange look on the young man's face. "What's the matter?"

"Sir, a couple of us began searching for the book as soon as we departed company," began the young man, the excitement level rising with each word. "We came to a weaponsmith's shop, and well, the shopkeeper confided a most interesting piece of information to us."

"What do you mean?" questioned Troy, intrigued.

"The old man had asked us why we needed such weapons and we told him of our quest, and —"

Troy gestured at the young man. "Soldier, please get to the point."

"Yes, sir! The man said that he is somewhat familiar with this 'bleeding book' legend. He believes that the scripture is around the area."

Troy said nothing, almost not believing what he had just heard. This was the first lead of any kind regarding the book.

"Sir, did you hear me?" asked the warrior after a few seconds of silence.

"Lead me to the man," ordered Troy.

The young fighter stood tall. "Yes, sir! Follow me."

Troy looked over at Teleios and smiled. "Finally," was all he had to say to convey his message to his advisor. Teleios nodded in acknowledgement and followed the two men out the door.

Troy's sentry led him to an old building with a plain sign above the doorway that read 'General Supplies and Weaponry.' The weaponsmith's shop was small, but served its purpose. The owner had many items displayed throughout the store, including some interesting pieces from the most remote places of the land.

Upon entering the establishment, the young general noticed the shopkeeper standing behind a display case. The person appeared well past the prime of his life and was counting the last of his gold pieces. The old man looked up to see Troy's soldier pointing him out.

The young general approached the counter. "My good man, I would like a word with you." Looking deeply into the old man's gray eyes, he said, "Word has it that you have knowledge of a legend regarding a bleeding book."

The balding man swallowed hard with anxiety, looking past Troy to Teleios, then to the soldier behind them. "I know of the legend, yes."

The older man used a frail, wrinkled hand to try and discreetly slide the gold pieces into a pouch behind the counter.

Troy watched the man handle his money. "Don't worry about your gold. If I wanted to rob you, I would have been finished by now, don't you think?"

The man stopped sliding his coins, not wanting to alarm his intruder further. Troy paused before continuing. "I want you to tell me all you know of this legend."

"There's not much to tell," said the man in a timid tone. "The story is probably nothing but fiction anyway."

Troy waved a hand at the man. "Nevertheless, I need to know everything you have heard."

The shopkeeper took a moment to gather his thoughts, then said, "Many years back, well before the birth of my ancestors, there was a dragon that would terrorize the countryside. For years, as the story goes, the winged beast would swoop down from the mountains and set towns ablaze with his breath of fire. Over time, the people had had enough. They assembled themselves and proceeded to hunt down the evil dragon."

"Is that all?" said Troy with a frown.

The man raised his hands. "Please, let me continue. Legend states that a brave knight led the charge against the dragon and delivered the fatal blow. After he had killed the mighty beast, they used its skin to bind a sacred scripture."

"To bind a sacred scripture," repeated Troy, with visions of the elusive book in his head.

The old man continued. "Legend has it that this binding will bleed the tears of the evil dragon for all eternity."

Troy's eyes widened, a smile stretching across his face. "Where did they lay the book to rest?" he asked with great anticipation. Teleios leaned closer to the counter as well, waiting for the answer.

The old man cocked his head. "Supposedly in some chamber below the surface of the earth."

Troy waited for more, but soon realized that the old man had finished speaking. "Is that all? Some chamber below the earth?"

The shopkeeper raised his palms to the ceiling, shrugging. "That's all I know of the legend. I'm telling you the truth!"

Troy felt annoyed at first, but his feeling of displeasure passed. "Hearing this story is more than I expected from this little town, I suppose." The young general then gazed at the man again with intent. "I would appreciate it if you told no one else of this legend."

The older gentleman flashed a sly grin. "I'm sure I could be convinced to avoid spreading any more rumors about this myth."

Troy nodded, then smiled at the elder. "Give him some gold," he said to his young fighter before turning to leave the shop. His soldier fumbled with a sack of coins before paying the shopkeeper and departing himself.

Outside the store, Troy addressed his advisor. "We must find the name of this brave knight. If we find out more about him, we'll get a better idea where the book might lie."

Teleios agreed. "I believe you are right. Troy, this is the break we have been waiting for."

The young general smiled. "I know. Let's find a place to digest this new information." The two men then left the weapon shop and returned to the inn to discuss their next plan of attack.

CHAPTER 10

○

Troy and Teleios returned to their room at the inn, ready to discuss their newfound information. Troy removed his armor and weaponry, then took a seat at a sturdy wooden table.

"What do you make of this knight, Teleios?"

Teleios fumbled with his backpack while he answered. "There have been many brave knights in this land." He paused for a moment before finding the elusive item.

"I might be able to find some clues within this scripture." The halfling leafed through the pages of the same old, tattered book he had gazed at before while on the ship from Dragon's Lair.

Troy gave his advisor a look of surprise. "You mean to tell me that that book has links to the past?"

Teleios continued to stare intently at the manuscript. "This sorcerer's book is ancient," he said, while thumbing through the pages.

"There are spells, stories, and historical references from the past. I've studied it many times and I remember something about a dual between a dragon and a knight."

Troy watched as Teleios continued his quest to find the passage. A moment later, he exclaimed, "Here it is!" Troy's advisor placed the book on the table.

The young general leaned over in anticipation. "What does it say?"

Teleios crinkled his brow, then began to read the section, using a finger to follow the text. *"The battle for Dragon's Quarters had reached its pinnacle. The wicked beast, Cedryicus, all but defeated the townspeople led by William the Great. That is until a highly decorated member of the Legion of Knighthood came to save the village. His tactical maneuvers proved mightier than his skill with the blade.*

"Using the mountainous cliffs to his advantage, he managed to corner the wretched creature and subdue him. This brave knight liberated Dragon's Quarters by capturing the beast and forcing it to become his slave."

Teleios stopped reading and leafed through a few more pages. Not finding anything further that pertained to the story, he said with disgust, "That's all there is."

"The story doesn't even reveal this knight's name?" Troy slammed his fist on the table in frustration. "What kind of historian would write about an important event and leave out the name of the hero?"

Teleios shrugged. "At least we have the name of the dragon." The halfling gazed up in thought. "Cedryicus does not sound familiar to me. How about you?"

"Not at all." Troy let out a deep sigh. "I suppose you're right. We have more information now and we can ask people about this dragon and the brave knight."

Teleios nodded. "I'm sure there is a legend to this story, especially in Dragon's Quarters."

Troy's eyes lit up with Teleios's last statement. "Yes, I'm sure there'll be a well-known myth there." The young general smiled. "This will coincide perfectly with our planned route."

Teleios smirked. "You see, I told you we were on the right track. You should believe in me more."

"You're right again." Troy stretched and yawned. "Let's get some sleep. We'll have plenty of work to do tomorrow."

"That we will." Teleios collected his things and headed for the doorway.

The next morning, Troy and his men spent several more hours information hunting, but left without any additional clues. Their next stop was the town of Rocklia, a solid day's journey from Lars. From there, they figured to get a better perspective on how the townspeople of the Great Forest region felt of their ransom. Troy also hoped that the lack of information he had encountered along the coastal towns would mean that an abundance of untapped knowledge would reveal itself from the inland villages. And maybe someone could help them decipher the legend of Dragon's Quarters.

Instead, two more days of frustration ensued. Troy and his band of soldiers traveled from Rocklia to the small town of Tigris, just outside of the Great Forest. His men began posting signs, just as they had done in the previous towns, as the cloudy sky darkened and the night began to creep in.

Troy looked about the small village. "This place is barely a town." The young general shook his head at Teleios. "There isn't even a dwelling suitable for us to lodge for the evening."

"We'll just have to make do here."

"I agree." Troy then gathered his men, who surrounded their leader. "We'll remain here for the evening. There's no place in Tigris large enough to house us for the night. Start erecting a campsite and settle in."

Troy's men heeded their leader's command and formed a small encampment on the outskirts of the town. While his men worked, Troy began to rummage through his backpack for much-needed food.

Teleios approached his superior. "I suggest we spend a minimal amount of time here." The halfling placed his pack next to Troy's and pulled out dried meats. "I can't imagine there being anything worthwhile coming from a town like this." After a long pause, he said, "Our next stop is Dragon's Quarters."

"That's where we'll find what we need. I just have that feeling." Unbeknownst to Troy, his good sensation would soon change forever.

While the rest of the men prepared their meals near the campfire, a soldier approached his leader. "General, this may not be pertinent information, but the owner of a local establishment remembers a rather rowdy party coming through the town about a week ago."

Troy continued to fiddle with his meal, not bothering to look up at the man. "I'm sure many rowdy parties wander through here often."

"This is true, but he said they needed a mage. He was not sure why, but he thinks he remembers that they needed this wizard to look at something magical that they had found."

Troy continued to cook his meal, placing vegetables in a pot that he had positioned over the campfire. "The owner said they arrived a week ago?" asked Troy, stirring the food.

"Yes, he did."

"If by chance they did find the book —" Troy paused a moment, using his spoon to taste his food. Continuing, he said, "and it took them a few days to get to this town, then that would coincide with the time the king felt the removal of the book from its resting place." Troy then turned his gaze to his soldier. "Even with all that, the probabilities are very small that this group would have the book."

"I understand," said the soldier, "but he also said that the mage left the next day with this group. The old wizard had lived in this town for the better part of his life and rarely ventured."

Troy suddenly took a stronger interest in his soldier's information. "You're saying that this mage, who has lived in this pathetic little town for so long, decided to leave with this group after meeting them for the first time?"

Teleios had listened to the whole conversation up until now and could see the direction of his superior's thoughts.

"Troy, I think your frustrations are getting the better of you again." Teleios shook his head. "You don't believe in all honesty that this group could have the book. This just happens to be a coincidence."

Troy peered at his advisor. "I suppose you're right. Good work anyway, soldier."

The young man was not ready to give up just yet. "But sir, this mage lives in a house down this street. The owner says his niece lives with him and she did not accompany him on his trip."

Troy looked over to Teleios. "I guess it can't hurt to inquire. This town is so small that this may be the only lead we get." Troy took another spoonful of food, then looked over to his soldier.

"As a matter of fact, I'll do the interrogation. I would like to question this person myself. After we're finished eating, you'll lead us to this mage's residence."

The soldier stood tall. "Yes, sir. I will be waiting for you." The young man then left his leaders to finish their supper.

Troy watched the fighter depart, then looked over to his advisor. "Would you care to join me?"

Teleios shrugged. "I might as well." The men then continued with their meal, not realizing what awaited them.

Tara had kept herself busy reading over simple spells that she promised her uncle she would learn before he returned from his journey. Every time she opened the book, she could not help but think of where her uncle might be. Her thoughts then drifted to Harrison and she wondered how he was doing, too. A sudden knock at the door interrupted her day dreaming.

Why would someone be visiting so late, she wondered as she made a cautious approach to the entranceway. Opening the door slowly, she saw three figures waiting in the doorway.

"What can I do for you, gentlemen?" she asked, before a look of shock overtook her face.

Troy, seeing the girl's panicked expression, tried to put her at ease. "Miss, please don't be frightened. We mean you no harm." Tara continued to stare at Troy, unable to say a word.

Troy gazed back to Teleios and his soldier with concern, before focusing on the young girl again. "We would like to ask you a few questions, if it is all right?"

Tara knew right away that something was gravely amiss. Mustering all of her courage, she said in a meek voice, "Am I in some kind of trouble?"

Troy let out a sigh of relief. "No. Not at all." The young general noticed the girl carefully looking them over.

"Let me explain why we're here. We're in the process of scouring the land in search of a special treasure," he began, hoping the girl would relax. "I know that our armor and weaponry have alarmed you."

Tara began to pull herself together. "I've seen men like you before," she said, never taking her gaze off Troy.

The young general nodded. "Good. Now, I need you to think back about a week ago. Did you notice a group of adventurers come through this town at that time?"

Tara knew just whom Troy alluded to. "Many adventurers have come through this town. I didn't recognize any group in particular."

"Do you remember the group that left with the mage that lives in this house?" asked the young general pointedly.

"A mage? In this house?" Tara's words sounded very unconvincing. She knew she had to try to cover up her knowledge of the book, but she just found herself becoming even more nervous.

Troy did not let up with his questioning. "The owner of the tavern down the street says you're this mage's niece. Is this true?"

Tara's face grew flushed and she knew that her expression was giving her away. "I suppose," she said in a shy manner, taking her apprehensive gaze to the ground.

"Then you do remember a group of adventurers leaving with him," pressed Troy, continuing with a comforting tone.

Tara took care in selecting her words. "Well, yes, he did leave with them."

The young general pressed further. "Have you heard of a ransom for a sacred book?"

Tara could not believe her ears. A sacred book, she lamented to herself. How could they have found out about that? Did something happen to my uncle? To Harrison?

The young girl pulled herself together once again. "No, I have not heard of any such ransom," she said in her best truthful voice.

"Why did these men need your uncle's services?"

"They had a map of some kind with symbols that they could not understand. They hoped my uncle could decipher them."

Troy nodded, squinted a bit, then said, "I see. And where will this map lead them?"

Tara thought up a quick lie. "Near the Great Ridge of King Solaris. I don't know what kind of treasure they are expecting to find." The young girl felt that leading these people in the exact opposite direction would help spare the group some time. She was wrong.

Troy smiled. "Thank you very much for your time, Miss. I'm sorry if we caused you any alarm." As the men departed, Tara closed the door as fast as she could, bolting the lock in the process.

"Do you believe her?" Troy asked Teleios, as the men began their trek back to their encampment.

"No. She is obviously covering up something. Her uncle has left and she is doing her best to lead us away from him."

Troy nodded in agreement. "My thoughts exactly. I think we should follow up on this. In the morning, we'll ask the owner what direction this group headed in and proceed from there."

"I agree." Teleios thought for a moment. "I think we might have something here, Troy. We need to take advantage of this new information." The three men then entered their encampment and continued with their tasks for the evening.

Tara began to feel at ease now that the door separated her from the soldiers. However, that leader's face! How could it be? Without noticing, droplets of perspiration began to form on her forehead.

She had a nagging feeling that the group had run into some kind of trouble. How could three soldiers appear on her doorstep and ask her about the scripture? Her uncle had left only ten days before. Had they not sworn themselves to secrecy? Did they volunteer their sacred information on their own or did someone extract it from them? Either way, Tara felt that she had to somehow alert the group of what had just occurred.

"I must get in touch with Gelderand and Harrison," she muttered.

With her mind racing, a plan began to formulate in her head. She went through her uncle's desk and found an ornate pen and black ink, then rummaged through the books on the desktop before finally finding a piece of paper to use. With pad and pen in hand, Tara quickly sat herself down at the kitchen table.

Composing herself, she began scribbling her important message. *Dear Martinaeous, my uncle Gelderand and four of his friends have journeyed for some days now. I am hoping that they have arrived at your home by the time you read this letter. Even if they have not, please inform them of this most important information as soon as they arrive.*

Three soldiers appeared at my door tonight inquiring about the treasure Gelderand's friends have found. I told the men that they uncovered a map that depicted a marking near the Great Ridge of King Solaris. I hope they believed me and will head in that direction. I am very frightened that these men might try to hurt my uncle and the rest. Please tell them to be careful; I am thinking of them every day. Give my love to my uncle, and Harrison, too. Tara.

She rolled the paper with care and, using the melted wax of her candle, affixed Gelderand's personal seal. Then she placed the message in a metallic tube and corked the top.

Tara lifted her gaze from the table to the open window. Outside, nightfall began to take its grip on the village. The nervous girl cursed the ensuing darkness, knowing it was too late to have her letter delivered.

"First thing in the morning I will get young Thomas to take this to Martinaeous. I hope I'm not too late." She sighed while she anxiously waited for the morning to arrive.

To Tara's dismay, the threat of rain delayed the appearance of the morning light. Sensing the lateness of the day, she rose from her bed and dressed herself in haste. The previous evening she had lain in her bed, tossing and turning the whole night through, in great anticipation with what she had to do today. After dressing, Tara approached the kitchen table where the metallic tube that held her urgent message awaited her. She snatched the container, placed it in a canvas pouch, then proceeded to the doorway. Slowly cracking the door open, Tara found Troy's men had remained milling about the town.

Tara shut the door in fear. "I can't let them see me! I will have to wait until they leave town," she lamented. She then began pacing inside her home, burning off some of her nervous energy.

"How long will they stay?" she asked herself, knowing there would be no answer. "What will they do if they see me deliver this note?"

Maybe they would do nothing. Maybe they believed her story and would just leave. Then again, maybe not.

Distraught, she decided to remain in the house until things settled down. If these soldiers did not leave by nightfall, then she would sneak to Thomas's residence and inform him of his duties under the cover of darkness. With sadness, she placed her pouch back on the table and began her daily chores.

"General, we have returned with the information you sought," announced one of Troy's men. Troy had sent his platoon into the small town to inquire about the group of adventurers who had come trampling through a week earlier.

"What have you found?"

"The men in question arrived from the Great Forest and proceeded to Johanssen's Pub, a local drinking establishment, where they scuffled with some of the townsfolk before being thrown out of the tavern. After that, they met a mage named Gelderand and left with him the next morning."

The information pleased Troy. "His name is Gelderand," the young general said, storing the new information in his mind. "This is good news. Now we can identify one of the members of this group. Very good, soldier. In which way did they leave?"

The soldier pointed in the direction of the woods. "The bartender said they followed the main path leading out of the town. They haven't been heard from since."

"Excellent." Troy nodded, smiling. "We'll proceed in that same direction. Tell our best scouts that I'll ask them to find tracks that are about ten days old. Give them the same information you have told me. After that's done, round up the men and tell them to be ready to leave as soon as possible. You're dismissed."

"Yes, sir!" answered the soldier, leaving to follow his leader's commands.

Teleios, who had overheard the conversation, knew that they had definitely found another solid lead. Still, he did not feel altogether convinced that this rogue party had possession of the book. His common sense told him to forget about chasing this particular group, but his gut instinct told him to hunt these men down. Maybe he was beginning to feel like Troy, tired of finding only bits and pieces to this mysterious scripture. On the other hand, maybe his instincts, which had proved to be correct many times before, would be right again.

"Troy, if we follow this party, we cannot make our evaluation in Dragon's Quarters as planned," he said, looking at his leader. "And, we will not be able to follow up on the myth of the dragon and knight."

Troy held his chin in his hand, stroking his face. "I've thought of that myself. We'll travel for a few days, then evaluate our progress. If we find no trace of this party, then we can go back to Dragon's Quarters.

"These woods take a good three days to travel through by foot. It'll take just as long with the horses due to all the underbrush. After we traverse this forest, we should be able to make a justifiable determination if we can find this group." Gazing over at Teleios, he said, "The myth can wait a few more days."

Teleios nodded in agreement. "Like I said before, we can amend our schedule as we see fit. The course of action you propose is sound and just."

"I'm glad you concur, Teleios." Troy then called for one of his men who stood close by. The soldier rushed over upon hearing his general's command.

"I have a special assignment for you," Troy started.

"After we enter the woods and have traveled out of eyesight of this village, I want you to circle back and watch the mage's house. Investigate any activity you deem suspicious by the young girl. If she has held back any information, I want to know about it immediately. Do you understand your mission?"

"Yes, sir!" responded the young man. "Sir, how will I find our platoon again?"

"Our advanced scouts can detail our proposed route through the forest for you. If nothing strange happens in two days, you are to return to the squad."

The soldier nodded. "I understand, sir. I will not let you down." The young man then went off to find his comrades.

Troy watched his men break down their camp and smiled. "Teleios, I have a very good feeling about this."

Teleios gazed at the men as well. "So do I."

After spending a final hour dismantling camp and gathering more supplies, Troy and his men finally ventured toward the outskirts of town. Several minutes later, the platoon had advanced far enough into the forest where they could no longer see the little town of Tigris.

Troy looked back at one of his soldiers and gave him a nod. The sentry acknowledged his superior and peeled off from the rest of the group. Being as stealthy as possible, the fighter headed back to the small village.

Tara had heard the horses trotting down the only road heading into the forest. She peered out of her window with care and patiently waited until they had disappeared into the depths of the forest.

"I will wait a little longer until I'm sure that they will not be back," she said to herself, all the while clutching the canvas bag in her small hands.

After waiting what felt like days, Tara began her mission of getting her urgent letter to the group. Leaving her home with a purpose, she sought out a young man who could help her cause. Passing several buildings along the way, she found the person she had looked for at last. Thomas, a young man about Tara's age, was busy combing his horse's mane.

Tara quickly walked up behind the boy and attempted to get his attention. "Thomas?"

The young girl's voice startled the boy at first. Thomas turned around and saw Tara gazing back at him with worried eyes. "What is the matter, Miss Tara?"

"Thomas, I have a most important favor to ask of you."

Thomas flashed a boyish grin. "Miss Tara, you may ask me anything."

"Could you deliver this message to someone in Valkala?"

"Valkala?" Thomas looked from side to side, fumbling with his words. "That's quite a ways from here. I don't know if that's a good idea. I have not taken my horse on many long journeys —" he rambled before Tara's plea interrupted him.

"Oh please, Thomas. I know it's far away, but I must have my uncle receive this letter." Tara knew that the young man had always paid her extra attention and she used her teary, blue eyes to her full advantage.

Thomas let out a deep sigh, then shrugged. "Well, I guess I could do this favor for you," he said, as a wide smile came across Tara's face. "Who should I deliver the message to?"

"My uncle's friend, Martinaeous. I don't know the exact location of his house; you'll have to inquire when you arrive there. Please be very careful with this." Tara handed Thomas the canvas pouch.

"I will. You can count on me, Miss Tara." The young boy then continued brushing his horse. "Allow me a little time to prepare myself for my trip, then I'll be gone."

"Oh thank you, Thomas." Tara leaned over and kissed him on the cheek, turning the lad's face a deep red.

"Do be careful." Tara then left the boy and his horse to head back to her home.

Neither of them knew that Troy's soldier had witnessed the whole encounter. Noticing the exchange of the small pouch was all he needed to see in order to know what his next course of action would be.

After some time, young Thomas mounted his steed and began his journey to Valkala. As he trekked through the woods, the armed horseman followed him from a distance far enough away that the young boy could neither see nor hear him.

A short time later, the soldier noticed Thomas entering a small clearing and knew that the time to react was upon him. Removing his sword from its scabbard, the fighter advanced to the young man's position with his horse at full gallop.

Thomas heard the sudden sound of hoof beats. With a quick jerk of his head, he saw the soldier bearing down on him. Pulling on his reins, the young boy tried to get his horse to evade the area. To his dismay, his animal could not match the skills of a seasoned warhorse and Troy's soldier made a quick advance upon him.

With a slash, the fighter's blade made a clean slice in Thomas's upper left arm. The boy released the reins in his left hand, causing him to lose his balance and fall to the ground. Dazed and injured, he clutched his bleeding arm, while he watched his horse continue off into the clearing.

Thomas tried his best to regroup, but felt a sharp pain in his right leg. "My leg! I think it's broke!" he wailed while he tried in vain to flee from the clearing.

As fate would have it, the soldier forced his horse to make a tight turn and galloped toward the injured lad again. Dismounting, the fighter cautiously approached the young man.

Thomas knew he could not defeat the soldier in his current condition, and furthermore he had stowed all the weapons and gear for his journey on his horse, which had now run off to the other side of the meadow.

With the fighter hovering over him, Thomas pleaded, "I have no gold! All that I own is on the horse!"

The soldier pointed to the object slung over the boy's shoulder. "Give me that pouch."

Thomas tightened his grip on the sack. Why didn't Tara tell me there could be some kind of danger? What did this message say anyway?

"No!" the lad exclaimed, as he tried to wriggle away from the soldier. Thomas squeezed his eyes and winced, the shooting pain from his injured leg forcing him to abort his getaway attempt.

"You are as noble as you are a fool." The soldier approached the young man, then lightly placed his foot on the boy's injured leg. Thomas's eyes widened with shock, knowing the great pain that would follow if the soldier applied more pressure to his wound.

"You are in no position to bargain!" barked the fighter. "I'm not going to ask you again. Hand over the pouch." This time Thomas obliged.

The soldier removed the scroll from the sack, then opened the metallic tube and scanned through the letter. Satisfied with its contents, he rolled the parchment back up and placed it in the cylinder.

"What town were you heading to?" the soldier commanded, applying slight pressure to Thomas's injured leg. The young boy gasped as he felt the biting pain. Still, he said nothing.

The fighter admired the boy's valor, but he had started to lose patience with poor Thomas. "It would be a shame to have to take the life of such a beautiful young woman, but I will if I do not hear the name of the town!"

Thomas glared at Troy's scout. "Don't you dare hurt her! She is the sweetest person in this whole land!"

The soldier cocked his head. "All the reason to answer the question, boy!"

Thomas understood the graveness of his situation. Feeling that he had failed Tara, he responded dejectedly, "I was heading to Valkala."

"That was not so difficult, now was it?" finished the soldier in a sarcastic tone, removing his foot from Thomas's leg. The fighter took the pouch with the letter and placed it inside his backpack, then went to his horse.

Thomas felt a momentary sense of relief, but soon realized that he was at this man's mercy. "What are you going to do with me?" he asked, the nervousness evident in his wavering voice. The soldier did not respond. Instead, he began to look for something on his horse.

"Did you hear me?" pressed Thomas.

The soldier gave the young boy a look of agitation. Gesturing to the trail, he said, "We'll round up your horse, then I will take you back to the main path. From there, you're on your own."

Thomas gave the man an incredulous stare. "What? My leg is broken! I cannot travel like this!"

The fighter did not seem to care about Thomas's predicament. "This path is well traversed. Someone will find you and help you get back home."

The soldier approached Thomas and helped the young boy gingerly get to his feet. Placing Thomas's arm around his shoulder, both men took cautious steps toward the awaiting horse.

"This is going to hurt, so prepare yourself." The soldier assisted the young boy in mounting the steed. Thomas wailed in pain as his injured leg careened through the air and thudded against the other side of the animal.

After a few moments, the two men were ready to travel again. "Hold on tight," said the soldier. "And don't yell in my ear."

Troy's soldier tugged at the reins and the horse began to move. Thomas clenched his teeth, not daring to let a whimper escape his mouth. Before too long, the two men gathered the boy's steed, left the clearing behind, and headed back to the well-traveled path.

CHAPTER 11

○

The last five days had been a struggle for Harrison and the group. The young warrior had regained feeling in his injured arm, but still could not grip a tankard of water, let alone his battle-axe. Gelderand and Swinkle had taken longer than expected to regain their strength due to the mental energy they had expended repairing Harrison's wound. Fortunately, Pondle's infliction healed faster than anticipated, though it too still felt a bit tender. Standing on the outskirts of Lord Nigel Hammer's land only compounded matters further.

Murdock and Pondle had led the party through the lightly wooded landscape without incidence. Now, they all stood on a small hill and looked to the west. In the distance, they could see a great wall that encircled a large city.

"Concur," said Harrison, his arm still in a sling. The rest of the men stared in silence.

Gelderand gazed at the city of Concur with the others. He knew that the town held bad memories for the group, but did not know to what extent. Breaking the uncomfortable stillness, he asked, "Please tell me again, just what happened to you the last time you visited that place?"

"We almost died there," said Harrison, maintaining his stare. "And it was my fault."

Swinkle came to his friend's defense. "You cannot take all of the blame. I was there with you and did nothing to stop the chain of events."

"I never saw Marcus so upset." Murdock turned toward Gelderand. "We just wanted to stop in Concur for food and supplies. Harrison had different plans though."

The young warrior heard his friend's comment, but his thoughts had shifted to the visage of a beautiful woman. Meredith had been so unhappy and so desperate for someone to save her. He could still see the pain in her blue eyes.

"Marcus also told us to find the sacred plate that Lord Hammer harbored," the young warrior said in his own defense. "In that respect, I succeeded."

Murdock had a different take on the matter. "If you mean escaping from the city as being successful, then yes, we did succeed. Otherwise we failed."

"We most certainly did not fail!" Swinkle again would not allow his friend to take all of the blame. "Harrison saw the plate."

"And she gave me this." The young warrior showed the group his ruby ring, which gave Harrison the power to move objects through the air. "Without it, I might have died."

Gelderand remained perplexed. "Why is this Meredith so important?"

"She's Nigel's woman." Harrison positioned himself to face the older man. "He doesn't like ordinary people visiting with her when he's gone, let alone warriors like us."

Gelderand frowned. "So, he is just a jealous man?"

Harrison shrugged. "You could say so. A jealous man with a well-paid army."

"Like I said before," said Murdock, nervously shuffling his feet, "they'll remember our faces."

Harrison took his gaze into the distance once again. "I wonder what they've done to her."

Murdock took a step toward the young warrior, pointing in his direction. "We're not going to find out! We have work to do and I'll be damned if we step foot in that city again!"

"Don't worry, Murdock," said Harrison, raising his hands. "I agree. The next time we go to Concur it'll be with an army of our own."

The ranger gave Harrison a look of approval. "That's more like it."

Gelderand persisted. "Again I ask, what is so special about Meredith?"

Harrison paused before speaking. "She's a special person that the entire city adores, yet Nigel keeps her locked away. When Lord Hammer and his army took over Concur, he made Meredith his prize. She's neither a queen nor his wife, only a trophy to him."

The young warrior sighed. "Meredith wishes to be liberated and to set her people free from the clutches of their wicked lord. But she can't do this alone. An underground resistance is gaining momentum. Someday they might topple Lord Hammer and reclaim their city. I hope to help her then."

Gelderand gave Harrison a look of surprise. "That is quite noble of you."

"I think it's sweet," said Murdock, his voice thick with his usual sarcasm. He then looked toward Concur. "We need to avoid that city as best we can. I suggest we continue."

Pondle stepped to the forefront, taking his cue from Murdock's last remarks. "What route shall we take?"

Murdock thought for a moment. From where they stood, Concur loomed directly in their path. "We can't go along the shore or we'll run right into the city." The ranger maintained his gaze on the metropolis before motioning with his hand. "We'll have to make a wide sweep to the south of the town. If we're lucky, we'll avoid any of Lord Hammer's men who might be patrolling the countryside."

Pondle agreed with Murdock's plan. "I don't think we have any other choice. Does anyone else have an opinion?"

Gelderand and Swinkle shook their head no. Harrison, agreeing with the aforementioned strategy, said, "Like you've stated, Pondle, we have no other choice."

"Good," said Murdock. "Follow our lead."

After a few minutes of trekking, Gelderand said in Harrison's direction, "Will Lord Hammer's men find us?"

The young warrior shook his head. "I don't know. His men are very skilled and I'm sure there's a bounty on our heads. We need to get through this land, and quickly."

Gelderand nodded, knowing Harrison told him the truth. "I can imagine what they will do with us if we are captured."

"That's why we can't allow that to happen." The men continued onward, all the while keeping an anxious eye toward Concur.

The wall surrounding Concur stood approximately thirty feet high. On any given clear day, all of Lord Hammer's sentries had an unobstructed view of about twenty miles. Today was no exception.

A young guard took his usual rotation and patrolled the eastern side of the city. From his vantage point, he could see the flatlands that led away from Concur. The sun had not risen to quite the perfect angle to see The Guard's River, which flowed about twenty-five miles away and had become the unofficial boundary between Lord Hammer's land and Gammoria. As he looked for the water body, he saw something else instead.

The young man squinted to get a better look at the person approaching the enclosed city. At first, the being looked like nothing more than a vagabond stumbling in the wilderness. Something, though, told him that this person was more than just a drifter. He watched the figure get closer, and as it did, he could tell that the man wore black, tattered armor.

The warrior continued his erratic approach toward the gate. The young sentry maintained his gaze on him, but did not alert anyone just yet. That would quickly change. The man now staggered close enough for the soldier to see that the intruder sported a beard.

The sentry then stood motionless, a stunned look overtaking his face. "It can't be," the young man muttered to himself, before turning and yelling to his fellow guardsman who patrolled a hundred feet away from him.

"Open the gate!" he shouted at the top of his lungs. "Open the gate!"

"What is it?" yelled the second sentry as he relayed the command to the gate operators.

The first man's face beamed. "It's Lord Hammer! He has returned!"

The thirty-foot tall double doors creaked while the men of Concur slowly opened the eastern gate. When enough room existed to squeeze through the opening, several of Lord Hammer's men seized the opportunity to greet their leader.

The first soldier reached Nigel and gazed upon him with a look of shock. "Lord Hammer, thank the gods you're alive!"

Nigel stopped in his tracks, then dropped to his knees. His body looked worn and his appearance disheveled. His armor was torn and ripped in several places; he carried no backpack and held only his long sword. Though no one would say it to his face, Lord Hammer looked very thin and drawn. His soldier placed an arm around his leader and helped him back to his feet.

"I have journeyed in this desolate wilderness for over ten days," said Lord Hammer in a shallow whisper.

"I've had to forage for food and water," he continued, his voice rising with each word, "stave off the beasts of the land, and return to my city in humility!"

By this time, a group of twenty soldiers had surrounded their missing leader. The first soldier spoke again. "My Lord, you have not returned in humility. On the contrary, you have returned in honor."

Nigel looked at the fighter, but his demeanor did not change. "I failed in securing the Treasure." Lord Hammer grimaced, then snarled, "Assemble the army! We have unfinished business to take care of!"

"Yes, sir!" said the soldier, before turning to the rest of the men. "You heard your leader! Assemble the army! And spread the word about the town – Lord Hammer is back!"

The soldiers cheered in unison, then made haste to start their new tasks. A few fighters remained with the first soldier and helped Nigel enter his city. Their leader spoke again, this time in a low hiss.

"Consider Harrison Cross a wanted man. I don't care if it takes a lifetime; I will hunt him and his friends down!"

No one said a word; they just nodded in approval. Nigel was not finished. Looking at the man to his left, he snarled, "Take me to my mansion and have Meredith wait for me in her chamber. She has much explaining to do."

The next day began with a very overcast sky. Troy and his contingent of men had ventured out of the Great Forest and were currently taking a break from their journey. The past few days had brought them precious few clues about the renegade band of adventurers that had left Tigris ten days earlier.

Troy took the uneventful travel in stride. As he looked at a map of the countryside, he reflected on the course of events that had brought him to his present position. He knew that the ransom signs posted by his men would generate interest in the townsfolk, and he trusted his instincts in searching for this missing group. Nevertheless, there remained a nagging feeling of uncertainty that clouded all of his decisions.

The young general-at-arms took a hand to his head and rubbed his brow, allowing the map to dangle in his other hand in the process. A light rain began to fall, so he quickly rolled up his favorite parchment and placed it in its canister. He looked out at the flat countryside and for a second he began to question his judgment.

Suddenly, Troy heard a commotion coming from several of his soldiers. The rain fell from the sky at a blinding pace as he stood from his position to get a closer look at the excitement. One of the young general's soldiers had galloped into their campsite and, upon closer inspection, Troy noticed that the sentry from Tigris had returned.

Troy's soldier was not about to allow foul weather to stop him from delivering his important message. After a difficult trek through the forest, he had reached his familiar convoy at last.

"General Harkin! I have returned with important news!" the soldier exclaimed.

Troy passed through his men in order to confront the scout. "What is it, soldier?"

Teleios, who had been resting in seclusion at the time, joined the rest of the men and stood by Troy's side. The look on this soldier's face could only mean that he had found something substantial.

"I watched the girl as you commanded and caught her giving a message to a young man." The soldier handed a parchment to Troy. "I managed to track the boy down and take it away from him."

Troy quickly unrolled the scroll and began to read it. "This is addressed to a Martinaeous and talks of a treasure," he said aloud as he scanned the letter. "She's trying to warn her uncle of our presence, as well as someone named Harrison, whoever he might be."

Teleios peered over his superior's shoulder. "Does it indicate their destination?"

"The writer states that this Martinaeous lives in Valkala." The rain came down harder, pelting the group. Troy used a hand to shield the parchment, in an effort to keep it dry. "We could be there in four days if we travel fast."

Teleios agreed. "That is exactly what we must do."

Troy turned his attention to his scout. "Good work soldier, you will receive a handsome reward. Assume your usual position in the convoy."

"Yes sir!" shouted the sentry, then left for his post.

Troy gathered the rest of his men. "Scouts! Lead us to Valkala. Push the horses as far as they can go — I want to arrive there in four days!" His men scrambled to their animals with haste in order to get ready for their new destination.

Troy and Teleios secured their belonging to their steeds. When they finished, the young general glanced over at Teleios, who prepared to mount his horse.

"We're getting closer, Teleios. Day by day, we're getting closer."

"That we are," said his advisor as he watched Troy mount his animal. "We now have some names to inquire about."

"That we do." Within minutes, the convoy assembled in their marching order and began their trek to the small village of Valkala.

Troy pushed their convoy hard through the pouring rain. The young general knew that he was several days behind his target and the only way to catch up to the unsuspecting party was to travel as fast as possible. The countryside they trekked through lay particularly flat and the visibility on a clear day was usually very good for miles. Today, however, the rain limited their field of vision.

Teleios yelled from his mounted steed. "Troy, we might need to slow down, for the horses' sake."

Troy took a moment to read the signals of his own animal. His horse drew ragged breaths, due to trudging through the muddy landscape. "We can journey a bit longer. We have a lot of ground to cover."

"That is your decision." Teleios started to say something else, but stopped abruptly. Instead, he squinted to get a better visual on something that stood right in front of their convoy.

Troy stared in the same direction. "What's that up ahead?"

"I would say it looks like a campsite."

The two men could see campfires struggling to maintain their flames in the rain, as well as carts, horses, makeshift tents, and people in the general vicinity, who took cover in a hurry, scrambling for their weaponry in the process.

"They've spotted us," said the young general. "I'm sure they're alarmed to see a band of warriors heading toward them." The men of the campsite assembled in a defensive posture as the group advanced closer to the encampment.

Troy turned to Teleios. "Follow me."

The young general guided his horse to the front of their convoy with Teleios following close behind. The rest of Troy's men stopped and allowed their leaders to advance.

The peasants immediately realized that Troy's platoon outnumbered and overmatched them. Instead of raising their arms to fight, several men from the campground approached Troy with caution, making sure that they had secured their weapons by their sides.

"We're sorry if we've ventured onto your land," said one of the men. Troy could sense the man's sincerity and did not intimidate him in any way.

"On the contrary," said the young leader, "this is not my country. We're merely traveling through the area as well."

Troy then took a closer look at the men. Their tents appeared quite new and their animals all seemed to be in relatively good health. Even the men themselves looked very well kempt and did not exhibit signs of a nomadic life.

The young general cocked his head and crossed his arms, resting them on his horse's neck. "Tell me, my good man, you don't look like the type of people who drift throughout the land. Where have you come from?"

The man stared back at Troy with a look of disbelief. "We are from Cyprus," he said, before looking back at his friends. "Have you not heard of the recent happenings there?"

Troy gave Teleios a curious glance before answering. "What kind of happenings?"

The man wiped the rain from his face. "Everything seemed normal until about ten days ago. Then the evil spirits swept through the town."

Troy and Teleios looked at each other in confusion. "I don't understand," said the young general. "Describe these evil spirits."

"That's not easy to do," said another of the men. "No one made any sightings of ghosts or anything like that."

"All of our literature disappeared," said the first man.

Teleios crinkled his brow. "All of your literature *disappeared*? How did that happen?"

The man shrugged. "I can't explain that either. One minute people were reading books and scriptures, and the next, all the text vanished." He paused a moment, allowing his new information to sink in. "This didn't happen to just one person, either. This happened to everyone in the town."

Troy thought for a moment. "You say this occurred about ten days ago?"

"Yes."

Troy looked over to Teleios. "Ten days ago."

Teleios knew just what Troy meant. "About the same time these adventurers arrived in Tigris."

"Which is the same time we left Dragon's Lair. These events are related to the taking of the book, I'm sure of it."

"I agree." Teleios motioned to the peasants. "What shall we do about them?"

"Nothing." Troy turned to the vagabonds. "Where are the rest of the citizens of Cyprus?"

The man shook his head. "Everyone fled in different directions. The place is deserted."

"Be careful out here," said Troy, "there've been a lot of unexplained occurrences in the past week and a half, and I have a feeling they're all related."

"We'll take that into consideration. You be careful yourself."

The young general nodded, then turned his attention toward his platoon. "Scouts, lead us onward to Valkala!"

Troy and Teleios returned to their usual spot in the convoy. "Let's go over the findings that we have uncovered," said Troy.

Teleios started, "First, the ancient scripture is removed from its resting place. The king sensed this on the onset."

"Correct. Then the shopkeeper told us a story about a bleeding book legend and that someone placed it in a chamber below the ground."

"As well as a brave knight who saved the town of Dragon's Quarters." Teleios nodded. "We cross-referenced that with the manuscript that I possess. Still, we have no name for this knight."

"I'm sure we'll find that out." Troy looked up in thought, the rain still soaking him, though he paid it no attention. "Next, we discover that a group of adventurers teamed up with a mage in Tigris.

"Then we intercepted a message to a person named Martinaeous, which also mentioned two more people, Gelderand and Harrison."

"Yes, Gelderand is the mage. We do not know who Harrison is, but we do know that they left for Valkala a short time ago."

"And now, we have this evil spirits situation in the town of Cyprus."

"All of the text to every scripture that exists in the city has disappeared." Teleios raised an eyebrow. "At, what looks like, the same time someone took the book from its sacred place."

Troy nodded, grinning. "Precisely. I'm glad that we have our facts straight."

Teleios leaned closer to Troy in an effort to be heard over the rain. "I believe this party we are after hold all the answers to the clues that we have found."

"I believe the same. That's why it's imperative to find them."

"I agree."

The two men then looked into the distance, not saying another word to each other. Both realized at that very moment that whoever was heading to Valkala most likely possessed the king's coveted prize.

C H A P T E R **12**

⊠

A light drizzle began to fall from the sky. Harrison gazed upward and saw thick, menacing black clouds that threatened rain.

"Looks like we're in for some bad weather, boy," he said to Lance, who walked beside him.

"Have I told you that I'm not too fond of rain," said Gelderand with a laugh.

"I don't think we have much of a choice." Swinkle looked back in the direction they had come and saw the dark clouds, too. "That's a fairly large storm system."

Harrison and Gelderand peered back at the storm that had started to catch up to them. "That looks nasty." The young warrior looked around the area, finding nothing except flatlands, without even a hint of a tree to hide under.

"We're all going to get very wet."

"That's an understatement," agreed Swinkle.

Murdock and Pondle had stopped their trek and headed back to the other members of the group. "We might as well keep moving." The ranger gazed upwards, watching the swift moving clouds fly by. "There's no use waiting for the thunderstorm and there's nowhere to hide."

"I hate water." Pondle shook his head while looking to the heavens. "Why must this journey test my will so?"

The rain changed from a sporadic drizzle to a steady shower. Harrison looked at his friends and saw their dry clothing soak up the unwanted liquid.

"Are you sure we don't want to just set up camp? At least until the storm blows through?"

All eyes turned to Murdock. The ranger looked at the ever-thickening clouds and knew that the weather might not change for hours. Shrugging, he said, "We only have a few hours until nightfall. We might as well set up camp now."

The rest of the men felt relieved, but only temporarily. Lance, sensing something out of the ordinary, turned his head to the east. A moment later, he looked up at Harrison and whimpered.

The young warrior raised an eyebrow, staring at the wet dog. "What is it, boy?"

Lance looked to the east again. "Noise."

"Noise?" The young warrior wrinkled his brow. "What do you mean, Lance?"

Pondle noticed Harrison's conversation with his canine friend. "What did he say?" he asked with a hint of worry in his voice.

"If I understand him right, he said 'Noise.' I don't know what he means though." Harrison shrugged. "It's probably thunder in the distance." Just then, the rain began to come down in sheets.

"Maybe so," yelled Murdock over the din of the rain, "but something tells me otherwise."

Pondle nodded, concerned. "Me, too."

The two brought a hand over their eyes, shielding them from the rain as they scoured the countryside. At first, they saw nothing, but that changed a moment later.

"Over there!" Pondle pointed due east. "Horses!"

Harrison's jaw dropped. "Carrying Lord Hammer's men! What are we to do?"

The thief motioned to his friends. "Follow me and stay as low to the ground as possible!" Pondle led the men as far out of the horsemen's path as he could. After a few minutes, he gave another order.

"Everyone! Get down!"

All of the men dropped to the saturated ground. Harrison grabbed Lance and pulled him down,.putting the dog beside him.

"Keep quiet, Lance," he said, fixing his stare straight ahead.

The rain continued its steady fall to the earth, while the sound of galloping horses engulfed the area. Harrison lifted his head ever so slightly and watched as the armored men rode by. With a peek toward the heavens, he knew the pouring rain was saving them at this very moment.

"They can't see us," he whispered to Lance, knowing there would not be a response. Harrison counted twenty warhorses before the stampede passed. Within minutes, Lord Hammer's men vanished into the distance and the group huddled alone again.

Harrison spoke first. "Are we all clear?" he yelled in Pondle's direction.

The thief took a moment to scan the area. "I think so."

Gelderand stepped to the forefront. "Where do we go now? We are vulnerable without any cover."

"Don't you have any kind of magic that can help us?" Murdock wiped the mud from his leather armor. "You're a wizard, right?"

Gelderand looked at Murdock in surprise. "Come to think of it, I do."

Murdock rolled his eyes and shook his head. "I have to admit that little trick you performed on Harrison's arm was impressive, but having to remind you that you're a magician is getting tiring."

The mage grimaced. "I told you, it has been a long time since —"

"Since you used your magic," said Murdock, shaking his head in disbelief.

Pondle appeared a bit more apprehensive than his ranger friend did. "I don't like being out in the open for this long. Or have you already forgotten that a platoon of soldiers just passed by."

"Pondle's right," said Harrison. "Gelderand, what can you do?"

The mage thought for a moment. "I can create a temporary sanctuary, something that will keep us invisible to outsiders."

The young warrior lifted his arms, soaked to the bone. "Will it keep us dry, too?"

Gelderand shook his head. "No, and it won't stop anyone or anything from entering the area. It will simply keep us out of view."

Harrison shrugged, trying to hide his disappointment. "I suppose that'll do for now."

The mage closed his eyes and clasped his hands together. "Give me a moment to concentrate."

Everyone watched while the older man mumbled a spell. A soft yellow glow encompassed a twenty-foot by twenty-foot area before making an abrupt disappearance.

Gelderand slowly opened his eyes. "That should do it."

Harrison looked about the area and noticed that nothing had changed. "How do we know it worked?"

"Swinkle," Gelderand pointed behind the young cleric. "Walk backwards that way."

Swinkle nodded, before walking away from the men. After a few steps, he said, "I can still see you."

Gelderand waved the young cleric back. "You need to go further away. You are still in the sanctuary."

Swinkle again nodded and continued his trek. After a few more steps, the other men saw his eyes widen in surprise.

"Now you're gone!"

A broad smile came across Gelderand's face. "Good. Come forward again."

Swinkle listened to the older man and took two steps before stopping. "I can see you again!"

Gelderand motioned the young boy over. "You've proven that it works."

Harrison placed a hand on the older man's shoulder. "Great job, Gelderand!"

Murdock, not an easy one to impress, came over to the mage, too. "Not bad, old man. Now can you make it stop raining?"

Gelderand gave the ranger a quizzical look. "Stop raining? That would take years of practice! I would need to study volumes of ancient spell books and gather countless rare ingredients."

"I'm only kidding," said the ranger with a grin. "Gelderand, you're going to have to figure out when I'm serious and when I'm joking."

The mage frowned. "I suppose so."

Murdock panned the area, gauging their situation. "How long will this spell last?"

"The magic will last through the night, but we still need to keep watch."

The ranger nodded. "We don't want Lord Hammer's men to walk right into our camp while we're asleep."

Pondle agreed with his friend. "No, we don't. We'll use our usual guard rotation, all right?" Everyone nodded in agreement. "Good, then let's set up camp and somehow get out of this rain."

The men then went about settling into their campsite. While Harrison fiddled with his backpack, Swinkle asked, "Where do you think those soldiers were going?"

Harrison brought his gaze to the horizon. "I've been wondering the same thing. They seemed pretty eager to get somewhere."

Gelderand overheard the younger men's conversation. As he fumbled with his wet belongings, he said, "We must be extra careful. They seemed to be on a mission."

The young warrior nodded. "That's how I felt, too. We'll be far away from Concur by the end of day tomorrow. I won't feel safe until then."

Gelderand and Swinkle took in Harrison's comment and knew he was right. With the ever-pounding rain causing them more havoc, the men quickly set up their campsite and settled in for the evening.

Troy's advance scouts saw the oncoming horses first. "How many are there?" asked Troy to his soldier.

The scout's eyes remained fixed on the intruders. "Twenty or so. What shall we do?"

Troy did not flinch. "Set up a defensive posture. No one attacks until I say so."

"Yes, sir!" The young man quickly relayed his commander's orders to the rest of the squadron and Troy's fighters maneuvered their horses in a tight circle around their leaders. Every man drew his weapon.

Troy peered through the pouring rain as best he could and found that the advancing platoon consisted of warriors in black armor, with their horses sporting body shielding as well.

"What do we know about the rulers in this part of the land?" asked Troy.

Teleios stared at the oncoming men. "This land is governed by a dictator of Concur. A ruthless man, I might add."

The oncoming brigade slowed as they approached Troy's group. Suddenly, the horses broke off and fanned into a wide semi-circle formation around Troy's men. The leader of the new army positioned his horse in front of his squadron.

The lead man brought his stare to Troy. "This land is owned by Lord Nigel Hammer of Concur. What is your purpose?"

Troy waited a moment before answering. Though fifty men and horses stood in the small area, the only sound heard was that of the pounding rain.

"We wish safe passage to Valkala. That's all."

The leader glared back at Troy. "You come with a platoon of soldiers with weapons drawn. How am I to believe that you don't have ulterior motives?"

"I have but thirty men." Troy cocked his head. "How can we be a threat to your great city?"

The Concurian did not waver. "How do we know there are not more of you scattered across the land?"

Troy began to grow impatient with this form of diplomacy. "What do you suggest we do to rectify this situation?"

The soldier thought for a moment. "Give us your weapons while you are on our land. We will escort you to our border and return them to you then."

Troy shook his head, barking, "That's unacceptable. I will not leave my men defenseless."

"All right then," said the leader. "You may keep your blades, but your swords must be sheathed and all other weapons left in your packs."

Troy looked over to Teleios, who gave him a nod of approval. "We will accept those terms. Everyone, withdraw your weapons!" His men obeyed their superior's command.

The young general then maneuvered his horse to the front of his men, motioning for them to allow him passage through their defensive alignment so that he could approach Lord Hammer's soldier. Teleios remained with the rest of the squad.

Troy reached the opposition's leader and extended his hand. "My name is Troy Harkin. We thank you for your cooperation."

Lord Hammer's soldier accepted Troy's offering. "My name is Haldor. I suggest we integrate our people, to insure no hostilities."

Troy nodded. "That's fine with me. Let me inform my men, then we can arrange ourselves accordingly."

Haldor nodded back in agreement. "I will do the same." Both men then went back to their respective groups.

Troy approached Teleios first. "We're going to integrate the armies. We'll advance with their leader."

Teleios appeared a bit skeptical. "Are you sure that this is a wise thing to do?"

The young general did not waver. "I trust in my decision. I have complete confidence in the fighting power of our men. If something does go wrong, we could defeat this platoon with ease."

Troy's advisor scanned the other group of soldiers. "I agree. Let us proceed then."

Troy broke away from Teleios and addressed his men. "We will march through the countryside with the men of Concur," barked Troy over the rain. "Keep your weapons by your side and obey my commands."

The young general gestured toward Haldor's men. "Let us break formation and advance toward them." Troy's brigade did as instructed and broke out of their circular configuration. The general-at-arms then led his men toward Haldor's platoon.

Troy approached the Concurian leader again, this time with his second in command. "Haldor, this is my advisor, Teleios." Teleios and Haldor shook hands.

"Teleios," Haldor said, squinting. "That's an odd name. Is it of a certain heritage?"

"My mother does have elven ancestry." Troy's advisor fidgeted and did not hide his discomfort well. "That is where my name came from."

"Interesting," said Haldor, before bringing his gaze to Troy. "We can escort you the twenty or so miles to our border. I intend to set up camp at nightfall."

Troy agreed with the Concurian man. "By all means. Teleios and I will journey with you."

"I figured as much." Haldor then addressed his men. "The red brigade will lead us in the direction of Valkala. Set our course and proceed!"

The Concurians quickly maneuvered into position, being careful to place themselves with one or two of Troy's men. Haldor waved his soldiers forward after they situated themselves.

The large platoon of men trudged through the sloppy landscape for several more miles until darkness forced them to cease operations for the day. The rain never let up and continued to fall heavily upon the warriors. Haldor instructed his men to set up a camp, with Troy doing likewise.

As the night progressed, Troy and Teleios found themselves eating by a campfire with the Concurian leader.

Haldor stirred some food in a bowl. "What is so special about your trip to Valkala that you have brought a large contingent of armed men with you?"

Troy chose his words with care. "Let's just say we have some unfinished business to perform."

"Enough said," said Haldor, before taking a mouthful of food.

Troy, always with his mission on his mind, decided to try to get information from the Concurian. "Have you heard of any happenings in Cyprus?" The young general gave his advisor a quick glance, who responded with a cautious stare.

The leader of the dark army nodded, chewing. "Now that you mention it, yes. A squadron of our scouts intercepted a convoy of peasants near the Guard's River. They went on about evil spirits stealing their literature."

Troy remained calm, trying not to let his rising excitement give himself away. "That's odd. We ran into a group of peasants also making the same claim."

Haldor leaned over and spoke in a hushed tone. "To tell you the truth, I think it has to do with the Treasure of the Land."

Troy stopped chewing his food and stared at the Concurian leader. The young general knew about the legend and understood that someone had found the Treasure. What he did not know was what Haldor harbored in his mind.

"What makes you say that?"

Haldor took a sip from his tankard. "Lord Hammer took over half the army in an effort to find the Treasure. No one has heard from him in over a month."

Troy appeared perplexed. "How does the Treasure figure into that?"

Haldor fiddled with his food as he spoke. "Lord Hammer maintains continuous contact with his city and always sends scouts to and from his position in an effort to retain his grip on Concur." The Concurian then took another bite of food.

After he swallowed, he continued, "Now, we have lost all contact with Lord Hammer. We fear that he might have been killed searching for the Treasure. Couple that with this strange occurrence in Cyprus and things start to add up."

Troy lost himself in thought. "Where in this land did Lord Hammer's scout deliver his last message?"

The Concurian looked up in thought for a moment. "He sent his sentry back to Concur to tell the people that he had started to head for the Dark Forest. The soldier left the following day for that region. We figured the Scynthians might have slaughtered him. You know how they have a foothold in that area."

"Yes, I do." Troy had taken in Haldor's information, but nothing seemed to bring him closer to his mission, until now.

"I wonder if Lord Hammer ever received his last message," said Haldor.

Troy crinkled his brow. "Why do you say that?"

"Well, it seems that his woman had invited a young man to his mansion while he was away," said Haldor, raising an eyebrow. "Nigel would not be happy if he ever found out about that."

"Did anyone find out this man's name?"

Haldor used a spoon to scrape the bottom of his bowl. "I think I heard that it was Harrison or something like that."

Troy almost choked on his food. "Did you say, Harrison?" he asked, looking over to Teleios, who also sported a stunned expression.

The Concurian squinted, not seeing a connection just yet, but becoming a bit suspicious nevertheless. "Yes. Are you familiar with him?"

Troy shook his head. "Not exactly."

Haldor pointed at the young general. "Because if you are, there is a price on his head. He and his friends escaped from Concur. But, since we have not heard from Lord Hammer, we do not know what to set the bounty at."

Troy knew he had to press for more information, hoping that it would not expose his mission's secrets. "Would there be people in Concur who could help us locate this man?"

"I suppose," said Haldor skeptically. "Why do you ask?"

Troy held his gaze on the Concurian leader. "Let's just say we have a vested interest in finding him, too."

Haldor flashed a sly smile. "I see what you mean. I have been away from Concur for almost three months, so I get a lot of my information second hand. I'm sure there are people who can help you."

"Good," said Troy. "Tomorrow, let's set our course for Concur. All right?"

Haldor shrugged, placing his bowl away. "Fine with me. It will be good to go back home."

Troy looked at his food, then said, "It's getting late. I'm going to go to my tent and settle in for the night."

The Concurian nodded. "Good idea." Haldor took a weary eye upwards as he said, "I hope it stops raining by tomorrow. We'll be leaving early."

"My men and I will be ready." Troy and Teleios excused themselves, then headed back to their part of the campsite.

Troy's advisor panned the area and when he felt Haldor would no longer hear them, he said under his breath, "Troy, you are taking a big risk going to Concur!"

"Teleios, this Harrison character will eventually be going to Cyprus." Troy looked from side to side before continuing. "Think about it. Someone removes the book, then all of the text disappears in the city. It's all related. Something is going on in Cyprus and Harrison needs to be there."

Teleios shook his head, uncertain. "You're taking a big leap, Troy."

"We can gather information on Harrison in Concur, then wait for him in Cyprus. I have a very strong feeling about this."

The two reached their area of the encampment and proceeded to enter Troy's tent. The young general turned to say something to his advisor and noticed him deep in thought.

"What is it?"

Teleios hesitated, then said, "I don't want to question your judgment, Troy, but I'm concerned about what the men might think."

The halfling's comment caught Troy by surprise. "About what?"

Teleios tried to get his point across as delicately as possible. "Well, it's just that we have changed our planned route several times in the past few days." He looked at Troy and saw that his leader waited for more.

"First we posted ransom signs, then we learned about the adventurers and started following them." Teleios made a slight pause, then continued. "Next, we learned about the happenings in Cyprus, followed again by the news of this Harrison person."

"I understand that, Teleios." Troy shook his head. "Our mission must remain flexible. I firmly believe that all our questions will be answered once we reach Cyprus."

"Troy, it is not as if I don't agree with you. However, think about the men. We have told them to journey to Dragon's Quarters, before changing the destination to Valkala. Now Concur is in our sights and I assume Cyprus after that."

Troy held his ground. "I am their leader. They must obey my commands without hesitation. It's not up to them to question my motives."

Teleios raised his hands in an effort to calm his leader down. "I'm just suggesting you gather them together before we leave for Concur in the morning and tell them your thoughts. They will be truly grateful if you do."

Troy thought for a moment. "That's not a bad idea. I'll heed your advice."

Teleios smiled, relieved. "Thank you. I'm going to go to my own tent now."

"Be ready to journey in the morning." Teleios turned to leave, but before he could exit the tent, he heard Troy say, "You know I'm right."

Teleios looked at his leader. "Yes, I do. I'll see you in the morning." With that, he left Troy and headed to his own shelter.

Troy watched his advisor leave. After his friend departed, he laid his belongings on the moist ground and tried his best to create a warm, dry area. First, he unrolled his backpack and placed it flat on the earth. Then, using a couple of his blankets, he managed to create a spot where he could sleep for the night. The rain continued to pound the earth, though, and no matter what he did, water still managed to seep into his sheltered quarters.

Taking care in placing a lit lantern on the ground, Troy began to rummage through his scattered belongings and retrieve his map. Being wary not to get it wet, he sprawled it out on his makeshift bed.

The young general looked at the towns that he and his men visited, then peered to their proposed route. Teleios was right. He had changed course too many times and his men would be unsure of their mission if the same activity continued. Rolling up the map, he placed it back into its container.

"I'll clarify our position to the men in the morning," Troy said to himself. "And I'll reinvigorate them to succeed." With that decision behind him, he began to ponder the next leg of their journey.

Concur remained a great unknown to him. Though Troy knew that a dictator ruled the city, he would now learn firsthand what went on behind the large walls of the metropolis. The young general also hoped that he would find out more about the group he was hunting down and maybe get more information about the strange phenomenon in Cyprus, too. As he continued to think to himself, Troy felt sleep begin to overtake his body. After a few more minutes of rest, he fell into a deep slumber and would not wake until the morning.

CHAPTER 13

O

The storm that soaked the countryside the night before had subsided by morning. Troy awoke to the sound of light rain pelting his tent. The night before, he had thought about the chain of events that had led him to his current position and he knew what he had to do next.

The young general repacked his backpack and put on his armor. After that, he pushed aside the covering that had blocked his way out of the tent. The weather had remained overcast with little sunlight. Nevertheless, he proceeded to his advisor's tent.

"Teleios," he called to his friend, who shuffled around inside of his shelter after hearing his name.

Teleios peeked his head out of his refuge. "What is it, Troy?"

"I'm going to assemble the men now and brief them on our discoveries."

The halfling smiled. "Give me another moment." After a couple of minutes, Teleios appeared from his tent and joined his leader.

The two men walked past several shelters and extinguished campfire sites. Many of his men had begun tending to their horses, feeding and preparing them for travel.

"May I have your attention," said Troy in the direction of his warriors.

His soldiers stopped their tasks and began to assemble near their leaders. Troy began to address them after the last of his men stumbled out of their tents.

"I would like to take this time to explain the latest change to our mission. I know what you must be thinking, but I assure you all the moves I have made will lead us to the book faster." He paused and looked over his men. They all stared back in anticipation.

"We are now going to journey to Concur." Troy noticed several of his men give a look of confusion. In an unprecedented move, he said, "Does anyone have any questions?"

No one said anything at first, but after a moment of uncomfortable silence, one of his men raised his hand.

Troy motioned to the young man. "What do you have to say?"

"Sir, many of us have been wondering why we have changed venue so often. We all believe that we will find the king's book, but we are not privy to the information you might have discovered."

Troy nodded. "Very well. As you all know, the king sensed that the book went missing about two weeks ago, which is the time he sent us on our quest. Since then, we have uncovered many clues to this mystery. Unfortunately, these clues have sent us in numerous different directions in a rather short amount of time."

The soldier pressed his superior for more information. "Are you at liberty to share these clues?"

The young general nodded. "I can tell you this. The book, the party we're following, and the peasants we intercepted from Cyprus are all related. The reason we're going to Concur is that one of the people in the group we're following is wanted there. We can inquire about him and possibly his doings when we get to the city."

The men seemed to be more at ease after Troy's explanation. "What is this person's name?" asked the soldier. "So that we may help in your investigation."

"His name is Harrison. I know nothing more than that. The message we intercepted from Tigris mentioned his name, as did the leader of the Concurian men last night. I feel that this person just might possess the book."

Troy scanned the looks on the faces of his men. They seemed satisfied with their leader's honesty. Feeling that he had finished with his explanations, Troy said, "Ready the horses and pack your belongings. We'll be leaving soon. That's all."

The platoon of men quickly disbanded and set off to handle their own tasks. Teleios, who had remained quiet while Troy spoke, approached the young leader.

"That was a very necessary speech. And you articulated it very well."

Troy smiled and nodded. "Thank you, Teleios. I feel I told them enough to restore their confidence in me."

Teleios agreed. "That you have. We can inform them about Cyprus after we learn more ourselves."

"My thoughts exactly. Come, let us seek Haldor and determine when we'll be breaking camp." The two left their soldiers and proceeded toward the Concurian men.

The two men passed through their encampment, then entered the area where Haldor's men had established their campsite. Troy noticed that the Concurian leader's men had cleaned their horses' armor and that their steeds were ready to journey. Troy found Haldor instructing his men about their trek back to Concur. When he saw Troy and Teleios, he dismissed his soldiers.

"We'll be leaving soon." Haldor walked past the two men to his own steed, then checked his horse's equipment. "The weather is not going to cooperate again."

Troy looked up into the drizzle. "At least it's not as heavy as yesterday. My men will be ready to journey. We're waiting for your cue."

"It'll be within the hour." Haldor tugged on his horse's reins. "We'll travel like we did yesterday."

"I anticipated that. Let me know when you're ready." The two men left Haldor and headed back to their brigade of soldiers.

Just as Haldor said, the Concurian men were prepared to leave before an hour's time. Troy maneuvered his platoon to join Haldor's and before too long, both parties ventured to Concur together.

Troy followed Haldor and his men through twenty miles of the Concurian countryside. Fortunately for them, the rain stopped halfway through their trek, allowing them to travel without the extra burden of foul weather.

After several hours, Troy could see the great walled city in the distance. His escort also looked upon his hometown.

"Concur," said Haldor, using his hand to shade his eyes from the afternoon sun.

"It'll be nice to be back home, won't it," said Troy.

"Yes, it will." Haldor maintained his gaze on the metropolis. "I've been away for quite some time." As the squadron of men moved closer to the city, Haldor called out to his scouts.

"Raise the red flags to alert the watchmen we are coming!" he shouted in their direction.

Upon hearing their commander's order, the advance scouts unfurled their red, triangular flags. In all, four of the banners waved in the light breeze.

As the group continued their march toward Concur, Haldor noticed a single horse galloping at them. He immediately recognized that a soldier dispatched from the city raced toward the assembly of men and horses, and after a few minutes, the fighter reached the platoon. The advance scouts intercepted the soldier, then called for their leader.

"Sir," said one of Haldor's men, "there is an urgent message from Concur."

"Everyone, halt!" commanded Haldor, before looking over to Troy and Teleios. "Wait here while I investigate this information."

Troy nodded in acquiescence. "By all means."

Haldor maneuvered his horse away from Troy and Teleios and positioned it next to the messenger. Troy watched in anticipation as Haldor conversed with his soldier. As he did, the young general noticed a surprised look come across the Concurian man's face.

Haldor nodded to the courier, then watched as the sentry sped back toward Concur. Haldor turned his horse to face everyone, then shouted, "I have great news! Lord Hammer has returned to his city!" All of the Concurian men hollered with delight.

Haldor walked his horse over to Troy's. "We must rearrange our marching order before we enter the city. I cannot have you walking in with me."

Troy again agreed. "I understand. What do you propose?"

"My men will encircle yours and we will march in that way. I will be with my advance scouts, leading us into the city."

Troy knew he really had no other option at this time. "Where will we be taken once we enter through the gates?"

"I'm sure Lord Hammer would like to speak to you. I will confirm that after we arrive."

Again, Troy was at Haldor's mercy. He knew he did not choose to be in this position, but under the circumstances there was nothing more he could do.

"All right." Troy stared with intent into his new ally's eyes. "I trust you, Haldor."

"Don't be concerned. Lord Hammer is fond of guests of your stature. I'm sure you two will have many interesting things to chat about."

Troy maintained his gaze on Haldor, before raising a hand in his direction, signaling him to wait. "Men," the young general yelled over his shoulder to his platoon, "don't be alarmed; our Concurian friends will circle us and guide us to the city."

Haldor nodded to Troy, then positioned his horse at the front of the pack. "Surround our guests!"

With that, Haldor's men positioned their horses and encircled Troy's platoon. When they had completed that maneuver, Haldor commanded his soldiers onward.

"To Concur!" he yelled, with his men cheering again. Troy looked over at Teleios and noticed a hint of concern in his eye.

"I know what you're thinking," said Troy to his advisor. "We have to play this one out."

The squadron of soldiers continued their trek to the great metropolis and, before too long, they had positioned themselves outside of the western wall of the city. The gatekeepers had already opened the western gate, which was customary during daylight hours. Though a ruthless leader ran Concur, he encouraged foreigners to visit and spend their money in the city. He also levied a tax upon them before they entered the municipality. Troy and his men were no different.

Haldor stopped the caravan at the entrance to the gate, then turned and called back to Troy.

"The cost to enter the city is ten gold pieces per person."

Troy gave him a look of surprise. "You would think warriors like us would be exempt from these ridiculous tariffs," he said to Teleios under his breath. He then looked to Haldor.

"Will three hundred coins suffice?"

Haldor make a quick scan of Troy and his men and counted thirty-two. "Three hundred and twenty," he said dryly. "I'm not about to have twenty gold pieces deducted from my wages."

Troy stared back at his fellow soldier with a blank face. "Three hundred and twenty it is."

The young general rummaged through his belongings until he found his gold, counted his tax amount, then called on one of his men. The young soldier approached his leader.

"Give him these." Troy handed his sentry a variety of coins, who then proceeded to pass the money to Haldor.

The Concurian man graciously accepted the tariff, but became perturbed after inspecting the coins.

"I have never seen this type of currency," he said in an angry tone. "I cannot accept this!"

"Tell your leader that these coins have come from Dragon's Lair," said Troy. "I'm sure he'll accept them."

"Dragon's Lair," said Haldor in surprise. The Concurian had heard stories about an eccentric king who lived on the island, as well as the tales of treasures carted there throughout the ages.

Haldor secured the coins in a pouch. "Your men can stay in our army barracks," he said to Troy. "You and your advisor will be housed elsewhere."

Troy nodded. "Thank you."

Haldor then commanded the men to follow him and enter the city. The town buzzed with activity with many shops open for business and townsfolk hurrying to do their daily chores.

The amount of commotion surprised Troy. Many people stopped their activities and looked at the large contingent of men entering their metropolis. He even saw several people point directly at him, then converse with their fellow man, but he did not think anything of it, since they were strangers to these townsfolk.

Up ahead, a large mansion sat in the middle of the city. Teleios motioned to the structure. "That must be Lord Hammer's residence."

Both he and Troy could see that the building definitely appeared different from the other edifices in the city. Landscapers had manicured the mansion's grounds to perfection, with brilliant plants and shrubs adorning the walkways. The building also sat upon an incline, which allowed the occupants a beautiful view of the waterways.

The central road leading to the mansion forked, with more shops and homes on the left and a large walled structure further down on the right. Haldor stopped the brigade short of the governor's building.

The Concurian leader pointed to the right. "The barracks are that way. My men will escort your soldiers there."

"Where will we go?" asked Troy, in reference to he and Teleios.

"You're the lucky ones," he said with a sly grin. "You get to meet Lord Hammer." Haldor then motioned to his soldiers.

"Escort these fine men to the barracks. Give them plenty of food and drink, and make sure each one has a place to sleep." With that, Haldor's scouts guided Troy's men in the direction of the army's quarters.

The Concurian leader pointed to Troy and Teleios. "You two, get off of your horses and follow me." Troy and Teleios dismounted, gathered their belongings, and accompanied Haldor.

"Your steeds will be taken care of as well," said the Concurian, as two of Lord Hammer's workers took hold of the horses' reins.

Haldor led the two men up the stairs of the mansion to the guarded doorway.

"What is this man doing here?" demanded one of the sentries, glaring at Troy.

The guard's tone took all the men by surprise. "They are here to see Lord Hammer." Haldor gave the guards an odd look. "Is there a problem?"

The first guard kept his gaze on Troy. "Does he come willingly?"

"Of course." Haldor turned to Troy. "Is there something I don't know?"

"No." Troy appeared just as confused at the guard's actions as Haldor. "I have never been here before."

Neither guard flinched. "Lord Hammer will be most surprised to see you back," said the second guard.

"See me back?" Troy crinkled his brow. "I told you, I've never been here before."

Teleios sensed something amiss. "I don't like this, Troy. Something is not right here."

Haldor tried to put the men at ease. "Don't worry about them. There is obviously a misunderstanding." The Concurian turned back to the guards. "Tell Lord Hammer we have arrived. He is expecting us."

"By all means," said the first guard before knocking on the large door. A moment later, the portal creaked open and a servant appeared in the entranceway.

"Guests for Lord Hammer," said the second guard.

"Please, come —" said the servant before stopping in mid-sentence. The frail man took a long look at Troy and remained speechless.

Haldor, witnessing the servant's astonished look, said, "Please, find us Lord Hammer."

"Yes," said the servant, never removing his gaze off Troy. "Everyone, follow me." The servant turned and led the men inside the mansion.

"My name is Percival," he said as he took the men up a large spiral staircase.

Percival brought Troy and Teleios to the second floor and led them to a room on the left. Inside, a large dining table sat in the middle of the room. Troy gazed at the ornate statues in the corners, as well as the fine tapestries that hung on the walls.

Percival glided across the room. "Now for the most beautiful view of them all."

The servant approached a double doorway and opened both doors into the room. Troy looked out and saw the scene that Percival had spoken about. The doorway led to a terrace that overlooked the harbor of Concur.

"This truly is remarkable." Troy could see the many boats docked in the harbor, as well as the scenic landscape across the inland waterway.

"Lord Hammer enjoys this room most of all," said Percival. "As does Meredith."

"Meredith?" said Troy, not recognizing the name.

Percival gave him an incredulous look. "Meredith is Lord Hammer's lady."

"I did not know." Troy took his gaze back to the scene. "I'm sure she adores this view as well."

Percival gave Troy a perplexed look. "I will tell Lord Hammer that you are here. Please excuse me." The servant then left the room.

Haldor approached Troy and Teleios. "I must leave now. I will make sure that my soldiers attend to your men and give them everything they might need. That goes for your animals, too."

"Thank you, Haldor," said Troy, extending his hand. "You have been very helpful and it won't go unnoticed."

Haldor shook Troy's hand. "I appreciate that." He then shook Teleios's hand, too. "Good-bye."

As Haldor left, another servant entered the room carrying two glasses and a carafe of fine wine.

"From Lord Hammer's wine cellars." The servant filled two goblets with a deep red liquid. "Enjoy," he said, as he exited the room.

Troy took a sip of the wine. "Delicious."

Teleios was not as impressed. "Troy, I don't have a good feeling about this place."

Troy understood his advisor's apprehension. "I know. I've been feeling funny ever since we entered this city. Is it me, or is everyone giving me a strange look?"

"Precisely." Teleios nodded with emphasis. "And by the way they have reacted to you, it does not bring back fond memories for them."

"Let's see how this Lord Hammer reacts." Troy took another sip of wine. "And let's not forget why we're here. We need to get information on the happening in Cyprus, Harrison, and the legend of the old knight."

"I haven't lost sight of that." Teleios drank from his goblet. "I'm glad to hear that you haven't either."

Nigel Hammer stood in his chambers, gazing at his appearance in a full- length mirror. He viewed a man who was thin, underweight. Worst of all, he noticed his own deficiencies. The journey back to Concur had taken its toll. But he was back.

A knock came at the door. "Enter," barked the governor of Concur.

Percival slowly opened the portal. "Your guests are waiting on the terrace for you, sir."

"Thank you." Percival tried to make a quick exit, but Nigel stopped him.

"Percival, how do I look to you?"

His servant knew that no possible answer could satisfy his boss. Instead of contriving one, he told him the truth.

"You need some time to get back to peak form, sir. You had an extremely hard journey. A lesser man would have failed."

Lord Hammer laughed at Percival's last remark. "That's a very good answer. Honest, yet direct. That is why you are my main servant. You are relieved."

Percival quickly left Nigel's chambers. Lord Hammer looked at himself in the mirror one last time. After he deemed himself ready, he proceeded to greet his guests.

Troy and Teleios were watching the sun sink lower in the western sky when Lord Hammer entered the room. Nigel had begun his trek to the terrace to join them when he saw Troy for the first time and stopped dead in his tracks.

"This cannot be," he muttered with skepticism. "He is not that much of a fool, is he?" Nigel took another moment before advancing to the balcony.

Troy saw the governor approaching out of the corner of his eye. Placing his goblet of wine down, he walked up to Lord Hammer.

Extending his hand, he said, "You must be Nigel Hammer. I'm Troy Harkin and this is my advisor, Teleios. It's a pleasure to meet you."

The governor shook Troy's hand and nodded to Teleios. "I hope you find everything to your liking." Nigel gazed deeply into Troy's eyes and knew at that very moment that he had never met this man before.

Troy nodded. "Your soldiers have been very accommodating."

"I have them trained well," said Nigel dryly, with a smirk. "Let us come inside and discuss our predicament."

Lord Hammer motioned for Troy and Teleios to come back into the main room and sit down.

Nigel sat at the head of the table, while Troy and Teleios positioned themselves to his right. "I don't usually allow convoys of soldiers to cross my land," said Lord Hammer in a very direct manner.

Troy raised his hands. "We were only traversing your countryside. We have no intentions toward Concur."

"I should hope not." Nigel took a sip from his goblet, then placed the cup down. "What business do you have in this area?"

Troy took care in choosing his words, not wanting to divulge their true mission. "We're heading to Valkala. There's some information that we're seeking and we feel that we can get answers there."

"What kind of information are you searching for?"

"There's a legend about a brave knight who saved the village of Dragon's Quarters many years ago. We wish to learn more about this man and the myth."

"I might be able to help you with that." Nigel sat tall in his chair. "His name was Sir Jacob and he was very influential to the rulers of the land at that time. From what I have found, he was the right-hand man to one of the ancient kings and a member of the Legion of Knighthood."

Troy gave Nigel a look of surprise. "That saves us time on our investigation. Thank you." Nigel nodded, accepting their gratitude.

Troy thought for a moment, then asked, "What do you make of the claims of evil spirits overrunning the town of Cyprus?"

Nigel shrugged. "I have only recently heard the rumors. Several of my soldiers have mentioned it to me. What do you feel that occurrence is due to?"

Lord Hammer felt it had something to do with the finding of the Treasure of the Land, and he hoped that Troy would confirm that for him.

"I'm not sure," said Troy, not wanting to let on about the coincidence between the happenings in Cyprus and the finding of the sacred book. "I find the whole situation to be odd." Troy then took an unplanned direction with his questioning.

"One of your soldiers, Haldor, said that you searched for the Treasure of the Land. Were you successful?"

Nigel held back a grimace. The question brought back feelings of failure and, as he stared at Troy, the ill will he felt toward Harrison.

"I believe that the Treasure is in the hands of someone else."

Troy felt the same, but he pressed further, wanting to convince himself that his assumptions about Harrison and the book were correct, asking if Nigel knew who might possess the treasure.

Nigel did not go for Troy's bait. "I have a person in mind." Changing the course of the conversation, Lord Hammer said, "It has come to my attention that you are trying to locate a group of adventurers who might be heading to Valkala." The governor stared with cold eyes at Troy, waiting for his answer.

Nigel's comment took Troy by surprise. He knew he had mentioned to Haldor that they were actively searching for a person named Harrison, and he did not think that that information would get all the way back to Nigel. Troy kept his answers short and concise.

"There's a person named Harrison, as well as a mage named Gelderand, that we wish to find."

Nigel glared back at Troy. This marked the first time that someone had uttered the name of the person who had beat him to the Treasure of the Land.

"What business do you have with Harrison?"

Troy felt Nigel's pressure towards this mysterious person. "We need to talk to him. That's all."

Nigel did not hold back his rage. "Harrison is a marked man! I wish nothing more than to have him brought back to me."

Troy could see that the mention of Harrison's very name brought Nigel to a fury. Still, he needed to know more about this man.

"May I ask why you have such anger toward him?"

Nigel shifted in his seat. "There are several reasons," he began. "I firmly believe that he is in possession of the Treasure that I have searched for. He was lucky to have found it before me."

Troy stared intently at Nigel. He now knew that Harrison indeed possessed the Treasure of the Land and he also knew, thanks to his king, that part of this treasure took on the form of a book. What he did not know was if Nigel knew the same.

"I can see that this possession is very dear to you. Why is that so?"

Nigel chose his words carefully. "Let's just say that I had researched the Treasure for years. I took the painstaking measures to hunt for clues, decipher artifacts, and assemble an army to find it," he said, raising his voice. "Only to lose it to a man your age!"

"It hurts when we set our goals so high, only to see them come crashing down by an unforeseen obstacle," added Teleios.

Nigel glared at Troy's advisor. "It does hurt, but I will find this man and take what is rightfully mine."

Troy furrowed his brow. "What makes you believe the Treasure belongs to you?"

"Have you not listened to me!" barked Nigel. "Harrison is a boy as far as I'm concerned! He had no more than six men and a dog with him, whereas I had a regimented army. He was lucky."

"Or maybe he is more skilled than you give him credit for," said Teleios.

Nigel glared in Teleios's direction again. "You were not in the catacombs. *I was.* If I did not possess superior fighting skills, I would not be alive today. Harrison was fortunate to have been in the position he was in."

"Be that as it may," intervened Troy, "he still has your prize."

"Yes," said Nigel, whose face reflected the coldness of a glacier.

"Don't you want to get it back?"

"Absolutely." Nigel gave Troy a skeptical look. "Are you proposing something?"

"We might be able to help you. May I have a word alone with my advisor?"

Nigel extended his hand. "By all means."

Troy and Teleios excused themselves from the table and headed to the terrace, closing the doors behind them so that Nigel would not hear.

"What are you thinking, Troy?" asked Teleios with an incredulous look. "I don't feel comfortable bargaining with this man."

"Neither do I." Troy glanced back at the closed doors. "He wants to find Harrison just like us. Nigel is in a position to offer more men and supplies, and more information I'm sure."

"What about us?" Teleios shifted nervously. "We know that Harrison will be heading to Valkala and we have very good reason to believe that he will end up in Cyprus. If we tell Nigel where Harrison will be, he will capture him and take the book."

Troy cocked an eyebrow. "He doesn't know the treasure's a book. I'm willing to bet he thinks it's some elaborate artifact. This plays to our advantage."

Troy's advisor thought for a moment. "You are right. I never thought about that. But how can Lord Hammer and his army going to Cyprus with us benefit our quest at all?"

"I have an idea and I think it'll work. Let's go."

Troy then led Teleios back into the room, with the two men taking their seats again at the table. Troy spoke first. "I think we can help each other out."

"How so?"

"You want this Harrison person. We know where he is right now."

Nigel's eyes widen. "Tell me where he is!"

"Not so fast," said Troy, thrusting his palm in Lord Hammer's direction. "We need to agree on a few things before we make any kind of deals."

"I'm listening," said Nigel as he leaned close to Troy.

"First of all, we know about Harrison, but it's the mage, Gelderand, who we seek," lied Troy. "The person who hired me has a vested interest in having this man brought back to him alive."

"The mage?" Nigel waved his hand. "He is yours."

Troy nodded and smiled. "I had hoped you would say that. Then it's agreed. When we find Harrison and his men, we will take Gelderand and you can take Harrison."

Nigel stared back at Troy. "Agreed. What about the rest of his men?"

Troy shook his head. "I have no use for them. You can do as you please with them."

Lord Hammer nodded. "Fair enough. Now, where is Harrison?"

Troy felt better about the situation. "He and his men are heading to Valkala as we speak and he might even be there now."

Nigel rose from his chair. "We must leave now! With the men that we have, we can apprehend him with ease!"

Troy motioned for Nigel to sit back down. "Wait, there's more. Please, take a seat."

Nigel reluctantly did as Troy asked. "Continue."

"Teleios and I feel he will be going to Cyprus. The town is deserted and we can ambush him there easier."

Nigel cocked his head. "Why do you believe this?"

"There have been a string of occurrences that have taken place in the past two weeks. We've made a thorough investigation into them and we've ventured to Concur because of what we have found. That's why we feel so strongly that Harrison and his men will wind up in Cyprus before too long."

Nigel thought for a moment. "You say the town is deserted?"

"From what we have learned, yes. Harrison and his mage will not suspect an army waiting for them. I have thirty men of my own. You have much more."

Troy stared at Nigel. "I can't believe that Harrison has anywhere close to the manpower we both possess. He'll be easily defeated."

Nigel let out an uncharacteristic smile. "You are convincing. All right, we can strategize about Cyprus, but I want to make this clear. Harrison is mine."

Troy nodded again. "By all means."

Nigel looked at Troy and Teleios, then felt satisfied. "It is already late. I suggest that the two of you get a good night's rest, and we can pick this conversation up in the morning."

"That is fine with us," said Troy.

"Consider the two of you guests of the city." Nigel turned toward the doorway and shouted, "Percival!"

Nigel's servant quickly scurried into the room.

"Percival, show these two gentlemen where they will be staying for the evening. Return back after they are settled in."

"Yes, sir," said the servant. "Please, follow me."

"And be sure they are fed well." Nigel stood as Troy and Teleios rose from their chairs.

"Thank you again, Nigel," said Troy.

"My pleasure." Lord Hammer watched as Percival escorted Troy and Teleios out of the room.

After they left, a scowl came across Nigel's face. He went out to the terrace where he looked over his harbor, which began to give way to the ensuing darkness. After several minutes, Percival returned.

"What may I help you with, my Lord?"

Nigel continued to stare out at the stars. "Fetch me Allard, the high mage of the Concurian Order."

"I will instruct your guards to do just that," said Percival. "Is there anything else?"

"No. But I want Allard here tonight. Be gone!"

"Yes, sir." Percival bowed and scurried out of the room.

Nigel maintained his gaze into the darkness. "Now it is time to find out who you truly are, Troy Harkin."

CHAPTER 14

○

Troy had just settled into his room when he heard a knock at his door. Opening the portal, he found Teleios waiting in the hallway.

"May I come in?" asked his advisor.

"By all means." Troy motioned for his friend to enter. "I figured you would come by to discuss the happenings with Lord Hammer."

Teleios tried to hold back his true feelings. "Troy, I think we have put ourselves in a difficult situation."

"How so?" The young leader frowned. "The way I see it, we have more manpower to corral Harrison and the book."

Teleios nodded in agreement. "That's exactly my point. We should have proceeded anonymously. I thought we had discussed bringing outsiders into our circle. We don't need Nigel or his men."

Troy sat down on his bed. "Don't feel that I didn't think this out. I needed Nigel's information about Harrison. I needed to be certain that this man has the book." The young general paused for a moment, reading his advisor's reaction. Teleios just waited for Troy to continue.

"Tell me, Teleios, if we had a priceless treasure, who would be in possession of it?"

Troy's question surprised the halfling. "That depends on the treasure."

"Fair enough. Let's say it was a magical sword, one that could rip through the flesh of any beast."

Teleios shrugged. "I would assume that someone like you, a warrior, would have it."

"Exactly! Who would you say would carry a magical item other than a weapon?"

"Probably a wizard or a mage —" Teleios's eyes widened, realizing where Troy was heading with his questioning. "Gelderand has the book."

Troy smiled. "That's what I'm thinking. Harrison is a fighter; you heard that from Nigel yourself. Why would he carry the sacred book? He would be too busy protecting the lesser members of his group."

"Yes," said Teleios, seeing Troy's rationale more clearly with every sentence the young general uttered. "A wizard would have spells to protect himself, something to keep his enemies far away."

Troy could see that Teleios understood. "The perfect person to carry the manuscript. That's why we want possession of him."

"And Nigel will get Harrison," said Teleios with a smile. "This is who he wanted all along."

"Precisely."

Just then, they both heard a knock at the door.

"Excuse me," said Lord Hammer's servant from the other side of the entrance. "Dinner is about to be served."

"Thank you," responded Troy. "We'll join you in a moment." The young general then rose from the bed.

"I suppose it's time to partake in that well-deserved meal that Nigel promised us."

Teleios nodded. The two men then left the room and followed Percival to the dining area.

Exquisite furniture, fine rugs, and tapestries decorated the master bedroom, which also offered a breathtaking view of the city. Unlike the other inanimate objects, the most beautiful possession in the room lived and breathed. Meredith sat on the bed while Nigel rummaged for something in the closet.

Lord Hammer had left his city for a long time, and Meredith cherished those days the most. Though she loathed the man, she felt compelled to offer her assistance.

"What are you looking for? Maybe I can help."

"That won't be necessary," came the voice from the closet. Nigel returned with a few articles and placed them on the bed.

Nigel's actions seemed to confuse Meredith. "Where are you going?"

Lord Hammer did not bother to look at the woman and continued with his chores. "That doesn't concern you. I'll be leaving the day after tomorrow."

Meredith felt a burden lift from her soul. Nigel's unexpected return from his adventure had caused her stress level to rise almost to the point of a nervous breakdown.

Trying not to show her enthusiasm, she said, "Why are you leaving so soon? You have only just returned a day ago."

Nigel looked into Meredith's blue eyes. "Don't sound so relieved," he snarled. "I've already located Harrison and I'm going to bring him back to Concur."

Meredith did not hold back her agitation. "I told you he did nothing wrong! Why must you persecute that poor boy?"

Nigel glared at his woman. "That *poor boy* has the Treasure! And *I* want it!"

"So you can terrorize the whole country, not just Concur?" Meredith stared back at Nigel. "Maybe Harrison is *supposed* to have the Treasure."

Nigel started to say something, before holding back. "I have somewhere to go. I expect to see you here later." Lord Hammer pointed to the bed. Meredith crossed her arms and turned away, not wanting to look at her heartless man any longer.

Nigel collected his things and proceeded to the doorway. "I will be back sometime tonight," he said, then left the room, closing the door behind him. After he departed, Meredith cried in her pillow.

Later that evening, a stagecoach rolled up to the governor's mansion. Lord Hammer's soldiers escorted a man into the building to take him to their leader's private study.

"Wait here," said a young soldier.

"As you wish," responded the hooded figure. The man pulled aside the black cloak in order to get a better look at his surroundings. Allard was the highest-ranking mage at the Concurian Order and respected by all. People all over the land knew of his wizardry and Nigel always consulted him before his major battles. Now, he waited for his town's leader.

Lord Hammer arrived in his library before too long. He opened the large double-doorway that led to his study and found Allard standing in the middle of the room. The wizard turned in the direction of the doors.

"Allard the Magnificent," said Nigel with a smile.

"You know I don't care for the designation," responded the mage, frowning. "It is not my fault that my magical abilities are so powerful."

Nigel approached the older man and held out his hand. "The people call you that out of respect," said Nigel, with Allard accepting the greeting. "You have earned that honor."

Allard maintained his skeptical gaze. "I'm sure I haven't been brought here to sample some of your fine wine." The mage removed his hand and turned away from Nigel.

"I must admit," started the magician, gazing upon the many bookcases that filled the room, "your adventures have brought you an astounding collection of literature."

Nigel stood next to the man and admired the ancient scriptures as well. "You can never have enough treasures."

Allard turned and faced Lord Hammer. "Nigel, why have you called for me?"

"I need a favor." Nigel gestured for the mage to take a seat at a large, oak table.

The mage sat down first and waited for the Concurian leader to situate himself. After a short pause, he said, "What kind of favor?"

"What do you know of The Prophecy?"

The wizard sat back in his chair, a mystified expression overtaking his face. "The Prophecy? Why are you concerned about that?"

Lord Hammer locked his gaze on Allard. "I know who has the Treasure, and I fear this person might try to start the process of becoming the supreme ruler."

Allard furrowed his brow. Motioning with a wave of his hand, he asked, "And how does this person simply start the process of ruling the land?"

Nigel could feel his agitation begin to rise. "If I knew that, I would be stopping this person right now," he said in a forceful voice. "But I don't, that is why I have asked you here today. What do you know?"

Allard looked up in thought, rubbing his cheeks in the process. "I know that part of the story states that a young leader will systematically take control of the land. He will guide an ever-growing army from city to city throughout the countryside until the conquest is complete."

Nigel listened to the wizard with great intent. He knew the average person would not consider him old, though he also was not young. "When you say 'young leader', would my age fit into that category?"

Allard looked Nigel over. "No," he said flatly.

Lord Hammer turned away in disgust. He could see Harrison's image in his mind — his young face, raw skills, and righteous ways — and knew the Prophecy was meant for him. He then faced Allard again.

"Can the Prophecy be stopped?"

Allard shrugged. "Anything is possible."

"I don't want possibilities!" Nigel snarled. "I want absolute facts!"

Lord Hammer's outburst did not seem to faze the magician. "Nigel, I am telling you what I feel I know, what I have heard. The only real way to get absolution is to find the Sacred Scrolls of Arcadia and read them yourself. Those scrolls hold the secrets you desire."

Nigel nodded, understanding. "Where are they now?"

Allard took his gaze to another part of the room, as he said, "Legend states that they are protected from humanity by — "

"Legend states!" interrupted the Concurian leader. "I am sick and tired of that phrase! Legend stated that the Treasure of the Land existed somewhere; legend states that a young warrior will rise to power; legend states these scrolls are protected from humanity! Do you hear me? I want to know what the Prophecy says! And I want to know now!"

Allard understood Nigel's urgency and did what he could to appease his leader. "I can do this for you. There are colleagues of mine who have researched the Sacred Scrolls and have a comprehensive understanding of what they entail. I can bring this information to you.

"But I must warn you, what I return with will be a compilation of notes and theories, not the actual text from the scrolls."

Nigel looked down in thought, holding his head in his hand and rubbing his brow repeatedly. "Are these friends of yours trustworthy?"

Allard nodded. "I would believe anything they say."

"Then ready yourself for your quest." Lord Hammer looked up again. "I want you to find out all you can about this prophecy and relay that information to me."

The wizard nodded again. "Very well. I will need about a week to gather all of the information. Will you be in Concur at that time?"

The Governor shook his head. "No. I am going to Cyprus. You will deliver the information to me there."

"Agreed."

Nigel rose from the table. "My men will escort you home." He held out his hand toward the mage once again.

Allard stood up and the two shook hands. "I will see you in Cyprus." The mage then turned and left the study.

Nigel continued to stand while thoughts raced through his head. How could it be that The Prophecy stated that an unproven warrior would rule over the land? Hadn't he shown his worth as a ruler of a city, as well as a feared general of his army? Hadn't he navigated through the catacombs and lived to tell about his tale, regardless if he obtained the treasure or not?

There was no question in his mind who he thought should be ruler. Moreover, Allard had stated moments ago that nothing said that the Prophecy had to happen. He could stop it and, if he were successful, he could take control of the land.

Nigel agreed with his final thought, then left the library. In less than two days, he would embark on an important part of his continuing journey. Together with Troy, he would confront Harrison in Cyprus, then bring the young warrior back to Concur where he would imprison him indefinitely. The Prophecy would end here.

C H A P T E R 15

Ο

Several more days of travel concluded with Harrison and his friends standing on the outskirts of Valkala. They took in the sight of the small village and the thick Valkaline Forest rising at its end.

Valkala was an intriguing town. Only humans inhabited the village and no more than ten buildings of trade existed. Resting on the outskirts of the vast woods, one would believe that tradesmen would bring back an abundance of articles from the forest and sell them on the streets of Valkala. This was far from the case.

The main reason for the scarce population of the town stemmed from what lived in the forest's depths. All who ventured in this part of the land called the inner region of the Valkaline Forest, Troll's Hell. Many a man had ventured into that area and the lucky few who escaped alive told of its horrors, for in the center of the massive woods lived the creatures that gave the place its name. Though the woodlands had its perils, for as long as the townspeople could remember, no beasts had ever ventured out of their safe haven.

Gelderand looked around the town with amazement. He knew it had been quite some time since he had last visited, but things had definitely changed.

"Where are all the people?" he wondered aloud, as he led the party towards Martinaeous's home. "There used to be many exquisite buildings and hoards of tradesmen. Now the place is almost deserted."

"This doesn't look too promising," chimed Murdock. "How long ago did you leave this village?"

"Fifteen years ago, give or take." Gelderand scanned the area for anything that could jar his memory. Nothing did.

"Take your time, Gelderand," said Harrison. "I'm sure a lot of things are different now compared to when you last studied here."

After a few more minutes of contemplation, Gelderand looked over to a dilapidated building. "If my memory serves me correct, I think this is the place."

The house they approached appeared very old and quite run down. Cobwebs filled all the windows and a thick green moss covered the outside walls of the house. Overgrown bushes and shrubs grew out of control all about the yard.

Gelderand took a closer look at the edifice. He could see visages of the past, things that seemed vaguely familiar, but nothing he could say for certain. The mage began to wonder if his old mentor was still alive as he continued to snoop around the battered home.

"I got the feeling we ventured this way for nothing!" exclaimed Murdock. "Are you sure this is the right place?"

The older man stared at the house. "I'm positive. I learned much magic here." The wizard then proceeded to the front door, but before he could give the portal a knock, he noticed it opened a crack.

Gelderand gave a cautious glance back before yelling, "Hello? Is anyone here?" No sound emanated from the home.

The mage shrugged and motioned for the rest of the group to follow him inside. Gelderand pushed the door and entered the house. By the looks of the surroundings, it became obvious that whoever lived there did not or could not keep the place in order. Thick dust and cobwebs appeared everywhere, as well as unclean pots and pans.

"Hello?" yelled Gelderand again while everyone scanned the surroundings for any source of life.

Harrison sighed. "I don't think anyone's here."

Before they could continue, a small, shadowy figure appeared in a doorway at the back of the house. Without warning, the being waved a small wand, emitting a dull red projectile. The missile sailed over Harrison's head, striking a pan that hung on the wall, causing it to come crashing down in a puff of smoke. Everyone ducked for cover, fearing that another projectile might come hurtling in their direction.

"Who dares to enter my home?" cried an elderly man. When the person came into the light, Gelderand recognized his old, familiar face.

"Martinaeous! It is I, Gelderand," he said, raising his hands and slowly rising up from behind a small piece of furniture.

"Gelderand?" replied the old man in amazement, lowering the wand. "Is it really you?"

Martinaeous had finished with Gelderand's training some fifteen years ago and he had not seen him since. At that time, Martinaeous had been a very prominent magician, and adventurers across the land had asked for his services. Not only did he comply, but he also had helped recover scores of ancient artifacts and treasures. As age caught up with him, he resigned himself to teach others of the powers he possessed.

Gelderand had been a young mage at the time they met. Martinaeous took to him quickly and his young apprentice's progress made quite an impression on him. When Gelderand left him upon completion of his training, Martinaeous at last felt he had found the man who could replace him as one of the elite magicians of the land.

"I should have come back long ago," said Gelderand. "I can't believe I am really looking at you after all these years." The two embraced like father and son.

"You should have stayed in touch," responded Martinaeous as the two separated. "What kept you away?"

"When I finished my training, I headed back to my home in Tigris," began Gelderand.

"From there, I learned that my sister had taken ill. Her husband died a few weeks later from the same illness and I found myself caring for their daughter. Fortunately, my sister recovered, but to this day, she cannot handle the burden of raising a child. I became Tara's only parent and raised her as if she were my own. Now she is a beautiful young woman and old enough that I can leave her alone. That is part of the reason why I am here."

Motioning to the rest of the group, he continued, "These are my friends — Harrison, Murdock, Pondle, and Swinkle, and the dog is Lance. We have most interesting news to tell you."

"I'm sure we will have plenty of time to talk." The old man then made a curious glance toward Harrison. "What is wrong with your arm?"

Harrison grimaced. "I foolishly allowed the Scynthians to capture me. The beasts cut off my arm before the rest of the group could save me. Gelderand and Swinkle made a heroic effort to reattach it for me. I'm making progress, but it has been very slow."

Martinaeous took a closer look at the young warrior. "I might be able to help you later. Why don't we all settle in?"

The old wizard moved as fast as his frail body would allow him, as he cleared away some of the accumulated debris from his dining table and chairs.

After finishing that task, he said, "Please, make yourselves comfortable." He then noticed something wriggling around in Gelderand's pack. "What's that in your bag?"

Gelderand swung the knapsack around, placed it on the table, then removed the contents from his pack. "Don't you recognize him? It's Rufus; you gave him to me when I left."

A wide smile flashed across the older man's face. "Well, I'll be! He was no more than a kitten when I gave him to you." Martinaeous gave the cat a scratch behind its ears.

Rufus meowed with approval. "Is he still trained for his tasks?"

Gelderand shrugged. "I believe so, but it has been a long time since we have gone on an adventure. One can never know for sure with animals."

The rest of the men helped Martinaeous straighten the area and upon completion, they all sat around a very old and dusty table. Martinaeous excused himself and walked over to the kitchen area.

"I am sorry about the mess," he said as he stretched for some mugs. "I am but an old man and have a little trouble getting around." After a few moments, he returned from the cluttered kitchen area, carrying a tray of dirty mugs filled with ale.

The old man held the tray in front of Murdock. "You all look quite thirsty."

Murdock, not one to refuse alcohol, looked at the filthy containers, then glanced in Harrison's direction. The young warrior gave him a discreet nod, signaling to the ranger to take the drink. With a look of dejection, Murdock took the pint, as well as everyone else.

"Drink up!" said Martinaeous. "I brewed the ale myself. You will enjoy it, I promise." After peering at their individual mugs, one by one each man began to drink. The bitter liquid slowly flowed down each of their throats, with everyone sporting the same look of disgust on his face.

Murdock slammed his mug on the table. "I'm sorry! This is horrible! I think I speak for the whole group, don't I?"

Martinaeous folded his arms, upset at the ranger's comment. "It is an acquired taste. You'll get used to it."

"Don't count on it," said Murdock under his breath.

Martinaeous waited until the ranger finished his outburst before turning to look at Gelderand. "Now, tell me, my friend, why have you and your colleagues traveled all this way? I am sure it's not to sample my ale."

Gelderand nodded in the old man's direction. "That is true, Martinaeous. I know you have heard the story about the Treasure of the Land," began the mage.

"These men have uncovered the treasure and I have helped in deciphering its cryptic code. There are several clues to finding additional pieces of a complex puzzle, and we want to know if you could assist us in any way. I told my friends that you have a mystical crystal ball that might aid in the search."

Martinaeous sat back in his chair after hearing what Gelderand had to say. After a moment, he said, with his eyes gleaming like a child's, "Tell me, what does the Treasure look like?"

Gelderand's eyes lit up as well. "It's the hoard of the ancient kings. There are weapons, armor, countless gold coins, and more scrolls than you can count."

The older mage nodded, figuring that royalty would possess such treasures as what his old pupil described. "Is it safely tucked away?"

Gelderand nodded. "Yes, save for one piece of the prize. And I'm not telling you where we stashed the rest."

A wry smile flashed across Martinaeous's face. "Good. I'd rather not know." The elderly man scanned the faces of the adventurers. "Do you understand what you are up against?"

Harrison leaned forward. "We know it'll be arduous, but we're willing to risk everything in order to put this puzzle together."

Martinaeous locked his gaze on the young warrior. "The Treasure of the Land is a very sacred thing indeed," he began.

"Not only have humans searched for it, but over the ages other humanoid races have sent out many fighters to help bring the Treasure back to their respective leaders. Halflings, Salinian Dwarves, Chowiaks, and even some Scynthian tribes have sent out armies to recover it. They will all kill you for a hint at what this treasure entails."

Harrison nodded. "We understand that and we're being very careful not to allow anyone to know that we have uncovered the bounty."

Martinaeous took his gaze to Gelderand. "Does Tara know you have this treasure?"

The mage sighed. "Well, yes. She had to know why I was leaving so suddenly."

Martinaeous smirked at his prized pupil. "There is your first problem. In time, she will tell someone, anyone, where her uncle set off to. It is only human nature." The old man scanned the group. "Who else knows?"

"No one else, besides you," said Gelderand.

Before anyone else could speak, Harrison said, "Nigel Hammer knows, too."

"Nigel Hammer!" exclaimed Martinaeous. "The Governor of Concur? Your task has just become impossible!"

"Now hold on a minute." Murdock waved his arms in protest. "First of all, we beat him to the treasure and have it in our possession as we speak. That certainly counts for something."

The ranger then looked to Harrison. "Second, Lord Hammer is dead in all likelihood. I'm sure those lions made a nice snack out of him."

"Lions?" Martinaeous looked toward Gelderand. "What about these lions?" Gelderand shrugged, he also ignorant of Murdock's meaning.

"Lord Hammer journeyed with us in the final stages of our quest," said Harrison. "Before we entered the Sacred Rooms, which a large pride of lions guarded, I asked their leader to give him safe passage out of the catacombs. I believe that they did, meaning he's still alive."

Martinaeous gave Harrison a blank stare. "You talked to lions and they left you unharmed?"

"I have a gift," said Harrison before shaking his head and waving his palms toward the group. "That doesn't matter now. What matters is finding out more about these clues."

Martinaeous continued to stare at the young warrior. "If you think Nigel is alive, then you know he will come searching for you."

"We understand that."

The older wizard sighed. "So, besides you, Tara, Nigel Hammer, and me, no one else knows you have the treasure?"

Harrison nodded. "We believe that's true."

Martinaeous shook his head. "Arduous is the least of the words that come to mind."

"Then you must help us now," Harrison pleaded. "Please tell us all you know of this treasure and its clues, then we can find it that much faster."

Martinaeous scanned the group before speaking. "I only know of scattered stories and legends. I might only confuse you more."

Harrison motioned to Gelderand. "What about this crystal ball Gelderand spoke about? Maybe it can show us something, anything."

"The crystal ball —" said the elderly man before putting his head down and running his frail hands through his gray hair.

Martinaeous brought his gaze to his old pupil. "Why did you put so much faith in that silly, magical object? The crystal ball might be able to show you the events leading to the placement of the treasure, and might show you what's to come, but to journey all this way for that is rather extreme."

Gelderand drew a heavy sigh. "We had no other leads. Can you at least try?"

"If I am strong enough," started Martinaeous, "you should be able to see the person or persons responsible for putting this whole treasure together.

"But remember, almost a thousand years have passed since the Treasure of the Land was laid to rest. There is a good possibility that you will see nothing. Nevertheless, follow me."

Martinaeous led the men to a small, dark windowless room. Like the other rooms they had seen, it too was a mess with all kinds of rubbish strewn about. The frail man cleared off a small, square table and covered it with a black cloth. Next, he went into a closet and retrieved a small clear sphere that measured about twelve inches in diameter. Martinaeous wiped off the accumulated dust, then placed the globe in a gold stand and motioned for the rest to sit around the table.

The elderly man then went rummaging through a small desk and found a candle, which he promptly lit. Next, he closed the door, allowing the room to fill with a soft yellow glow.

Martinaeous took his seat behind the magical artifact. "I will need to hold the treasure in my hand. Like I stated before, if we are lucky I will be able to see the last events leading up to the placement of the treasure as well as events to come."

Swinkle snatched the manuscript from his pack and handed it to Martinaeous. The old wizard gave the men a most curious look.

"A book?" he said as Swinkle handed him the scripture. "People have searched for centuries for a book?"

"Hard to believe, isn't it?" chided Murdock.

Martinaeous looked over the leather-like binding before saying, "I will need total silence in order for me to concentrate. I have not used my magic for a very long time."

"Sound familiar, Pondle?" whispered Murdock to his friend while the old man concentrated.

Martinaeous chanted the words to a spell while he tightly clutched the book in his hands. After several minutes, a thin, white smoke began to swirl around the inside of the sphere. The party members moved closer to the table as the mist engulfed the crystal ball. Suddenly, the glass object cleared, revealing the image of a chamber.

"Finally, something of worth from a magician," said Murdock under his breath.

The chamber appeared rather dark, with what appeared to be a bookcase filled with scriptures. Just then, they saw a hand removing a book from the shelf. Everyone looked at each other in surprise. The hand belonged to Murdock.

"Hey! That's me!" the ranger shouted with a laugh. "I guess I'm part of history now."

"Quiet!" responded Gelderand in anger. "The crystal ball will show the images in order, from the last person to touch the treasure to what is to come, if we are that fortunate."

Soon thereafter, the images of the party disappeared. Again, the crystal ball began to fill with the thin layer of white smoke. Harrison watched with amazement. He knew they had traveled a long way and the time had come to see what they should do next.

A large mountain range filled the crystal ball. The young warrior gazed at the peaceful scene and wondered what it meant. He did not have to wait long to see the image change. A split second later, a violent explosion filled the ball.

"The mountaintop blew right off," said the young warrior in a hushed tone.

"That's one of the clues," said Swinkle in a soft voice.

The image quickly changed to that of a middle-aged man. At first, the men could not decipher his actions, but that changed as well. The person began to leaf through the pages of his book, looking dumbfounded as he did. Without warning, droves of people began to run in every direction, all with a panicked look on their face.

"This is the first clue, but where is this taking place?" whispered Swinkle.

"Cyprus." Gelderand pointed at an obscure image within the crystal ball. "Look, that statue in the background —" he started before the scene altered again.

This time, all the men recognized the vision. A caravan of soldiers on horseback filled the ball, all with familiar markings.

"Concurian soldiers," said Murdock, looking in Harrison's direction.

"Did you expect anything else?" The young warrior shrugged. "I told you, Lord Hammer's alive. This proves it even more."

The scene inside the glass sphere morphed again. This time two small, but eerie red eyes stared out of the crystal ball. They began to get larger and brighter with each passing second. Suddenly, a large mouth filled with razor sharp teeth appeared, followed with the orange glow of fire. The flames swirled inside the sphere, taking several seconds to subside.

Pondle stared at the ghastly image. "I don't care for that clue."

The fiery image dissipated, replaced with a boat's bow. Beyond that stood a rocky shoreline shrouded in a thick mist.

"Where's that?" asked Harrison to no one in particular.

Swinkle stared at the scene. "That could be anywhere."

Before anyone could add his thoughts, the crystal ball filled with a thick, black smoke. Martinaeous leaned forward and dropped the book on the table, almost knocking the sphere over.

"Martinaeous, are you all right?" Gelderand jumped from his chair and went to his old teacher's side.

"I feel very weak," said the old mage in a raspy voice. "I need rest. Help me to my bed, please." Swinkle helped Gelderand lift Martinaeous out of the chair and the two of them escorted the elder man from the room.

After they had left, Harrison spoke first. "What are your thoughts on what we've just witnessed?"

"We saw a lot of images." Pondle shook his head. "I'm not sure where to begin."

"I'm still bothered by that army," said Murdock. "Harrison, we only have five men."

The young warrior understood Murdock's plea all too well. "I was hoping we had seen the last of Nigel Hammer for a while, at least until we uncovered the

Talisman." Just then, Swinkle and Gelderand returned to the room.

"Is Martinaeous all right?" asked Harrison.

Gelderand took his seat at the table. "He's a very old man. I would never have let him perform that spell had I known he would end up like this."

"He'll be all right, won't he?"

"He needs sleep," added Swinkle. "He's exhausted."

"We must stay here and watch over him for a day or two," said Gelderand. "It's the least we can do." The rest of the men nodded in agreement.

Harrison looked over to the mage. "You pointed to an image when we saw the people running in every direction. What did you see?"

"I saw a statue in the background."

The young warrior pressed further. "You said it was Cyprus. How can you be so sure?"

The mage sat back, scanning each group member as he spoke. "The statue of one of the ancient kings resides in Cyprus, which happens to be the birthplace of King Ballesteros."

Harrison's eyes lit up. "This coincides with the phrase 'the light of knowledge will be turned off in the town of Ballesteros'!"

Gelderand nodded. "Precisely."

"That's the first clue, too," said Swinkle. "Perhaps we should venture there."

"I tend to agree." Pondle added his thoughts to the conversation. "The other clues seemed a bit vaguer."

"Those soldiers weren't vague," said Murdock. "They're the ones looking for us."

The thief gazed at his friend. "I wouldn't be so sure about that. How would they know we've taken the book?"

Murdock shook his head and shrugged. "They don't, but I'm sure that Lord Hammer must assume that we uncovered the treasure. Especially if he survived."

Swinkle swallowed nervously. "What about the explosion, the fiery eyes, and the misty shore?"

"All indistinct images," reiterated Pondle. "I couldn't begin to tell you where they all occurred."

"I have to agree with him." Harrison pointed to the thief. "I'm surprised we didn't see an explosion of that magnitude. That must have happened in a remote part of the land."

"Furthermore," added Gelderand, "that rocky coast could be anywhere on the shoreline. Cyprus is our only concrete clue."

Harrison peered in Murdock's direction. "Cyprus is a long way from Concur, too."

The ranger nodded in agreement. "I suppose so. What's our next move?"

Gelderand interlocked his fingers and leaned forward. "We wait for Martinaeous to replenish his energy. He might have some more information as well."

Swinkle looked around the small room, noticing its dust and accumulated filth. "Maybe we can help Martinaeous clean his home."

"That would be a nice gesture," said Harrison. "We have to wait for him to recover and we have nothing else to do in the meantime."

"Wonderful." Murdock rolled his eyes. "We travel all this way to clean an old man's house."

"He will appreciate it, Murdock," said Gelderand, defending Harrison's decision. "When you get to be his age, you tend to let go of some things. Taking care of a house is a monumental task for Martinaeous."

The ranger shook his head. "Fine. Let's get started." The men left the small room and a few moments later began the menial chores of housework.

C H A P T E R 16

A heavy rain pounded against the roof, waking Harrison out of a sound sleep. Lance stirred next to his master, sensing his movements. The young warrior listened to the rain a bit more before he heard someone milling about the kitchen area. Martinaeous had slept for two consecutive days and the men had started to wonder if he would ever awaken. In the meantime, Harrison and his friends managed to make amends to the old man's home.

Using his strong arm, the young warrior lifted himself off the hard floor from which he had slept. He then noticed Martinaeous shuffling about the area, looking around in amazement.

Harrison made a cautious approach to the old mage, with Lance following close behind. "Good morning, Martinaeous. I'm glad to see that you've finally awaken."

Martinaeous did not acknowledge the young warrior. "This rain is coming down too hard. My garden will lose all its produce."

Harrison took another guarded step toward the wizard. "The weather will lighten up in time." The young warrior took Martinaeous's arm and guided the mage to the kitchen table. "Why don't you take a seat?"

After Martinaeous sat down, Harrison said, "Do you remember the actions of the other night?"

The old man gave him a vacuous stare and said nothing. At that moment, Harrison began to wonder if the spell that Martinaeous had conjured might have done some mental damage to the poor man. The wizard looked at Harrison, then down at the dog before answering.

"I saw many things," he began. "Strange things."

Harrison wrinkled his brow, not sure what Martinaeous meant. "What kind of images did you see?"

"Mountains and shorelines, armies and dragons," mumbled the old wizard. "I think I might have seen you, too."

Martinaeous's last comment surprised Harrison. "Me? I don't recall seeing any images of myself."

"Maybe you didn't, but I did." The old man looked about with ever widening eyes. "How did this house get so clean? I don't remember doing this."

Harrison tried his best to remain calm. "We all helped to straighten out your home while you recuperated."

"All?" Martinaeous gave the younger man a look of shock. "There are more of you?"

Harrison let out a heavy sigh. "Yes, my friends are here with me, but they're still asleep." He paused before saying, "Gelderand is with me, too."

The old man's eyes lit up. "Gelderand? He's dead, how could he possibly be with you?"

Harrison knew continuing the discussion with Martinaeous would be fruitless. "I'm going to awaken them, then we'll all get something to eat."

"That's fine with me." The old man continued to look around in wonderment.

Harrison went over to Gelderand first. "Gelderand," he whispered, lightly shaking him. "Gelderand, Martinaeous has woken up."

The mage tried to gather his bearings, wiping the sleep from his eyes. "Martinaeous is awake?"

"Yes, he is, and he's sitting at the table. I'm going to get the others up, too."

"By all means." Gelderand rose from his makeshift bedding and looked toward the kitchen, finding his former mentor mumbling in thought.

"Martinaeous," said Gelderand in a cautious tone. "How do you feel?"

Martinaeous looked at his old pupil. "I feel fine. Why is everyone asking me that?"

Gelderand could tell that Martinaeous was not back to himself just yet. "You performed an intense spell the other night, my old friend."

"I know." The old wizard shook his head. "I still feel very strange."

"I think I might have something for you." Gelderand tried to fish something out of his backpack. A moment later, he finished with his search.

"This will help to restore your health." Gelderand uncorked a small vial containing a purple liquid and gave it to Martinaeous. "Drink this."

Martinaeous took the potion from his old friend. The older wizard looked the vial over, then sniffed the opening. Satisfied, he chugged the liquid in one large gulp.

"Good," said Gelderand, taking the container from his friend. "The effects are almost instantaneous."

By that time, Harrison had rounded up the rest of the men who accompanied him to gather around the table.

Murdock took a seat first. "I'm glad to see that the old guy's still alive."

Lance came over to greet Swinkle, who patted the dog on the head. Looking in Gelderand's direction, he said, "We took a risk allowing him to conjure that spell."

The mage closed his eyes and nodded. "I know. I had reservations myself."

Suddenly Martinaeous's eyes appeared to focus upon everyone and everything in his home. "What have you done to my house?"

"I told you," said Harrison, "we helped clean it up for you."

"Now I won't know where anything is!" A look of agitation glazed the old mage's face. "Why must every person who steps foot in my home feel the need to rearrange it?"

"I would say your magic worked," said Murdock in a sarcastic tone in Gelderand's direction.

Gelderand again shook off the ranger's remark and addressed his old mentor. "Martinaeous, how do you feel?"

"I feel fine," answered the grumpy old man. "And yes, I remember the events of the other night."

"Good. Do you have any insights for us?"

Martinaeous thought for a moment. "No, I do not." The old man's simple response shocked the men.

"No?" Murdock gazed at his friends, his eyes wide and mouth agape. "What do you mean, no?"

"Just what I said, that I do not have anything concrete to tell you about what we all saw. I did not see anything different than any of you."

"I suppose we had hoped that you might have witnessed something we hadn't," said Swinkle in dejection.

"You said you saw me," said Harrison to Martinaeous.

"I said that?" The young warrior's remark surprised the old mage. "I'm sorry, but I don't remember that at all."

"At least we did see several images," said Gelderand. "And we know where we must go first."

"Cyprus." Martinaeous pointed at his old pupil, shaking a finger in remembrance. "I saw the statue, too."

Gelderand nodded. "Precisely. That vision coincides with the first clue."

Martinaeous raised his eyebrows. "Then what are you waiting for? You should have left when you came to that realization instead of cleaning some old fool's home."

Gelderand let out a laugh. "Do you really think that I would have left you alone in your condition?"

"You always were too compassionate." Martinaeous paused, then sighed with a slight smile coming to his face. "I do want to thank you all for what you have done for me."

"There's no need to thank us," said Harrison. "We thank you for your help."

Martinaeous looked at the young warrior, noticing again his injured limb. "You cannot leave here with your arm in that condition."

Harrison gazed at him with a look of exasperation. "I agree, but what else can I do? Gelderand and Swinkle did all that they could for me."

"That they did." Martinaeous nodded slowly. "Gelderand told me he used a regeneration spell coupled with a healing prayer from Swinkle to reattach your arm. Very ingenious indeed."

The old wizard stared deep into the young warrior's eyes. "But you haven't let me take a look at you."

"What are you proposing?" asked Gelderand, placing his hands on the table and leaning back ever so slowly, raising an eyebrow in the process.

Martinaeous gave his one-time pupil a wry look. "I think you know." The old mage then left the table and headed off in search of something. Gelderand followed him.

"Martinaeous, you have already done enough," lamented Gelderand, but to no avail.

"Remember when I taught you how to heal your wounds after a physical battle?" The older wizard peered about a cabinet as he spoke.

"Vaguely," answered Gelderand, while Martinaeous opened and closed drawers, searching for something that seemed just out of reach.

"You all have disrupted my organization!" shouted the old man to no one in particular, shaking his fist at the entire room.

Gelderand stood behind his mentor, waiting for the man to finish his search. "All I remember about healing myself is — wait, you don't mean —"

"Here it is!" Martinaeous yanked a black velvet sack from a cabinet. The old man then looked again in earnest for something else. By this time, the rest of the men had become quite curious about what the two wizards were searching for, Harrison in particular.

"Gelderand," said the young warrior, while he unwittingly caressed his injured arm, "what is he trying to find?"

"More ingredients to a spell," said the mage, sounding like a disapproving father to his child's actions.

Gelderand's answer did not leave Harrison with a warm feeling. "Might I ask why you sound so, I don't know, negative?"

Gelderand let out a sigh. "Let's just say I'm not sure I agree with Martinaeous's strategy."

"Here they are!" Martinaeous plucked two small burlap sacks from the bottom of a drawer. "These will cure you, that's for sure."

"These?" Swinkle appeared concerned for his friend's well being. "Are you trying to perform some kind of medicine, because I can help in that area?"

Martinaeous walked back to the table with the two sacks and placed them down. Just then, something inside one of the burlap bags began to wiggle.

"What's in there?" Swinkle pointed to the moving sack.

"Oh my," said Martinaeous, before moving the two bags away from each other, causing the burlap sack to mysteriously cease its motion. "The ingredients can become volatile if they are not handled properly."

Harrison gave Gelderand an incredulous look. "Please tell me what these bags contain and how they pertain to my arm."

The mage sighed. "They are leeches. By taking the leeches —"

"Leeches!" shouted the young warrior, backing his seat from the table.

"They're not just leeches." Martinaeous raised his hands in an effort to calm everyone down. "They're magical."

Harrison shook his head in protest. "Magical or not, I think you need to explain what you are about to do."

Martinaeous nodded in understanding. "After I combine the ingredients for the spell, the leeches will enter your body and find the damaged tissue. They will then mend your flesh. They're quite meticulous."

Murdock let out a laugh. "Just like that! These leeches just repair the severed nerves and tissue, then go on their merry way!"

Gelderand cocked his head from side to side. "Martinaeous is making the procedure sound a little more trivial than it is."

"How do the leeches enter Harrison's body?" asked Swinkle.

"I'd like to know that, too." A look of disgust flashed across Harrison's face. "I'm not going to eat them, am I?"

"Of course not," said Martinaeous with a laugh. "They will be placed on the injured part of your arm. From there, they will dissolve into your flesh. The whole spell should last no more than six hours."

Harrison opened his mouth, but no words came out.

"Let me get this straight." Murdock leaned forward, positioning himself to face the old man. "You do your little spell chant, sprinkle worms on his arm, and after a few hours he's magically healed?"

Martinaeous nodded matter-of-factly. "In a manner of speaking, yes." The ranger raised his eyebrows, sat back, and shook his head without uttering a word.

Gelderand tried to ease the situation. "Harrison, I know what you must be thinking, but I have witnessed Martinaeous performing this spell in the past, and I have seen positive results. I will be here to assist him."

Harrison remained unsure. "And you believe that this'll heal my arm?"

"Yes, I do."

"Harrison," said Swinkle, "I think this is your only real chance to save your limb. The procedure that Gelderand and I performed will not get any better than it is now."

Harrison looked at his injury again. The young warrior knew he could barely grip a mug, let alone flail a weapon in battle. With reservations, he said, "I'll let you attempt to heal me."

A smile came over Martinaeous's face. "Good. Give me just a few moments to prepare the spell."

Harrison and the others watched as Martinaeous went about his preparations. The mage took the burlap bag and dumped six of its contents onto the table. Harrison looked at the inch-long, curved pieces of clay-like material with wonder.

"Can you roll up your sleeve for me?" asked Martinaeous.

Harrison did as the mage asked, revealing a scar that encircled his arm just above the bicep. Martinaeous then placed the small objects in strategic places on the injured limb. Next, he took the black sack and began to mutter words to his spell. When he finished, he reached his hand into the pouch and took out a handful of fine, red powder.

Martinaeous sprinkled the powder over the clay-like pieces. Immediately, the objects turned a majestic red and took on a life-like form. The magical leeches began to wiggle about Harrison's arm.

"What are they doing?" asked Harrison in concern, while the others looked on in amazement.

"Trying to find the right insertion point," answered the old mage, all the while staring at the creatures.

A few seconds later, the leeches began to dissolve into the young warrior's body. Harrison could sense the miniature creatures enter his injured area.

"I can feel them inside of me!"

"Good," said Martinaeous. "The spell is working."

A controlled look of panic glazed Harrison's face. "What do I do now?"

"Nothing. As I said before, it will take the leeches about six hours to heal your wound. Be patient."

The young warrior gave the old man an incredulous stare. "That's easy for you to say!"

Martinaeous looked over to the rest of Harrison's friends. "Let Harrison be for now, I don't want to see him doing anything strenuous. I will examine him again after the allotted time is up."

"What shall we do while the spell is working?" asked Gelderand.

"Prepare yourselves for journey." The old mage scanned the group once again. "You will be leaving today. What will be your next course of action?"

Gelderand spoke again. "Like we said before, we will go to Cyprus to find the red jewel."

"How do you plan to get there?"

Gelderand looked over to the others with a look of surprise. "We have not determined our route of travel just yet."

"All I know is that we need to avoid Lord Hammer's army at all costs," said Murdock.

"Then I suggest you go due east." Martinaeous pointed in that direction.

"Are you suggesting that we travel through the Valkaline Forest?" Pondle glared at the old wizard.

"That's Troll's Hell," responded Murdock in a hushed tone. The ranger knew very well the dangers of the Valkaline Forest as he had lost many acquaintances due to the nature of the beasts that resided there.

Shaking his head, he said, "Why would we even consider venturing that way?"

"I'm not suggesting you bring five men and a dog through that wicked land," said Martinaeous.

Pondle thought for a moment. "Lord Hammer wouldn't bring his army into Troll's Hell."

"No," said Martinaeous with authority, stopping the thief's thought process. "I never would agree to that course of action. The trolls would slaughter all of you before you made it to the forest's midpoint."

"Why can't we go around it?"

"You can't risk being intercepted by Concurian soldiers."

Pondle shrugged. "We don't even know if they're going to Cyprus."

"You did see them on the move," said Martinaeous, "as did I."

"We can't take the chance of being seen." Murdock sat back in his chair, agitated.

"Stick to the outskirts of the forests." Martinaeous held up a crooked finger. "The beasts will not venture out of their land and you know Lord Hammer's army wouldn't be in the woodlands either. You would only have to worry about the open area in front of you."

Everyone took a moment to ponder Martinaeous's strategy. "The old man's right." Murdock leaned forward again. "No army would be foolish enough to go through Troll's Hell."

"And I'd be able to see an advancing platoon of men from quite a distance away," agreed Pondle.

"Does this mean that we don't need to go through that desolate forest?" asked Swinkle with hope.

Harrison looked over to Murdock and Pondle before answering. "Yes, Swinkle, we'll venture around the woods." The young cleric let out a sigh of relief.

"Then it's settled," said Murdock. "We might as well give Harrison time to heal before we set off for Cyprus." The ranger stood up and pointed to his friend. "Pondle and I will secure our supplies." The thief nodded in agreement, then both men gathered their belongings and set off for provisions.

"I'll stay with Harrison," said Swinkle. "I'm ready to leave now anyway."

"And I'm going to take the time to learn more from my mentor." Gelderand smiled as he gazed in Martinaeous's direction. "We still have much to catch up on."

The two older men excused themselves from the table as well and went off to another part of the house.

"Swinkle, do you believe that this will work?" said Harrison in a hushed tone, pointing to his arm.

The young cleric nodded.

Harrison looked at his limb and could see the flesh around his scar wriggling. "I hope all of you are right."

A feeling of fatigue began to overtake the young warrior. "I'm going to rest," he said with a yawn. "For some reason I'm beginning to feel very tired."

Swinkle smiled. "The spell is working. Rest. We'll be waiting for you when you awaken."

Harrison nodded and went off to where he had slept the previous night. Within minutes, he fell fast asleep.

Several hours passed before Harrison awoke. The young warrior shook the sleep from his body, then looked at his arm. The scar still stretched across his bicep and all appeared the same.

Harrison then peered over at the corner of the room where he had placed his weapon the night before. Taking hold of the axe, he gripped it firmly with the hand of his injured arm. To his surprise, he raised the blade to his face with minimal effort. Next, he held the weapon away from his body. Again, he felt no strain on his arm.

A feeling of adrenaline raced through the young warrior's body as he realized that Martinaeous's spell had healed his once devastating injury. Harrison wanted to tell his friends the good news, but as he looked about the house, he noticed that everyone had disappeared.

Before his concern level could rise, he heard voices coming from the other room. Walking over to the corner where Martinaeous had shown them the images from the crystal ball the night before, he found his friends seated at the same table. His brow rose to his hairline as he gazed into the room.

On the table stood Rufus meowing at Gelderand, while everyone else looked on. Harrison entered the room, clutching his battle-axe in his right hand.

"How did you sleep?" asked Swinkle.

Harrison shook his head, appearing confused at the question at first. "I feel great. My arm's back to full strength, too." He then raised his weapon to show his friends.

"That's wonderful." Martinaeous smiled, not really listening to the young man. "I told you the spell would work in time."

Harrison nodded, then squinted and looked at the orange tabby again. "What are you doing?"

"We are making sure Rufus still remembers his training," said Gelderand. "Lance has been a bit of a bother, though."

"It's been an interesting show of wizardry," said Murdock, his voice full of sarcasm.

The young warrior crinkled his brow. "Why, what's Lance doing?"

"I think he's jealous," said Swinkle. "Rufus is getting all the attention and he keeps breaking the cat's concentration."

Harrison shook his head again. "All right, someone just fill me in on what's going on."

Gelderand eased back in his seat. "If all goes well, I should be able to see through Rufus's eyes. What he sees, I should see."

"Really?" Harrison gave the mage a look of astonishment. "That trick can be very useful." The young warrior took a seat at the table. Lance quickly darted to his side and received a pat on his head from his master.

"But Lance keeps barking at Rufus," continued Gelderand, "and Rufus doesn't like that."

"I find that to be a problem," added Pondle, pointing to his wizard friend. "If his concentration is broken that easily, the spell will never work."

"Or it will come back to hurt Gelderand," said Martinaeous. "If Rufus is injured or killed while the spell is in place, there could be grave consequences for the caster."

Harrison took in the new information. "I have to agree with Pondle. If Lance's barking distracts the cat, there's no telling how other outside influences could sidetrack Rufus."

Martinaeous nodded. "Let's try again."

Gelderand nodded, then took hold of the cat. "Listen to me closely, Rufus. Focus on my voice."

The cat stared at its master while Gelderand spoke. Harrison patted Lance on the head again, preempting the dog from barking. The mage stroked the cat's fur and rubbed him briskly behind his ears. Rufus rolled his head, enjoying the caresses that the wizard gave to him.

Martinaeous then took out a fine, gray powder and offered a pinch to Gelderand. The mage accepted the delicate particles from his mentor and began to mumble the spell. Gelderand sprinkled the key ingredient over the cat, as well as his other hand that was stroking the animal. Without seeing anything visible, Gelderand felt a sensation course through his body. Likewise, Rufus shivered, signaling that the spell was in place.

Harrison watched Gelderand remove his hand from the cat, before shooing the animal off the table. The young warrior gazed at the wizard and realized that something appeared different about him. Gelderand seemed the same, but upon closer examination, he could see that his eyes had morphed into those of a cat.

"Rufus is heading into the other room," started Gelderand, all the while remaining seated and staring straight ahead with his cat-like eyes.

"Follow the cat!" Martinaeous pointed to Swinkle to perform the task. The young cleric scrambled out of his chair and followed the feline.

"He has jumped onto a piece of furniture," said the wizard again. "I see … I see … the ceiling. Now the floor — he just jumped down!"

Just then, Lance darted out of the room. A second later he began to bark.

"Rufus is on the table," exclaimed Gelderand. "I see Lance barking and Swinkle is trying to get the dog to stop." Just then, Gelderand jerked back in his chair.

"Rufus jumped from the table to the floor and now he's running under the furniture!"

Harrison closely observed Gelderand and could see beads of sweat beginning to form on his forehead. "Gelderand, are you all right?"

"Quiet," said Martinaeous. "Let him be."

"Lance is chasing Rufus!" said Gelderand, his excitement level rising. "He's running around the room! He's moving so fast! He's jumped again!"

Harrison looked at his friend with concern. The mage appeared a bit pale to him. The young warrior looked over at Murdock and Pondle; both men had the same look of worry.

"If I didn't know better," started Murdock, "I'd say he's about to —"

Before Murdock could finish his statement, Gelderand leaned over the side of the table and vomited on the floor. Groggy, he looked up again.

"Somebody stop that dog!" the mage said, sensing that Rufus had eluded Lance again and was running along the countertop.

"Lance!" shouted Harrison. "Get over here!" A moment later, the small dog came to the doorway and looked at his master.

"Come here!" said the young warrior in a stern tone. "Stay by my side. Now!" The small dog obliged and sat next to Harrison.

"Rufus has ... stopped." Gelderand appeared almost out of breath. "I see Swinkle ..." he continued between gasps. "He's holding ... Rufus and gazing ... into his eyes."

Martinaeous waved his hands. "That's enough. Swinkle! Bring the cat back in here!"

The young cleric reentered the room carrying Rufus, then gently placed him on the table.

Murdock, Pondle, and Harrison looked at the cat with disbelief. Gelderand took the animal and stroked its hair with care. Next he mumbled to himself and, a moment later, reverted to his original self. Everyone waited a moment to be sure the mage was all right.

"I would say we just witnessed a successful experiment," said Martinaeous.

"You call that a success?" Murdock shook his head, his eyes wide. "A man turns green and throws up, and that's your proof of accomplishment?"

"He saw what Rufus saw and felt what he felt," said Martinaeous. "Just like he was supposed to."

"That cat can still move pretty fast when he has to," said Gelderand, wiping the perspiration from his forehead.

The afternoon's antics still did not impress Murdock. "I think you need more practice. No way are you ready to perform this spell in battle."

"I'd say," added Pondle. "Look at you."

Gelderand knew the men were right, but he had proven to himself that he could perform the trick, which was enough for him. "I will be ready when the time comes."

"I think you will be, too," said Harrison, lifting the older man's spirits. "I think we've come away with more than we had anticipated from this journey. And it's time to leave on that note. Let's gather our belongings and set out before nightfall." At that, everyone dispersed to inventory their things and to prepare for the next leg of their journey.

Within the hour, the men assembled their respective packs and were ready to travel to Cyprus. They all stood in Martinaeous's home for the last time.

"You take care," said Martinaeous, taking his gaze to each of the men. "All of you. Go, before it gets dark. You have about three hours of sunlight."

After an uncomfortable moment of silence, Harrison said, "Pondle, let's get moving." The thief headed to the door, followed one at a time by his friends.

"Thank you, Martinaeous," said Harrison, brandishing his weapon to the mage, "from the bottom of my heart."

The old mage shook his head. "There is no need for thanks, my son."

Harrison, Lance, and Swinkle then departed, leaving Gelderand to say his final farewell. "I know what you think, but I am not too old for this quest."

Martinaeous gave his old friend an anxious stare. "Gelderand, be very careful. Your powers are there, but they have been dormant for a long time."

"I will be ready when the time comes." The mage saw a smile flash across Martinaeous's face. "Good-bye."

"Good-bye." The two men embraced one last time before Gelderand exited the house.

The men fell into their assigned marching order with Pondle and Murdock at the front, Harrison protecting the rear, and began to head in the direction of the vast woods. Harrison, Swinkle, and Gelderand turned to wave at the old man.

Martinaeous stood in the doorway of his rickety home and waved back. Knowing the next leg of their journey would be very difficult, he hoped that he would truly see them again.

"May the gods look favorable upon their quest," he said aloud as the last of the group left the outskirts of the town and disappeared from view.

CHAPTER 17

○

For two weeks, the men trekked across the land. Being wary to avoid any confrontations with Lord Hammer's army, the group traveled along the Valkaline forest, crossed the Guard's River, then hugged the outskirts of the Gammorian forest. From there, they ventured across the steppes of Gammoria, before stopping a day shy of Cyprus.

Harrison had used the time to hone his battle skills with his newly healed arm, while the rest of the men had focused on exploring how they might find the red jewel. The men took refuge beneath a group of shade trees in order to take a break from their journeying. Pondle had surveyed the area and made sure that no one would be able to sneak up on them.

Swinkle nodded his head after his prayer, then tossed a piece of dry meat over his shoulder. Lance scurried over to devour the young cleric's sacrifice, like he always did.

Oblivious to the dog's actions, Swinkle said, "I think I know what we need to look for once we reach Cyprus."

Murdock tore at a piece of dried meat as well. "What makes you so sure?"

"I have studied the clues from the sacred scripture during our rest times and I feel that the first entry is rather obvious." The young cleric paused after his statement.

Murdock waited for the young cleric to continue, and when he didn't, he gave him a wry look. "Well?"

Swinkle took the book out of his backpack and flipped through the pages. Finding what he was looking for, he said, "The passage states that the light of knowledge will be turned off in the town of Ballesteros, which is where the red jewel resides.

"Then it says *'Down you must travel, where those who are eternally asleep lie. You must dig for your treasure, but where you might say? It is where a treasure should be found, there are no tricks here.'* "

Swinkle lowered the book and looked at his friends. "Where do people in eternal sleep lie?"

"In a cemetery," said Gelderand. "You're right, Swinkle. That clue is rather obvious."

Swinkle continued with his argument. "We need to find a burial ground and when we do, I bet that we will find the ruby."

Harrison listened to his friend state his case. "The city should be deserted, too. We saw those frightened people running away in the crystal ball."

"You're making it sound like we can just walk into the town, find what we're looking for, and leave unnoticed." Murdock then pointed his finger at no one in particular. "I'm betting on it being a bit more difficult than that."

"I hope I did not give you the impression that it would be easy," said Swinkle. "We need to take precautions like we always do."

The ranger took a sip from his tankard. "Let me and Pondle survey the village. We'll find the burial ground and no one will see us, if anyone's there."

"That's a good strategy." Harrison frowned. "How long until we reach Cyprus?"

"We'll be there tomorrow," said Pondle, before scowling. "The worse part will be crossing that river."

Murdock smiled at his friend. "We can't seem to keep you away from water!" Pondle just glared at the ranger.

"Then it's settled," said Harrison. "Murdock and Pondle will continue to lead us to Cyprus, then they'll scout the town for a cemetery. Let's leave now!"

Pondle rose from his seat on the ground and started to secure his things. "We have half a day of sunlight ahead of us. I'm ready."

The other men prepared themselves, too. After making sure they had all of their provisions, Murdock and Pondle led the men in the direction of Cyprus.

The party approached the empty city the following day. Pondle took them to the banks of the Cyprian River before stopping.

"All we need to do is follow this river and we'll run right into Cyprus."

Harrison used a hand to shield his eyes from the sun. "How far away are we from the city?"

Pondle shrugged. "A mile, two at the most."

The young warrior gazed at his surroundings. The river cut through a wooded area that thickened in the direction they would be going.

"Is the covering like this all the way to the village?"

"Yes. The Cyprian Woods surrounds the city, with the denser forests looming to the north and east." Pondle looked at the water, which flowed toward them.

"Tradesmen pack their boats with treasures from the woodlands, then sail them to the Lake of Good Hope and destinations beyond."

"Will anyone see us coming?"

"Not if I can help it." Pondle gestured to Murdock. "We'll survey the land ahead of us and determine the best route into the city."

"We're not walking down the main street," added the ranger. "If that's what you're alluding to."

Harrison let out a sigh. "The town might be deserted, but you never know."

The thief nodded and motioned for the group to follow them.

Pondle and Murdock took the lead and began to follow the river bank. Lance darted in and out of the thickets along the way, his nose kept close to the ground. Harrison, Gelderand, and Swinkle followed fifty feet behind, scanning as best they could through the dense woodlands.

Another hour passed before Pondle and Murdock returned to the other men. "We can see some docks and buildings along the shore," said Murdock, pointing through the overhanging branches.

Harrison could make out the structures in the distance, while also noticing that the river measured a couple of hundred feet wide.

"How do we get across?" he asked with an exasperated look.

Murdock looked over to Pondle, who shrugged. "We haven't figured that out yet."

"Can we wade across?"

Pondle cringed at the thought. "The river's too deep and the current's too strong."

Harrison furrowed his brow in thought. "I guess we'll have to continue on until the water narrows."

"I'd have to agree." Pondle looked over to Murdock, who nodded in concurrence as well. "Everyone, follow us."

A short time later, Pondle and Murdock led the rest of the men to the stream's embankment. Harrison looked to the shore and noticed a small dock, constructed out of four wooden posts and ten-foot long timber planks. Four seven-foot tall oars, also made of wood, lay across the pier's decking. Likewise, a similar setup existed on the opposite side of the river.

Harrison appeared skeptical at the sight before him. "This looks too convenient if you ask me."

Murdock gave him funny look. "Don't be ridiculous. How else would you expect to cross the river?" The ranger looked up and down the stream. "This is where both banks are at their closest point. These docks have been here for a long time."

Swinkle and Gelderand approached the young warrior. "I wouldn't be so concerned," said Gelderand. "People from Cyprus would not expect visitors to wade across the river."

Harrison still appeared unconvinced, but knew they needed to get to the other side. "Let's just get over there as fast as we can."

Murdock took caution in approaching the dock. Scanning the area, he saw nothing out of the ordinary. Satisfied, he then waved to his friends to join him.

"Let's go." Pondle led the rest of the men carefully out on the pier.

Harrison looked over the area and noticed a ten-by-ten foot wooden raft secured to the dock. Murdock handed him and Swinkle an oar as soon as they stepped foot on the wharf.

"There are four of them," said the ranger. "You and me are up front. Pondle and Swinkle will push the raft from the back."

Murdock untied the rope that held the raft, and the men began their maneuver to the other side. Harrison felt very unsure about their situation. He thought back to his warrior training, how being on water was always a disadvantage to a fighter. Enemies could easily spot crafts sailing on lakes or seas, and trying to keep one's balance to fight on such vessels was always a chore.

The men reached the opposite shore with relative ease and quickly disembarked. Murdock tied the platform to the pier, then joined his friends who had taken refuge in the woods.

"That didn't take long at all," he said, looking back at the river.

Pondle still looked apprehensive. "We need to be very careful now. The town's about a half mile away."

Harrison scanned the area, but saw nothing of concern. Feeling a bit relieved, he said, "Lead us on."

Pondle, Murdock, and Lance led the men closer to the city of Cyprus along a well-worn path. Harrison knew that staying on the road increased the likelihood of being seen. After several minutes of trekking, he could see Murdock waving them onward from up ahead.

Harrison, Gelderand, and Swinkle reached the ranger at last. "We're about a hundred yards away from the outskirts of the town," said Murdock in a low voice, pointing in front of the men. "You can see the buildings from here."

Harrison strained his eyes to see through the overhanging branches, and soon could see the structures Murdock spoke of. Looking about, he noticed someone missing.

"Where's Pondle?"

"He's surveying the area." Murdock maintained his gaze toward the village. "He took Lance with him." After a few moments of waiting, he saw something in the distance.

"There he is! He's on his way back!"

Lance scooted past the thief and trotted back to the other men. Pondle approached his friends a second later.

"The place appears to be deserted," said Pondle, but his expression told his friends he felt otherwise.

"What's wrong, Pondle," said Murdock, reading his friend's face.

Pondle shook his head. "I don't know. Something just doesn't feel right."

"What do you mean?"

The thief searched for the right words. "I'm not sure, but there doesn't seem to be a person anywhere. I find that hard to believe."

"The happenings that occurred here probably convinced even the most skeptical to leave," added Swinkle.

Pondle still did not seem as certain. "Perhaps."

"We still need to find that jewel," said Harrison. "Did you see a burial ground?"

Pondle shook his head. "I didn't make an in depth search. This town is large and we need to investigate it carefully."

"What do you suggest?"

"Let me and Murdock have a look around." Pondle pointed to the town's center. "I think I noticed that statue you saw in the crystal ball over there."

Harrison grimaced. He knew Pondle was right when he said they needed to survey the area, but he was beginning to grow tired of sitting in the woods, protecting Gelderand and Swinkle.

In a bold move, he said, "We'll all go into the town. If it's really empty, we'll be able to find the cemetery that much faster."

Pondle yielded to his friends. "I know how you feel," he said, motioning with his head toward the town. "We'll approach those buildings over there, then we can fan out in different directions." The thief turned to his comrades.

"We'll meet back here in one hour. Remember, try and stay out of view." The men nodded in agreement before following Pondle and Murdock.

The small group reached the edge of the forest, then dispersed into the deserted city. Harrison took Lance with him to scout out the area. The young warrior scanned the buildings in front of him and determined that he stood in a residential part of the town. The homes resembled those that families would reside in, with their smaller buildings, gardens, and livestock pens.

While Lance sniffed around the compound, picking up the scent of the herded animals, Harrison took care in looking around the houses, but found nothing of worth. He continued to wander deeper into the town, looking for anything that resembled a clue. After passing his fifth building, he found a dirt trail that led farther into the city.

Harrison panned from side to side, in search of his faithful companion. Spotting the dog, he called, "Lance!" The animal lifted his head and ran to his master.

The young warrior bent down and patted the dog on its side. "Let's go this way," he said, pointing up the road.

Lance sprinted ahead of his master, while Harrison continued his reconnaissance. After several minutes of fruitless searching, he began to feel like his whole endeavor had been a waste of time. Just before he gave up all hope, he spotted something of interest.

Across the street from where he stood, Harrison noticed a flyer on the side of an establishment. Looking around to be sure that no one was watching him, he made a dash across the road, then turned around and surveyed the land behind him one more time. Sensing that no one had seen him, the young warrior felt free to gaze at the sign.

A wave of anxiety overcame him as he started to read the print. Troubled by what it said, he grabbed the sign, rolled it, and stuffed it in his belt.

Harrison frantically looked for Lance and, once he spotted him, shouted, "Let's go, boy! We're leaving!"

Lance ran to Harrison's side and the two retraced their steps to hurry toward the rendezvous point.

Harrison waited another ten excruciating minutes before he saw Gelderand and Swinkle appear from between two buildings. His anxious waving caused them to quicken their pace.

Swinkle reached his friend first. "What is the matter?"

"I've found something very disturbing." Harrison retrieved the scrolled parchment from his belt and unrolled it.

"Listen to what this says," he said, holding the notice in front of him.

"*Reward, 10,000 gold pieces for the return of a sacred book. General Troy Harkin will answer all questions regarding details of payment. The redeeming quality of this scripture is its leather-like covering — if it is scratched, it will bleed. It is imperative that this treasure is found immediately.*" Harrison then lowered the poster and gazed at his friends.

Both Gelderand and Swinkle's eyes widened with surprise. Without saying a word, the young cleric rummaged through his backpack to retrieve the book. Bringing the treasure to his face, he examined its leathery cover.

"Harrison, hand me one of your daggers." The young warrior removed a blade from his belt and handed it to Swinkle.

Swinkle took the weapon and made a small, diagonal slice across the binding. Droplets of blood dripped from the incision as soon as the blade pierced the covering.

A worrisome look overtook Harrison's face. "Who is this General Harkin and how does he know about this book?"

"Remember? One of the clues said 'It' knows we have the book," said Gelderand. "Maybe this Harkin fellow is the person the clue pertains to." Just then, the men saw Murdock and Pondle return from their mission.

The ranger also had his own look of concern. "We have trouble."

"Tell me about it." Harrison flashed the sign to Murdock and Pondle. When they had finished reading the message, they both looked over at Swinkle, where fresh blood stained the book cover.

"What did you find?" asked Harrison.

"There's a platoon of men on the opposite side of town," said Murdock, his gaze locked on Harrison. "And they bear the markings of Concur."

Harrison's face dropped. "Concur? That could mean Nigel Hammer is in the region, too!"

"But not all of the soldiers are from Concur," added Pondle. "We saw other men who did not have Concurian markings mixed in with Lord Hammer's men."

Harrison appeared confused. "I wonder if they're General Harkin's men."

Pondle nodded. "I'd like to know the answer to that, too. They might very well be. After reading that poster, it kind of makes sense." Everyone paused, deep in thought with the sudden turn of events.

Pondle looked back toward the town. "We did find something else of worth, too."

"The cemetery?" asked Harrison with hope.

"Yes. But, it's on the other side of the city and those soldiers are stationed around that area."

"How are they assembled?"

Pondle looked over at Murdock, who shook his head. "We don't know. We left as soon as we saw the soldiers."

Harrison thought for a moment, but before he could add another theory, Gelderand spoke. "I think I might have an idea."

All the men turned their attention to the mage. "I can send Rufus into the area and I will be able to see how they have convened."

Murdock raised an eyebrow and turned to face the wizard. "After what happened last time?" he said in a sarcastic tone. "That cat will do nothing but make you sick again."

Harrison ignored the ranger's comment. "I don't think that's a bad idea at all. Can you get Rufus to perform this trick?"

Gelderand crossed his arms and stood tall. "I believe I can."

Harrison looked at his friends. "It's worth a try. At least we'll know how many people we're up against and do this all from a safe distance."

Gelderand further conveyed his assurance. "I am more than ready for this task."

"If you say so." Murdock shrugged. "Pondle and I will lead us to where the soldiers are. Follow us."

Pondle and Murdock led their friends through a myriad of streets and buildings, all the time being careful not to spend too much time in plain view. After several minutes of darting from one structure to another, they saw the enemy before them.

The men held their ground behind an empty building. After waiting for a few seconds, Harrison peeked around the corner of the building to see between fifteen and twenty soldiers. He also could make out something of greater importance.

"Is that the cemetery beyond them?"

"Yes, it is," said Pondle. "They camped out away from the town's center, but unfortunately for us, they are close to where we need to go."

Gelderand placed his pack on the ground. "I am going to prepare for my spell. We should find a place to hide while Rufus is on the prowl."

"I agree." Pondle looked about the general vicinity and spotted a building with open shutters.

"Let's go over there," he said, pointing to the structure. "We can hide in that house while Gelderand monitors Rufus."

The men stealthily maneuvered away from the unsuspecting platoon. Pondle climbed through the open window to assure that the home was abandoned. Going to the back, he opened the door, then summoned his awaiting friends.

After everyone was safely secured in their hideout, Gelderand removed the ingredients he would need to perform his spell. First, he took Rufus and placed him on the ground in front of him. Next, he removed the fine, black powder from a sack and sprinkled the substance over the cat while reciting his spell. In a matter of seconds, his eyes reverted to those of a cat.

Gelderand picked Rufus up. "I can see through his eyes. The spell is working."

Harrison approached the mage. "We need to find a safe way into the cemetery. Have him find that for us." The young warrior gazed at the cat. "Rufus, I know you understand what I said. Do this for us, all right?" The cat stared at Harrison, cocked his head, and seemed to nod in comprehension.

The mage nodded as well, then brought the feline to his face. "Rufus, go."

Gelderand placed the cat on the floor and watched the animal scurry out the back door. He then found a chair and sat down. Harrison and Swinkle huddled around him while Murdock and Pondle peered out the window.

"There he goes!" said Murdock as he watched the feline stray about the buildings. "That cat's doing real good!"

"He's avoiding the soldiers." Pondle craned his neck to get a better look at where Rufus was going. "But he's starting to leave my line of sight."

Gelderand remained motionless in his chair. "I can see people off to his left. Rufus is trying to avoid them."

A moment later, the mage squinted and said, "I can see a fence and it surrounds the burial ground." The mage squirmed in his seat. "A soldier is pointing at Rufus. One of his comrades sees him, too."

Murdock and Pondle joined the others and hovered around Gelderand. The mage had a look of concern, then let out a sigh of relief. "They are letting him be. Rufus is approaching the fence."

The mage squinted further. "The fence is made out of metal stakes with sharp points on the top. Rufus squeezed in between two of the stakes — he's inside the cemetery."

"We can't fit between them if the cat had to squeeze through," Swinkle whispered.

Gelderand continued to stare straight ahead as he spoke, focusing on the cat's every move. "The grass is high and there are tombstones. There looks like some small mounds ahead of him." He paused. "He's approaching the back — wait!"

The wizard squinted hard and appeared as if he was trying to focus on something in particular. "I see a gate! There's an entrance in the back! Rufus is there now, he's looking up." He paused again. "It's latched, but not locked! That's our way in!"

Harrison peered over at Murdock and Pondle. "We know where to go now."

Murdock nodded. "I agree, but we still don't know where the ruby's hidden."

Harrison's face dropped. "I didn't think of that. I was so worried about finding the cemetery that I didn't think of *where* the gem might be."

Gelderand turned his gaze toward the young warrior. "I can help with that, too." Before he could continue, a look of concern glazed his face.

Harrison noticed the strange expression. "Gelderand? What's wrong?"

"The soldiers have spotted Rufus again! They're trying to catch him!"

"What?" The young warrior's face wrinkled with disbelief. "Why are they bothering a cat?"

Gelderand stared at no one in particular. "I see three men, boys I should say. One is bending down to look at Rufus. He's extending his hand."

"Why are they attacking him?" said Harrison with a sigh.

"They're not. They're playing with him!" Gelderand's body jerked from his seat. "Someone's got him by the scruff of the neck!"

Murdock stared at Harrison. "This isn't good! We need to do something!"

Harrison looked down while thoughts raced through his mind. He noticed Lance lying at his feet and suddenly got an idea.

"Lance," he called, his command causing the dog to spring to his feet. "We need you to distract the soldiers. Can you do that?" The dog tilted his head and appeared confused.

"They're outside and they have Rufus." The others heard Harrison, but looked at him with dismay.

"I thought sending the cat to provide surveillance was a stupid idea," snapped Murdock, "but I see you're trying your best to top that."

Harrison glared at the ranger. "We can't afford to be seen! Besides, they won't think seeing a dog is suspicious."

Murdock cocked his head and said with a sarcastic tone, "Oh really? A dog rescuing a cat is suspicious to me."

Harrison looked at the ranger, but did not say anything. Instead, he turned his attention back to Lance. "Distract them, boy. Go!" Lance quickly scampered out of the house and proceeded to run in the direction of the soldiers.

Gelderand continued to work his spell. One of the men turned Rufus around and looked right at him. The mage could see the young man's mouth moving as he spoke to his comrades. He saw the person laugh, then he had the feeling of being tossed in the air.

Another soldier caught Rufus and brought him to his face. Gelderand could see that this man was also quite young, but did wear the clothing of a warrior. Just then, something grabbed the boy's attention.

Gelderand could hear Lance's barking in the distance, but he could not see him through Rufus's eyes. The soldier dropped the cat in order to address his new problem. The mage could see that Rufus stood on the ground under his own power and that the soldiers had left him alone. The cat gazed at the commotion and could see a dog holding his ground some distance away, while it barked at the group of men.

"Lance has their attention," said Gelderand. "Rufus is free!" The feline quickly darted away from the platoon and began to run through an alleyway.

"Is he all right?" asked Harrison with concern. Murdock, Swinkle, and Pondle listened to the two attentively.

Gelderand shrugged. "I don't know. Rufus has run away."

"We need to help Lance!"

Gelderand reached over and grabbed Harrison's arm. "We need to find Rufus first. I must break this spell."

Harrison nodded, agreeing with the wizard, though he knew he needed to help Lance, too. "Can you see where Rufus is now?"

Gelderand focused. "He's running between two buildings."

"Can you point out any landmarks?"

"No. He's turning a corner." Gelderand straightened up in his chair. "Wait a second!" The wizard stood and approached the back door of the home. He peered outside, then dropped to one knee.

"Rufus!" The cat sprang into his arms, meowing. Gelderand scratched the animal behind its ears. "You had quite an adventure!"

The mage mumbled something aloud. Harrison looked at Gelderand and noticed that his eyes had reverted to their original state.

"The spell is broken. We know where we need to go."

Harrison spread his arms apart. "What about Lance?" he asked with concern.

Murdock spoke up first. "We should leave. He might lead those soldiers here, too."

"Murdock's right," said Pondle. "The cat retraced his footsteps and Lance might do the same."

Harrison sighed, but nodded in agreement. "Let's go then."

The men exited the house, making sure they stayed out of view. Harrison's worry level rose since he no longer heard Lance barking. Pondle led the men closer to the soldiers, then held up his hand, gesturing for his friends to stop.

"Wait here in the alleyway." Pondle hugged the building, then peeked around the corner. After a moment, he slowly removed a dagger from his belt.

Harrison, noticing Pondle's maneuver, clutched his battle-axe. "What is it?" he whispered.

"I don't see Lance, but the place is crawling with soldiers. I'm not taking any chances."

Murdock broke his silence. "This is ludicrous! We need to regroup and hide, not accidentally expose ourselves!"

"I agree," said Pondle. "Murdock, take everyone back to the point where we entered this town. I'll get Lance."

"What?" yelled Murdock. "I'm not leaving you here with all these soldiers running around!"

"Just go. It's not safe here. We can't even attempt to find this treasure until after nightfall anyway."

Murdock squinted and glared at his friend. "We'll discuss this later." The ranger turned to the other men. "Follow me."

Before Harrison started to follow the others, he told Pondle to be careful. The thief nodded and motioned for him to leave.

With Harrison gone, Pondle turned his attention to finding Lance. Being a former thief, he knew how to make himself almost invisible to others. Pondle used an elaborate route to stay as far away from the soldiers as possible, crisscrossing through alleys, hiding behind buildings, several times doubling back in order to cover his tracks.

Pondle finally reached a point where he could see the soldiers again. He scanned the area, but there was no sign of Lance. The squad of men appeared to be performing drills and preparing for something. At least he didn't hear them shouting after the dog — a good sign, he thought.

Maneuvering closer to the cemetery, Pondle saw what Gelderand had related to them. A fence with iron stakes surrounded the burial ground, with an opening on the opposite side. The thief kept low to the ground as he left the refuge of the last building and scooted behind a large tree. From where he stood, he figured to be about two hundred feet from the campsite.

Peering around the tree, he could see that the woods stood about a hundred feet beyond the entrance to the cemetery, while the soldiers camped to the left of that area. Still, he could not see Lance anywhere. He was about to give up hope when he saw the little dog trotting out of an alleyway between two buildings to his left.

Lance looked from side to side, appearing confused. Pondle fixed his gaze on the soldiers and waited for the right time to trek back to the buildings. Remaining unseen, he continued toward Lance. The dog started to head in the opposite direction, but Pondle called to him before he could get too far away.

Lance's head spun around and Pondle thought he saw a smile appear on the animal's face. The dog ran over to him and jumped up to greet him.

"Down boy!" said Pondle, acknowledging the canine's salutation. "We wouldn't leave you behind. Follow me." The thief guided Lance away from the soldiers and started their trek back to the other men.

Unbeknownst to both of them, another set of eyes watched their every move. "I told you there was something strange about those animals," said a soldier to two of his comrades.

"Good work," said the other sentry. "You two follow them. I'll inform General Harkin about this little matter." With that, the fighters separated to perform their new tasks.

CHAPTER 18

Troy was sitting behind a makeshift table drawing battle plans with Teleios when one of his guards allowed a sentry to enter his tent.

"Sir, we have seen several men enter the town," began the guard, looking straight ahead. "And we have followed them to their camp."

Troy looked up from his sketches. "Where are they now?"

The young soldier did not hesitate to answer his leader. "On the outskirts of town, near the Cyprian River. I have two scouts watching them as we speak."

Troy nodded at his soldier, taking in the information. "Good work. Be sure to watch their every move and relay that information back to me."

"Yes, sir." The soldier then left Troy's tent.

Teleios had heard all of the new details. "We could capture them now. I'm sure we have enough men to overtake them."

Troy started writing on his parchment again. "I know we haven't seen anyone lurking around this town in three days. But we don't know for sure if these are the people we have been waiting for." The young general looked up from his work and faced his advisor. "I'm not going to harass innocent townspeople."

Teleios nodded in agreement. "I suppose so. Maybe we should assign more men to this surveillance task, nevertheless."

"I think we have enough. I don't want to alarm these townsfolk in any way. If this Harrison person is in town, we'll know."

Teleios nodded again. "Shall we share this information with Lord Hammer?"

Troy pondered the question for a moment. "Not yet. There's no need in alerting him until we get all the facts. Let's finish off these plans."

Nigel Hammer's temporary residence sat adjacent to Troy and Teleios's. Not being a person with much patience, Lord Hammer tried his best to rest in his encampment. Just after nightfall, he heard the sound of hoofbeats near his tent, followed by the sounds of muffled voices.

The governor of Concur rose from his chair and lit a few more candles in order to provide additional light. Someone cleared his throat just beyond the entrance to his shelter.

"Sir, you have a visitor," came the voice of one of his guards.

Nigel stood tall. "Send him in."

A person dressed in a dark, hooded robe pushed aside the canvas that covered the opening. Once inside, the man pulled down his hood, revealing his face.

Nigel's eyes widened with surprise, recognizing the man instantly. "Allard!" he exclaimed, offering his hand. "How was your journey?"

The middle-aged man shook hands with his leader. "Not as bad as I thought it would be," Allard said, raising an eyebrow.

Nigel motioned for him to take a seat in one of his chairs, before sitting himself. With great anticipation, he asked, "Have you discovered the meaning of The Prophecy?"

Allard nodded as he spoke. "In a manner of speaking, yes."

Nigel frowned. "I don't understand. Did you or didn't you?"

"I did not find the Scrolls of Arcadia, but I managed to uncover enough information that I believe is true."

Nigel leaned forward, almost unable to contain himself. "What have you found?"

Allard retrieved four scrolls of parchment from his pack and began to unravel them. He looked from one to another, but did not answer just yet.

Lord Hammer watched the mage scan the scrolls and tried his best not to get agitated at his slow pace. Finally, Allard faced him to speak.

"I needed to cross reference much of my findings with old scriptures. Many ancient writings contained similar passages, but I could not find everything in one place."

Nigel slapped the table, his voicing rising. "I understood that before you left! Tell me, wizard, what have you found?"

Nigel's outburst did not faze Allard. Staring at Lord Hammer, he said, "The Prophecy states that brothers will reunite the land. They will assemble an army and advance using the same battle route as the ancient Four Kings. The war will be long and will culminate against a fortified city. Before the mighty fortress falls, another force will arrive, and all beings will be called to join the fight."

Nigel could not believe Allard's report. "How can that be? There's no mention of me in what you have said!"

Allard had become accustomed to Nigel's quick temper. Remaining calm, he placed the scrolls down and looked at his governor.

"Nigel, the prophecy foretells that a battle will occur against a fortified city. Is this not Concur?"

Lord Hammer looked up in thought again. He lusted to be the man who owned the Treasure, who ruled the land alone. But what if it was not meant to be? At least the scriptures mentioned a great battle must be fought and, if it were to happen in his city, he might be able to change the outcome of the future.

Nigel lowered his gaze to Allard. "If what you say is true," he started, holding back his rage, "then my being here is pointless. I need to go back to my city and prepare for what is to come."

Allard slowly nodded, sensing that Nigel had come to grips with his findings. "That would be the most prudent course of action."

Nigel scowled and squinted. "There is one problem," he said, rubbing his beard. "I have aligned myself with this General Troy Harkin to find Harrison, the one who has the treasure as we speak."

Allard gestured with a wave of his hand. "Nigel, it makes no difference who has the treasure now. You are not *supposed* to obtain it at this time."

The governor nodded. "You're right. We will leave tomorrow morning. I will inform Troy that you have arrived here to tell me of an emergency situation in Concur and that I must return immediately."

"That sounds fine to me. Be thankful you have been alerted to this now and not before it became too late."

Nigel's expression remained unchanged. "You may stay here tonight. I will speak to Troy in the morning." The two men then settled in for the evening and waited for daybreak to arrive.

Harrison and his friends had wanted to enter the cemetery under the cover of darkness, but they soon realized that would be impossible since they would need the benefit of torches, which would alert the soldiers to their presence. Instead, they awoke before dawn and readied themselves to enter the sacred sight while the soldiers still slept in their tents.

Pondle convened everyone together prior to trekking to the burial ground. "Be sure to follow me closely. I'm going to be able to see much better than any of you for some time."

"We'll be right behind you," said Murdock. "Are we ready to leave?"

The rest of the men did a final check of their gear and with everyone satisfied, they broke camp. Pondle and Lance proceeded to lead the group, followed by the others.

One of Troy's sentries noticed the group's movements. "They're leaving," he said to his comrade. "We'll follow them. You go alert General Harkin."

The second soldier hurried off to complete his task, while the two other scouts followed Harrison's group from a safe distance.

Pondle took the men on a wide, elaborate route through the city of Cyprus. The thief knew that the cemetery sat at the opposite side of town, which gave him the luxury of keeping him and his friends out of plain view.

Harrison recognized the scores of buildings, ranging from residential huts, to fine eating establishments and weapon shops. On their way through the town, Pondle brought them close to the statue they had seen in Martinaeous's crystal ball.

Though it remained dark, Harrison could tell that the bronze figure was that of a king adorned with a crown and royal robe. The young warrior strained through the darkness at the confident, regal face, as the figure proudly pointed into the distance. Harrison thought that the king appeared to look toward the future with hope and confidence.

The statue stood on a chiseled rock that contained a plaque. Harrison squinted through the shadows again and did his best to read the block lettering. *All hail, King Ballesteros. May his town remember him and all his good works throughout eternity.*

Harrison thought back to the ancient manuscript that Philius, his old mentor from Aegeus, had given him the night before his quest. He recalled seeing the king trying to flee his besieged castle and wondered if Ballesteros ever truly enjoyed his wealth and prosperity.

The young warrior passed the sculpture and started to head to yet another alleyway with his friends. Before continuing his trek, though, something sparked Harrison's subconscious and he turned to gaze at the figure again. Is he pointing to the future, or is he pointing to — the cemetery, thought Harrison. The young warrior looked in the opposite direction, where Pondle led them. He focused as best he could in the pre-dawn light and saw that, indeed, the burial ground sat in the direction Ballesteros pointed. A smile came to Harrison's face and he felt certain that they were following the right course.

"Assemble the men," said Troy, rising from his bed and fetching his armor. "But do so as inconspicuously as possible. I will alert Lord Hammer." The scout nodded in response to Troy's command and left the tent.

Troy was securing his chain-mail armor when Teleios entered his space. "What is happening?"

Troy picked up his gauntlets and placed them on his hands. "The party that we've been watching is on the move."

Teleios appeared confused. "I thought you did not want to harass innocent people?"

"My sentries saw them sneaking in this direction. It's awful early to be trekking, unless you don't wish to be seen."

Teleios shook his head, knowing that he could say nothing to change his leader's mind. "What are you proposing to do?"

"We'll intercept them," Troy said, retrieving his sword, "and question them about their intentions."

"They will become suspicious if they see all of the soldiers scurrying about," said Teleios, knowing Troy had not taken the time to think things through.

Troy took a moment to ponder what his advisor had said. "You're right. I'll pick a small contingent of men to come with us. The rest will fall back and wait for my orders."

Teleios agreed with his leader's rationale. "You better relay that information to Nigel."

Troy sheathed his sword. "I was about to do that right now. Let's go." With that, the two men left the tent and went to Lord Hammer's encampment.

Pondle approached the cemetery from the north and used his infravision to see the soldiers' campsites to their right, a good hundred yards away.

The thief scanned the immediate area. "All right, listen. There are a couple of homes in front of us, and behind them are the woods. We can go from building to building without being seen, but then we need to take cover behind those trees."

Harrison strained to see the landscape. The sun remained below the horizon and the pre-dawn sky had just started to glow. "I still can't see too far in front of me."

"Don't worry; I'll be your eyes."

The young warrior turned to the other men. "Gelderand, Swinkle, like always, stay close to me."

Before they could leave, Swinkle spoke. "What are we going to look for when we get to the burial ground? We need to find the jewel, then get away from there as fast as possible."

Gelderand stepped forward while the others pondered Swinkle's statement. "I am sure that whoever hid the ruby must have used magic. I must try to find where this aura is radiating from. We can locate the gem after I ascertain that."

"Can you do this quickly?" said Murdock with concern. "Those soldiers will be moving soon."

"I will try my best."

Murdock shook his head. "Let's get this over with."

Pondle took the ranger's statement as his cue to move the group closer to their destination. The men ventured as silent as possible to the coverage of the woods.

Harrison found the soldiers to be out of sight, with only a couple of sentries on duty. Behind the encampment stood the iron fence that enclosed the cemetery, as well as a thick mist that enveloped the grounds beyond the closed in area. Stealthily, the men trekked through the woods, getting closer to their goal.

Unbeknownst to them, Troy, Teleios, Nigel and their small group of men watched the party's every move.

"Let's surprise them now," said Nigel, squinting into the darkness. Though he did not mention it to Allard, he had hoped to confront Harrison again, even more so if his nemesis was one of the people they now watched. "We have the upper hand. They will be easily overtaken."

Troy gazed at the movements of the silent figures. "Not just yet," he said, not bothering to look back at Lord Hammer. "They appear to be maneuvering in some way."

Troy watched the lead man position himself on the opposite side of the burial ground, well away from his campsite.

"The first man is investigating the fence of the cemetery." Troy strained to focus on something else. "He has a dog with him."

Nigel's face went blank. Harrison had a dog the last time I saw him, he recalled. A rage began to boil deep inside the warrior, knowing that his adversary might very well be only fifty yards away.

Troy spoke again. "He's waving the others on. I see one, two, three — three more people are with him!" The young general squinted again. "This fog might hinder our surveillance."

Nigel tried to recall how many men traveled with Harrison, but he could not remember. "What do you plan on doing?"

Troy paused. "They're entering the cemetery! Let's use this mist to our advantage. We can surround the grounds with the rest of our men without them seeing us. They won't escape now."

Nigel began to rise from his position. "What are we waiting for? Let's advance from our position!"

"Not just yet," said Troy, looking back at Nigel. "They're obviously looking for something and they're trying to elude us on purpose. Let's let them find what they are looking for, then we can capture them and take their prize, too." Troy continued to peer at his advisor who nodded his approval.

Nigel crouched back down, grimacing. He did not enjoy taking orders from anyone, especially from someone Troy's age. "I agree with you on this strategy, too. Just remember our deal."

Troy gazed at Nigel and saw the older warrior glaring at him. "If this is the party we've been waiting for, you'll get your prisoner, then you can be on your way."

"Good." Nigel kept his stare on Troy. "Position your men."

Troy glared back at Nigel. Neither man flinched. Finally, the younger leader removed his gaze from Lord Hammer and toward one of his sentries.

"Go tell both camps to surround the cemetery. Tell them to do it quietly and not to enter the grounds until you hear my command."

"Yes, sir," said the soldier before scampering off to fulfill his task.

Troy looked over to Nigel again. "We'll wait until everyone is in position, then we'll go after them." Nigel nodded in concurrence and waited along with the others.

Pondle led his friends through the cemetery's entrance, comfortably away from the soldiers' encampment. After he guided everyone through the gates, he had them stop for a moment.

The thief looked about the area, noticing that the thick mist would help conceal the group. "We're inside. Gelderand, it's your turn now."

Gelderand took a couple of steps further into the burial site, gazing at the moss-covered tombstones and the high unkempt vegetation growth.

Turning back to his friends, he said, "I'm going to recite a spell that I hope will lead us to the exact spot."

Murdock looked at him with disbelief. "If there was magic here at one time, wouldn't it have worn off by now?"

"Magic doesn't wear off. The spell must be broken." The older man then closed his eyes and chanted. A minute later, he opened them wide. Without saying a word, he began to walk away from the men.

Harrison looked at the mage, then back at his friends. The others shrugged, not understanding what was happening either.

Swinkle saw the look of confusion on their faces. In a whisper, he said, "Quietly follow him. The magical aura is drawing him to it."

Gelderand continued his trek through the cemetery, passing tombstone after tombstone, moving closer to the larger mounds at the back of the burial site.

Harrison watched the mage maneuver and saw that he headed for one of three tombs. The mist made it difficult to see too far into the distance, but the young warrior noticed that the mounds stood about ten feet wide and rose ten feet high.

Gelderand walked down a small slope that led to the front of the grave to finally halt in front of the rightmost mound. A large black, iron door prohibited him from entering the tomb.

The older man shook his head, ending his spell. "This is it," he said, approaching the door. "There is a faint magical aura radiating from this entrance. I'm sure it is stronger on the inside."

Murdock joined Gelderand, as the two of them examined the portal. The ranger noticed a round, iron ring that posed as a handle on the right side of the door.

"Shall I open it?"

Pondle stopped his friend. "Wait. Give me time to check for traps."

Murdock nodded and moved away from the doorway. Gelderand did likewise. Harrison noticed that the older man continue to stare in thought at the portal.

"What's the matter?"

"I think this door is sealed."

Harrison looked at the closed entryway. "I can see that it is."

The mage shook his head. "No, I mean magically."

Pondle stepped back. "It appears to be trap free. Murdock, try and open the door."

The ranger grabbed the handle and gave it a firm tug. The door did not budge.

Murdock looked back at his friends, then encircled the ring with two hands, but no matter how hard he pulled, the door would not move.

After struggling for a moment, he shook his head in disgust. "That door is shut tight! We're not going to get it open this way."

Gelderand held his chin in his hand. "That's because it's magically sealed, like I expected."

Murdock shot him a look of exasperation. "Then why did you have me go through all this trouble?"

Gelderand smiled. "Because you always think in physical terms instead of mental. I told you I sensed an aura here."

Murdock frowned, knowing the mage was right. "Do what you need to do."

Gelderand approached the door again and positioned his hands on the cold exterior, then leaned closer, placing his right ear on the metal surface. He lightly tapped the portal, hearing a faint echo on the other side.

The mage went into his backpack. Finding the necessary ingredient for his spell, he took the dough-like substance in his hand and smeared it on the doorway near the handle. Next, he placed both hands on the door and began to chant.

Harrison watched as the mage mumbled in what sounded like a foreign tongue. A light purple hue began to envelope the portal, with a darker concentration appearing around the ring.

The young warrior gazed at the wizard and noticed beads of sweat springing from his brow. The older man continued his mantra, then began to shake.

Suddenly, Gelderand stopped his chant. A faint depressurizing sound emanated from behind the doorway before the mage fell to the ground.

"Gelderand!" said Harrison as he and the others came to the wizard's aid. The young warrior held Gelderand in his arms and peered into his eyes.

"Are you all right?" he said, the worry evident in his voice.

Gelderand's words came out as a whisper. "I have negated the magic," he said, before swallowing and closing his eyes. "Open the doorway."

Harrison looked up at Murdock and Pondle, who had heard the wizard's statements, too. The young warrior nodded and the two men approached the entrance.

Harrison peered back at Gelderand. "Are you sure you're all right?"

"I will be. I need rest now."

The young warrior smiled. "I told Tara I would keep an eye on you and I'm not going back on my word now."

Gelderand chuckled, happy to hear Harrison mention his niece. "You go with the others. Have Swinkle stay with me."

Harrison nodded and allowed his friend to care for Gelderand. "Let me know if you need anything."

"I will," said Swinkle, helping Gelderand get comfortable.

Harrison looked over to Murdock and Pondle. "Open the door."

The ranger grabbed the handle and pulled with all his might. This time the doorway opened with ease.

Pondle peered in first. "It's very dark, but a staircase leads down. You two will need torches to see."

Harrison fumbled through his pack, retrieved the items, then lit them. After handing one to Murdock, he gazed at the thief and said, "Lead us on."

Before Pondle entered the tomb, Harrison called to Lance. "You stay with Gelderand and Swinkle. If anything happens, come and get us." The dog barked once and wagged his tail.

Harrison nodded at Pondle, and with that, the three men started their trek. The young warrior entered the tomb last, following Pondle and Murdock. He held his torch high, providing enough light to see the buildup of cobwebs inside the dank, muddy grave. To his surprise, he did not see a casket or anything that would resemble the resting place for a king. Instead, a dirt staircase led them deeper into the tomb.

The stairs were small and the passageway tight. After only ten steps, the three men found themselves in a dirt corridor that went deeper under the ground.

Murdock strained to see ahead of him, but all that existed were cobwebs and earth. "Pondle, is there anything up ahead?"

The thief hesitated before answering. "It's opening up. I see something!"

Harrison followed his friends into a larger room. Pointing with his torch, he said, "That's exactly what I expected to see down here."

A casket sat on top of a stone structure, but even as Harrison looked at it, he still could not believe that a revered ruler rested here. "Does this look fitting for a king?"

Pondle examined the casket. "Not at all."

Crafters had forged the box out of a metal alloy, but he could not find anything that would signify the resting place of royalty.

"I expected to see ornate designs, fine craftsmanship, or something like that." The thief shook his head. "I would expect to be buried in something like this!"

Murdock noticed something on the wall behind the casket. "What's this?" he asked, walking around the structure. He placed his torch near the dirt barrier, allowing enough light for all to see a cobweb-covered plaque. Taking his hand, he removed the webs, revealing a stone tribute.

Harrison gazed at the inscription before speaking aloud. *"Here lies the body of our great king, Ballesteros. For it is he who fought off the Scribes and Gammorians, preserving our land with his lords Solaris, Nicodemus, and Holleris.*

"May the land and all its good, shine as bright as the mountain of King Solaris for all eternity. For those who understand, the Eye of the Crown lies with the light."

Murdock spoke first. "That last line is a clue!"

Harrison reread the writing to himself. "I agree, but a mountain doesn't shine, right?"

Murdock crinkled his brow in thought. "That doesn't make sense to me either."

Pondle walked over to the plaque and pointed to the word "bright." "It does make sense. Remember, one of the clues stated that a huge explosion has taken place. I bet you it happened on this King Solaris's mountain."

Harrison heartily agreed. "Yes! That has to be it! It makes perfect sense now!"

Murdock nodded in agreement. "Fine, I can live with that, but aren't we forgetting something? Where's this red jewel?"

All three men looked at the casket, then at each other. "It's in there," said Harrison, pointing to the box.

Pondle surveyed the resting place of the king. "I don't see anything out of the ordinary." Shaking his head, he said, "But there must be magic here."

Murdock approached the casket. "I agree, but we haven't come this far to turn back now. Harrison, help me lift this cover."

The young warrior placed his hands on the lid along with Murdock. On a count of three, they raised the cover, allowing a soft red radiance to emanate from the box.

Harrison's eyes widened. "Well, I'll be —"

"I'm not surprised by this at all," said Murdock, shaking his head in awe. Instead of seeing the remains of King Ballesteros, a large ruby hovered inside the casket, casting an eerie red glow throughout the room.

Suddenly, the sound of Lance barking startled the men. Harrison looked toward the passageway. "That can't be good. His barks are getting closer!"

Pondle rushed to the entranceway. "He's entered the tomb!" The thief ran to the casket. "Let's take this gem and leave!"

Murdock looked at his friend's worried face. "Grab it!"

Pondle snatched the jewel from its resting place. The red light ceased, but another transformation started.

"What's happening?" asked Harrison.

Before anyone could venture a guess, Lance entered the room, followed by Swinkle's voice. "Someone help us!"

Harrison and Murdock raced to the passageway and intercepted Swinkle and Gelderand. Lance continued to make nervous yaps.

Gelderand had his arm slung over the young cleric's shoulders. "Swinkle, what's the matter?" asked Harrison with concern as he rushed to help his friend.

"People are advancing toward us!" he said in a panic. "We're trapped!"

Pondle let the others tend to Swinkle and Gelderand while he examined the mysterious wall to the right of the casket. The dirt was slowly transforming into a translucent state, then disappearing altogether to reveal a new room.

A bright flash appeared, followed by a constant dim light. Pondle raised his hands to protect his face, afraid that something might fly out at him. Instead, a pylon appeared in the middle of the room.

"Give me a moment," the thief said as he approached the new room. He noticed that the pylon sat on a circular pattern on the floor, and ten smaller markings containing five-pointed stars surrounded that one. Looking up, he noticed another plaque on the far wall.

Just then, everyone heard the sounds of people storming the tomb. "Hurry, everyone get in here!" yelled the thief.

Murdock ran in first, followed by Lance. Harrison and Swinkle helped drag Gelderand to the back of the room. The three fighters then drew their weapons.

Swinkle gazed at the pylon and patterns in bewilderment. "What does this mean?" he lamented. The sounds of heavy steps became louder.

Gelderand looked up and read the inscription to Swinkle. "State the name of the Treasure's creator."

The young cleric gave the older man a quizzical look. "What?"

"It says to state the name of the Treasure's creator." Gelderand mustered all the strength he had to get up. "Everyone, stand on a circle!"

Harrison, Murdock, and Pondle looked back at the mage. "What? Why?" asked the young warrior, keeping an eye on the doorway.

"No time to explain," said the mage between ragged breaths. "Do it!"

The three men did as Gelderand commanded, with Harrison positioning Lance on a pattern of his own. Just then, the first intruder entered the space. His eyes locked onto Harrison's immediately.

Harrison recognized him at once, but instead of a confrontation, the man gave him a look of utter confusion. The expression soon disappeared from his face. Lord Nigel Hammer pointed his sword at the young warrior.

"Harrison Cross, your days of adventure are over!" Just then, several more men entered the tomb, but instead of charging, they held their ground in disbelief.

Teleios entered the area next, followed by Troy. Everyone stood in stunned silence. Nigel glared at Harrison, then back at Troy. The men were identical.

"What is the meaning of this?" Lord Hammer demanded.

Troy and Harrison locked their gaze on each other. Harrison's mouth fell open, unable to speak. Troy remained frozen in his spot.

Gelderand broke the uncomfortable silence, whispering to the young warrior, "Harrison, who created the Treasure?"

The young warrior snapped out of his trance. "Huh? Maligor, why?"

At that instant, the stars glowed green followed by a bright flash, then Harrison and his men disappeared. A moment later, the star-like patterns vanished from the ten circles and the pylon transformed into solid rock, resembling a stalagmite in a cave.

"No! Wait!" exclaimed Troy as he raced into the room. He desperately searched the area, but the men were gone.

As Nigel watched Troy, he recalled what Allard had told him that brothers would unite the land and knew he must leave Troy, at this very moment.

"Troy!" he barked. "They are gone. There's no use scouring for them here."

Troy looked at Lord Hammer, then Teleios. Sporting a wicked scowl, he walked over to Nigel with a purpose.

"You knew all along about this! Why didn't you tell me?" Troy stood to glare at Nigel, no more than a foot away.

The governor did not back down. "I needed to be sure myself! I could care less if Harrison is your twin or not!"

Troy let Nigel's comment sink in, but still stared at him. "You deceived me."

Lord Hammer let out a small laugh. "Deceived you? On the contrary, I brought you closer to him and his men than you would have on your own." Both men kept their stare. "Harrison is gone and my city needs me. This alliance is over. We both failed."

"So be it," said Troy. "I will find them without your assistance." Nigel held his gaze for another moment, then turned away and headed out of the tomb.

The young general watched the older warrior depart, before taking his stare to the rocky formation. Teleios felt his commander's confusion and came by his side.

"We need to press on," said Troy's advisor. "There must be a clue here. The king would not want us to stop."

Troy took a deep breath and raised his head, but stared straight ahead. "The king must know about this, too. Why would he have kept this from me?"

Teleios did not know what to say. "I'm sure the king had no idea —"

"Don't stick up for him," snarled Troy. "Something's not right about this whole situation. I can feel it." He paused, then looked around the room. "We must find Harrison and his group."

Troy turned his attention to the casket and the plaque above it. He read it to himself, then asked Teleios, "What do you think this means?"

Teleios reread the scripture. "I don't know. I've never heard of a mountain of King Solaris, but the range in the southern portion of the land is named after him."

"The Eye of the Crown lies with the light," Troy mumbled to himself. "Teleios, we will head for that mountain range."

Troy's advisor gave his leader an incredulous stare. "Troy, it will take us weeks to travel to that part of the land! If this group of men did end up there, they might be gone before we'd even arrive!"

The young general understood his advisor's rationale, but he had other plans. "This is where we must go and we will." Troy paused. "There are a lot of questions that need answering."

Troy ordered his men, other than Teleios, out of the tomb. After they departed, he looked around one last time before staring at his advisor.

"The king has a lot of explaining to do." The two men then exited the room and prepared for their southern trek.

CHAPTER 19

Harrison stood in amazement. No, more in total shock. Did I just see my identical twin or did I witness some kind of illusion, he wondered. Everyone glued their eyes on the young warrior, as they all stood in the exact position that they had in the room just seconds ago, except now they found themselves in an area filled with overgrowth.

Swinkle approached Harrison first. "I saw what you saw," he said, searching for the right words.

Harrison stared straight ahead, his hands still clutching his weapon. "That was my … *brother!*"

The young warrior did not remember ever having a brother, or any siblings for that matter. His parents never mentioned a twin, as far as he could recollect. Nevertheless, burned into his memory was the image of the man in his exact likeness. Just then, Pondle joined the two.

"Harrison," he said calmly, "he belonged with those men who were milling about Cyprus. They were searching for the book that we possess. He'll be back."

Pondle waited to see if the young warrior's expression would change, but Harrison's demeanor did not.

Gelderand and Murdock stepped forward as well. "We have to leave this area," said Murdock with urgency. "Those men might manage to work that device the way we did. They could be here any moment."

Pondle agreed with Murdock. "We need to take refuge now."

Harrison panned from side to side, snapping out of his trance. "I know, I know. Let's find a place to hide in case they do appear."

Pondle, sensing that the young warrior was thinking clearly again, said, "Good. Everyone, follow me."

Pondle led the men to a spot where the underbrush thinned the most, guiding them about a hundred yards away from the site. Feeling a bit more secure, he had them stop.

The thief positioned the men behind him, then peered back in the direction from which they came. "Let's wait here and see what happens."

Away from the others, Swinkle approached Harrison. "Gelderand is withdrawn and out of breath. He needs complete rest."

The young warrior looked back at the mage and could see that he struggled to stand. "We must secure the area, Swinkle. Until then, he needs to keep his guard up."

Swinkle gazed back at his friend. "We need to talk about this episode later."

"Indeed."

Pondle and Murdock joined the two men. "We're going to survey the area and try to get a fix on where we are," said the ranger. "You two stay with Gelderand until we get back."

Harrison nodded in agreement. "We'll keep Lance with us, just in case." The little dog sat by his master's side.

"Fine with me. Pondle, let's go." With that, the two men disappeared into the thickets.

Harrison lowered his weapon and his pack. Swinkle and Gelderand made themselves comfortable as well. The young warrior sat on the ground, using his backpack for support, then stared into the woods, deep in thought.

Swinkle spoke to his friend. "Harrison, I know you must have a million thoughts running through your head right now."

"You can say that again." The young warrior turned and faced Swinkle. "Tell me the truth, was that man for real or was he an illusion."

"He looked real to me."

"Most definitely," added Gelderand.

Swinkle tried in earnest to help Harrison as best he could. "Did your parents ever mention a brother?"

The young warrior looked up in thought, recalling his earliest memories of his parents playing with him when he was a very little boy. "There never was a hint of another child. Never. I can't remember an instance in my life where I could even question this."

Swinkle crinkled his brow in thought. "Could it be we are mistaken? Maybe he just had a strong resemblance to you."

Gelderand responded before the young warrior could. "No. That person is Harrison's twin. Did you see the look on the soldiers' faces, on ours, on his?"

"And Lord Hammer's," said Harrison. "How does he fit into all of this?"

Swinkle shook his head. "I was wondering that myself."

"Could he have had some prior knowledge of my twin?"

The young cleric shrugged. "I don't know, but my gut feeling is that he does not. He also had a brief look of shock on his face."

Harrison remained silent for a moment. "I wonder what his name is."

"I have the feeling we will find out before too long."

Just then, Lance stirred from his seat on the ground. He sprang to his feet to head off in Pondle and Murdock's direction.

Harrison grabbed his battle-axe. "You two stay here." Lance suddenly reappeared from the brush, followed by their two friends.

"We found some interesting designs," Murdock said, slinging his quiver of arrows off his shoulder. The ranger pointed into the woods. "Ten stone circles, about the same size as the ones we left in that chamber."

Harrison squinted, thinking. "We must have used them to get here."

"That's what Pondle and I believe, too," the ranger said. "We waited to see if those soldiers would reappear, but they never did."

"I wonder why that is."

Gelderand spoke from his seat on the ground. "When we uttered the appropriate word, we triggered the teleportation spell, as well as negating its magic."

Harrison stared at the mage. "So they can't use the device either?"

Gelderand nodded slowly. "That's what I believe. They're not following us, at least not in the manner we arrived here."

Pondle stepped forward. "Which leads us to the next question. Where is here?"

The men looked at each other, all with the same blank expression. Harrison let out a sigh. "It's still early in the morning. Let's give Gelderand a chance to regain his strength before we continue on."

Everyone agreed with the young warrior, and while Pondle and Murdock set up a makeshift camp, the rest of the men pondered their new predicament.

Gelderand felt much stronger by mid-morning and after a large meal, the group began their search for a way out of the woods. Pondle guided his friends through the thickets and, before too long, he found a well-worn path.

Pondle examined the markings on the ground. "We're close to a town, that's for sure." Footprints, horse tracks, and cart impressions littered the dirt pathway.

"Let's follow this trail," said Harrison. "With a little luck, it'll lead us to a place we know."

The men spent less than an hour following the footpath until the woods opened up to a larger area. Harrison looked around in amazement.

"This place is a mess," he said, scanning the immediate countryside. "Are those homes or shacks?"

The dilapidated buildings surprised Swinkle, too. "They appear to belong to the townspeople."

Harrison shook his head in disgust. He saw the battered huts, unkempt landscaping and free-roaming livestock. Several horses stood tied to posts with short leads. Harrison could see the ribs of the poor beasts and wondered how long they had been deprived of food.

The young warrior kept a hand on the hilt of his weapon as they wandered past the buildings. Chickens clucked and darted across the muddy path, goats bahhed and roamed free, while mangy dogs barked at the men as they strained from short leashes secured to iron posts. Even Lance held back, sensing the suffering in the animals.

Harrison avoided a pile of slop. "This place is despicable!"

"The sooner we find out where we are the better," said Murdock.

Just then, a man wielding a small hand axe came through a door from one of the buildings. "Git off my property!" he yelled, waving the weapon.

Harrison looked at the disheveled, middle-aged man with disbelief. Gazing at the residence, he could see little heads peeking through the half-closed shutters and a women glancing from the doorway.

The young warrior took a step toward the person. "We mean you no harm," he said, while his friends stopped and held their ground. "We only wish to pass through."

The man came closer, a crazed look in his eye. Using a hand to brush his uncombed hair away from his eyes, he exclaimed, "That's what y'all say! Git out! Git out!"

Harrison raised his battle-axe. "Back down! This is your only warning!" The man's eyes opened wide upon seeing the glistening blade.

The fellow lowered his much smaller weapon, then let it drop from his hand. Harrison could see a look of desperation on the poor soul's face.

"There ain't no more to take," he said, on the verge of tears. "Please, take me and leave my family alone."

Harrison glanced back at his friends with a look of confusion. "We don't want anything. We just want to find out where we are."

The man sighed. "Roxburg," he said. "You're in Roxburg."

Murdock spoke first. "Roxburg?" He scanned the area, finding nothing but filth and battered structures. "I thought Roxburg was an elite city."

The man shook his head. "Many years ago that mighta been true. Not now." Again, he appeared as if he wanted to cry.

"The elders take my land, my crops, and leave me to fend for myself. I ain't got the strength to fight'em and I gotta wife and three kids to feed. They'll be back later today to take whatever else they want."

Harrison felt great pity. "I'm sorry but there's nothing that any of us can do to help you." The man nodded, sensing the truth in his statements.

The young warrior reached for a sack on his belt, untied it, and let three gold pieces fall into his hand. "We've been venturing for a while and our supplies are running low. These coins are for you if you can lead us in the direction of a supply shop."

The man's eyes widened at first, then he sighed and looked to the ground. "There ain't but a few stores that you speak of. Everyone here shares the same heartache."

"Not even one?" Harrison could not believe that no stores existed.

The man raised a finger. "I suppose there's one good ole honest man I could lead ya to. His name's Philip Stoneham. He's gotta shop a little ways up the trail." The townsman looked at Harrison. "Keep to the outskirts a town. The elders don't have a likin' to strangers."

"Thank you." Harrison held out his hand. "Take the coins."

The man seemed embarrassed at first, but quickly snatched the money from the young warrior. "Rememba, keep outta sight as best you can."

Harrison and his friends bid the man thanks and proceeded further into the town. "How can these people be living in squalor?" asked the young warrior to no one in particular.

Swinkle shook his head, just as amazed. "Oppression can break one's spirit." Several downtrodden townspeople cast guarded glances toward the men entering their town.

From an alleyway, a large dog lunged from his thick chain with vicious barks aimed toward Lance. The small dog nervously yapped back.

Gelderand tried not to make eye contact with the people. "We must heed that poor man's advice. I don't like the looks of this place."

Harrison took in the sights around him. "I agree."

Pondle and Murdock, who advanced several steps ahead of the others, made an abrupt stop. The ranger pointed to a sign a few buildings up.

"That must be the place." A tattered sign with a broken hook leaving the placard to dangle in a precarious position hung from a pole off one of the buildings.

"Stoneham Supplies," said Pondle. "The man mentioned a Philip Stoneham, right?"

Harrison nodded. "Yes, he did."

The group approached the doorway and entered the shop. The men ventured in separate directions, looking for anything that appeared usable.

The messiness of the store took Harrison by surprise. The young warrior walked over to a table and picked up a small, rusted sword. Bringing it close to his face, he examined the damage to the hilt, its blade broken and unsharpened.

"How can the owners expect anyone to buy this garbage?"

Swinkle inspected some stacks of grain. "These bags are torn. They will rip if I even attempt to pick them up."

At that moment, a disheveled-looking teenage boy entered through a doorway behind the main counter. He panned the room with nervous eyes, before saying, "You need help with anythin'?"

Swinkle approached the counter. "I am trying to find some medicinal herbs and my friends are looking for supplies to take into the wilderness. Unfortunately, I don't see anything of worth lying around."

The boy remained uncomfortable, looking past the young cleric and at the warriors. "We don't got herbs here. We only got whatcha see."

Swinkle nodded in acknowledgement before something caught his eye. On a shelf behind the boy rested a cobweb-covered piece of wood. Swinkle squinted, trying to get a better feel for what the artifact looked like.

There is something familiar about that relic, he thought. "Thank you," he said to the young man, who nodded but kept his eye on the others.

Swinkle turned around, took a few steps back, then went into his pack. Retrieving the sacred scripture, he leafed to the pages that contained the clues to the treasure. Once there, he stared at one page in particular, then looked away in concentration.

The young cleric gazed at his friends, watching them mill about the shop with disgusted looks on their faces. He closed the book and put it back in his knapsack.

Turning back to the boy behind the counter, he pointed to the artifact and said, "Might I have a better look at that piece?"

The young man's face dropped and his coloring faded. "You wanna look at this?" The boy pointed at the relic, his eyes wide and his hand shaking.

Swinkle appeared very confused. "Yes, I do. Is there something wrong?"

The boy attempted to speak, but no words came out. Instead, he raced from the store through the door behind the counter.

Swinkle heard the stomping of his feet as he ran off. "Papa!" came a muffled voice. "Come to the store! Come to the store!"

The young cleric peered back at his friends, who seemed oblivious to the sudden strange course of events. Lance poked his head from around a table and Swinkle waved him over.

Lance sat next to the young cleric, who gave the dog a gentle pat on his head. "Stay next to me, just in case."

Swinkle heard the rumbling of heavy feet approach the doorway, followed by a deep voice. "What is it, boy? Whatcha want?"

"In the store," came the younger man's voice. Then in a hushed tone, "They wanna see that old piece a junk."

Swinkle leaned over the counter to better hear the muffled sounds coming from behind the door. After a brief moment of silence, he heard the deeper resonance again.

"You mean the one on the shelf?"

"Yes."

A heavy-set man burst into the room, almost knocking Swinkle off his feet and causing Lance to jump back. He scanned the shop, taking in the startled faces from all corners of the room.

The owner looked over to the boy. "Who asked to see the thing?" The frightened youth pointed to Swinkle.

A large smile, revealing several missing teeth, appeared on the unshaven face of the storeowner. "You wanna see this?" he said, pointing to the artifact.

Swinkle nodded. "Yes." By this time, the other group members began to congregate about the counter.

The burly man peered at the advancing men. "They with ya?" he said, shifting his eyes to the others.

Swinkle gazed back to see apprehensive expressions on his friends' faces. The young cleric saw Harrison make a subtle move to the hilt of his weapon.

The young cleric faced the owner again. "Yes, they are." Swinkle wrinkled his brow. "Is there a problem?"

The man smiled again. "I'm Philip Stoneham," he said, extending his hand. "It's an honor to meetcha!" Swinkle took hold of the man's hand, who in turn gripped it hard and gave it a vigorous shake. Philip pointed to the young man.

"This is my boy James." The teenager gave a sheepish nod of acknowledgement. Philip turned to his son. "Lock the doors!"

At that command, Harrison spoke up. "Why are you closing the store?"

Philip gave the young warrior an incredulous look. "We don't want anyone else comin' in! Don'tcha understand?"

Harrison shook his head. "Understand what?"

Philip leaned over the counter, looking side to side as if he were going to tell the young warrior a secret. In a hushed voice, he said, "The legend."

Harrison cocked his head, recognizing what the man alluded to. "I think we know what you're getting at. Tell me what you know of this legend."

Philip stepped back. "Not here," he said, then motioned for his son to lock the door. The shopkeeper grabbed the relic from the shelf and told the men to follow him.

James disappeared through the door behind the counter, followed by his father and the rest of the men. Harrison squeezed through a cramped hallway filled with worthless items and strewn debris. Philip led them up a rickety staircase that led to another part of the building.

James reached the top of the stairs first and opened the only door in the foyer. Philip followed next. "We live up here," said the elder Stoneham before shouting into the room. "Victoria, we have company!"

Philip looked back at Harrison. "Come on in."

Harrison led his men into Philip's home where he found yet another mess. Aged artifacts lay around the old furniture with stacks of useless items filling tables. Just then, a woman of about thirty-five entered the room. The young warrior gazed at the woman's worn face, sensing that her hard life had stolen the beauty of her youth.

"Did ya say —" she started, but stopped in mid-sentence when she saw the adventurers. "Philip, how couldya bring these people up here!"

Philip flashed a wide smile. "These are them! The ones!"

Victoria's dark brown eyes lit up. "Did ya say the ones? Like in the stories you been tellin' me all the time?"

Philip nodded empathically, almost unable to contain himself. "Yes! These are them!"

The woman gave the men a closer look. Shrugging, she said, "I guess I expected somethin' more."

Harrison still appeared confused, but looking at these people, he could see that years of oppression had taken a toll on them. A little girl, no more than four, tiptoed into the room and clung to her mother's leg.

Philip beamed. "This is my baby, Crystal." The little girl gazed up at the men with big, brown eyes. Wisps of russet hair shaped her face. Locking her gaze on Lance, she waved to the little dog. Lance wagged his tail.

Harrison turned to the man. "We appreciate you welcoming us into your home, but I have to tell you that we're all still a bit confused."

"Even more so when you say that we are the ones," added Swinkle.

Philip extended his hand. "Please find a seat."

Harrison could only see one chair and he dare not try to sit in. "That's all right, I prefer to stand."

Gelderand walked over to the tattered piece of furniture and sat down, while Swinkle took a seat on a makeshift couch. Murdock and Pondle positioned themselves close to Harrison.

Philip closed the door behind the men and locked it. "Suit yourselfs."

Harrison spoke again. "Philip, can you please explain what you know."

Philip took a deep breath and held the artifact in his hands. "This relic's been in my family for years. I'm thinkin' a thousand or so. The legend spoken to my family and me says that the land's greatest warriors will someday come and ask for the thing.

"Now this might mean nothin', but I do think I rememba that a knight first owned this piece a wood. What I rememba's that he gave it to his cousin to hold until you showed up."

Harrison scanned the room and saw the same confused expressions. "Do you remember the name of this knight?"

The man frowned, looking up in thought. "Sir Jack or somethin' or other."

"Sir Jacob," said Victoria, shaking her head. "We never heard a no Jack!"

"Jacob!" exclaimed Philip, pointing a finger in the air. "That's it!"

The men stared at each other in disbelief. Harrison raised an eyebrow and pointed to Philip. "You're a blood relative to Sir Jacob?"

"Sir Jacob of Roxburg! That I am!" Philip thought hard again. "I seem to recall he bein' an important man."

Harrison looked at these people and found it hard to believe that royalty and nobility flowed through their veins.

The young warrior squinted. "You're sure that you're a direct blood relative to Sir Jacob of Roxburg?"

Philip looked down to the floor. "Well, some people married into the family."

"I'm the blood relative," said Victoria. "My papa told me the story first."

The men turned their attention to the woman. Victoria picked up her daughter before stepping further into the room.

"Papa said we got rich blood, but I never believed a stitch he said." She took a wisp of her daughter's hair and tucked it behind one of her little ears.

"He told me, Tori, you gotta protect a legend someday. I married Philip just before Papa died. He gave me that thing and said keep it in the shop and never touch it.

"Then he says if you and Philip die, be sure James or Crystal keeps it there. Someone's comin' lookin' for it." She kissed her little girl on the cheek.

Harrison still had a hard time believing what he heard. "Might we have a look at the artifact?"

Philip did not hesitate in handing it to the young warrior. "Take it! We're honored!"

Harrison looked around and saw a junk-covered table. Motioning with his head, he said, "Swinkle, move those things."

The young cleric cleared the piece of furniture, then Harrison eased the relic down. Swinkle took a closer look at the artifact. The wooden structure looked flimsy, but he recognized the soundness of its construction.

"This wood is from Salinia," he said. "The dwarves used it exclusively." The young cleric examined it further, before retrieving the sacred book from his pack.

Turning to the appropriate page, he gazed at the clue, then at the piece. Three vertices attached to the base, with each arm holding a wooden bowl.

Swinkle pointed to the cup-shaped appendages. "These three pieces hold the jewels." He returned his gaze to the book.

Next, he pointed to the center of the structure. "This rounded area holds the candle, where the dragon's blood will go." He waved his finger around another part of the artifact.

"This area holds the book," he said, placing the scripture in the right spot. The manuscript fit perfectly.

Harrison stared at the relic and let out a deep sigh. Turning to Philip, he said, "You have fulfilled your family's duty with honor." Then, trying to hold back his grimace, he asked, "How much do we owe you for this thing?"

Philip raised his hands and shook his head. "Nothin'! Take it! Take it!"

Harrison protested. "No. We must give you something!"

Philip looked deep into the young warrior's eyes. "My papa-in-law said hand the relic to the next great kings and that's what I'm intendin' ta do."

Harrison still felt wrong about taking the piece, but before he could speak, Philip said, "All I ask is that some day you all could free us from these wicked elders. Please."

Harrison looked into Philip's eyes and saw his pain. He could see the same aspect of anguish in Victoria, James, and even little Crystal.

Harrison nodded with assurance. "That we will do."

Without warning, a pounding came on the outside door of the store. "Stoneham!" yelled someone from outside. "Open up! Your taxes are due!"

Philip's shoulders sagged. "I forgot! The elders were comin' today!" The shop owner gazed at his wife and saw a look of fear flash across her face.

"How much do you owe?"

Philip trembled. "Twenty-five pieces of gold, and I got only eight."

The taxman yelled again. "Stoneham! Don't make us break the door down!" Philip walked over to the window and opened the shutters.

"I got to go get it!" he shouted at the three men on horseback. "You don't think I carry monies like that on my body!"

"Make it fast! We got three more stops to make!" Philip backed away from the window. He stood thinking, tapping his fingers together in front of himself.

Harrison felt nothing but great pity for the poor man and his family. Without a second thought, he removed a sack from his belt and dumped gold coins into his hand. The young warrior glanced back at his friends, who reluctantly did the same. After collecting the coins, Harrison handed them to Philip.

"Don't even say no," said the young warrior, placing the gold in the man's hands.

Philip held his head down, embarrassed to have to accept the tribute. "Thank you."

The disheveled man walked to the window and yelled down. "Here's your taxes!" He then threw the money out the window and onto the awaiting men.

One of the men ordered his subordinate to collect the coins, before taking his gaze back up to Philip. "Next time have it in a pouch!" The shopkeeper waved his hand in disgust at the man.

The taxman pointed a finger up at the townsman. "Keep your eyes out for foreigners! People say they've seen strangers milling about. I better not catch you harboring anyone!"

Philip gazed at the elders one last time, then closed the shutters. After fastening them, he turned to Harrison and his friends.

"You can't stay here. You heard the bad man."

Harrison nodded in understanding. "We'll leave immediately. We don't want to get you into any trouble."

"Rememba what I said to ya. Free us."

The young warrior gave the peasant a look of assurance. "That we will do."

"There's a back way outta my home that takes ya to the forest. I use it to hide from the elders." Philip motioned for the men to follow him.

Harrison grabbed the artifact from the table and, along with the others, walked through two more cluttered rooms, before coming to a door at the far side of the house. Philip opened the door, which led to a rickety staircase that descended to the ground.

"Go that way," he said pointing into the depths of the forest. "The city goes the other way."

"Thank you, Philip. We will return." The young warrior led his friends down the stairs and into the surrounding woods.

Stopping when he felt they had ventured far enough out of sight and suspicion, Harrison said, "Pondle, can you point us in the right direction?"

The thief scanned the area. "I know Roxburg lies west of the Killer Swamplands. The Great Ridge of King Solaris is in a southwest direction from here. If we head that way, we should run right into that mountain range." Pondle located the mid-morning sun, then started to guide the men away from Philip's home.

Harrison attempted to secure the artifact in his backpack and, to his surprise, it collapsed perfectly on its vertices, making it easy to stow. Turning to Swinkle, he said, "We got more than we bargained for from this place."

"That we did." Swinkle stared at Harrison. "The more successes we make on this journey, the more people who will seek us."

Harrison concentrated on Swinkle's last remark. The young warrior knew his identical twin was one of these people and he felt confident in his belief that this man would search for him.

"We need to maintain our focus and handle whatever comes our way. We'll deal with these treasure seekers when the time comes."

The men fell into their usual marching order, leaving the outskirts of Roxburg and beginning their trek to the Great Ridge of King Solaris.

CHAPTER 20

🞓

Ten days of travel brought the men deep into the Ontarian Territory. Pondle and Murdock had guided their friends through the numerous lightly wooded forests and open grasslands without a hint of trouble. Though no one in the group had ventured this far south in the land in their lives, they all had heard stories of the majestic mountains of the Great Ridge of King Solaris.

The late afternoon sun started to hover on the horizon and Pondle figured now was as good a time as ever to stop for a much-needed break. He looked around the area and found a place that would hide them in the underbrush while they rested.

Harrison removed his battle-axe and heavy pack from his shoulders, dropping them on the ground. Stretching out his back, he said, "It feels good to finally take a rest. My legs are exhausted."

Murdock did the same. "You can say that again. We must have traveled for ten hours today."

"At least." Lance sprawled out next to Harrison. "Even poor Lance is worn out!"

Murdock looked at the dog and shook his head. "I can't believe that mutt has traversed the countryside with us."

Swinkle and Gelderand took the time to find a place to rest alongside the warriors, with the mage allowing Rufus out of his cramped backpack to stretch his legs and roam about a bit.

"We should set up camp and discuss our next course of action," said the young cleric. "Didn't Pondle say we were close to Ontario?"

Pondle, who had been busy looking for sticks to start a campfire, overheard the conversation as he wandered back into the area. "I'm thinking Ontario is another day's trek from here." He cleared an area on the ground and arranged the branches appropriately.

Harrison fumbled for some dry foods from his pack and tore off a piece of meat, giving part of it to Lance. "What should we do when we get there?"

Pondle fiddled with his flash and tinder. "Find someone who can lead us in the direction of that so-called explosion we read about in the book." A spark appeared near the thief's hands, followed by the soft glow of a flame. "We can't just ask someone to point us to the latest blast."

Swinkle said a short prayer, then tossed a piece of his meal over his shoulder. Lance saw the maneuver and quickly ate the sacrifice. "I'm sure if we phrase the question properly, no one will feel suspicious."

Murdock gobbled his food before speaking. "Why should anyone suspect anything?" he asked. "We just need to know what mountain in that range had its top blown off."

Gelderand spoke next. "Murdock is right. I think you all are putting too much thought into nothing." He paused to stir something in his bowl, then took a spoon to his mouth for a taste. Satisfied, he continued, "No one but us know the real reason to venture to the blast site."

Harrison drank from his tankard, then said, "That might be so, but I'd rather be overcautious —"

"Than have anyone find our actions suspicious," interrupted Murdock. "We get it, Harrison."

Harrison gazed at Murdock and shook his head, but did not say another word. He took another sip from his flask, then looked over his left shoulder, as if he had heard something. Scanning the group, he noticed that his friends had sensed the same thing.

Pondle slowly rose from his position. "I'm going to investigate." Lance sprung to his feet and followed the thief.

Murdock stood up too, reaching for his longbow. "Not without me."

Pondle raised his hand in protest. "No, stay here with the others. Let me look into this."

Murdock shook his head in disgust, but knew the twilight would hinder his sight in the woods and that Pondle had the clear advantage over him. "Don't take any chances."

Pondle nodded, then disappeared into the underbrush with the dog. Harrison, standing now too, clutched his weapon.

The young warrior positioned himself beside Murdock. "I thought I heard a grinding sound."

The ranger stared into the thickets. "Me, too."

Off in the distance a recognizable neigh filled the area. Harrison looked at Murdock. "Horse drawn carts?"

"That would be my guess." The ranger lowered his weapon, knowing that traders littered the countryside and that their venturing might have steered them close to a well-used path.

Harrison lowered his axe too, feeling the anxiety in his body wane. A minute later, Pondle re-emerged from the woods with Lance.

The expression on Pondle's face surprised the group. Murdock gazed at his friend. "Is it more than just horses and carts?"

"You could say so."

When his friend did not continue with a comment, Murdock shrugged and shook his head. "What then?"

The thief stared at his friends. "They're Scynthians."

Harrison's eyes widened. "What? There must be a mistake!"

Pondle shook his head. "There's no mistake. A couple of large horses are pulling a cart. I didn't see them, but I heard them and I read the tracks."

"How many warriors?"

"No more than four." Pondle raised an eyebrow in the young warrior's direction.

Harrison took a deep breath, contemplating the thief's last statement. He knew they could surprise and overtake four Scynthian warriors with ease. "What are you thinking?"

"The ruts in the ground are deep. They're hauling a significant amount of items."

Murdock added his opinion to the conversation. "They might have ambushed some traders and now have control of their loot."

Pondle agreed. "And we could use that for barter."

Harrison considered the information, knowing that they might need significant supplies in order to venture into the mountains. "How far ahead of us are they?"

Swinkle had kept quiet until now, but hearing the change in plans convinced him to speak up. "Are you suggesting ambushing those Scynthians?"

Murdock rolled his eyes and looked skyward. "Here we go."

Harrison turned to the young cleric. "We don't have much gold left and what we do have isn't enough to buy adequate supplies. Especially for trekking in the mountains."

Swinkle folded his arms the way that a parent would when they do not hear an answer to their liking. "So we just steal from those brutes, even though they have done nothing to us."

"Steal?" Harrison tried to respond, but all he could do was shake his head with an exasperated look on his face.

Murdock pointed his finger at Swinkle. Speaking forcefully, he said, "You have to stop treating those beasts as our equal! They wish nothing more than to destroy us. I'm tired of this conversation with you!"

Swinkle did not cower. "It's not right," he said, holding his gaze. "And you know it."

Murdock fixed his stare on the young cleric. "I don't care."

Harrison stepped between the two. "Let's stop this right now." The young warrior looked at Swinkle. "What can make this situation right?"

"Nothing. We have the opportunity to steer clear of the Scynthians, yet we are making plans to intercept, steal, and commit murder against them."

Murdock threw his hands up in disgust. "It's not that cut and dried."

Harrison held his ground. "How about if we investigate these beasts, see what they are carting and maybe determine how they got it."

Swinkle did not back down. "That is only an attempt to put ourselves in a position where we might have to defend ourselves, creating the illusion that what we might do is right."

Harrison let out a sigh. Swinkle was right, but deep down, he agreed with Murdock. "I know how you feel, but our journey might hinge on finding out what these beasts have."

Swinkle shook his head. "I'm following you either way, but you won't convince me this is just."

Harrison stared at his friend. "This is something we have to do. Trust me." Swinkle did not say another word.

The young warrior peered back toward Pondle and Murdock. "What do you think?"

The thief pondered for a moment. "They're about two hundred yards ahead and moving real slow. We should be able to loop in front of them and wait for them to come to us."

Murdock chimed in, holding up his longbow. "I can take them out with my arrows before we even engage them in hand-to-hand combat."

Pondle nodded, agreeing with his friend. "That's a good idea. I can survey the land and find the best ambush point."

Both men looked over to Harrison. The young warrior considered the plan, then nodded. "Sounds good to me. Let's follow Pondle."

The group gathered their things and trailed the thief through the underbrush. Harrison could hear the grinding of the cart's wheels as well as the heavy breathing of the steeds. They're hauling something big, he thought.

Pondle took his friends on an elaborate route around the unsuspecting Scynthians before finding a small, hilly area where the brush thinned out. The thief maneuvered his friends over the incline.

"They'll come this way," he said, pointing to a spot between the hills. "Murdock, I'll signal you when to shoot."

The ranger peered over the rise. In the distance, he could see small trees shaking due to the horses plowing through the underbrush. Satisfied with what he needed to do, he looked over at Pondle and asked, "Where will you be?"

Pondle pointed to a large tree about fifty feet to his left. "Over there. I can take Harrison with me. You'll be able to see us clearly."

Murdock looked at the tree, then his friend, and nodded his concurrence without saying a word.

Pondle turned his attention to Gelderand, who had collected Rufus and held him in his arms. "We might need a diversion from you if things don't go as planned."

The mage understood the thief's rationale. "I figured as much," he answered while scratching the cat's little head. "I will be ready." Gelderand then secured Rufus in his pack, in order to keep him close by in case things went awry.

Harrison gazed at the young cleric. "Swinkle, you stay with Gelderand. You know we'll need you at some point, too."

Swinkle scowled. "In case you injure yourself during the ambush. I understand."

Harrison shook his head, knowing he must press forward even if it meant disagreeing with his friend.

Pondle looked over to the young warrior. "Can you get Lance to bark when the Scynthians come into view? They might drop their guard if they're looking at the dog."

"I'm sure I can." The young warrior dropped to one knee and looked at his canine companion. "Lance, we need you to bark when you see the beasts come into view. Understand?"

Lance cocked his head, then yapped, "Beasts?"

Harrison grimaced, not knowing what words to use to describe the horses, carts, and Scynthians. A thought came to the young warrior and he pointed to Murdock. "He'll say 'Now!' That's when you bark."

Lance gazed up at the ranger. "Yes."

Harrison patted the dog on the head. "Good boy!" The young warrior stood up and said, "He's all set, Murdock. Just tell him when to start his job."

Murdock secured his longbow. "Good. Let's get moving."

Pondle waved Harrison over and the two of them left for the tree. Meanwhile, Murdock lay on his belly and peered over the crest of the hill, while Gelderand and Swinkle positioned themselves out of view. Lance lay next to the ranger.

Murdock could see the swaying branches in the distance and knew his enemy would be coming into view. A few seconds later, a figure leading a horse appeared out of the thickets. The ranger squinted in order to get a better fix on the situation.

He squirmed up the hill a bit more and gazed toward Pondle. The thief had positioned himself behind the trunk of the tree, with Harrison crouched down in the underbrush. Pondle held up his hand, signaling to Murdock to wait.

The ranger removed an arrow from his quiver. Now he could see his enemy clearly. Two horses pulled a large cart, while a Scynthian guided another horse. Two warriors flanked the wagon on either side, with a final one bringing up the rear.

Murdock set his sights on the warrior with the horse. He peered over at Pondle, who still had his hand raised. The ranger clutched his bow, ready. Just then, Pondle lowered his hand. The ambush was set.

Murdock told Lance, "Now!"

The little dog sprang to his feet and gazed over the crest of the hill. Upon seeing the horse-drawn cart, he began to bark at a feverish pitch.

The sudden sound of the animal startled the Scynthians, who in turn stopped their procession. Murdock rose to one knee from his position and fired at the lead savage. The arrow whistled through the air, hitting its mark in the beast's chest.

The Scynthian released his grip on the horse's reins and fell to the ground. The steed appeared confused at the sudden actions and galloped away.

A second arrow flew through the cool air, dropping the savage to the left. By this time, the two other warriors scrambled to take cover.

Harrison and Pondle, hiding no more than thirty feet from the cart, sprung from the thickets and joined the ruckus. The beast that had followed the wagon felt the cold, steel blade of Harrison's battle-axe enter his midsection and dropped without ever putting up a fight.

The final Scynthian turned to run, only to feel an arrow penetrate the flesh between his shoulder blades. The beast fell in agonizing pain.

Pondle rushed by the cart and approached the last surviving enemy. The savage lay spread out on the ground, wheezing. Pondle kicked the beast's sword away, leaving the Scynthian unarmed.

Murdock and Lance scampered down the small incline to join their friends, with Gelderand and Swinkle following. The ranger grabbed the horses' reins, not wanting them to run off like their counterpart.

After securing the animals, Murdock looked over to Harrison. The young warrior had gone to the back of the cart, then stood motionless with a look of horror.

Seeing his friend's expression, Murdock said, "What is it?"

Harrison tried to speak, but no words came out. He covered his mouth, turned and gagged.

Gelderand and Swinkle reached Murdock and gazed at Harrison with obvious concern. With a frown, the ranger handed the reins to Swinkle. "Keep them still."

Murdock made a cautious approach to the back of the wagon. Harrison still had his back to him, trying to regain his composure. As the ranger gazed at the contents of the cart, his eyes opened wide with shock.

The savages had piled human carcasses three bodies deep. Severed arms and heads littered the remaining torsos. Bloodied sacks of grain and meal, along with backpacks and belongings of the victims, lay strewn all about the wagon.

Murdock put his hand over his mouth as well, his eyes glued to the gruesome scene. The buzz of flies and the stench of decay filled the air.

Pondle approached his friend and stared at the carnage. A flush of rage overtook the thief's initial emotion of anguish. Going back to the Scynthian that lay on the ground, he used all his might to turn the beast over. The arrow snapped due to the savage's immense weight, forcing a gasp to come from his mouth.

"What level of Hell did your race come from!" exclaimed Pondle, before taking his fist and pummeling the beast with punches. The Scynthian remained expressionless, clinging to life.

At that time, Gelderand and Swinkle proceeded with caution to the back of the wagon, wary of the expressions they had seen from their friends.

Gelderand looked first and turned his head away in disgust. Swinkle followed and stared wide-eyed at the scene.

Murdock gazed at the remains, his face grief-stricken. "Do you still believe there are any redeeming qualities in these beasts?"

Swinkle could not find the words to say how he felt. "No," was all he could manage.

The ranger faced the young cleric and said with conviction, "I don't ever want to hear you speak of these savages as our equal again."

Swinkle had never seen Murdock so serious in his life. "I won't."

Just then, a body shifted, startling the men and causing them to jump back. Next, a groan.

Both men stared at each other in shock. Murdock looked around at his friends. "Harrison! Pondle! Someone's alive!" The two men rushed to the back of the cart, with Gelderand joining.

Murdock gazed at the pile of corpses. In the left-hand corner of the wagon a small pile of the carnage moved ever so slightly. "Help me move these bodies!"

The ranger took care in scaling the cart, trying his best to maneuver around the corpses and keeping his head clear from the stink. Harrison and Pondle jumped on the wagon, too, and hovered over the same spot, covering their noses.

Murdock brushed aside a severed arm, while Pondle grabbed a headless body. A moment later, both men stopped their actions. A young woman, no more than twenty, lay in a pool of blood. Her eyes were wide open in a state of shock, her skin as white as a ghost.

Harrison stared at the girl, wondering how she could still be alive. Then she blinked. The sight caused the young warrior to stumble backwards. Stepping on more severed limbs, he fell on the mound of human flesh.

Pondle pushed aside a large torso that lay across the girl's body. "Murdock, help me lift her off the cart."

The ranger positioned himself on the other side of the girl. Looking for a spot to place his hands, he made another gruesome discovery. "Her left arm is gone."

Pondle closed his eyes, trying to hide the pain he felt. "Let's lift her."

The two men picked up the young woman, with Harrison supporting her legs. The poor girl gasped in abominable agony, as the three men gently placed her on a blanket that Swinkle had laid out from his pack.

The girl's torn clothes revealed her almost naked body. She had cuts and bruises everywhere, and caked blood knotted her hair. Aside from having her left arm cut off, Swinkle could tell that the savages had broken her right leg and her other arm appeared severely distorted. Now, she began to sweat, panting to try and alleviate the pain that engulfed her body.

Swinkle made a quick examination of the girl, prayed over her, then folded the blanket covering her as best as he could. He took a cloth from his sack, soaked it in holy water, then lightly rubbed the bloodstains from her cheeks and forehead. At one point, the girl's eyes shifted and focused on the young cleric. Without saying a word, she thanked him.

Swinkle smiled, then approached his friends. The young cleric gazed back at the girl before speaking in a hushed tone. "She has lost too much blood. She will die soon."

Harrison hung his head. "No one deserves this." He looked over at the young woman, straining to remain conscious. "Maybe we should try talking to her."

Swinkle glanced at the girl, too. "She's in shock. I doubt she will say anything, but it's worth a try."

The men walked over to where the girl lay. Swinkle bent down on one knee to address the young woman while his friends watched. "Can you hear me?"

The girl stared upward, before shifting her eyes to Swinkle. Her mouth opened and her lips quivered. She tried to speak but could not. Tears formed from her brown eyes and began to stream down her face.

Swinkle wiped away her tears. "It's all right. You're safe now."

The girl attempted to speak again, this time succeeding. In a frail voice, she said, "Beasts. Hundreds."

Swinkle looked back at his friends with a grimace. Facing the girl again, he said, "Hundreds of Scynthians did this to you?"

"Yes."

Swinkle spoke in a soothing tone. "Where did you come from?"

A steady stream of tears rolled down the girl's pale face. "Ontario," she said before swallowing. "Savages killed everyone. They're coming this way." The girl's face cringed and she started to sob uncontrollably.

Swinkle carefully reached down and hugged the girl, lifting her ever so gently and holding her close. Running his hands through her bloodied brown hair, he said, "Don't worry. We will protect you now." The girl's body heaved as she cried. Swinkle held her tighter.

The girl's crying subsided after a few minutes and the young cleric gently placed her back down. Gazing into her sorrowful eyes, he said, "My name is Swinkle. What is yours?"

A slight smile came to her face. "Larissa."

Swinkle smiled back. "It's nice to meet you, Larissa. We're going to get you back to your family." Tears formed in the young girl's eyes again.

Swinkle caressed her cheeks, then stood up and faced his friends. "We need to get her back home. Immediately."

Harrison shuffled closer to his friend. Speaking from the side of his mouth in a quiet voice, he said, "Swinkle, will she last that long?"

The young cleric shook his head. "I don't know. But we must try."

"How are we going to get her there?"

Murdock overheard the two. "Never mind that. What do we do with the carcasses?" All the men looked at the cart.

Swinkle stared at the carnage again. "We take the bodies with us. They deserve a proper burial, plus family members would want to know the fate of their loved ones." The young cleric looked at Harrison. "I will ride on one of the horses while I carry the girl."

Harrison peered at the steeds. They appeared strong enough for the task, but he was not as sure about his friend. "Will you be able to do this? We're about a day's trek from Ontario."

Swinkle remained defiant. "I will be more than able."

"Can she handle the pain?"

"I know it will be almost impossible, but I will keep her as immobile as I can." The young cleric sighed. "It's what I must do for her."

Harrison nodded and shrugged. "All right. Does anyone object?" The young warrior scanned the others and found them all shaking their head no.

Pondle interrupted with a question. "What do we do with the Scynthian?"

Murdock peered over to the half-dead savage. "Let's throw him on the cart and let the Ontarians pass judgment."

Harrison nodded. "Fine with me."

Pondle and Murdock went around the cart and grabbed the Scynthian. Not bothering for his well being, they threw the beast in the wagon. They were about to join their friends when Murdock made an important discovery.

"Pondle, look at these markings." The Scynthian wore a tattered red armband.

The thief made a closer examination of the beast. "If I didn't know better — "

"These savages are part of the same tribe that took us captive a short time ago!" exclaimed Murdock.

A wave of anxiety tore through the group. All the men looked on in horror, with everyone but Gelderand remembering their captivity at the hands of these beasts. Fresh in their minds was their unexpected surrender and capture by a band of Scynthians just like the ones that had stood before them. The four men wondered if they might have found themselves on a similar cart if not for their friend Aidan's dramatic transformation into a werewolf, and whose subsequent antics inadvertently saved them from certain death.

Harrison's eyes widened. "First Tigris, now Ontario! This is a very bad sign!"

Gelderand had kept quiet, not understanding what the others had meant. "What do you mean these beasts held you captive?"

The young warrior turned to the mage, expressions of disgust and pain overtaking his face. "A short time ago, a group of Scynthians with similar markings took us as their prisoners. They beat us, chained us together, and if it wasn't for our good friend Aidan, they would've sacrificed us like these poor souls." The older man nodded, recognizing the ill will his friends had for the savages.

Murdock secured his backpack. "Let's get out of here. The girl said there were hundreds of these beasts. We've faced only four."

Harrison turned his attention to the ranger and nodded. "Yes, let's go."

Pondle made a quick trek back to their original site and doused the campfire, while the group prepared to leave. Swinkle secured his belongings before his friends helped Larissa into his arms. Harrison and Gelderand took hold of the horses' reins and walked beside the steeds. Pondle and Murdock, along with Lance, surveyed the area ahead.

Harrison gazed up at Swinkle and gave him a nod of approval. Larissa's face stayed ash-white and the young warrior did not know if she would survive the trip. Looking into the distance all he could see were low-hanging branches and thickets. The ensuing nightfall would make the journey even longer, but they had to press forward. Larissa did not have much time.

CHAPTER 21

◘

Larissa died in Swinkle's arms at some point during the long night. The young cleric had held out hope that the girl would survive her devastating injuries. Even non-stop prayers to his savior, Pious, could not save her. Today, he and his friends would have to break the news to the unsuspecting townsfolk of Ontario.

Found in the heart of the Ontarian Territory, Ontario served as the region's unofficial capitol. Though many years ago the village had thrived as the area's fur trading center, fewer and fewer tradesmen and adventurers returned from the Great Ridge of King Solaris. Harsh winters and rough terrain were the general reason that the townsfolk gave when asked why trading had lessened over the years, but the cruel reality was the ever-growing presence of the Scynthians. With greater numbers and sporadic outposts, the evil beings had begun to populate the great range, as they did in the Empire Mountains, and hoped to control the region in order to call it their own.

Murdock and Pondle had informed the others that the town of Ontario stood just beyond the shade of the coniferous trees that now littered the landscape. The men heard the serene sounds of a rumbling river.

Pondle motioned for his friends to halt the horses. "There's a crossing to our left over the stream, which feeds directly into the town."

Harrison waited a moment before responding. When they entered the village, he expected to see anguish on the faces of the townspeople after they discover the gruesome cargo. The young warrior played out in his mind what he would say to comfort the tormented souls, but no words of solace could ever express how he felt.

Harrison let out a heavy sigh. "Let's get this over with." Pondle directed the men forward to cross the bridge.

The young warrior looked about the area and noticed that the town of Ontario consisted of old buildings and homes. Situated just to the west of the Great Ridge of King Solaris, the young warrior had figured the land would be thriving with tradesmen and adventurers. That was not the case.

People milled about the streets, unaware of the solemn procession consisting of horses and a creaking wagon traversing the river. Harrison brought his gaze to several children playing, then watched as their faces turned from surprise to horror upon seeing the mutilated bodies. Two little boys ran to their home, screaming for their parents.

A moment later, a disheveled young man wielding a club emerged from the doorway where the children had disappeared. Harrison stared at the person and noticed the man's face shift from him, to Swinkle, then to the contents on the cart. A look of utter disgust overtook his face.

The men continued their slow march down the path, passing dated shops, pubs, and inns. By this time, more and more townsfolk noticed the atrocities being carted into their quiet village and an ever-growing mob, with their faces a myriad of twisted anguish, began to follow Harrison and his friends.

The small crowd lagged behind the men, without anyone saying a word, as they entered the town's center. Harrison's anxiety level began to rise, knowing a confrontation was inevitable. The young warrior gazed at the edifice in front of him. Horses patiently stood tied to posts, waiting for their owners who congregated inside the building. By the looks of the steeds, Harrison figured that local fighters or adventurers like themselves gathered here. Several people from the crowd rushed inside the establishment and within seconds, men brandishing swords dashed outside.

Harrison and his friends stopped their march as the crowd formed an anxious circle around them. Eight men, dressed in padded leather armor, wearing helmets and carrying shields, drew their weapons and glared back at the adventurers, while scores of others watched in anticipation. The sounds of sobs and suffering permeated the air.

One of the armored men stepped forward, shifting his gaze between Harrison and his friends. Without saying a word, the young warrior gestured for Swinkle to hand him the girl's limp body. The young cleric obliged, carefully placing Larissa in Harrison's arms, then dismounted the horse to stand next to his friend. Gelderand, Murdock, and Pondle joined both men. Lance huddled next to his master.

Swinkle approached the person first. "Words cannot describe the feelings you must have at this moment." The young cleric motioned for Harrison to step forward, too.

The young warrior joined his friend, still cradling Larissa's broken body in his arms. Swinkle had covered the girl's face with his blanket when she passed, but now revealed her to the man.

The townsman's face dropped as tears welled in his eyes. "Larissa!"

Another of the men moved to the forefront, brandishing his sword. "What have you done to her and the rest?" he snarled. A collective rage began to simmer throughout the crowd.

Harrison stayed focused. "My friends and I ambushed a band of Scynthians who were pulling this cart through the forest. We killed all but one of the beasts."

Swinkle spoke next. "Larissa was still alive when we encountered them." A gasp came from the crowd, followed by sobs and sniffles. "I did what I could to save her, but her injuries were too grave."

The first man, with tears streaming down his face, nodded at Swinkle in affirmation, then reached for the girl. Harrison gently placed the frail body into his awaiting arms.

Larissa's body weighed no more than ninety pounds, but upon accepting her corpse from Harrison, it appeared to feel as if it had weighed a ton. The man's knees buckled and he buried his face in the young girl's hair. "Those beasts will pay for their vicious deeds," he cried between sobs.

"We have one of the savages on the cart." Harrison glanced at the bloodied wagon. "And he's still alive."

All eyes shifted to the back of the wagon. The remaining Scynthian lay motionless on top of the human remains.

"Get that beast off our people," yelled a voice from the crowd. The angry mob converged on the savage, pulling him off the cart. Fists pounded the Scynthian, while feet kicked and stomped the motionless body.

The Ontarian holding Larissa looked up at Harrison. "We thank you for all you have done." He brought his gaze back to the girl again and tried his best to hold back his pain. "Larissa's family accompanied her on their journey."

Harrison felt the man's grief. "We thought you would want to give your people a proper burial."

The person nodded. "That we do."

Several of the weapon-wielding townsfolk approached the wagon and led the horses and the cart away. Harrison watched the men go about their morbid task, barely giving him notice. The young warrior felt invisible, overshadowed by the townspeople's incredible grief.

The townsman clutched Larissa's body tighter and followed the cart. After taking two steps, he turned back around to the adventurers. "Please, come with us. You are a part of this tragedy now and we wish to learn from what you saw."

Harrison nodded. "By all means." The young warrior gazed at his friends before following the sullen procession.

The mob led the horse-drawn cart down the main road before halting in front of one of the larger structures in the village. Harrison gazed at the building's two large doors, noticing its fine wooden craftsmanship. The builders reflected the same style when it came to the spiral protruding skyward from the edifice's center. Upon arriving at the temple, the whole crowd bent on one knee and bowed their heads.

Unsure of what to do next, Harrison stood with his arms hanging by side. Gelderand motioned that they should bow down too, and all mimicked the crowd. A man left the throng of people and entered the building, returning a few moments later followed by three others, two women and one man, adorned in red robes.

The monks bowed their heads in prayer, then approached the wagon. All three mumbled softly while making small circles with their hands over the dead bodies.

At that time, the townsman holding Larissa approached the cart. The heavyset, bearded clergyman stopped and gazed at the poor girl. Placing both hands on her head, he prayed for her soul. When he finished, he motioned to the man to step back and addressed the remaining corpses on the wagon once again.

A few moments later, the rotund monk addressed the crowd. "My brothers and sisters, we shall mourn two weeks for our friends. During that time, all of our energy must go into preparing the way for our dead to reach the land of the afterlife.

"Go now to grieve. There will be assemblies each time the bell tolls. May the gods have mercy on their souls."

The townsfolk rose from their positions after the monk concluded his speech and left their fallen behind.

Swinkle watched the people pass him by, then turned to witness the monks perform more religious acts on the dead. Motioning his head, he said to Harrison, "Follow me."

Swinkle did not want to interrupt the monks' prayer service and patiently waited for them to finish. One of the holy people saw Swinkle and stopped what they were doing. The holy man asked, "How may I help you, my son?"

"We are very sorry for your loss," began the young cleric. "Is there anything that we can do to help?"

The middle-aged man gazed back at Swinkle, then smiled. "Tell me, my brother, what order are you associated with?"

Swinkle smiled back. "I am with the Benevolent Healers."

The clergyman gave the young cleric a look of surprise. "That's the first I've heard of them." The monk smiled again. "I am Brother Lorenz. These are Sisters Clairese and Jada."

Sister Jada, a woman also about middle-aged, gave the men a shy nod, never making direct eye contact. Her counterpart, Sister Clairese, appearing much younger than the other two monks, gazed with her teasing green eyes at Harrison and Swinkle, then gave them a sorrowful smile from under her red hood.

Swinkle nodded and introduced his friends. "It is a pleasure to meet all of you, though the circumstances could have been better."

Brother Lorenz closed his eyes and nodded, while the women exchanged pleasantries before going back to their tasks at hand. The clergyman remained with the adventurers, asking, "One of the men told me that you intercepted the savages. Is this true?"

"Yes, it is." Swinkle sighed. "We fear there might be more bad news."

The monk crinkled his brow and raised his palms to the sky. "What could be worse?"

Harrison gazed at the holy man. "Larissa said that hundreds of Scynthians attacked them."

The man's face went blank. "Hundreds?"

The young warrior frowned. "Yes. They could be anywhere."

Brother Lorenz shook his head. "Please, come inside. We must discuss this matter further." He then took his gaze down to Lance. "Your dog must remain outside our holy sanctuary."

Harrison nodded. "By all means." The young warrior looked into the dog's eyes. "Stay outside, boy. We won't be long." The little dog let out a whimper, but understood his master.

Gelderand swung his backpack around, revealing Rufus's head. "Him, too?"

The monk appeared startled to see the cat. "He is also an animal; therefore, he must remain outside as well."

The mage rested his pack on the ground and set the feline free. "Go with Lance, Rufus," he said, pointing to the dog. "He will keep you safe for now." Rufus gazed at Gelderand, then over to Lance. With a meow, the feline walked over to the dog and rubbed up against him.

The wizard smiled, then said, "The animals are all set."

The holy man nodded and turned to escort the adventurers inside their temple. His companions followed. The lack of decorations inside the hallowed place surprised Harrison. The creators of the sacred building had arranged hard wooden benches in a semi-circle around an altar. The young warrior had expected to see religious items, paintings, scriptures — anything to symbolize their religion, but nothing to the contrary existed.

Brother Lorenz motioned for the men to enter a room off the main area. Inside, a large table with eight wooden chairs sat in the middle of the room. The décor reflected the same blandness as the temple.

The monk extended his hand toward the furniture. "Please, have a seat." After the men took their places at the table, Brother Lorenz said, "I'm very concerned about these Scynthians. Have you seen anything like this before?"

Harrison looked at the others before speaking. "We've witnessed their horrible acts firsthand." The young warrior rolled up his sleeve, showing the monks his scar. "They severed my arm less than a month ago."

Harrison's injury took the religious folk by surprise. Sister Clairese pointed to his limb. "How did you reattach it?"

"Gelderand and Swinkle used a combination of prayer and magic to fix my arm," said the young warrior as he rolled his sleeve back down. "Then another mage healed me further by using magical leeches."

The monks stared wide-eyed at each other. Brother Lorenz turned to Harrison. "You are very fortunate."

The young warrior nodded. "I know. A couple of months back, a band of Scynthians also took us captive, but we escaped." Harrison gazed at his friends, then the clergy people. "The Scynthians we ran into last night wore red armbands. Those are the same markings we saw in the Great Forest region."

"This is most disturbing. Where are they coming from?"

Harrison leaned forward, resting his arms on the table and interlocking his fingers. "We think the Empire Mountains. We saw loads of them when we trekked through the Dark Forest."

"You've mentioned the Great Forest, the Dark Forest, and now you are in Ontario. And you said you've been to all of these places recently. May I ask why?"

Harrison made a subtle glance toward his friends, where he saw Murdock open his eyes wide and shake his head no. The young warrior ignored his friend's antics and faced Brother Lorenz again, saying, "My friends and I are looking for a treasure that has taken us all over this land. We believe it exists in the mountain range to the south of your village. That's why we're here and that's also how we've managed to encounter so many Scynthians."

Brother Lorenz stroked his bearded cheeks. "I see. What do you suggest we do?"

"You must keep a constant lookout for these savages. They're around and it sounds like they have huge numbers. How many warriors live in Ontario?"

The monk let out a nervous laugh, pointing at Harrison. "Warriors? You mean like you?" He shook his head and closed his eyes. "Our people own rudimentary weapons and no one is trained at a warrior level. We're common people and wish not to engage in warfare."

Murdock chimed in. "You better start thinking otherwise or the Scynthians will overrun this town."

Brother Lorenz looked at his counterparts and shrugged. "We can only do so much. Most of our brothers and sisters are at our retreat in the mountains. But we fear for their lives as well."

Harrison crinkled his brow. "Why is that?"

"A violent explosion happened a couple weeks ago." The monk sighed. "The ash from the eruption finally stopped falling just the other day."

The men all looked at each other, knowing what had to be asked next. Harrison leaned closer. "Where did this blast take place?"

"We have a cloister many miles into the mountain range. The eruption happened very close to the reservation."

Harrison pressed further. "Would your people know how to get to this site?"

Brother Lorenz nodded. "Of course. We visit the area many times a year."

The young warrior placed a finger to his lips and turned away in thought. A second later, he said, "What if you escorted us to the blast site? We could help you find your people in exchange for guiding us to the impact area."

Brother Lorenz shook his head. "Not for two weeks. I've declared a fortnight of mourning for our deceased."

"Two weeks! We can't wait that long!" yelled Murdock.

Harrison agreed. "He's right. That's a long time to delay our journey."

The monk continued to shake his head. "I'm sorry, you'll have to wait. I can't go against our core beliefs."

Sister Clairese squirmed in her chair, wringing her hands. "Perhaps I could escort them."

Brother Lorenz stared at his fellow monk. "You? I'll need you here."

The woman protested. "Sister Jada can handle my duties." The clergywoman lowered her gaze to the table. "You know how I've wanted to check on our people."

"I can cover her responsibilities," added Sister Jada. "I have no problem with that."

Brother Lorenz' face showed mild agitation since he knew he and Sister Jada could handle all the responsibilities, but his concern lay more with allowing a woman to venture alone in the wilderness with five strangers.

After contemplating, the monk said, "Are you sure you feel comfortable about this?"

Sister Clairese nodded. "I do. These men seem honest enough, and I cannot trek through the mountains alone." The sister nervously tapped her fingers on the table, awaiting Brother Lorenz' response.

The monk sighed, knowing that no real reason existed for Sister Clairese to stay. Furthermore, he had wondered often in the past couple of weeks about the well-being of his fellow clergy people and knew far too much time had already passed without someone going to look for them. With a silent nod, he gave Sister Clairese his blessing.

A smile graced the sister's face. "Wonderful," she said, then turned and faced Harrison. "I suggest we find supplies and clothing for a mountain trek. The temperatures get quite cool, especially after sunset."

"We are running low on food and the like." Harrison agreed. "But, we don't have much gold and I don't think we can afford to buy adequate supplies."

Brother Lorenz interrupted. "You need not worry; providing protection for Sister Clairese more than pays for your things. Consider it done."

Harrison could not help but smile. Not only did they have a seasoned guide to help them venture through the rugged terrain, they also received free gear.

"We'll make sure your colleague returns safely. You have my word."

The monk nodded and smiled. "Good. I hope your findings are not as solemn as the ones you discovered yesterday."

"Me, too." Harrison faced the sister. "When do we leave?"

"At dawn. We have at least a seven-day trek to the eruption area." She glanced at Brother Lorenz. "It won't take me long to pack. Let me help you today with our burial preparations."

"Thank you, Sister." The monk addressed Harrison a final time. "Go into town and find supplies. Tell them Brother Lorenz has sanctioned the sales and if they have a problem, tell them to see me directly." He pointed a finger toward the men. "Be sure to get plenty of furs. It's cold up there."

Harrison nodded. "Thank you, sir." The young warrior squirmed in his seat.

The monk noticed the look of apprehension on the warrior's face. "What is it, my son?"

Feeling a bit foolish, he answered, "We have no place to stay and we don't want to impose."

"Nonsense," said the clergyman. "You will stay here with us. Now, go off and get what you need."

Harrison and his friends rose from their chairs. "We thank you again." The young warrior told Sister Clairese, "We will meet you here in the morning." With that, the men exited the room in search of supplies.

After the group left, Brother Lorenz remained staring at the doorway. "You feel comfortable enough with them?" his question directed to Sister Clairese.

"Yes, I do. We need to find out the situation with our friends."

The monk nodded and leaned back in his chair. "I agree. It has been long enough." He paused. "Be careful. You don't know them at all."

"I will, Brother."

Brother Lorenz nodded. With a heavy sigh, he said, "Time to tend to our dead."

Over the course of the day, the men gathered food and water, acquired gear to keep them warm, and additional blankets for nighttime. Harrison could not erase the images of the villagers' agonizing faces from his mind. In all, the Scynthians had butchered fifteen people from the town of Ontario. The outpost only had about a hundred and fifty residents, and each person had intimate recollections of the poor slaughtered souls.

By nightfall, the men took up positions inside the monastery and went through their belongings. Harrison knew he had everything he required for his journey into the highlands and made sure Lance had all he needed, too. He thought of the poor little dog that remained outside of the holy grounds and figured that the time had come to feed him one last time for the night.

The young warrior turned to see if Swinkle would like to accompany him, but found him staring at the group's sacred scripture. Harrison walked over to him, but before speaking, he gazed at the book in Swinkle's hands, marveling at the leathery binder.

"Sister Clairese is going to lead us exactly where we need to go."

Swinkle peered from behind the cover. "I know," he said, lowering the scripture. "This is all too coincidental."

Harrison looked around the room and saw the others fiddling with their things. He squatted down, balancing in front of the young cleric on his toes. "I feel that way, too. What do you think?"

Swinkle smiled. "Pious is leading us."

Harrison raised his eyebrows. "I never thought of it that way."

Murdock overheard the conversation. "I call it luck." The ranger pushed his backpack against the wall and faced the younger men. "Let's just have the woman lead us to the blast site, let her take a look around at her reservation, and bring us back home."

"It's not that simple." Harrison rose from his position.

Murdock shook his head and crinkled his brow. "Why?"

"She's going to witness us finding the jewel, if we're lucky enough to uncover it."

The ranger waved a hand in Harrison's direction. "You're over thinking again. We told them we're looking for treasure. Finding a jewel qualifies as that, and she doesn't need to know the real reason."

Pondle walked over to the men. "Plus, we're escorting her and providing protection. That's an even swap."

Harrison shrugged. "I suppose."

Gelderand finished with his things and joined his friends, too. Looking at the young cleric sitting on the floor, he asked, "Swinkle, have you found anything more about the green jewel?"

Swinkle gazed at the book, then read the passage containing the clue. *"A beautiful, majestic explosion has taken place; its traces can be seen from great distances. Here is where the green jewel resides. Get by the heat and wear on your feet, and the prize will be yours."*

Lowering the book, he said, "That's it. It doesn't pinpoint the location."

Gelderand was not so sure that he agreed with Swinkle's assessment. "Maybe it does and you don't see it."

The young cleric appeared confused. "What do you mean?"

The mage walked behind Swinkle, crouched down, and pointed at the passage. "Right here it says a beautiful, majestic explosion has taken place. We've located the area where this has happened.

"Then it states that the green jewel resides here. It has to be the epicenter of the blast."

Swinkle cocked his head. "I see what you mean. The creators of the treasure would not send us into a mountain range without any point of reference."

Gelderand smiled, knowing Swinkle understood his rationale. "Precisely. Now, finding the exact point of the explosion might be difficult. The area will be large and the jewel small."

Murdock spoke up. "We'll worry about that when we get there. I hope this sister is up to the task."

Harrison reached for his pack. "I'm sure she will be." The young warrior looked toward the doorway. "I need to give Lance something to eat."

Swinkle closed the scripture and placed it in his backpack. Rising, he said, "I'll join you."

The two young men left their friends in the temple and headed outside. The sun had already set when they found Lance curled up under a tree a little way from the building. The little dog jumped to his feet upon seeing his master and raced over to him with his tail wagging. Rufus recognized the men too, stretched his back, and trotted over to join the small group.

Harrison rubbed the dog briskly. "I missed you too, boy!" Lance licked the young warrior across the face. Harrison laughed. "Not that much though!"

Gazing at the cat, then back to Lance, he said, "I see you did a good job protecting Rufus." Lance barked once in affirmation.

Reaching into his backpack, Harrison found a sack of fatty meats and bones that he had purchased specifically for Lance. Placing them in his hand, he said, "Here you go."

The little dog gobbled up the meat, then snatched the bone and began gnawing at it. "If I didn't know better, I'd say you were starving," Harrison said with a laugh.

The young warrior also had a little bit of fresh meat for Rufus, which he placed in front of the cat. The feline sniffed the offering, then began to pick at the food.

Swinkle tugged on his friend's sleeve. "Harrison." The young cleric motioned with his head for his friend to look behind him.

Harrison had not noticed the procession of people congregating at the outskirts of town. The townsfolk had started a slow, solemn march toward them, with each man, woman, and child holding a lit candle.

Harrison recognized Brother Lorenz, Sister Clairese, and Sister Jada flanking a cart pulled by two horses. As the procession moved closer, the young warrior realized that the people had used the same two horses and wagon that he and his friends had found to haul a cargo. The silence was deafening, save for the creaking of the wheels and the grunts of the steeds. The soft candlelight illuminated the area and as the crowd walked by, Harrison could see fifteen wooden coffins on the back of the cart.

The two young men stood motionless while the mob passed them by. Brother Lorenz halted the procession about a hundred feet from the temple. Harrison noticed that the Ontarians had cleared an area to the left of the religious structure. Four townsmen helped to remove the crates from the wagon and placed them in this vicinity, alongside fifteen freshly dug graves.

Sobs and uncontrollable crying emanated from the crowd. After all the coffins lay in place, Brother Lorenz addressed the huddled mass of people.

"My brothers and sisters, we have lost our friends and loved ones to a ruthless and hateful enemy. We will mourn for them, but never forget the impact that they made on our lives.

"However, we must stay strong and persevere through this time. The Scynthians will be back and we must be ready to fend them off. Don't let what happened to our fellow Ontarians happen to us."

The monk went to each coffin and administered a final prayer. When he finished that task, he motioned to four men for the lowering of the boxes into the graves and, after the townsmen placed all of the caskets in their rightful position, they began the solemn chore of burying their friends.

Thirty minutes later, fifteen mounds of fresh earth with makeshift headstones lay beside the temple. Brother Lorenz sprinkled holy water on each pile as he mumbled a prayer.

The monk stepped back from the new gravesite. "May our friends rest in peace."

Harrison and Swinkle watched the crowd approach the graves. The young warrior could understand the pain these people felt, since he endured the same hurt when he had to bury his slain parents.

Glancing at his friend, he said, "Swinkle, we should leave and let these people mourn for their friends."

Swinkle nodded. "You're right. This is not our place."

The two young men, along with Lance and Rufus, left the solemn scene and returned to the temple. Both adventurers knew morning would come soon enough and that their own journey needed to continue.

CHAPTER 22

○

Harrison and his friends awoke just before dawn, ate a hearty breakfast, and waited for Sister Clairese. A short time later, the woman appeared at the temple.

Knocking quietly on the door jam, she said, "Is everybody ready to go?"

Harrison peered toward the doorway. A look of surprise crossed his face upon seeing the woman. Instead of wearing a red cloak as she had yesterday, Sister Clairese was dressed in hiking gear, carried a backpack, and looked the part of a knowledgeable guide. Her naturally curly hair, no longer hidden by her hooded robe, bounced around her shoulders.

Harrison nodded in her direction. "I believe so."

The sister smiled. "Good. The mountains stand about 7000 feet tall, but there are many passable trails. If we're ready, let's leave."

The rest of the men followed Sister Clairese out of the temple. Before they could get too far, Murdock stopped the woman. "We usually lead the group," he said, using his thumb to point at Pondle. "What did you have in mind?"

The monk gazed at Murdock and Pondle with big green eyes. "The trails are straightforward, but you should follow me."

Since he enjoyed his role as the team's tracker, Murdock tried to hide his displeasure. "If the paths are that easy to navigate, I'd feel more comfortable ahead of the others. Right, Pondle?"

The thief agreed. "So would I."

The woman rolled her eyes. "If your manhood tells you that you must lead the group, then so be it. I'll tell you which way to turn if we come to a fork in the passage." Murdock stood in his place speechless, his mouth agape.

Harrison snickered, never having seen a woman put his friend in his place before. "Sister Clairese, why don't you point out to Murdock and Pondle the direction you want us to go in?"

The woman pointed to the only path that led away from the village. "That way." She then addressed the men. "And please, all of you drop the 'Sister' part of my name. Call me Clairese."

Harrison grinned and nodded. "Clairese it is." The young warrior motioned to Murdock and Pondle. "Lead the way." The two men tried to hide their scowls as they turned and appeared to lead the party into the wilderness.

Clairese removed a walking stick from her pack as she hiked with the others, while Lance scooted before them.

Swinkle, being a fellow person of the cloth, maneuvered alongside her. "What type of order do you adhere to?"

The woman glanced at the young cleric. "Type of order? We don't have any singular god, we more or less believe in the peacefulness of nature."

Swinkle, being a devout follower of Pious, appeared confused by Clairese's statement. "What do you mean you don't have a god to pray to?"

Clairese huffed. "Nature is a strong force; her beauty and strength are undeniable. The precious balance between positives and negatives instills an even harmony."

Swinkle remained perplexed. "Who created nature? Surely you must have thought of that?"

"I don't know! I never really thought too hard about that."

The young cleric's eyes widened in surprise. "I'm sorry if I pried too deep into your religious beliefs."

The woman stopped and faced Swinkle. "Look, I'm sorry if I jumped at you. To be honest, I'm not a very religious person at all." Clairese turned and started her trek again.

Swinkle looked at Harrison, his brow crinkling with confusion, and asked her, "Are you not a woman of the cloth?"

Clairese sighed, but stared at the path that began to take a subtle turn upward. "Not by choice. If I had my way, I'd leave Ontario." She looked at the young cleric with her round, green eyes. "Why do you think I practically begged to guide you into the mountains?"

In Clairese's face Swinkle could see the pain of a woman who had spent too long in a place she did not want to be. "You're older than us; you could have left long ago."

Clairese narrowed her eyes, shooting the young cleric a look in regard to the age reference. "I'm not *that* old. I'm thirty-two," she said shaking her head. "And I love the wilderness. Nature is my god, she's my soul, my livelihood." Clairese waved her arm outward. "Look at all this beauty, listen to the birds, smell the fresh air."

Swinkle took in the sights around him. Hawks flew overhead in search of their daily meal, the sun's rays glowed behind the peaks in the distance, and he even witnessed Lance scurrying around playfully in the underbrush. At that moment, he understood just what Clairese meant.

Swinkle gazed at the woman. "I suppose you're right." Still he questioned her further. "Can you perform any clerical tasks?"

"Like what?"

"Well, I can help heal injuries sustained in battle or create sanctuaries if necessary."

Clairese shook her head. "No, I cannot. But I'm a great cook." The monk flashed a wide smile.

Swinkle smiled back. "And a wonderful guide, I'm sure."

"That I am." Clairese pointed to the first mountain of the great range that stood before them about ten miles away. "Our journey gets interesting once we reach there. Enjoy the morning hike, it'll get tougher later."

The group hiked for five days, trekking deeper into the Great Ridge of King Solaris. Harrison marveled at the stunning sights that Clairese pointed out to the men along the way. The young warrior wore fur skins over his armor, as did his friends, now that the temperature dropped to very cool levels.

Clairese described to the men the mountaintop sanctuary that the Ontarians had constructed, how it sat on a small plateau and faced a gorgeous sunset day after day.

The hikers were traveling along a worn path when they came to a fork. Murdock and Pondle reached it first and looked back at the group.

The ranger pointed to the path on the left. "I know this way is steeper, but it looks easier to pass."

Clairese and the others reached the men. The woman stared at the crevice between the mountains. A cool breeze swept through the group, ruffling her dark, wavy hair.

Maintaining her gaze on the trail, she said, "No, we take the path to the right."

Murdock raised his palms to the sky, shrugging in the process. "Why? That path goes around the mountain." The ranger pointed to the rightmost trail. "It'll take us twice as long going that way."

Clairese glared at Murdock. "No!" Her eyes became glassy and she appeared to hold back tears. "We go to the right!"

"All right, all right." Murdock raised his hands in a calming manner. "We can go the other way." The ranger looked at Pondle with a look of confusion.

Gazing to the path on the left, Harrison said to the woman, "What happened here?"

"Have you ever heard of Shalimar's Pass?" Harrison shook his head, while everyone else listened closely.

"That's it," Clairese said, swallowing hard and pointing up the mountainside. "It rises about a quarter of a mile before you reach the top, then it harmlessly connects on the other side."

"Did someone die here?"

Clairese let out a nervous laugh and faced the young warrior. "The question is how many people have died here." She looked toward the path again. "Listen."

Harrison and his friends stared at the passage and listened as best they could. A faint clanging noise emanated in the distance.

"I hear a sound," said Harrison. "What is it?"

The woman kept her gaze fixed on the rise. "That sound means it's too late."

"Too late for what?"

Clairese maintained her stare toward the mountaintop, her face sporting a blank expression. "You'll see."

The men glued their eyes to the summit as well. All of a sudden, a massive cloud formed at the top of the peak, followed by a rush of cold air. The wind blew through the trail, bending back the coniferous trees and swirling dirt, rocks, and anything else in its path. After thirty seconds, the air returned to its calm state once again.

Unimpressed at the event, Murdock turned to face Clairese and said, "Is there anything else that's supposed to happen?"

Clairese frowned and shook her head, all the while gazing at the path. "You don't understand." She took her gaze to the ranger. "That air is so cold it will turn your body to ice on contact. Then the force of the wind knocks you over, hurtles you into the mountainside, and splatters you into a thousand pieces. You won't even know you're dead."

Everyone stared at the passage again in disbelief. Harrison still seemed perplexed. "What was that sound we heard?"

"That's a massive wind chime." Clairese gave him a wry smile. "We erected it there some time ago. You see, this pass creates utter destruction only when the wind is strong enough to move the bells."

"What if you're in the pass when you hear the signal?"

Clairese let out a laugh under her breath. "You have thirty seconds, give or take a few. After that, death." The men continued to stare at the bypass.

"Murdock, Pondle, you can direct us that way." The monk pointed to the trail on the right. "The path is a little steep, so be careful." The men nodded and took the lead.

Harrison walked beside Clairese again. "If you weren't here, I'm sure we would've taken the shorter route."

"That's what happens to so many people. The devastation is so complete that no remains appear at this point to warn other hikers. Either you know not to attempt to cross the trail or you're just plain lucky."

Harrison agreed with a nod, knowing they were very fortunate indeed to have Clairese as their guide.

Three days after they reached Shalimar's Pass, they encountered another ominous sight. Harrison bent down on one knee and picked up the soft substance that had started to accumulate on the ground.

Squeezing it in his hands, he said, "Ashes."

Clairese pointed in front of them. "It's all over the trees."

"They look like they're covered in snow."

Just then, Lance darted from the thickets. He stopped a few feet from his master, then shook the accumulated debris from his coat.

"Look. Even Lance is covered with the stuff."

The woman gazed over to the young warrior. "I'm sure it gets worse." Clairese directed the men further into the mountainous forest, all the while the ash getting thicker.

By midday, the group began to see the devastation of the blast. Strong repercussions had knocked over trees, pointing them away from the epicenter of the explosion. Carcasses of deer and smaller animals littered the landscape. Where a vast evergreen forest once stood, now lay a desolate wasteland.

Clairese stopped her trek and looked around the general vicinity. The young warrior noticed her actions and approached her.

"What's the problem?"

The woman's eyes started to tear. "The sanctuary is another mile ahead, but I fear we'll find nothing left of it."

Harrison agreed, but tried not to show it. "Stranger things have happened. Don't give up hope just yet."

Clairese sniffled, then gave him a weak smile. "You have a big heart for such a young man." She turned to where the trail used to be. "Let's not stop now."

The group marched forward another hour. The thickness of the ashes hindered their progress, but they trudged through it nevertheless. Finally, after over eight days of travel, the landscape leveled out and Clairese stopped their trek.

The monk gazed about the immediate area. To the west, she could see the vast coniferous forests that grew along the mountainsides and in the distance the faint visage of the sea at the horizon. Clairese had sat on the reservation's stone patio and watched the sunset from here many times over. Now, nothing but crumbled walls of the sanctuary existed.

The young woman took a few steps toward the fallen structure, stopped, then started to cry.

Harrison put a hand on her right shoulder. "I'm so sorry, Clairese."

The woman turned and buried her face in his chest, crying. "They're all gone," she said through heavy sobs. "All of them!"

Harrison did not know what to say. "I'm sure they didn't feel any pain. They would've died quickly."

Clairese nodded, sniffling. "I'm going to miss them so much."

Pondle and Murdock took it upon themselves to investigate the area. After a few minutes, Murdock approached the two. "I wouldn't give up so soon."

Clairese stared at the ranger. "What do you mean? Did you find something?"

"It's just the opposite." Murdock pointed to the broken walls. "I can see how the building got destroyed, along with everything in it, but I expected to find bodies."

Hope started to fill the woman's heart. "You think they survived?"

"I didn't say that," said the ranger. "I'm just saying, I don't see any corpses lying around."

Pondle and the others joined in the conversation. "There's too much ash everywhere," said the thief. "I can't draw any conclusions from what I've seen."

Clairese looked wide-eyed around the compound. "But there's a chance they escaped — before the explosion!"

"I suppose," said Pondle. "Some tremors probably preceded the blast. If they started soon enough, it might have given your friends ample time to evacuate."

Murdock tugged on his backpack. "Still, don't get your hopes up." The ranger gazed toward Harrison. "We need to start looking for this jewel."

Harrison nodded in agreement, then looked into Clairese's eyes. "Thank you for guiding us here, but now we have to search for what we came for. Why don't you have a look around yourself, put your mind at ease."

"I'm going to see if I can find anything of worth. I'll be around the sanctuary site for awhile." With that, Clairese ventured to the battered enclave, while the men discussed their next course of events.

Swinkle started first. "The scripture stated that the green jewel resides where a magnificent explosion took place. That's here."

"We know that," snarled Murdock, "but where up here?"

"The book didn't state that."

The ranger shook his head. "Wonderful."

Harrison looked about the area, with the ash and broken forest. "Maligor wouldn't have sent us here without a clue." The young warrior scratched his head. "Something has to be up here."

"Clue or no clue, we need to comb this area." Murdock pointed to the west. "Pondle and I will start that way. You guys search the other way."

The duo set off to look for anything that seemed suspicious, leaving Harrison, Gelderand, and Swinkle to fend for themselves.

The young warrior peered in the opposite direction, seeing nothing but leveled forestation. "Where do we start?"

Swinkle gazed at the same nothingness. "I don't know. The jewel has to be here though."

"We're looking in the wrong place." Gelderand stepped forward in between the two young men. "You don't think the mountain would have belched an emerald onto the surface, do you?" Harrison and Swinkle looked at each other, wondering if that were true. "Of course not! The makers would have placed the gemstone in something safe."

Harrison cocked his head and squinted. "And it would be in something that would survive the eruption."

The mage nodded. "Now you're thinking."

Swinkle took his hands to his head and slowly massaged his temples. "What could withstand a blast like this?" he said, concentrating.

Gelderand appreciated the intense thought processes of the two lads, waiting for an answer. Without one coming, he said, "Something magical, don't you think?"

The two young men peered sheepishly at each other. "Of course," said Harrison.

"So, let's start searching, but look for something out of the ordinary." The mage turned his head to the west, noticing the sun's position. "We're going to be in store for a beautiful sunset. I suggest we take advantage of what little time we have left today."

The men heeded Gelderand's advice and began searching in earnest for the green jewel.

CHAPTER 23

○

Nightfall brought an array of stars across the cloudless sky. The adventurers huddled around a campfire, wrapped in their blankets as they attempted to fend off the bitter cold. After an unsuccessful first day of searching for the elusive emerald, the group patiently listened to Clairese tell them about the wonders of the ruined sanctuary and the many things that the blast had destroyed.

The monk pointed to an invisible wall that now housed the image of the moon. "Over here we tacked a drawing that showed us the exact time of day, based on the position of the sun." The woman swiveled to her left, subtly waving her index finger left to right as she squinted in thought.

"Let me see," she said before pointing over Harrison's head. "Right there is where we made the holes in the wall! It took quite a while to figure it all out."

The young warrior tried his best to appear interested, but his thoughts drifted to the treasure. Somewhere on this mountaintop hid a sacred gemstone, but two hours of searching proved fruitless. Even Gelderand couldn't detect any magic, he thought. How am I going to find the stone?

Harrison waited for a lull in Clairese's story, and when it came, he asked, "Have you or your friends ever found anything unusual up here?" The young warrior wrapped his blanket tighter around himself while the other men listened.

The woman paused a moment in thought. "Not really. The forest thinned out quite a bit. I think we would've seen something strange. Why do you ask?"

"It's this treasure we're looking for," he said, shaking his head. "Did any of your friends know how to perform magic?"

"Magic?" Clairese laughed. "We didn't have time to learn silly religious things like that."

The men all looked at Gelderand, who frowned after hearing the girl's words. "Magic is not silly, nor is it a religion. It is a very powerful thing."

Clairese blushed. "I didn't mean that the way it sounded."

The mage nodded. "It's all right. I know you didn't."

Regaining her composure, the woman questioned, "Why do you ask about magic anyway?"

Harrison sat up straight. "A very powerful mage hid the treasure and we think that magic protects the jewel somehow."

The woman shrugged. "I suppose that could be true. How do you find magic?"

Gelderand spoke again. "You do not find magic, you detect it. Swinkle and I are fortunate enough to be able to do that."

"Have you detected any?"

The mage shook his head. "No."

Clairese thought for a moment, trying to get a better feel for what these men sought. "Where have you looked for this aura?"

"All around this site." Gelderand looked over to Murdock and Pondle. "They went a ways further, but couldn't find anything either."

A strange look glazed Clairese's face. "Have you checked in the sanctuary?"

Gelderand looked at Swinkle, who shook his head no. "No, we haven't."

The monk appeared as if she was trying to recall something. "This might mean nothing, but I always got a strange feeling around this place, especially near the mountain overlook. I always assumed that a higher spiritual being was releasing its energy upon us."

The men suddenly took a much greater interest in the woman's story. "Go on, Clairese," said the mage.

"Well, we're sitting in the sanctuary, but the patio is over there." The woman stood up, clutched her blanket tighter, and looked over her shoulder. The dark valley loomed precariously beyond the terrace.

Clairese walked through the missing doorway and stepped onto the stony overlook. "We laid these stones down to create as natural an area as possible."

The men followed her onto the patio, too. "Where did you feel the sensations?" asked Gelderand.

Clairese stepped deeper into the terrace, moving closer to the edge. She then walked to her left, as if trying to pinpoint an exact spot. "I always felt them out here." The woman made an abrupt stop. "Wait."

The monk gazed past the men to where the building used to stand, then looked to the ground. She began to push away the ash in an effort to find the rocky floor. Satisfied, she sat cross-legged on the ground and peered at the horizon.

Perplexed by her actions, Gelderand asked, "What are you doing?"

Clairese maintained her forward gaze. "This is where I'd sit and watch the sunsets. The rays would filter through the holes in the wall, pointing to our solar clock with fiery fingertips." She turned and faced the men. "And this is where I felt the strongest sensations."

The mage approached the woman. Gelderand looked at the heavens taking in the stars and moon, then peered at the dark line separating the earth from the sky.

"Light your torches," the wizard said to the men, who heeded their friend's command, then walked alongside the mage. "Start clearing away this ash. I suspect what we are looking for might be under our feet."

Harrison dropped his blanket into the dirty cinders and helped move away the debris. After fifteen minutes, the men had cleared away the area around Clairese.

Gelderand touched the woman lightly on the shoulder. "Do you sense anything now?"

Clairese closed her eyes and tried to imagine the times she sat on the mountaintop at sunset. Nothing came to her. "I feel the same."

The older man stroked his beard, thinking, then reached for his pack. Finding the right ingredients, he chanted a spell. The mage paced about the immediate area, hoping to feel anything unusual, but he also sensed nothing.

Distraught, he asked, "Swinkle, can you sense anything?"

The young cleric recited a prayer, but just like the wizard, he too could not feel a magical aura. Swinkle gazed back at the mage, shaking his head to relay his somber message.

Gelderand shook his head. "This makes no sense," he muttered to himself. A moment later, he looked at the ground. Peering closer, he could see that the creators had placed stone slabs of varying shapes in a mortar mix.

"Clairese, are these stones laid in any special way?"

The monk looked at the flooring. "Not particularly. Why?"

Gelderand held his chin in his hand, still thinking. "Is it possible that something can be under here?"

The woman shrugged. "I suppose. I wasn't here when they laid the foundation."

The wizard told his friends, "Take out your weapons."

Harrison gave the mage a look of surprise. "What for?"

Pointing to the ground, Gelderand said, "Use the butts of your weaponry to find a hollow spot."

"It's worth a try," said the young warrior.

The men went about tapping the slabs, hoping to hear something echo. The young warrior had his doubts, but that all changed a few minutes later. Taking the hilt of his battle-axe, Harrison pounded a slab behind Clairese. Instead of hearing a thud, a reverberation came from below.

Clairese looked up at Harrison, noticing the look of surprise on his face. "I heard that, too." The rest of the men came over.

"What can it be?" asked Harrison.

Pondle dropped to his knees and began to examine the stone pieces. "This looks just like the stone slabs in the Seven Rooms! I should have recognized the similarities!"

Recalling how he had helped his friends navigate through one of the sacred rooms on their quest to find the Treasure of the Land, the thief pulled out a dagger and began to jam it between the slabs. This time, the mortar prevented the blade from penetrating.

After a few minutes tinkering with his knife, the thief said, "The sealant is too thick."

Harrison leaned closer to the stone to take a better look also. "Pondle, Maligor didn't design this. Clairese's people did. We need to shatter the stone somehow."

Pondle rose from his kneeling position. "I think you're right."

The young warrior stood near the rocky surface again. "Stand back." Taking his axe, he hit the stone harder. It shattered. Grabbing a torch from Swinkle, the young warrior dropped to his knees and peered into the newly created hole.

Harrison called to his friends over his shoulder. "I see a staircase!"

"Now that sounds like something Maligor created," said Pondle. "Let me lead the way."

Pondle cleared away as much debris as he could, then squeezed through the opening and carefully descended the stairs. He counted thirty steps before stopping and gazing upward. "There's a long way to go," he yelled up to his friends. "You might want to come down here with me."

Murdock heard his friend's plea. "I'm going down there." The ranger stepped into the hole before he felt someone grab his arm.

"Do you think it's a good idea that we all go into this passage?" Harrison's face had a look of obvious concern.

Murdock knew it would be wise to leave someone behind, but something told him otherwise. "I have a feeling we'll need all of our talents."

The young warrior agreed. Looking back to Gelderand and Swinkle, he said, "Keep your torches lit and stay close behind."

Clairese did not know what the group had in store for her. "What about me?"

Harrison let out a sigh, having momentarily forgotten about the woman. "Come with us. You might recognize things down here since you've been to this sanctuary so many times before."

The monk nodded and accepted a torch from Gelderand. "You'll need this." Clairese took hold of the torch and waited for the men to make the next move.

Murdock made one last check of the situation. "Are we ready?"

"Wait." Harrison called for Lance. "You go up ahead with Pondle, boy." The little dog approached the opening, sniffed, then scurried past Murdock.

After the dog disappeared, Harrison said to Murdock, "Tell Pondle we're coming." The ranger relayed the message and began his descent into the darkness.

Lance reached Pondle in no time. The thief placed a caring hand on the dog's head. "It's so dark I can barely see," he said to the dog, not knowing if Lance could understand him.

Pondle continued down the steps, counting a hundred before reaching a passageway. Lance ventured only a few feet in front of the thief, since very little light emanated from the advancing torches.

The corridor tunneled deeper into the mountainside, taking Pondle and the men farther from the staircase. The thief scaled the rocky walls and felt the passage bend to the right. With each step he took, he could sense that the path made a sharper turn. Suddenly, he heard Lance yap several times from up ahead. A faint glow emanated from around the corner.

"Maligor," muttered the thief to himself, recognizing the great wizard's signature of a magically lit room. Pondle walked around the curve and stood before a vast stone cavern. The thief gazed about the area and figured it to be about fifty feet wide by thirty feet deep. Taking his look upward, Pondle estimated that the cavern roof rested a good twenty feet above him.

Catching his eye, though, was the sparkling green jewel that hovered over a stone pedestal in the center of the room. A beam of light shone down from the ceiling, while the gem rotated ever so slowly.

Harrison and the others reached Pondle a moment later. The young warrior gazed about the area in wonderment. "Pondle, have you checked for any traps."

"Not yet. I'm sure there's more here than meets the eye."

Harrison gazed at the jewel in the middle of the room. "Be careful."

Pondle crept down the three steps that led into the cavern, then went off to make his examination while the others took in the sight.

"That stone is beautiful." Clairese could not take her stare away from the precious item.

"Like Pondle said, I'm sure there's more here," said Harrison, looking about for anything out of the ordinary.

The thief scrutinized the pedestal, keeping a close eye on the emerald that rotated a foot above him. The platform looked like nothing more to Pondle than smooth stone with no abnormalities.

Looking back at his friends, he said, "I don't see any traps. Shall I reach for the jewel?"

Harrison gazed at the thief with a worrisome feeling. Maligor had erected the setup for the ruby without any consequences to the finder, but he also constructed the elaborate Seven Rooms where they had lost one of their comrades.

The young warrior nodded to Pondle. "Be ready for anything."

Pondle took his gaze to the stone. Its shimmering green radiance teased him, begging him to pluck it from its resting place. Pondle rubbed his hands together in an effort to burn off his nervous energy, then reached for the gem.

The thief's hand intercepted the beam of light, took hold of the emerald, and pulled it close to his chest. The light disappeared from over the pedestal and an eerie quiet enveloped the cavern. Pondle raced over to his fellow adventurers, clutching the gem tightly.

Harrison and his friends surrounded Pondle, hoping to get a better look at the stone. "It's beautiful, just like the ruby," said the young warrior, peering over Pondle's shoulder.

Swinkle went into his pack and removed the red stone, then placed it next to the gem in Pondle's hand. "The cuts are identical."

Pondle agreed. "The same person forged these stones." Before anyone could say another word, a low rumble echoed throughout the cavern.

Harrison looked across the room and noticed that the far wall had started to change form. "Something's happening," he said, pointing in that direction.

Ten seconds later, a recognizable object appeared secured to the wall. Harrison gazed at the item along with the others. "A sword?"

"I'll check for traps." Pondle cautiously approached the weapon and searched for anything more unusual, but found nothing. "Come on over."

The rest of the group joined Pondle and gazed at their latest clue. Harrison took a step closer to the sword, marveling at its shiny blade and golden hilt. Secured to the wall next to the blade rested the sword's scabbard, adorned with smaller versions of rubies, emeralds, and diamonds.

The young warrior looked back at his friends. "I'm going to take it." Harrison removed the sword from its resting place, along with the scabbard. The blade was massive, larger than any weapon he had ever seen, but its weight felt less than twice that of his battle-axe.

Startled, Harrison gripped the hilt with two hands and swung the weapon back and forth. "It's as light as a feather!"

Murdock stared at the two-handed sword. "Do you realize how powerful that weapon can be for someone like you?"

A smile stretched across the young warrior's face. "I bet you one of the ancient kings wielded a weapon like this."

Suddenly, the beam of light reappeared over the pedestal, but this time an open book rested on the platform. The group looked at each other in surprise, then made a slow advance to the podium.

Swinkle reached the scripture first and read the text. *"Behold the Sword of Dracus. The keeper of the jewel must now slay the beast of fire and collect his blood. Behind you rests the receptacle you will need in order to gather his life force."*

Everyone turned around to find another oddity where the sword had lain. Another beam of light shined from the ceiling and an object hovered within it. Again, the group approached the new phenomenon.

"What is it?" asked Murdock, his brow crinkled.

"Don't touch anything!" Swinkle fumbled through his pack to find the ancient manuscript. Leafing through the pages, he found the passage he was searching for. The young cleric went over the writing with his finger as he read to himself. When he finished, he looked up.

Murdock gave him an exasperated look. "Well?"

"I just wanted to make sure the container is for Dracus's blood." The group fell silent. "The book states the same thing as that scripture, meaning that we will need to collect the beast's life force and place it in this lantern." Swinkle closed the book, placed it back in his sack, then approached the object.

The young cleric studied the lantern, noticing that four one-foot long gold rods held a clear, circular glass container.

A golden, cone-shaped lid screwed into the top, and a wick poked out from its peak.

On a count of three, Swinkle took both of his hands and carefully grabbed the artifact. Just as the light disappeared when Pondle snatched the emerald, the same happened when the young cleric took the lantern.

Swinkle brought the artifact close to his face and studied its gold features. "Filling this with the blood of a dragon is going to be a daunting task."

Harrison secured the scabbard to his belt and placed the sword inside it. "I'm sure that's what this weapon's for." The young warrior gazed at his friends. "We should leave this place."

Pondle headed for the exit. "I agree. All this magic stuff gives me an unsettling feeling. Follow me."

The group followed Pondle to the corridor leading out of the cavern. Harrison left the area last. The young warrior looked back a final time, gazing at the podium with the open book.

"Two more pieces of the puzzle to go," he said, before turning and leaving the room behind.

C H A P T E R 24

The group waited until morning to break camp and begin the next leg of their journey. The skies had cleared and the sun shone brightly over the mountaintops.

Harrison gathered his cinder-covered pack and secured his weaponry. Before he called Swinkle, he took another look at the sword that hung from his belt. Removing it from its scabbard, he brought the blade to his face. The forged steel gleamed in the morning sun.

"It is impressive," said Swinkle, who had approached Harrison without the young warrior noticing.

Harrison gazed at the sword. "What are we in store for?"

Swinkle shook his head. "I can only imagine," he said, his voice trailing off.

"We'll get through this. Somehow."

Swinkle was not as convinced. "How do we slay a dragon with one weapon?" he said under his breath. Making sure no one else was listening, the young cleric continued, "We can't defeat a beast like that with just the five of us."

Harrison placed the sword back in its protective covering. "I thought about that all night, too." The young warrior sighed. "I don't know how to kill a dragon either."

Swinkle looked over his shoulder and noticed the other members of the party readying themselves to leave. "We should join them." Harrison nodded and motioned for Swinkle to lead the way.

Clairese stood with her walking stick. "Are we ready to leave?"

Pondle raised a finger in the air, signaling her to wait. "What's our game plan? We haven't figured out where to go next."

"I know where we must go." All eyes turned to Gelderand. "The town of Dragon's Quarters rests at the base of the Ridge of Dracus. The townsfolk know all too well about the beast. How else do you think the town got its name?"

"Can we find more information on Dracus there?" asked Harrison.

The mage tucked Rufus into his backpack, readying him for their journey back to Ontario. "I'm sure of it," he said, securing the pack so that only the cat's little orange head remained visible. "But, first we must escort our guide back to her hometown." The men looked at Clairese.

"Thank you," said the woman. "Before we leave, I want you all to know that I'm happy to have been part of your journey. I wish you all the luck in the world." Clairese pointed away from the tattered sanctuary. "We need to go that way."

"How long until we get to Ontario?" asked Harrison.

"It should be a little quicker, going downhill and all. A week should do it."

"Let's use the same strategy that got us here." The young warrior motioned to Murdock and Pondle. "You two go first."

The two men started off in the direction that Clairese indicated, followed by the rest of the group.

Harrison walked alongside the religious woman. "Let's keep an eye out for your missing friends, too."

The monk flashed a caring smile. "Thank you."

"Like Murdock and Pondle pointed out, we didn't find any bodies."

Clairese's eyes watered. "There's always hope." The woman peered one last time at the remains of her reservation, then turned and never looked back again. "I'll cherish the good times here."

Harrison smiled. "Let's concentrate on getting you home." A few moments later, the sanctuary became a distant memory.

Two days passed without incident for the adventurers. Over the course of that time, the men had pondered what it would be like to encounter a vicious beast.

"So, do you think Dracus is a fire-breathing dragon?" Harrison asked Swinkle.

The young cleric nodded, keeping his gaze fixed on the landscape ahead of him. "The book in the cavern mentioned that we had to slay the beast of fire. It only seems reasonable."

Clairese overheard the two. "What does the emerald have to do with killing a dragon?"

Harrison and Swinkle's eyes locked. "It's all part of an elaborate treasure," answered the young warrior.

The woman shook her head. "Jewels, swords, dragons, it sounds like something pretty important."

The young warrior nodded. "That it is."

Clairese started to say something else when something caught her attention. Sniffing, she said, "Do you smell that?"

The two men stopped and sniffed the crisp air as well. "Smell what?" asked Harrison with concern.

"Fire." Gelderand approached the three from behind. "Something's burning."

Clairese agreed. "It's not a forest fire, though."

The mage furrowed his brow. "How can you tell?"

The monk squinted in the direction in front of them. "I'd expect more smoke, maybe see flames in the distance." Clairese looked around. "Where did your friends go?"

The three men scanned the immediate area. There was no sign of Murdock or Pondle. Even Lance had vanished.

Harrison took hold of his battle-axe. "It's not like them to disappear unless they were investigating something. That goes for Lance, too." The young warrior took a step forward. "Everyone, follow me."

The small group hastened their pace and descended the trail. Harrison did not want to panic, but having the others out of sight for this long troubled him.

The path twisted to a small crest, then dropped at a steeper angle. Upon coming to the top of the rise, Harrison raised a hand, signaling for the others to stop. In one smooth motion, the young warrior raised his blade.

"Run!" he shouted at the top of his lungs. A second later a Scynthian warrior swung a large club toward Harrison's midsection. The young warrior blocked the attack with his blade and engaged the brute in battle.

Clairese witnessed the melee with wide eyes. In an instant, she recalled seeing these strangers cart the dismembered body parts of her friends back to town, knowing the Scynthians caused their deaths.

With panic in her voice, she yelled to Gelderand and Swinkle, "Follow me!"

The three frightened souls ran away from Harrison and off the highly visible trail. Clairese led the men into the underbrush, looking for the right place to assess their situation. While they dashed through the woods, a horn bellowed in the distance and a dull thundering sound filled the forest.

The monk found a towering evergreen tree and hid behind its massive trunk. Peeking around the base, the nervous woman found too equally scared humans scampering toward her, but no sign of the enemy. Gelderand and Swinkle sprinted to the woman who bent over, gasping for air.

"What are we to do?" hollered Clairese through ragged breaths.

Gelderand leaned against the tree to take off his pack, his older body aching and his lungs yearning for oxygen. "We must go back to Harrison and find the others!"

Swinkle bent at the waist, his hands on his knees, out of breath also. "Where are Murdock and Pondle?" No one answered.

Clairese began to shake. "I have no weapons! Those savages are going to kill us!"

The young cleric raised his head, still breathing heavy. "We need you to guide us out of here."

The woman tried to regain her senses. Taking a few deep breaths, she nodded while saying, "All right. All right."

In the distance, the three of them heard weapons clashing and the trampling sounds of very heavy footsteps.

Gelderand stood tall. "We must go now. I have a few spells that can help us." The mage placed his hand in his pack to make sure Rufus was still safe. The cat gazed back at its master with wide eyes and a very anxious expression. Satisfied, Gelderand slung his backpack over his shoulder.

Swinkle looked at Clairese with a look of fear on his face. "Are you ready?"

"As ready as you are." The young woman crouched down while advancing back through the brush, with Gelderand and Swinkle following close behind.

Harrison swung his axe and sliced his enemy across the midsection. The savage dropped to the ground, but before the young warrior could savor his victory, a second brute attacked him.

The young warrior stood his ground on the crest of the hill, deflecting the Scynthian's advance with his battle-axe. As his mind churned during the heat of battle, Harrison realized that he and his friends unwittingly stumbled upon a Scynthian gathering. The anxious fighter looked beyond the savage and could see many figures scurrying up the rise, as well as a fiery glow down in the valley.

The creature swiped at Harrison with his mace, hitting the young warrior on his left side. Harrison absorbed the wallop and recovered in time to use his blade to beat back the beast. The savage swung at the human's head, but this time Harrison ducked out of the way and counterattacked with a devastating blow to the creature's leg. The young warrior's axe cut through the savage's skin and severed his femur, dropping the Scynthian to the ground. The beast wailed in pain.

Harrison stared at the pathetic soul as it writhed in agony. The young warrior peeked down the hill to see seven Scynthians advancing a good hundred yards away and dozens more charging further beyond them. With his enemy incapacitated, and its reinforcements a distance away, Harrison took the time to sling his axe over his shoulder and remove the two-handed sword from its scabbard. Grasping the hilt of the blade with two hands, he raised the sword over his head and in one motion drove the tip into the awaiting beast.

The young warrior pushed the razor sharp edge into the creature, but instead of tearing through flesh, the blade left the Scynthian unscathed, never cutting its skin, finding the ground instead.

Harrison brought the weapon to his face, dumbfounded. This time he hacked at the savage, but just as before, the blade seemed to slide through the beast and hit the earth. The Scynthian, breathing heavy, gazed up at Harrison with a look of utter disbelief.

Just then, Clairese, Gelderand, and Swinkle reached the young warrior. Harrison saw them stop several yards away from him, their eyes glued to the wriggling savage on the ground.

Harrison peered over the hill, seeing the countless figures advancing and gaining on their position. Without another moment to spare, the young warrior gazed at his enemy on the ground and said, "You're lucky this time." He then turned his attention to his friends. "Clairese, get us out of here – fast!"

The monk spun around, panning aimlessly at the landscape. "We want to stay on this trail! It will take us back to Ontario!"

Harrison looked over his shoulder again and grimaced. The initial seven beasts had made it halfway up the hill, albeit at a slower pace due to the steepness of the rise. Beyond the original savages scaling the hilly area, many more Scynthians scurried about the valley.

The young warrior stared hard at the clergywoman. "In a matter of minutes this area will be swarming with Scynthians! Hurry!"

Clairese closed her eyes and concentrated. She knew the passage cut through the forest and led back home. Just then, a thought came to her mind. "How many creatures can you see?"

Harrison gazed down the slope. "Twenty or thirty. It's hard to tell."

Clairese joined Harrison and glanced at the other side of the valley. In the distance, she could see where they needed to go. The landscape resembled a horseshoe, with the trail winding around the perimeter of a steep valley. Thick coniferous trees littered both sides of the trail, including the descent down the slope.

Pointing, the monk said, "We must get to the other side of this ledge. We can hide ourselves in the underbrush."

The young warrior hesitated, taking in the information. Harrison took a second to look at the advancing beasts trudge up the hill, then turned to Gelderand. "We need a diversion."

The mage peeked over the crest as well, then gazed back at the young warrior and nodded. Gelderand went into his pack, maneuvered Rufus out of the way, and collected the necessary ingredients for a spell.

A moment later, he rejoined Harrison. "Stand back."

The wizard chanted and waved his hands in the direction of the oncoming enemy. Without warning, three fireballs flew from his fingertips and hurtled toward the unsuspecting savages.

The projectiles slammed into the trees near the Scynthians, exploding in the process. Screams of anguish permeated the area, while dried pine needles and underbrush caught fire.

Harrison peered over the rise and found that the Scynthians had halted their charge and seemed to have ducked for cover. With precious little time to waste, he took his gaze over to the other side of the valley, a good quarter mile away. Seeing the area devoid of their dire enemy, he yelled, "Let's go!"

The young warrior led the charge, running away from the path and into the ensuing brush. The evergreen trees stood tall, while the underbrush hid the humans better than they could have expected.

As they dashed closer to their goal, Harrison watched the befuddled Scynthians meander in the valley. The young warrior could now see what had caused the smoke — a Scynthian bonfire. Harrison felt his arm tingle in the spot where the beasts had severed it, and as anger began to boil in his veins, he vowed to himself never to be captured by Scynthians again.

After advancing a few hundred yards, Harrison stopped behind a group of smaller pine trees and waved his friends over. The young warrior surveyed the area while the others caught their breath.

"I wish I knew where Murdock and Pondle drifted off to," muttered the young warrior.

"This is not good, Harrison," said Swinkle through breaths. "They don't know our plan."

"I know. I'm hoping they saw the fireballs."

The young cleric had a more somber thought. "I'm hoping they haven't been captured."

Harrison looked at his friend with concern. "We can evaluate our position once we get to the other side." Turning to Clairese, he asked, "What's over there?"

The monk gave the young warrior a blank stare. "Shalimar's Pass." The group stood silent upon hearing the woman's statement.

"I thought you said that passage was extremely dangerous."

Clairese nodded. "It is, but it just happens to be our only hope."

"This is too risky!" objected Swinkle.

The woman pressed further. "We need to lure those beasts into the Pass."

"Using ourselves as bait?" Harrison raised an eyebrow.

"Yes."

Harrison covered his face with his hands, then slowly ran them through his blonde hair. "You should have mentioned that before. How are we to inform Murdock and Pondle about this?"

Clairese shook her head. "I was hoping you'd be able to figure that out."

"I don't like this one bit." Frustrated, Harrison turned to his friends. "But, we have to move on."

The group left the security of the trees and started trekking again. Harrison led the party onward until they reached a point where the underbrush thinned considerably. The young warrior motioned for the others to stop at the point where the brush began to wane.

Harrison peered into the valley and saw Scynthians scouring the area. He then brought his gaze across to where the woods thickened again, some fifty yards away. We'll be exposed, he thought, not wanting to alarm the others, but also knowing there was no other way to flee. Furthermore, looking down into the gorge, the young warrior noticed that the angle from the base to where he stood now had leveled significantly. The Scynthians will catch up to us a lot faster this time, he thought.

The young warrior faced his friends. Pointing in front of him, he said, "We need to get over there. From that point, we hook around until we reach the top of that hill."

Swinkle looked at the open land. "Those beasts will see our every move!"

"We have no other choice." Harrison stared into his friend's eyes. "The Scynthians have already covered the ground behind us. There's no turning back. We must press forward."

Not waiting for an answer, the young warrior turned to face their next challenge. "On a count of three, everyone follow me. One, two, three!"

The young warrior had not taken more than three steps when he heard a horn bellow. Peeking over his shoulder and into the valley, Harrison saw several beasts point at their position, then charge.

Harrison's heart raced as he picked up his pace and reached the thickets first. Peeking back, he could see Clairese and Swinkle, with Gelderand three paces behind them. Beyond the mage charged the enemy up the flatter terrain, closing the gap between both parties with every step.

We're not going to make it, thought Harrison, as his friends approached him. "Clairese! Run to the pass! Everyone follow her!"

The young warrior readied his battle-axe, allowing his friends to continue onward. Harrison waited for the savages, who numbered twenty by now. Several of the beasts saw the young warrior, but seven others split off and took an alternate route in the direction of his unarmed friends.

"Oh no!" said the young warrior, knowing the others had no chance against the Scynthians. Instead of holding his ground, he decided to follow his friends.

Clairese raced through the forest, her lungs burning for more air, her legs becoming heavy. Swinkle and Gelderand followed close behind, but thunderous footsteps fast approached.

The woman turned her head to see if Swinkle and Gelderand were still following her, but found that they had halted and sported looks of horror. Clairese turned in the direction she was previously running and found herself crashing into an awaiting Scynthian warrior.

The savage did not attack her with a weapon; instead, he took his massive arms and clutched the surprised woman. Clairese screamed and kicked in vain, but she could not match the sheer strength of the beast.

The cloaked men stared wide-eyed at the poor girl, each one feeling helpless. Three more Scynthians surrounded the two and readied to pounce on them as well.

Before they could, one of the savages bellowed in agony before buckling to his knees. Harrison pulled his battle-axe out of the creature's back and stared at the two men. "Run!" he yelled before rushing toward another Scynthian.

The two remaining Scynthians turned their attention to the human warrior, leaving the perceived weaker beings alone, allowing Swinkle and Gelderand to dash past the beasts.

The young cleric caught a glimpse of the savage carrying their screaming guide deeper into the woods. "Gelderand, we must save her!"

The mage peered back at Harrison, seeing the young man use flawless maneuvers to attack the two beasts. Knowing Clairese stood no chance of survival on her own, he said, "Go after her!"

Clairese screamed repeatedly, not so much out of fear, but to alert the others to her position. The Scynthian was strong, but his heavy body was not built for sprinting and he started gasping for air.

The woman continued to try to wiggle free, but the beast held her tight to his chest. Clairese tried to bite the savage, but his leather armor protected his limbs.

From the corner of her eye, the scared woman saw two more Scynthians advancing to her position. She tried to look past the beast, but saw no sign of her friends. Feeling all was hopeless, she began to cry.

"There are two more behind you!" bellowed one of the savages in his native tongue to the beast that held Clairese.

The Scynthian motioned with his head for them to go onward. "You handle them; I'll take this one to the compound."

The two beasts nodded in agreement and were about to start their trek when a small dog appeared out of thin air in front of them. Standing fifteen feet before them, the animal began to bark frantically.

The Scynthians stopped for a moment, startled by the sudden appearance of the canine. Before either one could react, two arrows penetrated their upper torsos, dropping both to the ground, writhing in pain.

Pondle appeared from out of the thickets and, wielding a dagger, slit the throats of the shocked Scynthians, ending their misery.

The thief yelled at the savage that held Clairese. "Let her go!"

The look of surprise left the beast, replaced by an expression of defiance. "Never!" he said in an understandable language, then ran again with the woman.

The beast took four steps before feeling the steel tip of an arrow enter the small of his back. The Scynthian fell forward, landing on top of Clairese.

Murdock readied another arrow from his quiver and approached the savage. The ranger stood over the creature and yelled, "Get up!"

The beast raised himself to his knees, enabling Clairese to squirm out from under him. The Scynthian turned his head to face Murdock, his breathing heavy. The ranger did not say a word; instead, he planted a second arrow in the chest of the creature, killing him instantly.

Clairese remained on the ground, coughing and crying. Murdock raced over to her. "Are you all right?" The woman nodded, sobbing.

The ranger looked over his shoulder to find Gelderand and Swinkle rejoining him and Pondle. Lance teleported over to the scared woman, nestling his snout in her midsection.

"This isn't over yet," said Murdock, grasping Clairese by the arm in an attempt to get her to stand. "There's more Scynthians on the way."

Clairese regained her senses, recalling what she had told Harrison. "We must get to the Pass. We need to draw those beasts there."

Murdock did not have time to think. "Let's find Harrison first." The ranger helped Clairese to her feet, then looked beyond the group. Coming into view was a familiar sight.

"Harrison!" shouted the ranger with relief.

The young warrior appeared disheveled, sweating profusely, with cuts and gouges on his body. "We can't stay here," he said through heavy breaths. "They're right behind me!"

Clairese looked into the distance and could see more dark figures advancing. Pointing, she yelled, "Here they come!"

Harrison waved the group forward. "Make a run for the pass!"

Clairese took the lead, running as fast as she could toward their destination. She knew the perils of Shalimar's Pass, but also its many quirks. On any given day, the passage remained calm without any hint of its treacherous history. Today she hoped for the region to live up to its legacy.

The group continued to run, increasing their distance between their foes with every step. After what felt like an eternity, the landscape pitched upward and the forest thinned out.

Clairese recognized a very familiar sight. A massive wind chime, standing over twenty feet tall, stood at the crest of the hill. She walked over to it, running her hands over one of the smooth iron poles.

Harrison reached the rise next and stared in awe at the object. From his perspective, four metal cylindrical pipes of varying length hung off thick chains from an inverted L-shaped bar.

"How does that thing work," he asked, as the rest of the party reached the hilltop.

Clairese pointed to the structure. "When the wind blows, the hollow chimes slam into each other over and over again. The sound can be deafening." In the distance, she heard the Scynthians coming. "We need to enter the pass."

Harrison took hold of the monk's arm and looked deep into her eyes. In a direct, but non-threatening voice, he asked, "Will we be safe?"

Clairese stared at the young warrior, but remained silent. She stepped to the crest of the hill and gazed down

Shalimar's Pass. In front of her stood a breathtaking view of the mountain range and the greenness of the open landscape beyond the valley. Clairese took her gaze downward to the harmless looking slope.

Finally speaking, she said to Harrison, "Let's just say we need to get through this passage as fast as possible." The woman got the attention of the other men.

"Listen to me. All of you must run as fast as you can through this pass. I know the trail is a bit rocky and steep, but if we're lucky, we can make this quarter-mile run in less than five minutes."

Clairese read the worried expressions of the men, but that did not stop her. "We must leave now." With that, she motioned for the adventurers to follow her, then turned to head down the mountainside. Lance sprinted after the woman.

Harrison never felt his heart beat so hard. The descent went rather quickly, due to the steep angle, almost causing him to fall. Less than a minute later, he heard the shouts from the Scynthians at the crest of the rise. The young warrior peeked over his shoulder and saw scores of beasts enter the passage.

Clairese maintained her lead, followed by Lance and Harrison. Murdock and Pondle caught up to the young warrior in no time, but Harrison noticed that Swinkle and Gelderand fell further behind.

The young warrior knew he could outrun the others with ease and reach safety first, but his warrior pride told him he must protect his weaker friends. Making an abrupt stop, he shouted to Murdock and Pondle, "I'll meet you at the base!" The two men shot him a brief look of concern, but continued onward.

The young warrior closed the gap between himself and his two slower friends. "You need to run faster!" he said in Gelderand's direction.

The wizard had already started gasping for air. "I won't make it!"

"Yes, you will! I won't let you fail!"

The young warrior glanced up the hill and saw the Scythians advancing at a rapid pace. If that image was not bad enough, the sight of a cloudy mass at the peak of the hill caused him even more concern. A moment later, he thought he heard the subtle sound of metal striking metal.

Swinkle, three steps ahead of the other two men, turned to Harrison with a look of panic. "That's the wind chime! We must get out of the pass now!"

Harrison ran stride for stride with Gelderand, while Swinkle raced farther ahead. In front of the young warrior, he could see Lance in the distance along with Clairese, Murdock, and Pondle. Behind him, the roar of Scythian warriors filled the chasm.

The young warrior noticed that the passage flattened out about two hundred yards away. A cool breeze wafted over him from behind, not a hard wind, but one whose chill bit at the young warrior's neck.

Harrison peered over his shoulder again. The cloud grew dark and the chimes started to clang. Thirty seconds, he thought, recalling what Clairese had told him days ago.

Ahead, the young warrior could see that his friends, other than Swinkle, had reached the end of the passage and motioned for the rest to hurry.

The din of the chimes grew louder. Harrison felt a colder draft sliding down the mountain pass. His exposed hands started to stiffen and the skin on his face tightened in the cold.

Harrison watched Swinkle reach the end of the trail, but he and Gelderand remained thirty yards away. A deafening crash came from the top of Shalimar's Pass as the hollow metal chimes slammed into one another. A thunderous whoosh emanated from the top of the passage and proceeded to flow down the trail.

The young warrior felt the ground beneath him level and he practically pushed the old wizard to the spot where his friends stood.

Clairese, near hysterics, waved at the two. "Get off the path! Get off the path!"

Harrison watched Clairese dive to the right and into the underbrush, while Lance scampered after the woman. Murdock and Pondle followed their lead, while Swinkle rushed to the left. The young warrior grabbed the mage and hurled him into the thickets with him.

Harrison rolled twice, then regained his orientation. Taking his eyes to the pass he found that thirty Scynthians ran toward them, still over a hundred yards from the end of the passage. The dark cloud gushed from the peak and a few seconds later, engulfed the entire mountainside. Screams of anguish stopped abruptly, followed by a cold, stiff breeze.

The young warrior covered his head and curled up in a ball, allowing the wind to pass him by. The icy cloud had dissipated as fast as it had appeared. The young warrior peered toward Shalimar's Pass, but there was no sign that the Scynthians had ever existed. The chimes had stopped clanging and the sun's rays warmed the trail.

Gelderand groaned from his spot on the ground. "Is everyone alive?" Rufus wiggled out of the mage's pack and limped around the area, his master's tumble having squashed the poor feline while he nestled anxiously in the safety of Gelderand's sack.

Harrison scanned the area and saw the rest of his group wander out from the brush. "I think so." Just then, Lance bolted from the woods and greeted his master.

"Thank goodness you made it, too," said the young warrior, scratching the dog behind his ears.

Murdock approached the young warrior. "The Scynthians are all gone. There's not even a hint that they were ever in the pass." The ranger motioned toward the passage with his head. "Clairese didn't lie to us. This place is brutal."

Pondle interrupted the two. "We're not out of the woods yet." The thief pointed away from the descending path. "The Scynthians' camp is over there. I think we need to at least see what they're up to."

Clairese overheard the men. "What? Are you kidding me? We're lucky to still be alive! Let's leave this place before more of those beasts come looking for us."

Harrison understood both points. Facing the woman, he said, "We need to see what these savages are planning. Don't worry, we'll observe them from a distance."

The monk shook her head. "I'm not going anywhere near that compound!"

Harrison nodded in concurrence. "I agree. You take Gelderand and Swinkle down the trail and we'll meet up with you in a little while."

Swinkle understood his friend's rationale, but he had other ideas. "Harrison, if you are captured, we cannot save you. I highly suggest we leave like Clairese said."

Harrison approached his friend. "I know how you feel, but we need to see just what the Scynthians are doing down here. I have to tell you, Swinkle, all this activity in these remote parts of the land is very disturbing. Remember what Marcus and Jonathan told us — that the Scynthians are organizing. This is just more proof."

Swinkle nodded, recalling the days that the group had spent with his former leader, Marcus Braxton, and his good friend, Jonathan Winston. Both men were convinced that the Scynthians were planning something, and what had transpired today just solidified that belief in the young cleric's mind.

Making as strong a point as he knew how, Swinkle said, "No more adventures! Take a look around, then come back, all right?"

Harrison smiled. "All right." The young warrior faced Clairese and pointed to the trail behind her. "You're going to stay on this path, right?"

"Yes."

"Hike for a half-mile, then get off the trail. We'll meet up with you in twenty minutes." The young warrior looked at his canine friend. "Send Lance to find us and he'll lead us back to your location."

Clairese nodded. Looking at Swinkle and Gelderand, she said, "Follow me."

Harrison bent down on one knee and addressed the dog. "Lance, you stay with them. You'll find us when the time's right."

The dog yapped, "Yes."

The young warrior looked over to Pondle and Murdock. "Let's go."

The three left their friends behind and followed the path away from Shalimar's Pass. The trail cascaded along the mountainside, leading the men closer to the Scynthian-controlled area.

Harrison feared what they might find. Since embarking on his journey to find the Treasure of the Land, and now the Talisman of Unification, he had witnessed firsthand the many Scynthian outposts that had cropped up throughout the countryside. He now refuted the belief that the Scynthians were unorganized; if an outpost existed here, they were definitely up to no good.

CHAPTER 25

🗘

The three men took every imaginable precaution on their way to investigate the Scynthian compound. Harrison followed Murdock and Pondle through the underbrush away from the main trail. As they circled back to the complex, Harrison could only wonder what they might find.

The Ridge of King Solaris is way out of the Scynthian's territory, thought the young warrior. But, after finding camps in and around the Great Forest, anything was now possible.

Pondle had taken the lead and held up a hand, signaling a halt. The thief positioned himself behind a large bush and carefully peered around it. A moment later, he removed his sword from its sheath, trying to make as little noise as possible.

Harrison saw his friend wave Murdock and him to his location. The young warrior stayed low to the ground as they reached the thief, who gestured for them to keep down as they approached.

Harrison took a good look at Pondle and could see something was wrong. "What did you find?"

Pondle gave his friends a blank stare. "Nothing can prepare you for what you'll see."

Harrison and Murdock gazed at each other with concern. "Show us," said the ranger.

Pondle nodded, then pulled back enough branches to allow the other men to see into the Scynthian compound.

Harrison's mouth dropped open, aghast at the gruesome scene. Besides the typical Scynthian layout of buildings, the young warrior saw eight poles encircling the smoky remains of a bonfire. Impaled on each stake rested a human body.

"Who are these people?" Harrison felt his rage boil, clutching the hilt of his weapon with a firm grip.

Pondle maintained his stare at his friends. "I'm willing to bet they're Clairese's friends."

Feelings of anxiety, sorrow, and anger raced through the young warrior's body. "These savages must pay for this! We can't allow them to keep slaughtering innocent people!" he said through clenched teeth.

Murdock grabbed the young warrior's forearm. "I'm just as enraged as you, but what can we really do?" The ranger locked his gaze with Harrison's. "There're only three of us."

"This has to end!" Harrison could feel an unstoppable wrath coursing through his veins. "This *must* end!"

Murdock and Pondle always knew Harrison had a strong will, but both of them knew their situation was hopeless this time.

"Harrison, listen to me," began Murdock, "I want nothing more than to make these bastards pay for their actions, but we can't do it now. Not yet."

"Then when?" The young warrior squeezed his weapon tighter. "After they've murdered every man, woman, and child? When?"

The ranger shook his head. "Just not now," he said, his voice trailing off.

Harrison looked at Murdock and could almost see a look of defeat. He then took his gaze to the campsite, to the impaled people. Murdock was right. His anger would only get them killed without the chance of saving others in the future.

Pondle tried to reason with Harrison. "We need to leave, to get to safety. The camp's deserted right now, but that can change at any moment." He paused, then pointed to the compound. "And I don't want to get captured and end up like that."

Harrison understood Pondle's rationale. Staring at his friends, he said, "Both of you promise me that once we find this treasure and figure out how to use it, that we'll do all that we can to rid these savages from this world."

Murdock nodded. "You have our word."

Harrison nodded back, seemingly looking through his friends. "I'll tell Clairese."

A look of sorrow and despair flashed across the faces of both Murdock and Pondle. "Let's get back to the others," said the thief, motioning for his friends to follow.

Harrison gazed back one last time, taking in the disgusting scene. "I *will* avenge your souls," he said softly to himself, then ran off with his friends.

The three men scampered along the trail, keeping an eye out for unwanted Scynthian attention. Five minutes into their trek, they saw a small animal off the side of the trail. The little creature recognized the men.

"Lance!" exclaimed Harrison as the dog bounded toward his master. "Where are the others?"

The dog yapped once, then turned and led the men off the main trail. A couple of minutes later, Harrison found Swinkle, Gelderand, and Clairese hiding amongst overgrown bushes.

Swinkle stood up to greet his friends. "I'm glad you all made it back alive. What did you find?"

Harrison gave Clairese a quick glance before speaking to the young cleric. "There's a large Scynthian compound," he said under his breath, "with several slain humans."

Swinkle swallowed. "Could Clairese have known them?"

"That's what I'm thinking." Harrison peeked over to the woman, who noticed the men watching her.

"Are the Scynthians over there?" The conversation by the two men concerned the monk.

"They have established a base near Shalimar's Pass." Harrison faced the woman, not sure what to say next.

Clairese wrinkled her brow. "What's wrong? There's something else, isn't there?"

The rest of the men stared at Harrison. "Your other friends are dead. We saw their bodies in the Scynthians' camp."

The woman covered her mouth and appeared on the verge of tears. "Are you sure it was them?" she asked, her voice wavering.

"They wore the same clothing as you and your friends back in Ontario." Harrison paused. "It has to be them."

Tears streamed down Clairese's face, her voice barely a whisper. "Why?"

"I don't know." Harrison shook his head and embraced the pained woman.

Between sobs, she said, "We need to go after them. To give them a proper burial."

"We can't." The young warrior tried his best to take in account the monk's feelings. "It's too dangerous. With all the Scynthians running around here our best bet is to leave this area as soon as possible. We must get back and warn your people."

"First you cart a wagon full of mutilated bodies into our town," Clairese began, sniffling. "Then this. We're defenseless in Ontario."

The young warrior used a soothing voice. "All the reason to get back there and warn them."

Clairese nodded, understanding what needed to be done. "I'll get us back in double time."

"Good." Harrison glanced in Pondle's direction. "Let's keep clear of those beasts."

"Understood." Pondle motioned for the other men to gather their packs. Within minutes, everyone was ready to travel.

Clairese tightened the fasteners on her backpack, then grabbed her walking stick. "I'm ready. Follow me."

The group followed the determined monk back in the direction of the main trail and began their return trek to Ontario.

The party hiked for four days without any further worries from the Scynthians. By mid-afternoon on the last day, the adventurers approached the outskirts of Ontario. Not many people wandered the streets, as far as Harrison could tell.

Clairese guided the men back to the temple. Upon entering, she found Brother Lorenz alone, kneeling in prayer. The woman gestured for the men to stay back and waited patiently for her fellow monk to finish.

A moment later, the man stood up and faced the group. He smiled when his eyes met Clairese's. "Sister, it is good to have you back in one piece. How was your journey?" The monk waved his hand toward the room off the temple, urging the people to go there.

Clairese took a deep breath, then said, "My trip has been successful, though very sorrowful."

"What do you mean?" Brother Lorenz took a seat at the table and gestured for the others to do likewise.

"The eruption ruined the sanctuary, Brother, but it allowed our friends to find their treasure."

The monk cocked his head. "Finding the treasure was a good thing, no?"

"Yes, it was, but we couldn't find any of our people at the site."

"Their bodies weren't near the reservation?" Brother Lorenz scanned the men for answers. "Maybe they avoided the blast."

"No." Clairese let out a heavy sigh. "Harrison saw their corpses at a Scynthian camp."

"What?" The monk's eyes grew wide.

"There's a large Scynthian compound about a four day's trek from here," said Harrison. "They were all over the mountainside."

Brother Lorenz asked, "How large of a compound?"

The sister shook her head. "Large. Hundreds of savages roamed the area near Shalimar's Pass."

"That can't be!" The man sat back in his chair, dumbfounded at the information. "What are we to do?"

"You must leave." Harrison leaned forward to put emphasis on his words. "All of you."

"All of us?" Brother Lorenz seemed unable to comprehend the danger. "It's not as easy as you make it sound."

"If you stay here, you risk an attack from the Scynthians. They'd slaughter the village."

"You saw what they did to Larissa and her family," added Clairese.

Brother Lorenz looked at the sister and nodded. Turning to Harrison, he said, "What do you suggest?"

Harrison thought for a moment. "Pack up all of your belongings and move away from the mountains. Arcadia might be able to help."

The monk shook his head in disbelief. "You're talking over two hundred people, leaving their town, their homes, their way of life."

"It's either that or die." Clairese started to wring her hands.

Brother Lorenz directed his next question to Harrison. "Can you help us?"

The young warrior, surprised at the request for help, took his gaze to his friends. "Um, no, we can't. We're not prepared to lead a convoy of townspeople through the countryside. Besides, we have other things we need to attend to."

The monk nodded. "I understand. I shouldn't have asked you to take on such a burden."

"You're not a burden," said Harrison, fumbling for the right words. "But don't you think it should be you who leads your people to safety? How would your fellow Ontarians feel putting so much trust in people they don't know?"

The monk nodded. "You're right. The sisters and brothers of this temple will coordinate this effort." Brother Lorenz took his gaze to Clairese. "Thank you for returning our Sister to us safely."

Harrison smiled. "There's no need to thank us. We'll be leaving in the morning." The young warrior looked at his friends, who nodded in agreement.

"You can stay here for the night. It's the least we can do for you."

The young warrior and his friends thanked Brother Lorenz, then took advantage of the remains of the day to gather food and supplies. After a good night's rest, they readied themselves to leave the small village.

"Dragon's Quarters is about a three-week trek through the Arcadian countryside," said Pondle, securing the last of his things.

Harrison nodded. "Good. It'll give us some time to think about what we need to do next." As the men prepared to leave, Harrison noticed a woman approaching them.

"Good morning, Clairese." The young warrior smirked. "Where's your red cloak?"

"I told Brother Lorenz what I saw and gave him my honest opinion about my life. He understood completely and has given me time to reflect." Clairese smiled at the young warrior. "I enjoyed our journey together. I'm glad I was able to help you achieve your goal."

Harrison nodded in thanks. "More than you can imagine."

Clairese smiled again. "My people are going to decide what we are to do tonight."

"I hope they realize the dangers that are around them."

"I do, too." The woman's face lit up. "I've decided to venture to Arcadia and take up residence there. I'm going to help my people first, though."

Harrison smiled. "Good for you, Clairese. There'll be more opportunities for you there, I'm sure."

"Yes, there will be." The woman looked toward the forest behind Harrison. "You better get on your way." She then leaned over and kissed the young warrior on the cheek. "Thank you and take care."

Harrison's face went flush. "I hope to see you again sometime."

"Sometime." Clairese smiled, then turned away. After a few steps, she glanced back and gave the group a wave.

The young warrior watched the woman head back into town, then turned to his friends. "It's time to go. There's a dragon waiting for us."

C H A P T E R 26

¤

The adventurers trekked across the Arcadian countryside for over a week without a hint of trouble. On many different occasions, they passed tradesmen and herders, but no one caused them any concern.

Harrison gazed upon the open plains and could see more rolling hills in the distance. The sun began to sink low in the sky and twilight fast approached. Calling ahead to Pondle, he said, "How much longer are we traveling today?"

The thief turned to face him. "We can stop any time since we've journeyed all day. I'm ready for a break."

The men regrouped and Pondle secured the immediate area. "As usual, we can make a small campfire," said the thief. "I don't like having to spend so many nights on a wide open plain." Everyone settled in around the fire to eat and rest their weary legs.

Harrison gave Lance a piece of dried meat, then turned his attention to Gelderand. "Tigris is a short distance from Dragon's Quarters. What stories have you heard about the place?"

The older man hand fed Rufus, who sat by his side. "The village is small, but quaint." After finishing with the cat, the mage took a sip of water from his tankard before continuing. "The town is an oddity, actually."

"What do you mean by that?" Swinkle tore a piece of dried meat, gave thanks to Pious, then tossed the food over his shoulder. Lance eyed the beef and scurried over to gobble it up.

"Well, what I mean is that the village is more of a gathering place for adventurers like you." Gelderand pointed to Harrison.

"Warriors have heard stories of Dracus, the fire-breathing dragon, and come with visions of slaying him. Most of the time they just get drunk and go back from whence they came."

"Are you telling me that Dracus is nothing more than a myth?" Harrison shook his head in disbelief, while his friends listened to the conversation the young warrior had with the older man.

"Oh, I didn't say that," said the mage, wagging a finger in the young warrior's direction. "Dracus is real and has terrorized the village for centuries."

"Then why do people stay there?"

"For the mystique, for the thrill of living at the base of a mountain range that is home to such a volatile creature." Gelderand sipped from his water skin again.

"So, he's alive?"

"Very much so."

"How do we defeat him?"

The mage exhaled with a heavy sigh, shook his head and looked down. "That, I don't know."

The young warrior finished the remainder of his food, then grasped the hilt of his two-handed sword and pulled it from its sheath. The razor-sharp blade glistened in the firelight.

"I'm sure this weapon is needed."

Gelderand nodded. "Finding that sword was not a coincidence."

Harrison gazed at the blade, then to the three jewels embedded in its hilt. "I just wish I knew what I was supposed to do."

"Again, you will find out in due time."

The young warrior waved the massive weapon in front of him, reveling again at how light the blade felt. When finished, he placed the sword back in its sheath. "What other stories have you heard about Dracus?"

Gelderand looked up in thought. "There are so many, but this one I know to be true. Every twenty years or so, the red dragon swoops down from the mountains to reek havoc with the townspeople. Each time he has burned their buildings, charred their crops, and killed their livestock. And, he is overdue."

The young warrior furrowed his brow. "How do you know this?"

"I was there the last time he torched the village. People scattered into the forest while their homes burned. Men tried to slay the wicked beast, but that only infuriated the creature more. Many people lost their lives that day.

"That's why the area is inhabited by warrior types, so that they will be there when Dracus strikes again. At least the villagers will have a better chance to defeat the beast."

Harrison was about to ask Gelderand another question when he saw Lance spring to his feet.

Pondle grabbed his sword and looked to the east. "I see torches advancing!" A low rumble began to fill the area.

All the men jumped to their feet with weapons drawn. Lance raced to the edge of their camp and began to bark at a feverish pitch.

Harrison looked in the dog's direction. In the distance, he saw small orange fireballs bobbing against the dark horizon. The unmistakable sound of hoof beats started to fill the general vicinity.

The young warrior looked around his campsite. The landscape offered the adventurers no place to hide. The openness left them unprotected to whomever the campfire, which served as a beacon in the night, drew toward them.

As the horses drew nearer, Harrison said, "Let's not draw any conclusions just yet. Don't force any actions."

The men watched as twenty or so warhorses advanced on their position. With expert maneuvers, the horsemen circled their camp, surrounding the men in the process.

Harrison, Murdock, and Pondle surrounded Swinkle and Gelderand, while Lance barked at the intruders. The young warrior stared at the young faces of the soldiers, wondering what their next move would be.

Just then, two horses entered into the ring. The lead horseman maneuvered his steed closer to Harrison.

The young warrior's jaw dropped. "You again!"

Troy Harkin gazed upon his mirror image. "I've scoured the land in search of you. I have many things to ask."

"That makes two of us!" Harrison held his battle-axe in a defensive posture. "Who are you?"

"My name is Troy Harkin and I wish to speak with you and your men." Troy brought his horse closer to Harrison.

The young warrior kept his stare locked on Troy. "How can this be? How can you look just like me? This must be some trick!"

"I assure you there's no trick." Troy tried to put the men at ease. "I want nothing more than to talk to you and try to find answers to both of our questions."

While Harrison pondered the man's request, Murdock voiced his opinion. "I don't know, Harrison. This is all very strange."

"I know," said the young warrior under his breath, "but I need to know what's going on."

Harrison addressed Troy again. "What do you suggest we do?"

Troy dismounted, leaving his weapon on his horse. "I wish nothing more than to speak with you one-on-one."

A thousand thoughts raced through Harrison's mind. Part of him wanted to flee the scene, in order to regroup with his own thoughts, while another piece yearned for answers.

"First, back your men away from our camp. After that, we shall speak alone, unarmed."

Troy nodded in agreement. "Fair enough. Where will your men be?"

"Equally away from us, except Lance comes with me."

The young general cocked his head and squinted. "Lance?"

"The dog," said Harrison, nodding his head toward Lance. "Just in case."

Troy peered at the canine, then back to Harrison. "Deal." The soldier called to his advisor. "Teleios, take you and the others a hundred yards away from their camp."

Teleios gave his leader a look of concern, but nodded and heeded his wishes. A few moments later, Troy's men had departed the immediate area.

Troy then turned to Harrison. "Your turn."

Harrison hesitated. "Murdock, Pondle, take the others away from the campground."

"I don't like this, Harrison," said the ranger, still wielding his weapon.

"Just leave us alone." The young warrior called over to Lance. "Stay with me, boy." The little dog came to his master's side.

Troy pointed to Harrison's battle-axe and sword. "Give them your weaponry."

Again, Harrison hesitated, not wanting to relinquish his blades. Without taking his eyes off Troy, he lowered his axe and handed it to Murdock. He did likewise with his sword, giving that to Pondle.

Turning toward the thief, he said in a whisper, "Guide them no more than a hundred yards away."

Pondle nodded, then waved his friends onward, using his infravision to lead them from the two warriors. A minute later, the twins found themselves alone in the Arcadian countryside, the crackle of the fire the only sound.

Troy motioned to one of the backpacks that lay on the ground. "Do you mind if I take a seat? We've been riding hard all day."

Harrison shook his head. "No, go right ahead. That's my pack anyway."

Troy sat down, followed by Harrison. Lance lay by his master's side.

Troy removed a flask from his belt, uncorked it, and took a swig. "Would you like a sip?" Troy held the flask out to Harrison.

The young warrior felt compelled to oblige. "Sure." Harrison took the flask to his mouth and felt the liquid scorch his lips. Without trying to cough, the alcohol burned his throat while making its way to his stomach.

Troy looked over to Harrison and laughed. "The king likes his whiskey well fermented."

"I can tell." Harrison handed the container back to Troy, coughing. The young warrior then gazed at the man in his identical likeness. "Tell me about yourself."

"What's there to tell? I'm a warrior like you, searching this land for treasures."

"No." Harrison shook his head. "Where do you come from? Where do you live? Who raised you?"

"Ah." Troy nodded. "I live off the coast on Dragon's Lair. I was born and raised there, and still call the place my home. The king has treated me very well."

"The king?"

"King Holleris rules the island." Troy paused, reading Harrison's face. "He really exists; he's not a myth."

Harrison recalled the stories that Philius had told him, how King Holleris had turned evil and banished his fellow lords. The young warrior also knew that the Talisman they seek would involve this regal ruler to a certain degree.

"What role do you play in his army?"

Troy locked his gaze onto the young warrior. "I'm his general-at-arms."

Harrison had not expected that answer. "I see. Then what business do you have with me?"

"I believe you know that answer." Troy continued to stare at Harrison. "But I don't care about that now. I want to know who you are and why you exist."

"I exist because my parents brought me into this world."

"Tell me about your parents," said Troy.

Harrison looked up at the starry sky. "My parents were beautiful people. Mom loved her artifacts and treasures, and Dad would cart them to her every day." Harrison let out a little laugh recalling them. "I'd go with them on their trips between Aegeus and Argos, up until the time I joined the Fighter's Guild."

Troy noticed Harrison's face change. Frowning, he asked, "What's the matter?"

Harrison felt anguish deep in his soul. "One day my parents set off on an expedition with five other couples. Scynthians attacked and murdered them. I was only twelve." The young warrior looked to the ground and began to scratch Lance on his head.

"I'm sorry, Harrison."

The young warrior jerked his head up. "How do you know my name?"

"Nigel Hammer and I had an allegiance, and your name came up. He wants nothing more than to capture you."

Harrison shrugged, not surprised at the news. "He's a wicked man who will be dealt with in due time." The young warrior paused. "How did you find me?"

"We arrived in Ontario six days after you left. I had my men comb the countryside, leaving no stone unturned."

The young warrior flashed a smile to the man in his likeness. "Your men are very good."

Troy laughed. "I've trained them well."

Harrison gazed at his twin. "Tell me about your parents."

The young general turned his face away. "I lived on the island with them. For as long as I can remember, I was training for our army. I didn't see them all that much."

Harrison found the information odd. "Really? How well did you know them?"

"Up until the age of eight, I stayed with them every night. After that, I spent my time in the barracks, training to become a warrior." Troy fidgeted, uncomfortable to continue.

"I never really had a childhood with parents and siblings. I was always told that I would be the king's favored son."

Harrison squinted. "Why is that? How come the king took such an interest in you?"

"King Holleris told me that the Harkin lineage dated back to the original Overlords, to the days of the Four Kings." Troy paused, looking toward the campfire. "He always told me that someday I would return to him the greatest treasure this land had ever known."

Harrison felt a chill race through his body. The young warrior knew that he and his friends possessed the prize Troy had sought. "Can you describe to me the treasure you seek?"

Troy stared at Harrison. "I believe you have it with you."

The young warrior knew he had to do something at this very moment. "If we do have this treasure, will you still return it to King Holleris?"

Troy did not respond right away. No one had ever challenged his loyalty to the king — until now. In his heart, he needed confirmation before making such a drastic decision.

"Harrison, I must know if you are truly my brother. Is there anything that you can show me to convince me that we are?"

Harrison thought hard. His parents had never mentioned another son and no indications of another baby existed in their home.

The young warrior shook his head no. "I lived in Aegeus my whole life. Do you recall anybody mentioning that town?"

Troy shook his head as well. "No. My journeys have always taken me to the Great Forest and points south of that."

The young warrior pondered the situation. "Do you remember anything specific from your youth that seemed odd?"

Troy concentrated, but came up with nothing. "No, other than my extensive warrior training." Suddenly, a thought sprang to his mind. Holding up a finger, he said, "Wait, there is something."

The general-at-arms removed a chain from around his neck. "My mother gave this to me when I was very young. She said to always keep it with me, for someday its true meaning would be exposed."

Harrison's eyes opened wide in shock. The young warrior likewise removed a chain from around his neck. In his palm rested the hand-carved ivory dove that his mother had given him, identical to the one Troy held in his hand at that very moment.

The two warriors stared at each other, neither saying a word. Harrison broke the uncomfortable silence. "Mom made this for me when I was born. I wore it on a bracelet when I was a baby, but she put it on a chain as I got older."

A sudden sadness overtook Troy. "I wish I had known our mother," he said, accepting the fact that Harrison was indeed his twin. A deep anger began to replace his sorrow. "Why did the king take me away?"

Harrison shook his head. "I don't know. That's something you must ask him yourself."

Troy looked away, rage boiling in his blood. "He stole my youth, my livelihood, my identity! For what?" He clenched his teeth. "I need more than answers!"

Harrison tried to calm his brother. "My friends and I can help you, but we'll need to work together."

The thought of the sacred treasure popped into Troy's mind. "The king wants me to bring you back to Dragon's Lair, to see who acquired the prize."

Harrison appeared skeptical. "He's an evil man, Troy. The king's dangerous."

Troy nodded. "This might be true, but I must confront him nevertheless. There are many things he needs to explain."

Harrison thought of the treasure he possessed and what the scriptures stated. "King Holleris is the keeper of one of the pieces to the puzzle."

The young general crinkled his brow. "How do you know?"

"The ancient book revealed that in a clue."

Troy's eyes widened. "Did you scratch the book? Did it bleed?" Harrison nodded in affirmation.

"Then it's true!" Troy took a closer look at Harrison. "Armies of men are looking for this book. My army, Lord Hammer's army, yet you and your four friends found it? How?"

"There were more of us before, but only four of us survived the Seven Rooms." Harrison paused, recalling the losses of Marcus Braxton, Jason Sands, and Aidan Hunter along the way to finding the Treasure of the Land. "Finding the next piece of the puzzle has been a burden as well."

"Maybe I can offer you and your men help."

Harrison pondered Troy's offer, knowing where they were heading next. "We could use all the help we can get. Our next course of action is to slay Dracus and obtain his blood."

Troy appeared puzzled. "Dracus?"

"Dracus is a dragon."

"How in the world do you expect to slay a dragon with five men?"

The young warrior shrugged. "After we found the last part of the treasure, a sword appeared in the chamber. It's huge, yet weighs less than a pound. I'm thinking it's needed for our next battle."

"A sword?" Troy raised a brow. "One sword versus the strength of a dragon? You are brave, Harrison."

The young warrior nodded sheepishly before his eyes lit up. "You have seasoned soldiers. With you and their help, we could defeat this beast!"

Troy agreed. "Our chances would greatly improve. But it's still risky."

"In order to obtain the treasure we must slay the dragon. There's no way around it."

"Then it must be done." Troy gazed into Harrison's eyes. "What are you proposing from this point forward?"

Harrison knew he must answer this question before they could embark on their journey. After a moment of thought, he said, "Help us find the remaining pieces of the puzzle, then we'll venture to Dragon's Lair together. But, Troy, you'll have to somehow trick the king into giving us the final clue. He possesses it."

"Leave that to me." Troy stood up and extended his hand. "It would be an honor to enter upon this quest with my brother."

Harrison stood as well. "Yes, it would." The two men shook hands, then embraced.

"We'll need to congregate the men and let then know what we've decided," said Harrison.

"Let's bring both parties over." With that, Harrison and Troy called for their respective groups to meet at the campfire area.

Before Troy's soldiers approached the campground, Harrison explained the arrangement with his friends. "We've made a deal to find the treasure together."

"What?" exclaimed Murdock. "You had no right accepting anything from him without consulting us first!"

"Calm down, Murdock! We need Troy's help in order to defeat Dracus. Plus, he will get the last jewel from the king."

"King? What king?" asked the ranger, folding his arms.

Harrison looked past his friends and could see the soldiers approaching. "It's a long story, but the fact of the matter is he's my brother and he has offered his assistance in helping find the Talisman. This'll work out for everyone."

Murdock glared at the young warrior. "Is he to partake in the riches we have stashed away, as well as what's to come?"

The young warrior knew that he had to convince his friend of his actions. "We didn't get into specifics, but I suppose."

The ranger squinted. "You do realize he can defeat us with his army of soldiers, yet you still made this deal with him."

"Murdock, he's my brother."

The ranger closed his eyes and shook his head. "Harrison, this better not backfire on us. We've come too far and have endured too much for someone else to take this treasure from us."

Harrison raised his palm outward in a calming gesture. "You have my word."

Just then, Troy and his men approached the campsite. Teleios joined the young general, and the two of them approached Harrison and his friends.

"It will be an honor working with all of you," Troy said to the group of adventurers. "This is my advisor, Teleios." The halfling nodded after Troy mentioned his name.

Harrison introduced his fellow adventurers and suggested to Troy that his men assemble around the camp. The soldiers set up their tents and tended to their horses a short distance away from where Harrison's group had constructed their site. After the soldiers situated themselves, Troy and Teleios joined Harrison and his friends around the fire.

The general-at-arms, along with his advisor, passed out flasks to each of Harrison's cronies. "Where are you heading?" asked Troy to Harrison.

"Dragon's Quarters. Dracus lives in the mountain range just to the east of the village."

Troy nodded in understanding. "I see. What kind of attack plan have you devised?"

Harrison's eyes bulged once again after sipping the liquid. Murdock took a big swig and began to cough uncontrollably. After a moment, he said with a hearty laugh, "This is some good whiskey!"

Troy smiled. "I'm glad you like it. The king enjoys it strong."

Harrison felt his eyes watering. "We don't have an attack plan just yet since we don't know what the terrain is like near his lair."

Teleios leaned over and whispered to Troy. The young general said something back under his breath and nodded, then Teleios left the men.

Harrison watched Troy's advisor leave. "Where's he going?"

"Teleios seems to remember something about a dragon and a knight." Troy replied. "He thinks he recalls it had something to do with Dragon's Quarters."

A moment later, Teleios returned holding a large, tattered scripture. "If I'm not mistaken," he said, flipping through the pages, "this book mentions a battle plan used by a knight. Here it is."

Teleios began to read the scripture. *"The battle for Dragon's Quarters had reached its pinnacle. The wicked beast, Cedryicus, all but defeated the townspeople led by William the Great. That is until a highly decorated member of the Legion of Knighthood came to save the village. His tactical maneuvers proved mightier than his skill with the blade.*

"Using the mountainous cliffs to his advantage, he managed to corner the wretched creature and subdue him. This brave knight liberated Dragon's Quarters by capturing the beast and making it his slave."

Teleios closed the book. "The historian never mentioned the knight's name."

Harrison looked over at his friends, then back to Troy and Teleios. "I'm willing to bet this knight was Sir Jacob. He was a member of the Legion of Knighthood and an important historical figure."

"The author says he used the cliffs to his advantage," said Troy. "We should ask the locals about any stories that their ancestors passed down to them."

"That's just what we intend to do." Harrison frowned. "The scripture mentioned the name Cedryicus, not Dracus."

Teleios nodded. "Dracus could be the offspring of this Cedryicus."

"That would explain why he terrorizes the village from time to time." Murdock shared his views, then took another sip from his flask. "I'd be pretty upset if some knight enslaved one of my parents."

"Murdock might be right," said Harrison. "Either way, we must defeat him."

"Then I suggest we formulate a plan on our way to Dragon's Quarters." Troy finished the liquid in his flask. "Teleios is an expert in devising such schemes."

Harrison glanced at Troy's advisor. "We're looking forward to working with you."

"As am I." Teleios turned to face Troy. "Perhaps we should get some rest, then depart in the morning."

"Sounds fine with me." Troy checked Harrison to see his take on the proposal.

"Sounds good to me, too."

After the two left the campsite, Murdock said, "Is everyone comfortable with this arrangement?"

Everyone looked at each other for assurance. "Troy seems trustworthy," said Swinkle. "I feel he is being sincere."

"I get the same feeling." Gelderand shuffled in his seat. "His men will be a great asset for us in confronting that creature."

The ranger stared at Gelderand. "And you don't think he might have a hidden agenda?"

"Not that I can see."

"We talked for a long time." All the men listened to Harrison. "He's realizing he's a lost soul. The king deceived him since the day he was born. His world changed after seeing me. Now he knows he has a brother and he wants to help us succeed." The young warrior paused. "I know in my heart we can trust him."

Murdock rubbed his face. "Is this what we all want?" The ranger scanned the faces of his friends, who nodded in assurance. "All right then. Let's slay this dragon."

The men then settled in for the night, all of them secretly pondering the agreement they just made.

CHAPTER 27

◘

Harrison did his best to keep his horse in marching order with the rest of Troy's men. The young warrior had practiced numerous battle activities at the Fighter's Guild, but riding mounted steeds was not high on his list of achievements. As he yanked on his horse's reins, he sensed his twin watching.

"Haven't ridden in a while, have you?" Troy said with a smirk.

The young warrior glanced behind him and found Murdock cursing under his breath, he too having trouble controlling his horse. "My men and I usually travel by foot."

Troy laughed. "That's noble of you, but traversing the countryside on horseback is much quicker."

Harrison nodded in agreement, knowing that if they had had the backing of a king, their journey would be much different. Changing the subject, he said, "We planned on spending some time in Dragon's Quarters before hunting Dracus. The villagers, in all likelihood, will have first hand experience in dealing with the beast and we want to gather as much information on him as possible before doing something foolish."

"I tend to agree." Troy motioned to Teleios. "Let's give my advisor a little time to survey the landscape. I'm sure he'll come up with a fine battle plan."

Harrison nodded. "As long as we have final say on any procedures."

"Agreed." A sudden wave of anger coursed through Troy's body. "I need to keep a clear head once we get back to Dragon's Lair."

The young warrior had an inkling of how his brother felt about his newfound predicament, but he wanted to learn more from his sibling. "Why's that?"

Troy knew Harrison could never understand the pain he felt in his soul. Looking at his brother clouded his head with uncertainty and broken promises. King Holleris had appeared to be his friend and confidant, but in reality he was only using Troy to secure his precious treasure.

The young general shook his head. "I'm not sure what the king has in store for us, for me. What was he going to do with me and my men after we handed you over to him?"

Harrison shrugged, unsure. "I couldn't begin to tell you."

Troy thought hard about what the king did to him and his family. "I can't trust him, Harrison. He lied to me, took me from our mother and father, and forced me to live a military lifestyle." Troy's voice trailed off. "I never made any choices for myself."

Harrison stared at his brother and could feel his pain. The young warrior, using a low, soft voice, said, "Troy, I'll be there with you and we'll deal with this evil tyrant together. I promise you that."

Troy gazed at his brother and smiled. "I know you will. But let's not jump ahead of ourselves. We have a very difficult task in slaying a dragon. It's not out of the realm of possibility to fail, you know."

Harrison looked out toward the horizon, agreeing with his brother's last statement. "My deepest fear exactly."

The convoy of adventurers and soldiers trekked across the Arcadian countryside for the next six days, not in any particular rush to get to Dragon's Quarters, understanding that a great beast unknowingly waited for them.

On the seventh day, they arrived at the small village at the base of the mountain range, aptly named the Ridge of Dracus. Harrison and his team congregated with their horses.

Gelderand spoke first. "I'm a little more familiar with this area. Let me see what I can find."

Harrison nodded in approval. "Are you sure you're all right with the decision not to go back to Tigris."

Gelderand wanted more than ever to check in on Tara, since the little village of Tigris sat nestled on the outskirts of the Great Forest, a short trek from Dragon's Quarters. However, they all had agreed that taking a small army to a place where a king's ransom resided could prove foolish.

"I'd love to see my niece, but I'm satisfied with our decision."

Murdock looked back to Troy and his men. "Why don't you let Pondle and I do what we do best, too."

Harrison gave the ranger a wry smile. "What's that, find a tavern with the best ale?"

"No. We'll snoop around town and talk to some adventurers who've trekked around these parts."

Harrison looked over to Gelderand and Swinkle. The two men shrugged, appearing at ease with Murdock's remark.

"Very well." Harrison wagged a finger in his friend's face. "Just stay out of trouble."

Murdock cocked his head, nodded and smiled. "Let's go, Pondle." Both men turned and headed toward the direction of the small wooden buildings at the base of the mountains.

Harrison watched his friends leave their gathering spot. "Why do I always worry about them?"

"Because you have to," said Swinkle, gazing in Murdock and Pondle's direction also. "But they will be fine. For some reason they don't seem to get into too much trouble."

Harrison sensed someone approaching. Turning, he found Troy and Teleios advancing to them. Lance scurried to Troy's side to greet the visitors.

Troy pointed away from their position. "Teleios and I believe it would be in everyone's best interest if we set up camp on the outskirts of the town."

Harrison nodded in agreement. "I don't have a problem with that."

Troy looked over to Murdock and Pondle. "Where are they going?"

"To gather information." The young warrior secured his backpack, confident that his friends would be fine.

The young general appeared skeptical. "Do you think that's a good idea?"

Harrison gazed at his friends. "I trust them more than anyone else. They'll uncover something about Dracus, though I'm sure they won't use the protocols you're accustomed to."

Troy looked at the darkening sky. "I suggest we establish camp, and if it's not too late, we can venture into the village."

"Fine with me. And, maybe Murdock and Pondle will bring back something of interest."

After about an hour of milling about the edge of town, Swinkle approached Harrison. "Looks like we have some company," he said, pointing to a group of about twenty people heading towards them.

Harrison glanced in the direction Swinkle indicated. "Let's see what they want."

The two men took the initiative to meet the intruders halfway. The young warrior could tell by the armor and clothing they wore that this group was not a bunch of town dignitaries. Both parties stopped ten feet from each other.

After a few uncomfortable seconds, a scraggly, older warrior spoke. His aged and weathered face told the young warrior that he had seen more than his share of battles.

Pointing a jagged sword at Harrison, he said, "What business do you have with us?" The man peered past the younger fighter after his statement and looked over at the new encampment.

The young warrior knew this might be his only chance to solicit information about Dracus, and if all went well, have some of these men help with their battle.

"Our journey has taken us to Dragon's Quarters because we have been told a mighty dragon lives in these mountains."

The man held his stare on Harrison. "You mean Dracus."

"Yes, that's the name we've heard time and again. What do you know about him?"

"The beast is a ruthless killer who has no care for any living being." The tired warrior squinted to make his point. "What could you possibly want with him?"

Harrison peered over to Swinkle before answering. As usual, he saw the look of apprehension on the young cleric's face. "We must slay Dracus and retrieve a vial of his blood."

The man's mouth opened, but nothing came out. A second later, he burst into laughter. "Did you hear that, men? They've come to slay Dracus!" The man and his cronies continued to laugh hysterically.

Harrison did not take well to these people poking fun at his predicament. "This is no joke, I assure you!"

The leader tried to gather himself. "That's what makes your statement even funnier!" Before he could summon another guffaw, one of the man's friends tugged his arm and pointed behind Harrison and Swinkle. Everyone's laughter ceased.

Two horses approached the small mob, followed by ten others. "I take it my brother has spoken of our intentions," said Troy from his steed.

The man gazed at Troy, then back to Harrison. "Well, I'll be. Twins."

Troy pressed further, taking control of the situation. "What is you name?"

The man stood tall and proclaimed, "I'm Gunther Slue and I'm the leader of these fine men."

The young general gazed over the battle-scarred veterans. After a moment, he continued, "Can we count on you to give us a detailed insight to the moods and dealings you have had with this mighty dragon?"

Gunther cocked his head. "If the price is right."

Troy did not miss a beat. "Name it."

"One hundred gold pieces for each of us and we'll tell you all our tales."

The young general did not flinch at the outrageous request. "Five hundred gold pieces to you alone and you can decide how to disperse the spoils."

The older warrior nodded slowly. "Deal. We'll meet at The Dead Man's Casket. I'm sure you'll be able to find the place, which has more than enough room for all of us to 'talk.'"

Troy nodded in agreement. "Very well. We'll meet you there in an hour."

"Yes, one hour." The man turned to his friends. "Let us be on our way. The ale will be flowing tonight!" And with that, the group of twenty departed the area.

Troy dismounted from his horse and approached his brother. "Harrison, I hope you understand that I have extensive training in dealing with people like this."

Harrison tried to hold back his true feelings. Swiveling to face his brother, he fixed his stare on him and said, "We need to determine who's in charge. Right now."

Harrison's tone took Troy by surprise. "In charge? We should handle this together."

The young warrior shook his head. "No, Troy, that isn't going to work. My men won't take direction from you, and I'm sure your soldiers won't listen to me. Furthermore, we need to decide who does the talking to people outside of our team."

Troy nodded, coming to understand wholeheartedly how his brother felt. "Agreed. Let's have both of our camps take directions from only you or me, and we can work as a team for all other meetings."

"Like the way we worked together just now?" Harrison's voice was thick with sarcasm. "I'm going to feel like a fool, like the lesser brother, when we meet these men again."

"I'm sorry that I put you in an awkward position. I only meant to help the situation."

Harrison let out a deep sigh. "I know you were only trying to help, too. Just be mindful of the circumstances before you attempt to take it over."

Troy chuckled. "I guess I'm just used to being the person in charge. I'll do my best to share this responsibility in the future."

"Starting in one hour."

"Yes, starting in one hour."

By the time Murdock and Pondle rejoined Harrison, Swinkle, and Gelderand, the carousing at The Dead Man's Casket had already reached a feverish pitch.

"We stopped by this place a long time ago," said Murdock, trying his best to prepare Harrison for what he would soon encounter. "The people here are nothing but a bunch of drunks and old warriors who've seen more than enough battles in their lifetime. We should proceed with caution."

Swinkle looked over to Harrison. "If Murdock thinks the establishment is hostile, then we better take extra precautions."

The ranger peered in the same direction. "Diplomacy will be … how should I say … very secondary to hard currency."

"You better bring gold and a strong sense of conviction," added Pondle. "These guys don't care about anything but themselves and their reputation, which as far as I could see is to be the toughest warrior in this part of the land."

"I'll keep that in mind." Just then, Harrison saw Troy, Teleios, and a small contingent of men approach him and his friends.

Troy looked confident and prepared for the evening's events. "Are you ready to interact with these men?"

"Ready?" responded Harrison. "I hope you're up to the task, brother."

"Don't worry about me, Harrison. I'm —"

"Trained for events such as this," interrupted the young warrior. "Yeah, I know." Harrison took charge. "Take my lead tonight."

Harrison's strong headedness took Troy by surprise. The young general looked over to his trusted advisor, who gave him a subtle nod. "By all means, you lead the conversation."

"I'm glad you agree." Harrison gazed at Lance, who sat by his master's side. "Go back with the soldiers, boy. This is no place for a dog." Lance whimpered for a moment, then turned and left for the safety of the encampment.

The young warrior motioned to Gelderand. "You better leave Rufus with Lance as well." The mage nodded in concurrence, swung his pack around, and allowed the feline to wiggle out of the sack.

The mage pointed to the dog. "Go with Lance, Rufus." The cat took a moment to register his master's command, then scooted over to Lance.

With the well-being of the animals settled, Harrison told Murdock and Pondle. "Lead the way to The Dead Man's Casket."

"No problem, boss," said Murdock.

It took the mixed group of adventurers and soldiers a little more than a minute to reenter the town of Dragon's Quarters from their encampment and stand before the doors of the tavern.

Murdock gazed over to Harrison. "Remember, these people are, how should I say," the ranger fumbled for the precise words, "unruly, even by my standards."

Harrison looked over to Gelderand and Swinkle, who reflected a feeling of apprehension. "This is where we must go. There's no turning back now."

Murdock nodded, then opened the door to the tavern. The name of The Dead Man's Casket proved fitting. All activities — dart playing, drinking games, deeply engaged conversation — all revolved around the large central bar where drink upon drink of finely brewed ale poured freely.

Gunther Slue's head turned toward the entrance as soon as the foreigners entered the tavern. Placing his hand on his broad sword, he removed it from his sheath and slammed it on the table where he was drinking with his cronies. The blade crashed on the wooden structure, making a hideous sound and causing all onlookers to jerk their heads in his direction. When all conversation ceased, he pointed his weapon toward Harrison, Troy, and all of the others who had entered the establishment.

"It's about time you showed your cowardly faces! We have much to talk about!"

Troy looked to Harrison, who gazed upon the members of his small group. The time had come for the young warrior to ascertain himself and he was not about to let himself down.

Taking a line out of his old mentor's vocabulary, he said, "My good man, the time has come to discuss our strategy."

Flashing a toothy smile, Gunther said, "Come, youngster, and partake in some fine ale."

Murdock grabbed Harrison's arm. "You take the lead, but watch me. Got it?"

Harrison knew just what Murdock meant. "Line up the drinks, Gunther. We have a long night ahead of us."

A wide grin appeared on the older warrior's face. Gunther peered over to the bar. "Finius, glasses for everyone! And put it on the other twin's tab!"

The bartender poured mug upon mug of ale, with scantily clad barmaids delivering the amber liquid to a long table. Harrison and his friends positioned themselves on one side, while Gunther and his buddies gathered on the other.

Harrison waited until the wench delivered all of the mugs to his friends, paying special attention to Swinkle. The poor cleric gazed upon his flagon with a look of grave concern.

The young warrior raised his glass. "We drink as one, except for him." Harrison pointed to the young cleric. "By the end of the night, he will hear you deepest confessions and absolve your sins!"

Gunther shrugged. "Whatever." Raising his mug, he said, "To the death of Dracus!" A loud roar encompassed the room, followed by the chugging of bitter ale.

Troy raised his mug and guzzled the liquid. Murdock and Pondle finished their drinks even before the young warrior started.

Casting a caring gaze to his friend, Harrison whispered, "Swinkle, I spared you tonight. Keep a close eye on me." The young cleric closed his eyes and gave Harrison a subtle nod.

Gelderand also peered over at Swinkle. "Look after me, too, Swinkle. Harrison seemed to forget my age when he relieved you of tonight's duties."

"I'll do my best. Just be careful," replied the young cleric.

Gunther slammed his mug down on the table. "Another round!" His cronies cheered for more, their flagons crashing onto the tables as well.

Troy grabbed Harrison's arm. "Dictate the action. Don't let these people run the show."

Harrison slid his mug away and nodded at his long lost brother. "Gunther, it's time to talk."

The older warrior used his sleeve to wipe the foamy ale from his lips. "As you wish, young one."

Gunther then gave a high-pitched whistle, silencing his friends in the process. "Quiet, everyone! Our high-priced friends have something to say!"

The tavern grew eerily still and everyone waited for Harrison to speak. After a tense moment, the young warrior started. "First, before anything else, another round of ale for everyone!"

The crowd roared with approval. Barmaids hurriedly retrieved more ale and distributed the alcohol to the willing patrons. After everyone received another mug of the amber liquid, Harrison raised a hand, signaling for quiet. When everyone settled down, he continued.

"A notorious beast, which I don't have to elaborate on, lives in these mountains. We wish to destroy him, with your help, of course."

Shouts came from the crowd. "You haven't drank enough!"

Another said, "Who's foolish enough to speak these words?"

A third added, "Are you ready to die, young one?"

Harrison expected the negativity. Keeping his resolve, he continued. "I assure you, our intentions will not change, no matter how much ale we consume tonight."

Gunther stared at the young warrior, alternating his gaze from Harrison, to Troy, Teleios, Murdock, and Pondle. Rising from his stool, he shouted, "Quiet! I believe these men and everything they say!"

The rancor died down to the point where no one spoke another word. Gunther continued, looking at Harrison. "I have someone who can relate to your cause." He gestured to another battle-scarred veteran.

A shorter, stockier warrior stepped forward. All those around him moved out of his way, creating a path to Gunther. The man looked at Harrison. The young warrior deduced that a battle from this man's dark past must have led to the blindness in his right eye, a deep slice visible from his eye socket down to his cheek.

The man slammed his mug down, followed by his battle-axe. "I am Haren the Wise, and Dracus unmercifully slaughtered my father and grandfather. A family debt, I owe this creature of hate."

The young warrior asked, "Is there anything you can propose?"

Haren took a long look at Harrison and his friends. "What is your true motive, warrior?"

Harrison hesitated before answering. "The death of this creature, then unknown riches."

"Fair enough. The destruction of this beast is more than enough for me."

"Do you have any insight in how to defeat this monster?"

Haren thought hard, but his face told Harrison all he needed to know. "If I knew how to defeat him, my father and grandfather would still be alive."

The young warrior tried his best to resolve the situation. Before taking too much time to think, he heard someone clear his throat behind him. "I might be of some assistance."

Teleios had retrieved his old tattered manuscript from his backpack and now laid it out on the table for all to see. "This scripture details the steps an ancient knight took to subdue Cedryicus, a dragon who inhabited these mountains a millennium ago."

Haren stood frozen, his mouth agape. "Dracus has uttered the name Cedryicus in conjunction with restoring dignity to his ancestors."

"Could Cedryicus be Dracus's parent?" asked Troy's advisor, raising a curious eyebrow.

Haren and Gunther exchanged glances. "It's possible," said Gunther. "But there's no proof to the contrary."

"Then we'll have to take it as truth," said Harrison. "Our scripture mentions a path that leads to Dracus's lair where we can attack him without incidence."

"I wouldn't say that we could hold our ground without incidence." Teleios stared Harrison down.

Haren the Wise added to the conversation. "But there is a way to enter his lair through an overhang." He paused. "An oversight if you ask me."

Harrison cocked his head. "An oversight?"

"Yeah, a place where we can attack the beast. It's been there for a very long time."

The young warrior gazed at Haren, dumbfounded and waiting for more.

"Dracus's lair sits at the top of the highest peak." Haren took another long sip from his mug before continuing. "There, the beast rests in a large cave, waiting to wreak havoc upon us again. The opening of the cave is huge, large enough to fit three dragons side by side, and deep enough to house ten more."

The warrior paused, cocked his head and pointed a bent finger at the young warrior. "But there is a back door."

Shaking his head, Harrison asked, "A back door?"

Everyone remained glued to their spots, listening like children to a scary story, waiting for Haren to speak more. "The opposite side of the mountain is steep and a large overhang exists behind the back wall of the cave. Over there is a crevice, large enough for a man, but too small for a dragon. We can use this entrance to attack."

Harrison remained skeptical. "How can we simply attack a dragon one warrior at a time?"

"You can't."

The young warrior placed his elbows on the table, then held his face in his hands. Massaging his temples, Harrison brought his gaze to the older man and said, "This information is nice, but it really doesn't help all that much."

"Have you ever seen evil, son?" Haren gazed deep into Harrison's blue eyes.

The man's comment took Harrison aback. "Well, sure, yes, I have."

"Really?" Haren's gaze intensified. "This evil is like nothing you've ever seen before. This beast will know we're coming. It will sense our moves, feel our presence, and will never stop."

Harrison gulped. "Never stop what?"

"Hunting us down until each and every one of us is dead. This evil is *relentless*. It feeds on our fears and takes joy in our failures. And, I assure you, we will have more than our share of those."

The young warrior felt his heart beat faster. "If this evil is as persistent as you say it is, then how are you standing before me? Shouldn't the beast have killed you by now?"

"We beat the bastard back." Haren laughed and shook his head. "We always do. But, Dracus is very smart. He'll slay a score of us, torch the rest and leave us in ruins. He always keeps us weak, always at a disadvantage."

Gunther stepped forward. "This time, we have you and your men, and Dracus doesn't know this."

Haren waved his hand and shook his head. "You're wrong, my friend. He knows these men are here! Haven't you heard a word I said! He senses *everything!*"

At that very moment, a thought came into Harrison's mind. "Does he sense this?"

Using two hands, the young warrior removed his mighty two-handed sword and brandished it in front of all the men. A gasp came from the crowd upon seeing the weapon.

Haren's eyes widened. "Tell me that this is the sacred sword! The one the legend speaks of!"

"Which legend?" Harrison's travels had brought him on countless quests, each one with talk of legends and folklore. Keeping them all straight had started to take its toll on him.

"The one he spoke of is true." Haren pointed to Teleios. "An ancient knight saved the town from the evil of Cedryicus and left behind a sword of dragon slaying."

The young warrior peered over to his friends, hoping that this legend of Sir Jacob had substantial meaning to their current quest. "How can we be sure this sword is the one?"

"Raise it over your head."

Harrison took both hands and lifted the weapon with little resistance.

The old warrior shook his head. "No. Use only one hand."

The young warrior looked at the blade. Surely, not even the strongest man in the world could lift a two-handed sword forged from steel with a three-foot blade over his head with only one hand, he reasoned to himself. But this was no ordinary sword. Removing his left hand from the hilt, Harrison suspended the weapon above him with ease.

"You might be strong, laddie, but not *that* strong! This is Dracus's weapon of death!" Haren sported a broad smile.

Harrison lowered the blade to his side. "What more do you know?"

The older fighter shrugged. "Only that the weapon is weightless. You've proven that now."

Harrison knew that they had discovered the weapon in a cavern where the green jewel resided. He knew finding it was not a coincidence and that he would need it for something — that something being to slay Dracus.

"How do we get close enough to kill him?"

Haren smiled, then laughed. "That, my boy, is what we need to figure out."

At that time, Troy entered into the conversation. "I have thirty soldiers who can fight with your twenty men. Add Harrison's team and we should have more than enough manpower to overtake Dracus."

The old warrior cocked his head from side to side. "One would think."

"You don't sound convinced that we can."

Pointing his finger at the fresh young faces that stared back at him, the older warrior said, "This beast is crafty. He'll see us, hear us. We can't be so bold as to rush up the mountain and entice him into a fight of life or death."

"We need to out think him." Teleios added his thoughts to the conversation. "I can help devise a plan, but I'll need the assistance of people who know the terrain."

Haren recognized some disturbing Scynthian traits in Troy's advisor. "Yes, we will have to come up with a very good plan."

Teleios continued with his line of thinking. "First, I suggest that we send a small team to the summit to survey this beast's lair. That way we can make a better assessment of what we need to do."

The old warrior shook his head in disagreement. "No, we all go at the same time. We only get one shot at this. Gunther knows of some trackers who've been close to the dragon's lair. I stress, 'close.'"

Teleios conceded the argument. "Fine. We all go together."

"My team's ready to go up there with you, Troy," added Harrison. "We didn't come all this way for nothing." His brother pursed his lips and nodded, figuring as much from his twin.

"As you wish," said Haren. "Just be prepared to witness evil like you never have before."

Harrison projected an air of confidence. "We'll be more than ready."

Troy asked the next question. "For when should we plan this mission?"

Haren looked at Gunther. "Day after tomorrow. We need to gather things and say our good-byes."

"Good-byes?"

Haren smiled wide. "Not all of us are coming back."

CHAPTER 28

○

The men took advantage of their extra day to gather supplies, retool their weaponry, and survey the mountain base. Harrison stood in their encampment with Swinkle, Gelderand, and Lance, gazing at the imposing peak before them.

The young warrior shielded his eyes from the sun. "What do you think we'll find up there?"

"Besides a vile beast?" answered Gelderand, while he shuffled Rufus into his backpack, the cat meowing with delight. "I only know of the local folklore and it's not good."

The young warrior brought his gaze to the mage. "What have you heard?"

The wizard tapped his temple in thought. "When I was younger, I recall a story about Dracus and the way he would go about his rampages. The beast would let out a hideous screech, almost letting everyone know he was coming."

Gelderand patted Rufus on the head, then stared at his friends before continuing. "He wants to see terror on the faces of people he kills. And … he's confident that he will win."

Swinkle swallowed hard. "Can we really defeat Dracus?"

The mage shrugged. "The more men the better, but what can we do against a huge beast that can fly, torch us with his breath, and out think our every move?"

"Not to mention we'll be going to his lair," added Harrison. Gelderand nodded in agreement.

The young cleric appeared visibly shaken. "Not to quote Murdock, but this sounds like suicide."

"This is our next step to gathering the Talisman. We must try." Harrison searched for more words. "I believe all of this has happened for a reason – us attaining the Treasure of the Land, you discovering the sacred book, me finding a brother I never knew I had – all of this."

Swinkle knew that his friend spoke from his heart, but he still had reservations. "You heard Haren; we are not all coming back alive."

Harrison nodded. "It's a chance I'm willing to take. Swinkle, if you want to end your journey with us, by all means, that's all right with me."

The young cleric shook his head. "No, I made a vow to help you on your journey and I plan to stick by it. I just wished our tasks were not so arduous."

"It's more fun that way!" Harrison laughed.

The young warrior's comment brought a smile to his friend's face. "Somehow you are always able to make difficult things sound so simple."

"Just look at the bright side. After we slay this dragon, we'll liberate these poor people from his evil clutches, we'll have another piece to our puzzle, and we'll be able to go with Troy to get the final jewel."

Swinkle shrugged and turned his head away. "Just like that?"

"Just like that."

The young warrior looked beyond Swinkle to see Murdock and Pondle heading their way. Lance noticed them, too, and ran over to greet them.

"We need to regroup with Troy and his men," said Murdock. "Our buddies Haren and Gunther are ready to discuss a battle plan."

"Why," asked Harrison, "don't I like the sound of that?"

Murdock nodded with a smirk. "Finally, your insights are sharpening."

The small group of men found Troy and Teleios bent down, examining their supplies. They both stood when they saw the approaching men.

"Good morning," said Troy. "Are you ready for our big day?"

Harrison nodded. "Yes, but I hear the men of the village are prepared to discuss our battle plan."

"Really? What did they say specifically?"

"Only that they want to go over our battle route," intervened Murdock. "They're at The Dead Man's Casket awaiting us."

Troy shook his head in amazement. "These 'warriors' are already drinking and it's not even noon! How can we depend on them in battle?"

"We won't need to depend on them," said Teleios. "I suggest we meet with them and go over what we know."

"I suppose." Troy faced Harrison and his team of men. "Lead the way."

Pondle and Murdock escorted the group of men to The Dead Man's Casket, where they found Gunther and Haren. To their surprise, the two men were enjoying an ale in relative quietness. When they saw the familiar faces advancing, the elder war veterans waved them over.

Gunther raised his mug. "A nice crisp drink in the morning really gets you going all day, don't you think?" The warrior slurped the amber liquid.

"Not to me," said Troy, "but who am I to say what's right and what's wrong?"

Gunther cocked his head. "True."

Troy waved Teleios to the forefront. "My advisor has worked on this plan all night." The young general pointed to a larger table in the back of the room. "Why don't we all go over there and discuss what he's found?"

The group of men took their seats at a large rectangular table. Teleios removed a container from his backpack, unrolled a parchment, and spread it on the tabletop.

"I surveyed the base area of the mountain and the general vicinity," he started. "This is what I came up with."

Harrison gazed at the map and noticed a myriad of dotted lines leading up to the summit. The young warrior pointed to the dashes. "What are these?"

"Possible routes up the peak."

The young warrior stared at the top of the mountain, noticing that no symbols marking vegetation existed. "Why are there so many bare spots at the summit?"

"Because that's above the tree line." Teleios sighed. "There're no hiding places for a good two hundred yards."

"Not bad work," said Gunther, listening to the two men converse. "Do you want to hear our take on your assessment?"

"By all means," said Teleios.

Gunther swigged the last of his ale and put his flagon down. "This map is worthless. You've charted the wrong paths to the summit."

Teleios stood tall in his seat. "I take great pride in my work, sir. I based all of my calculations on observations I had made about the surroundings of Dragon's Quarters. I've mapped out our best case scenarios."

"In your opinion. Did you not listen to Haren the other day? We need to attack Dracus's lair from the opposite side of the mountain. That's where the crevice lies."

Teleios pointed to the dotted lines on his map. "These paths go up to certain points. We can deviate our course when we get there."

Gunther smiled as if he knew something the others did not. "You didn't have time to journey around the base of this great peak. The opposite side of the mountain is steeper, but the foliage is much denser. The pine trees will prevent Dracus from swooping down from the heavens and attacking us. And, they're tougher to ignite, minimizing his fire breathing tactics."

"And the crevice faces the back side," reiterated Haren. "Trust us, we've made this trip before." The warrior slurped the final drops of his ale, too.

Teleios scrambled for words, knowing that his strategies, though strong, were wrong. Nodding, he said, "I see your point. I might have been a bit presumptuous in my outline. Of course there might be better avenues to traverse this summit from the opposite side."

Haren squinted and shook his head. "Why do you talk like that?"

"Like what?"

"'I might have been presumptuous, there might be better avenues to traverse'," said Haren in a condescending tone. "We're not idiots! Talk to us like a human!"

Teleios felt the sting of Haren's comment. His whole life he tried to hide his Scynthian heritage, studied to be the best he could, trained to fight better than his peers, and now an ale-swilling, battled-scarred warrior called out his one flaw.

"I'm sorry if I make you feel uncomfortable. This is how I talk."

Haren maintained his stare. "Well, I don't like it."

Teleios glared back. "Get used to it. I'm not changing for you."

Haren sat back a bit and reached for his sword's hilt. Smiling, he shouted, "That's more like it! You catch on quick."

Teleios did not flinch; instead, he wanted to continue their discussion. "What do you propose as a battle route?"

"Do you have something to write with?" Troy's advisor handed Haren a writing utensil.

The older warrior flipped over Teleios's map and began to draw. After a minute of scribbling, he turned it around so all the men could see.

"This is Dragon's Quarters," he began, pointing with his pencil to the dot at the base of the mountain. Tracing a solid line with the writing tool, he continued, "We follow this path until we get here." He stopped at a point on the mountain's backside.

"From this point, we go straight up the mountainside, being careful to stay hidden under the cover of the trees." A crooked line separated the tree line and the peak. "We camp out here at the fringe of the woods and make our trek to the top at nightfall."

Teleios nodded, accepting the fact that Haren knew the terrain better than he did. "What about this crevice?"

"That's a little more tricky," started the ale guzzling warrior. "First, we have no coverage from the forest to the backside of the cave."

Troy's advisor cocked his head, agreeing. "Thus your rationale for attacking at night."

Haren wagged a finger at Teleios. "Don't get ahead of yourself. We'll attack during the day. Let me explain.

"We need to position our men at the crevice during nighttime and wait until daylight to strike. I don't know about you, but I can't see in the dark and Dracus will see our advancing torches from miles away."

Teleios, knowing the infravision capabilities he and Pondle possessed, made a subtle glance at the thief who gave no indication of voicing his own ability. Instead of mentioning his powers at this time, Troy's advisor nodded and let the man continue to speak.

"With those men in place, another group of us will push forward from the entrance of the cave. Our goal is to trap Dracus in his own lair by attacking from the front and the back. We can use the rest of the men as reinforcements in case the beast gets the best of us."

Haren scanned the group of men, then said, "We're all dead if Dracus escapes from his cave. He'll take to the air and torch us from above. There'll be no hiding from him then."

Teleios nodded and silently gave Troy reassurance that the man's plan seemed sound. "This all sounds fine, but I have to ask you. Have you employed this tactic before?"

Haren and Gunther exchanged glances. "Yes," responded Haren.

Teleios waited for more of an answer, and when none came, he pressed, "And the outcome was?"

"We lost almost all of the men." Haren shook his head in dismay. "But, we didn't have seasoned fighters. Villagers, men with wives and children, they made up the contingent of soldiers we used the last time we attempted to take down Dracus.

"We were foolish enough to think we could slay the beast. Our downfall was allowing the dragon to escape from his cave."

Teleios shook his head, angry. "Then we cannot employ the same attack plan! If Dracus is as smart as you say, he'll know exactly what to do!"

"Not unless we surprise him. Listen, the summit is barren, there's nowhere to hide. We must trap the beast in the cave. It's our only hope."

Teleios looked over at Troy, who then took his gaze to Harrison. The young warrior shrugged, not sure of what else that they could do. Troy's advisor sighed and said, "If this is what you think, then I say let's try it."

Murdock agreed. "Enough talk! Let's get this battle underway. We can figure out what to do when we get closer to the peak."

Troy drew a deep breath. "I have to agree with Harrison and Murdock. If Teleios feels that your plan is correct, then I say we proceed." He could see his brother nodding in agreement.

"We leave within the hour then!" bellowed Haren. The two older warriors rose from their seats. "We'll alert our men. I promise you, they're ready."

"We'll meet you back here in an hour," said Troy, as he, Teleios, and the rest got up from their seats as well.

Before they could leave the building, Haren added, "Find a place to keep your horses; they're not coming."

Troy shot the older warrior a concerned look. "Why do you say that?"

Haren smiled. "Dracus particularly likes the taste of horseflesh. I'm surprised he hasn't smelled them by now." With that, Haren and Gunther exited The Dead Man's Casket and searched for their friends.

After the two fighters had left the establishment, Troy muttered to no one in particular, "I don't like the sounds of this whole plan."

Murdock overheard the young general's comment. "Lighten up, Troy. Not every battle can be drawn up and executed as planned." The ranger then followed his group out of the tavern.

Troy waited a second, then whispered to Teleios, "I still can't understand how these guys secured the king's sacred book."

"Maybe Murdock's attitude is what we need," said Teleios. "I don't like creating carefree battle plans, but it just might work for this group."

Troy followed his advisor out of the establishment. "I hope you're right."

After an hour of equipment gathering and instruction giving, Troy and Harrison assembled their respective men in front of The Dead Man's Casket. As usual, they found the establishment buzzing with men drinking and carousing. Before either brother could enter the tavern, the place became strangely still. Next, a loud roar came from inside followed by the sounds of sheathing weapons and the clanging of armor.

Gunther and Haren exited the bar first with two dozen men in tow. Gunther approached the twins, facing them both. "We're ready to destroy this beast once and for all. Haren will lead us to the spot on the mountain just below the tree line."

Harrison gestured to his friends. "I want Pondle and Murdock to advance with your scouts."

"I also have a few men that should lead the way, too," added Troy.

Gunther and Haren laughed at the exuberance of the two younger warriors. "Scouts?" asked Haren. "I'm your scout!"

Harrison and Troy gazed upon the men who accompanied Gunther and Haren. Both could see that they were nothing more than old war veterans, townspeople dressed in armor and, more than likely, drinking buddies of the two older men.

Troy turned to his brother. "I have thirty seasoned soldiers and your men are made of solid stock. Gunther and Haren's friends will help us when we charge Dracus."

Harrison nodded. "I agree. Just remember, we have to control this battle."

Troy nodded in agreement, then turned to the older warriors. "Haren, how do you foresee us advancing from here?"

Haren rubbed his thick beard. "Hmm, let me think. I'll lead the way with whoever you want to walk with me. Gunther will stay with you two," the older man pointed to Harrison and Troy. "Arrange the others how you deem fit."

Harrison faced his brother. "Murdock and Pondle will go with Haren, and I think the rest of us should stick together. You know your men better than I."

"Agreed. Teleios will stay with us and I'll position my men accordingly." Troy then proceeded to place his men in a typical marching formation; one that he knew would be most beneficial for trekking in the woods.

After he finished arranging his men, Troy looked over to Haren and said, "Take us to Dracus!"

Haren removed his sword from its sheath and raised it in the air. "Our three day trek starts now, and on that third day, Dracus shall live no more!"

All of Haren's men shouted in unison, raising their weapons in the air in a similar fashion. The older warrior yelled to Murdock and Pondle.

"Let the fun begin!"

The ranger spoke to his friend in a hushed tone. "An old one-eyed warrior who reeks of alcohol is going to guide us to the most dangerous battle of our lives." Murdock shook his head. "Wonderful." With that, the contingent of men began their trek to find Dracus.

CHAPTER 29

◘

The men spent the first day hiking about the perimeter of the tallest mountain. Harrison had enjoyed the beautiful view of the cascading peaks, but he knew an evil lurked at their summit. While he listened to Haren's tales, filled with wicked words describing the dangerous beast, an unmistakable chill coursed through his veins. The young warrior had fought many battles, but he knew that the fight of his life stood before him.

Swinkle approached his friend as they started to climb the rocky terrain. "I sense a great evil in the area; the likes I've never felt before."

Harrison kept his gaze forward, watching Lance dart in and out of the underbrush. "It's Dracus. Only he could generate that kind of feeling in everyone."

"It's more than that." The young cleric searched for the right words. "I can sense everyone's fears, their worries. This dragon has already affected us and we have not even encountered the beast yet."

"That's how he wins most of his battles, Swinkle." The young warrior chopped at an overhanging branch. "Dracus feeds off our fears and plays them against us. If we let our worries get the better of ourselves, we'll make mistakes, we won't think straight, and that will get us all killed in the end."

Swinkle still did not feel at ease. "I'm afraid of this creature."

"So am I." The young warrior turned to face his friend. "We all are. You felt it yourself. We just can't let it get the best of us."

Swinkle nodded, understanding what his friend said, but fearful nevertheless. Just then, the two could see a commotion ahead of them. The young men quickened their pace and reached the small group of warriors.

Harrison arrived first, finding Murdock and Pondle sifting through the remains of a wayward party. "What did you find?"

Pondle stood up. "Three bodies." Pointing to an overturned cart, he continued, "And everything they had is gone."

"This is Dracus's work!" yelled one of Haren's men.

The thief stepped forward. "No, it's not." Pondle approached one of the bodies, flipped it over, and pointed at slashes that ran across the torso. "Weapons inflicted these wounds, not claws."

"Who could have done this?" asked Harrison to no one in particular.

Pondle sighed. "Scynthians."

"They're around here, too?" Harrison shook his head, dumbfounded.

Haren drove his sword into the ground and leaned on it. "The beasts have advanced against us before. We defeated them handily."

"That's beside the point. The last thing we need is to worry about fighting them while we hunt Dracus."

"Don't worry about those brutes. If they show up, we'll take care of them." Haren pulled his sword out of the ground and put it back in its sheath. "Let's move on."

The men trekked for the remainder of the day without incidence. The terrain had begun to get steeper, but ample foliage kept them hidden for the most part. Murdock and Pondle suggested a site to camp out for the night and all of the potential dragon slayers settled in for the evening.

After the men ate dinner around small campfires, Harrison sought out his brother. Troy and Teleios were enjoying a hot meal when the young warrior approached them.

Harrison took a seat next to the fighters. "I think we should get together and discuss our next steps."

Troy swallowed the last of his food, then said, "That's a good idea. We're a little more than a day away from the summit."

"We should include Gunther and Haren as well."

Troy nodded, placing his bowl to the side. "Let's get everyone together."

The three men wasted no time in gathering all of the appropriate members for the discussion, then settled around the main campfire. Harrison sat with his party members, while Troy and Teleios positioned themselves next to them. Gunther and Haren found a spot across from the warm glow of the flames.

Harrison spoke first. "We're a good day away from the mountaintop. What can we expect from here on in?"

Haren looked to Gunther before speaking. "Everything's going according to plan. Like we told you before, we'll halt our procession at the tree line."

The young warrior still felt apprehensive. "I'm a little more concerned at not seeing any signs of this beast. Shouldn't we have seen something by now?"

Haren flashed a wicked smile. "That's the beauty of Dracus. He gives you nothing to go on, then — POW! — he's flying overhead and swooping down on you." The old warrior took out a flask and unscrewed the top. "Rest assured, he knows we're coming." Haren then took a swig.

Harrison's face became red with anger. "I'm sick of hearing this! Are we just sitting ducks, waiting for this creature to surprise us?"

Haren raised his palms toward the young warrior. "Hey, calm down."

"Don't tell me to calm down! You've given us nothing to go on! Just sneak up the backside of the mountain and surprise a beast that *knows we're coming!*"

"Look, that's the plain truth. You're going to have to trust us on this one, son. We're still living and breathing, and we've been here more than once in our lives."

Harrison gave the older men an incredulous look. "And your success rate is what?" Not bothering to wait for an answer, he continued with his rant, saying, "I'll tell you — zero percent!"

Haren cocked his head and in a sarcastic tone said, "All right, Mr. High and Mighty, what do *you* suggest?"

The young warrior fidgeted, knowing he had no concrete answer. "I don't know," he said feebly.

Haren held his gaze on Harrison for a moment longer before speaking again. "That's what I thought. We'll continue as we have."

Troy let the situation subside before adding his thoughts. "I think we all share in Harrison's frustration. We all know a lethal and volatile beast is awaiting us and that thought alone is daunting. But we need to persevere and stay strong, physically and mentally." He took his gaze to his brother, hoping to calm him in the process.

Haren stared at Troy. "We'll continue as we have. We know what we're doing."

Teleios leaned over to Troy. "Let's discuss the strategy at the summit again."

"What do you want to know?" Haren asked before either man could question him.

Teleios shifted in his seat. "The legend documented in the manuscript said that the brave knight used the cliffs and overhangs to his advantage to subdue the dragon. What can you tell us of these features?"

The one-eyed warrior shrugged. "Those formations are only around the mouth of the cave."

Teleios's eyes widened. "Are there no overhangs above the crevice's opening?"

Haren shook his head. "Not anything we can stand or fight on, but underneath the lair's entrance there are some places we can hide."

"Maybe we can station men there and use them to surprise the beast," said Troy's advisor.

Haren nodded. "We've successfully attacked from those positions in the past. Ten to fifteen men can fit around that area."

"How many can enter through the crevice?"

"I'm not sure about that. We found the crack in the mountain when we retreated and didn't have time to investigate."

Troy shook his head in disbelief. "So we don't know what to expect from this plan of attack?"

"Look, this is the best form of a sneak attack." Haren let out a deep sigh. "We've never tried this before so Dracus won't be expecting it. It's our only hope."

"I might have a way to determine what the crevice is like." Gelderand fumbled for his backpack and pulled out an orange fur ball. Rufus meowed as the wizard scratched the animal on the head. "We'll send the cat into the crevice."

Haren gave Gelderand an exasperated look. "And what's the kitty going to do? Go in the cave and come back with a map of the area?"

The mage cocked his head. "Well, not quite in those terms. I'll cast a spell over Rufus that will allow me to see through his eyes."

"Then we'll know how many men we can fit in the crevice, as well as where the beast is positioned!" Haren's interest in the cat took a sudden, drastic increase.

Gelderand raised his hands. "Don't get ahead of yourself. Rufus might be too scared to give us any information."

"Then I suggest you prepare the feline for his task. We only get one shot at this."

Gelderand nodded. "Understood."

Haren sat back and smiled. "Then we continue as we have. We'll halt our trek near the tree line."

The rest of the men gazed upon each other, then nodded in agreement. Harrison stood up and said, "Let's get some sleep; we'll need it."

"Sleep tight," said Haren with a laugh. "But not too tight! And keep your weapons close by in case Dracus decides to awaken you with a sweet little kiss." Gunther joined in with laughter, too.

Harrison smirked. "I'll keep that in mind."

A full day passed with no signs of a dragon, much to Harrison's chagrin. The young warrior had privately hoped to have seen or heard the great beast, anything that would give this journey something tangible to believe in. Instead, they all had to wonder if Dracus was even in his lair.

Swinkle could sense his friend's apprehension, as did Lance, who kept close to his master's side for the latter part of their trek. "What's worrying you, Harrison?"

"Isn't it obvious?" The young warrior shook his head in agitation. "There are too many unknowns for my liking."

Swinkle nodded in agreement. "I think Dracus is in hibernation."

"Hibernation? Are you insinuating that dragons hibernate?"

"I recall reading in my literature at the monastery that certain types of dragons will sleep for long periods of time in order to conserve their energy. Maybe Dracus is one of them."

"We can only hope." Harrison peeked over at Gelderand, who was trekking ten yards behind and speaking with one of Troy's men. Motioning with his head in the mage's direction, he asked, "What do you think of Gelderand's plan?"

Harrison knew his friend's answer before the young cleric spoke. "I must admit, I am very nervous."

The young warrior glanced back at Gelderand again. "I remember the episode at Martinaeous's home, the way he got nauseated when Rufus started running around. What do you think that cat will do when it sees Dracus?"

"Run for his life," deadpanned Swinkle.

Harrison sneaked another peek behind him. "If his strategy fails, Dracus will know we're here before we can even begin to fight."

A nervous smile flashed across Swinkle's face. "I thought he already knew we were here."

The young warrior let out a little laugh. "Yeah, I forgot about that."

Twilight forced the men to end their adventuring for the day, since no one dared to light a torch so close to the summit. After an hour of setting up camp, the men settled in once again for their final evening before what they assumed would be a long day of fighting; a day where many men might perish along with their dream of slaying a brutal and evil beast.

Troy and Teleios addressed their men before joining Harrison and his friends. Before too long, Gunther and Haren strolled over, too. There would be no friendly fireside chat tonight.

"Gather your halflings. Now!" Haren's look left the men speechless.

Harrison responded first. "Why? What's going on? And, what makes you think we have halflings?"

Haren pointed to Pondle and Teleios. "They ain't like us! I could see that the minute we met." Haren directed his next comments to the two men. "Am I right in believing that you can see in the dark?"

The two halflings gave each other a look of surprise. "Yes we can," answered Pondle. "What do you have in mind?"

Haren smiled, while Gunther tightened his grip on his sword's hilt. "I think you know."

Harrison's eyes widened. "I thought we were going to attack in the day! So we could all see!"

"Plans have changed!" The scarred warrior pointed to Gelderand. "Get that pussy cat ready for battle!" The mage stood mouth agape, and with a blank expression staring in Harrison's direction.

The young warrior corralled his emotions and spoke forcefully to the two older warriors. "Now wait one second! We didn't trek all this way with an assumed battle plan, only for you two to change it at the last minute! We all want some explanations."

Haren glared at the young warrior for a long second to see if the boy would snap. Harrison never removed his stare.

"Very well. Dracus is asleep, which is something he does often, and when he slumbers, he does so for weeks on end. The time is right to make a bold move and we shouldn't waste it."

"Then why not wait until daylight? If he's asleep, what's the difference? Plus, we'll all be able to see without needing torches."

Haren raised an eyebrow in surprise. "Torches? No one's lighting up anything until we give the signal."

"You never mentioned a signal or this plan of attack for that matter!" Harrison felt his blood begin to boil.

Troy had heard enough as well. "What makes you think that you're in any way leading us? We'll give the orders around here!"

Haren gazed at the brothers, then to his friend. "Is that so? Did you hear that, Gunther? These boys don't want to listen to us."

"I say we leave'em here," said Gunther.

Troy raised his hands in protest. "Wait one second! Before anyone does anything rash, I want to hear your reasoning for these plan changes."

"I always have to spell everything out for you people." Haren took a hand and rubbed his temples. "This is how we proceed. The tree line is no more than an hour's trek from here." The old warrior pointed to the moonlight peeking through the trees. "We'll use her light to guide us humans along. Once we reach the vegetation limit, the wizard sends his cat to the crevice. The feline pokes his head around the lair and gives us a read of Dracus's cave. Follow me so far?"

Everyone nodded. "Good. We position our men, enter the lair and slay the wretched beast."

Harrison followed the man's logic until his last statement. "But you left out how we slay Dracus?"

Haren closed his eyes and shook his head. "Some answers you must find in the heat of battle. Let's get moving."

Harrison turned to his friends. "Are you all satisfied with what he said?" Murdock and Pondle nodded in affirmation, whereas Gelderand and Swinkle looked at each other and shrugged.

The young warrior took two steps toward Gelderand. "Do you feel comfortable with your task?"

The mage sighed. "I didn't come this far to turn back now. Rufus and I will be up to the challenge."

Harrison nodded, then asked Troy, "How about you?"

"My men will do what I say." Troy made a subtle look to Teleios, who gave him a nod. "This plan just might work."

The young warrior faced Haren and Gunther again. "I'm assuming your men are ready for battle."

"Have been for ten years and counting," said Haren. "Get the halflings ready. And remember, no torches."

Harrison knew there were no more decisions to make. "We can all regroup in fifteen minutes." With that, all parties went back to their respective camps and gathered their belongings.

After securing his things, Swinkle approached Harrison, who had just finished packing his knapsack. "Can this plan succeed?"

Harrison did not look up. "It has to, Swinkle." The young warrior brought a confident gaze upon his friend. "Remember the room with the minotaurs? How grave those battles were and how we felt like we'd never escape alive? This will be worse."

Swinkle stared straight ahead. "We lost Jason to those beasts," he said, his voice trailing off.

"And we'll lose men tonight," said Harrison in a hushed tone. "Pray it's not someone close to us."

The two young men convened with Murdock, Pondle, and Gelderand, who in turn met up with all the other men. Teleios and Pondle assumed the lead, followed by Haren and Gunther who served as their guides. Everyone else fell into position behind them, each one harboring a secret wish for this battle to finally begin.

CHAPTER 30

¤

Pondle and Teleios forged through the diminishing underbrush with the contingent of men following a short distance behind. Just as Haren had said, the trees thinned out quickly after about an hour's worth of hiking. Everyone started to feel the effects of the high altitude, their lungs straining due to the thinning air and steep climb.

Pondle caught Teleios's attention and pointed up ahead. "The trees end less than a hundred yards away."

Troy's advisor nodded. "I'll alert the others." Teleios retreated to inform everyone of what lay ahead. After a couple of minutes, the large group of warriors and soldiers congregated together.

Pondle took the lead. "The tree line's just ahead of us. What's our next move?"

Haren peered in Gelderand's direction. "That pussy cat ready?"

The wizard nodded. "He will be. How far to the summit?"

The old warrior gazed toward the peak, making a mental calculation. "About an eighth of a mile."

Gelderand winced. "That's too far away for Rufus. He won't know where to go."

Haren pointed his sword at the mage. "I thought you said you can see what that cat can see!"

"Yes, that's true, but I can't tell him where to go." Gelderand sighed. "He's only an animal, you know. I need to lead him in the right direction and I can only do that if we are close to the crevice."

Harrison interrupted. "Let me talk to Rufus."

The one-eyed veteran gave the young warrior a wry look. "And I suppose you think that kitty cat can understand you."

Harrison gave Haren a condescending look. "Actually, he can." The young warrior brought his gaze upon the feline. "Rufus, listen to Gelderand and he will point out where you need to go."

The cat meowed. "I understand."

The young warrior panned over to the older men. "Rufus is ready."

Gelderand nodded his approval. "Good, but we still need to be nearer to the mountaintop."

Haren shook his head, removed the flask from his belt, and took a quick swig. "Then we'll get you closer."

Gelderand gazed back at the men standing behind him. "All of us?"

The one-eyed veteran shook his head. "No, only a small team. We can assemble everyone else after we determine the layout of Dracus's lair."

Harrison spoke next. "I want all of my men with us."

"Teleios and I will join you, too," added Troy. "I can have my men positioned here and await our return."

Haren agreed with the makeup of the group thus far. "Gunther and I will also come. Our friends will stay back with your soldiers."

"Let me address my men again, then we can leave." Troy explained the new plan to his soldiers, who heeded their leader's commands. Haren's men mingled with Troy's soldiers and formed a perimeter around the waning vegetation.

With the men set, Haren gave Harrison and Troy his final instructions. "The halflings will lead us up the mountainside. How close to the crevice do we need to be?"

All eyes turned to Gelderand. "Close enough that I can point out to Rufus where I want him to go."

Haren raised his eyebrows. "Forty yards? Fifty yards?"

"I was thinking more like twenty."

"Twenty yards it is." Haren removed his sword from his sheath. "We go up the mountainside, but we must be quiet — no talking, no loud noises. If we wake up Dracus, we're all in trouble."

The two halflings led their friends to the tree line, then scanned the immediate area with cautious eyes.

Pondle could feel his counterpart's apprehension. "Something's not right here."

Teleios concurred. "I sense it, too. Let's be extra careful."

The terrain became very rocky, with large boulders jutting out of the ground. Loose rocks made up the bulk of the surface area, causing the men to slip from time to time.

After ten minutes of hiking, Pondle stopped. Peering at the summit, he pointed at a fissure in the side of the mountain. "That must be the back entrance Haren spoke about."

Teleios nodded. "I'll call him forward."

Troy's advisor went back to the other men, brought them to their forward position, then addressed Haren. "Is that the crevice?"

Haren did not have to think twice. "Yes, it is." The older warrior summoned Gelderand. "Wizard, it's your turn."

Gelderand struggled to gain adequate footing as he came to the front of the group. The mage gently placed his pack on the ground and removed Rufus from his resting place.

Before setting the cat on the ground, he said, "Why haven't we heard anything from Dracus?"

"I told you before, he's asleep." Haren's face showed his agitation. "Why doesn't anyone believe me?"

Gelderand stroked the cat's fur. "We've all been through a lot. Seeing no action from such a volatile beast is a little unsettling to say the least."

"I know what I'm talking about." Haren scowled. "Now get that cat up there and it'll prove my words."

The mage removed a small pouch from his backpack and mumbled a spell. A moment later, with his eyes transformed, he took the cat and placed him on the ground. Pointing to the crack, Gelderand said, "Rufus, enter the crevice and show us what's in there."

The cat looked at the fissure, meowed, and trotted up the incline. Jumping from boulder to boulder, the feline quickly ascended the mountain.

Gelderand felt a slight queasy sensation as Rufus approached the opening. "He's almost there."

Rufus placed his paws on flat, solid rock as he walked into the entrance. An excited expression overtook Gelderand's face. "He's inside!"

Harrison felt his heart rate quicken. "What do you see?"

The mage mimicked the cat's movements as Rufus trekked some more. "The passageway appears wide enough for one person at a time. He's going in deeper."

The young warrior hung on Gelderand's every word. "Keep telling us what you see."

The mage squinted as he focused through the cat's eyes. "It's getting dark; the passage winds to the right." Gelderand waited, allowing the cat to advance some more. Suddenly, a look of confusion flashed across the mage's face. "I see light."

"Light?" Harrison shook his head, confused. "Why would Dracus need light?"

"I don't know." Gelderand paused before speaking again. "It's getting a little brighter. I see small glowing orbs!" The mage focused a second time, this time his eyes widening. "And chests of coins and artifacts! Piles of gold, too!" All the men gazed at each other with smiles beaming on their faces.

Gelderand continued. "I see a large, padded cushion with a deep indentation." The mage waited yet again. "Now I see the opening of the cave."

Harrison started to get concerned. "Are there any other rooms?"

The mage peered deeper into the lair. "Not that I can see."

The young warrior's eyes panned the small group. "Then where's Dracus?"

A hellish roar came from just below the tree line, followed by a gigantic orange glow. Next, screams of anguish erupted from the same place.

Harrison and his friends heard the commotion and immediately turned their heads in Gunther and Haren's direction.

"What was that?" yelled Harrison, knowing all too well what created the sound.

Haren gazed at the fires sprouting all about the vegetation line. "I think you know what's happened! We're completely vulnerable up here and we must get back to the forest!"

Gelderand rose in protest, still entranced in his spell. "I can't leave without Rufus! That cat is linked to me for better or worse!"

"You're on your own now, wizard. The plan's changed," yelled Haren as another violent glow burst through the woods below.

Without hesitation, Gunther and Haren began their scramble past the group of adventurers. Harrison grabbed Haren's arm as he raced past.

"We're not through up here! Take the others down to the tree line. I'll stay with Gelderand."

Troy overheard his brother's command. "You can't stay up here alone!"

"We don't have time for this," barked his twin. "Take the others to safety!"

Troy was not about to leave his brother to fend for himself. The young general turned to his advisor and said, "Teleios, take Pondle and guide the men down the mountainside. Regroup with our soldiers and prepare a counterattack. We'll be with you soon."

Troy noticed the look of protest appearing on his lifelong friend's face. "This is not open for debate! It's an order! Now go!"

Teleios could see the intensity in Troy's eyes and did not try to change his mind. Turning to Pondle, he said, "You heard him! Let's get out of here!"

Pondle hesitated, gazing past Teleios and over to the young warrior. "Harrison, you can't do this alone!"

"Take Lance with you! Go!" The young warrior caught the stares of Swinkle and Murdock, too. "I know what I'm doing!"

Murdock shook his head. "You don't have to prove your bravery! You can't slay a dragon with just three men!"

"Don't worry about us! Regroup with the others and fend off that beast!" Harrison grabbed Gelderand's arm and forced him forward. "Follow Troy and me."

Harrison did not bother to gaze back to see the looks of anguish from his good friends. Instead, he positioned the mage between him and Troy and forged forward.

The young warrior helped the mage focus. "What do you see now?"

Gelderand shook his head, clearing his senses in the process. "Rufus is standing at the precipice of the cave, gazing out of the entrance." The mage almost commented on the surreal beauty of the sight before screams of pain and agony permeated the tense atmosphere.

Troy pushed Gelderand forward, nudging him along. "We must hurry!"

Harrison reached the crevice first. The crack was dark and he could not see inside. "I need my torch."

"No!" protested Troy. "Dracus must already know that someone would try to enter his lair."

"I didn't see any obstacles when Rufus trekked through the passageway," said Gelderand. "Feel your way inside."

The young warrior did just that, using his hands to feel the coarseness of the stone walls, guiding him through the blackness. The passage veered to the right before widening.

Harrison could see a faint light, remembering that Gelderand had said that he saw orbs in Dracus's den. Taking a few more steps forward, the young warrior entered the dragon's sacred lair.

"Unbelievable!" exclaimed the young warrior as he gazed at the abundance of riches that littered the cave. A moment later Gelderand and Troy entered the same area.

Troy approached his brother, awed at the treasures, too. "We'll have to come back for this another time, but right now we must succeed in our mission."

Harrison nodded, albeit reluctantly. "To find the cat."

"Rufus! Rufus!" said Gelderand in a hushed tone, not wanting to bring attention to them in such a dangerous place. Seconds later, he heard the familiar meowing of the orange tabby.

"Rufus!" exclaimed the mage with joy. Bending down, he scratched his little friend's head. "Now to break the spell."

Gelderand removed a pouch from his pack, took out the ingredients, then mumbled something inaudible. A moment later, the wizard's eyes reverted to their original state. "The spell's broken!"

The mage scooped the cat and placed him in the backpack, being careful to allow Rufus's head to protrude out of the top.

Harrison realized that Gelderand had finished his task with success. "Now it's time to help our friends. Troy, lead us away from here." Troy did as his brother asked and guided the men back through the crevice.

The young warrior followed the mage and a minute later, they stood at the end of the passageway. "Gelderand, what would have happened to you if Dracus had attacked Rufus?"

The magician drew a heavy sigh. "I would have felt what he felt. If he died, there was a possibility of me dying, too."

Troy interrupted the conversation. "We need to get down this mountainside. Are you ready?"

"Let's go," said Harrison.

The three men headed down the slope. In front of them, fire rose from the forest floor, spiraling into the early morning sky. Harrison gazed at the dancing flames, wondering if anyone survived the attacks. Before they could get halfway to their destination, the adventurers heard a thumping sound coming from their right.

The young warrior looked skyward to see a dark, winged silhouette flying high into the night. "Run! Dracus is getting ready to attack!"

The three men scampered down the shifting, stony ground, all the while the sound of massive flapping wings grew louder. Harrison could see the beginning of the woods, some thirty yards away. He peered over his shoulder, admitting to himself at that instant he had made a mistake to look back.

Dracus swooped down and released a cone of flames from his mouth. The intensity of the heat ignited the closest trees and singed the young warrior's exposed clothing. Harrison gazed back again, watching the immense beast rise high into the night in order to avoid impaling itself on the trees.

Knowing he had precious little time, the young warrior checked on his friends. "Are you two all right?"

Gelderand and Troy both had burn marks on their clothing, but appeared safe. Troy waived to his brother to continue onward into the forest.

Harrison took the lead, steering clear of the fires that began to rage about the area. After several steps, the young warrior stopped and gazed in horror at the charred corpses that lay on the ground before them.

"No!" said the young warrior in a hushed tone as he bent down and tried to recognize the body. The fire had burnt the unfortunate soul beyond recognition.

Harrison turned to find his brother investigating two more unfortunate souls. "These men are not my soldiers."

Gelderand bent down to look at the bodies along with Harrison. "They are not our friends, Harrison. These men are heavier than Murdock, Pondle, or Swinkle."

Harrison nodded and breathed a sigh of relief. "Where are they, then?"

Before the mage could give an answer, another hellish roar came from the heavens. The young warrior looked toward the sky and saw Dracus flying toward the forest. A moment later, the great beast rested on the ground and out of sight of the adventurers.

Troy grabbed Harrison's arm. "Keep moving forward! And keep in mind that the flames won't affect Dracus!"

The three men pushed onward, doing their best to stay away from the destructive fires. Along the way, Harrison heard a familiar sound — a very welcome, familiar sound.

"Lance!"

Harrison started to run in the direction of the barking dog. "Lance! Where are you?"

The little dog heard his master's plea and sprang through the thickets, running to Harrison's side. The young warrior dropped to one knee and greeted his furry friend.

"Lance, you're all right!" Harrison noticed burn marks on the dog's back and side. "Looks like you survived the worst of it." The young warrior stared in the direction Lance had come. Gazing intently into the dog's eyes, he said, "Where's everybody else?"

Lance looked behind him. "Big tree."

Harrison gazed in the same direction and saw an immense coniferous tree about a hundred yards away. "Lead us there!"

Lance scooted away with the men in tow. Moments later, the young warrior recognized the outline of a ranger.

"Glad to see you're alive," said Murdock. "We have a problem."

Harrison's face dropped. "What is it?"

The ranger looked over to Troy. "You've lost a lot of men."

The young general nodded, figuring that his men would have sustained heavy casualties. "Where's Teleios?"

Murdock gazed into the forest behind him. "Attending to Pondle. That advisor of yours is a brave soul."

Troy nodded with confidence. Though not many people recognized Teleios's talents, he always respected them, especially in the heat of battle. "What's the matter with your friend?"

"Burns. The dragon scorched his legs. Swinkle's prayed over him, too."

Troy glanced from side to side, seeing nothing but smoke and flames. "Let's get everyone together."

Murdock and Lance quickly escorted the men around the hulking pine, where they found Teleios, with Swinkle's assistance, caring for the thief's needs.

Harrison noticed the familiar white glow emanating from the young cleric's hands. Moving closer to the scene, he asked, "What happened?"

Swinkle finished his prayer, then moved away from Pondle. Harrison could see the burn marks on the thief's legs and his scorched clothing.

Swinkle used a hand to wipe the accumulated perspiration from his brow. "Dracus incinerated half of Troy and Haren's men even before we made it to the forest. But Teleios saved us all."

Troy's advisor dismissed the young cleric's comment and moved away from Pondle. "Your friend needs rest, but we don't have time for that."

Swinkle continued, "Dracus entered the forest and chased us down." The young cleric shook his head, worried. "The beast was so quick, we couldn't outrun him ..."

"Teleios stared down Dracus. The creature took in a deep breath, getting ready to spew flames again when he blinded the beast with a spell. Dracus averted his eyes and missed his target."

"The dragon torched the trees next to us," said Troy's advisor. "One of the larger limbs burned and fell, hitting your friend in the process. We managed to relocate him away from Dracus."

Swinkle looked over at Teleios. "Don't be so modest. You carried Pondle away, hiding him until he regained his senses. Then Dracus saw Haren's men and went after them, allowing us to escape."

Teleios closed his eyes and nodded once, accepting the praise. "Temporarily. We must keep moving."

Harrison agreed. "We heard Dracus land behind us not far from here. Thank you, Teleios, for saving my friend."

Troy's advisor nodded, taking in the young warrior's appreciation. "Like I said, we are far from through with this battle." Teleios faced Troy. "Our troops are thin, but we must find them."

The young general agreed wholeheartedly. "They must be wondering where their leader has gone." Troy addressed the rest of the men. "I suggest we maneuver together. We won't be able to kill this beast with just us. We'll need whatever's left of my soldiers as well as Haren, Gunther and their men."

Murdock shook his head in disgust. "Don't count on them. Those cowards ran away."

Troy shook his head in disbelief. "Even Gunther and Haren?"

"They didn't even bother to find their friends."

The young general grimaced. "Where are they now?"

Murdock brought his eyes to the surrounding forest. "I'm sure they're running aimlessly through the woods."

Troy's concern began to elevate. "Do you know where my soldiers are?"

Murdock shook his head. "Everything's in chaos. They're around here somewhere." The men heard a roar followed by screams a short distance away. "We need a game plan. Now!"

Troy scanned the immediate area. Aside from the fires burning around him, the darkness of the night hindered his sight too much. "Teleios, Pondle, we need you to be our eyes. Take us to where you feel my soldiers might be."

The two halflings exchanged glances, neither one sure who should take the lead before Teleios took the initiative. "We left our men near the tree line. Let's head that way and see if we can follow their tracks."

Pondle nodded in agreement. "Good idea. Murdock and I can scour the vicinity, too."

"You need rest!" The ranger glared at his friend. "Or did you forget about the scorches that mark your body?"

"I might not be a hundred percent, but I can still handle my tasks." Pondle waved his hand at his friend, dismissing his scowl. "I'll be fine."

"And don't forget, we have a horrible beast waiting to kill us." Teleios gave his counterpart a wry smile.

"Don't remind me."

The two men led the small contingent of adventurers away from the large tree and headed in the opposite direction, to where they felt the vegetation limit existed. All the men could hear Dracus's movements in the distance, getting further from their current position. After about five minutes of tense trekking, the woods appeared to thin.

Teleios pointed in front of them. "No trees left up ahead."

"We've reached the end of the line," said Pondle, looking back to the rest of his friends.

Teleios began to investigate the area around them. Pondle and Murdock did likewise, scouring the ground for tracks. What they found scared them.

Murdock bent to one knee, straining his eyes to identify the markings on the ground. "I definitely have boot tracks here. They go in all directions."

Teleios joined the ranger. Using his infravision, the halfling could make out the exact details of the print. "We equip our soldiers with boot treads like these." Teleios looked up at Troy. "Our men were here."

The young general peered over the shoulders of the trackers. "Where did they go?"

"Everywhere," Teleios said with a sigh. "They ran deeper into the woods after Dracus attacked."

Troy shook his head in dismay. "You know what we have to do, right?"

His advisor slowly nodded, a grimace appearing on his face.

Harrison had stood back, listening to the conversation, but now he too wanted to know their next move. "What do we have to do?"

"Find Dracus," said Teleios. "He's chasing our men, so it only makes sense that he knows where they are."

The young warrior let the halfling's comments sink in, knowing that his rationale was right. With Dracus chasing the soldiers through the forest, finding the elusive beast would lead them right to the other men.

Harrison gripped the hilt of his two-handed sword. "We didn't come all this way to invite Dracus to a tea party. It's time to destroy him."

Murdock and Pondle stood by the young warrior. "Count us in," said the ranger.

"My men will be more than willing to seek vengeance on this beast." Troy glanced at Teleios. "Any suggestions before we leave?"

Troy's advisor turned his gaze to Gelderand and Swinkle. "What powers do you two possess that can help us in this battle?"

"I can create fireballs that explode upon contact," said Gelderand.

Teleios shook his head. "That won't help. He's a fire-breathing dragon. Attacks using fire will only feed into his strengths."

The mage realized the incorrectness of the words he had just spoken. "How about electric bolts?"

"That might work. But what we need is something that's the exact opposite of his strengths."

"Like ice or frost?"

Teleios nodded. "Exactly."

"Fear not, I can help!" The mage smiled.

"Good." Turning to address Swinkle, Teleios said, "What about you?"

Swinkle appeared very nervous about his role. "I'm a cleric, not a magician! I can only bless our weaponry, heal our wounds, or create dancing lights and the like. I don't have anything to offer!"

Teleios put a hand on the young cleric's shoulder. In a soft, calm voice, he said, "You have more to offer than you think. You'll display your powers at the right time."

Troy intervened. "Are we ready?"

Teleios nodded.

The young general turned to his brother. "It's time, Harrison."

The young warrior looked at the sky, seeing the flames climbing higher into the night. Turning to Pondle, Teleios, and Murdock, he said, "As Marcus used to say, lead the way."

With their weapons firmly in hand, the small group of men started their trek to find the others and commence with the battle of their lifetime.

CHAPTER 31

◘

The forest burned all around the men. As they scampered through the woods, they found tracks from Troy's soldiers, as well as footprints of other men, presumably Haren and Gunther's people. Most disturbing of all, though, were the abundance of claw marks created by an enormous beast.

A loud shrill permeated the air to the left of the small group. Harrison looked in that direction, shading his eyes from the light of the flames. "Dracus is that way."

Troy agreed. "Let's move — quickly."

The men made haste in trekking deeper into the forest, steering clear of the intensity of the flames. Minutes later, they all froze.

In the distance, they saw a massive creature lunge forward, snatch a person in its jaws, then crush the poor soul with its razor-sharp teeth. Dracus allowed the body to fall from his mouth in two perfect halves.

"That monster just killed one of my men," said Troy through clenched teeth.

"We need to proceed with caution." Harrison rested a caring hand on Troy's shoulder. "Let's gather your people."

Dracus stomped forward from his position, moving further away from the group of adventurers. Swiveling his head to the right, the great beast found more targets.

Troy pointed in the direction that the dragon headed. "Look, he's chasing someone! We must go that way, too."

Pondle and Murdock led the small group away from the beast, swerving deeper into the forest in order to keep from the dragon's view.

Pondle pointed up ahead to the running figures silhouetted against the flames. "There they are!"

Ten men ran at full speed away from the advancing monster. Dracus took two gigantic steps forward and was upon the men immediately. The beast's serpent-like neck rose high into the night, then spewed fire from its mouth. Troy's men dispersed away from the flames, running in all directions in an attempt to avoid the intense heat.

Using his hands, Pondle motioned for the men to follow him. About twenty yards ahead of his position ran five soldiers.

"Hey! Stop!" yelled the thief.

The soldiers looked for the source of the command, and when they saw their leader near Pondle, they reversed their direction.

One of the armed fighters sought out Troy to apprise him of their situation. "General, thank the gods you're still alive! We all feared the worst."

Troy saw nothing but fear in the young man's eyes. "How many are still alive?"

Clearly shaken, he answered, "No more than twenty." A roar came from the woods to their left, causing the boy to jerk his head in that direction. "Sir, we must leave!"

Troy held up his hand and looked toward Harrison. "We must find them. Without all of the soldiers there's no way we can defeat Dracus."

"Sir, if I may," said the fighter. "The group of men from Dragon's Quarters is still in the woods."

The young general squinted. "I thought they retreated."

"They did, but they fell back to more familiar ground."

"Do you know where that might be?"

The young man nodded and started to leave. "Yes, follow me."

"Wait!" ordered Troy. "First, we save the men you separated from." The young general turned to Pondle. "Lead us toward the beast."

The thief gave a reluctant nod, then slowly put one foot in front of the other to start the solemn trek toward the flames. Further ahead meandered the large body of the great dragon and in front of him scurried Troy's men.

Pondle continued to lead the small group away from Dracus, all the while making headway toward the escaping soldiers. Another bellow from the imposing creature preceded a cone of flames spewing from his open jaws. A large tree came crashing to the ground, igniting the underbrush around the men.

The thief took the group away from the new obstacle, only to find four soldiers running toward him.

"Run!" yelled the closest one, a clear look of panic overtaking his face.

Without warning, Dracus pushed over a smaller tree and appeared no more than thirty yards away. The creature saw the huddled mass in front of him and raised his neck.

Harrison recognized the maneuver. "He's going to spew fire!"

Before the huge beast torched the landscape again, Harrison, Swinkle, Gelderand, Lance, and three soldiers dispersed into the woods on the right, while the rest of the contingent darted to the left. Just as they split apart, a wall of flames scorched the ground where they had just stood.

Swinkle caught up with his friend, grabbing his arm. "Harrison, what are we to do!"

The young warrior continued running, as he said, "Don't worry about that now! Just take cover!"

A crash came from behind the fleeing men. Dracus bowled over two saplings before gaining on the small group.

"Run, wretched humans!" he declared in a demonic voice that echoed throughout the woods. "You will never escape my wrath!"

Harrison did not bother to look back, knowing full well who uttered the sinister words. A little ways ahead, the forest opened a bit, before thickening again. The young warrior and his friends sprinted through the small clearing and into the denser woods. Upon reaching the condensed area, Harrison briefly stopped to look back. He saw nothing.

Harrison panned his head in every direction. "Where did he go?" asked the bewildered young warrior. Before anyone could answer, they all heard a whooshing sound coming from overhead.

Swinkle pointed skyward. "Dracus is circling above us!"

Harrison stared upward, only to see the thick limbs of the coniferous trees. What followed next terrified him. A ball of flames struck the treetops, igniting them upon contact. The heat reached the ground, forcing the men back into the open area.

Harrison understood Dracus's strategy. "He's trying to flush us out into the open!"

The young cleric reluctantly agreed. "We can't go deeper into the woods!" Fire consumed the underbrush in the thicker part of the forest, leaving the opening as the only escape route.

Gelderand came to the forefront. "Let me go first. Make a run for it after I distract Dracus."

Harrison crinkled his brow. "What are you going to do?"

The mage moved Rufus aside and removed the vital ingredients for his spell from his pack. "You'll see. Wait for my mark."

The wizard exhaled deeply to relieve his nervous tension, then headed out of the thicket. Dracus hovered about thirty feet overhead. The sheer size of the creature astounded the mage.

The menacing beast saw Gelderand and careened his neck lower. "You're next to die, old man!"

Keeping his fear in check, the wizard recited the words to a spell, then waved his hands skyward. Three large, icy white balls flew from his fingertips and hurtled toward the dragon. All three hit the creature in its underbelly, causing Dracus to screech and alter his flight path.

Harrison took his cue and led the men across the clearing, back from whence they came. Seconds later, Gelderand followed.

The young warrior could barely contain his excitement. "Nice work, Gelderand!"

The mage waved his hand, shaking his head. "There's no time for accolades. We must move on."

Harrison heeded the older man's advice, knowing Dracus would return and with a vengeance. The frightened group of men ran across familiar ground before realizing that they had no idea where their other friends had taken refuge. To make matters worse, they could hear the sound of massive flapping wings advancing in the distance.

Before all was lost, Harrison recognized a voice calling out to him in the woods. "Harrison! Over here!"

Pondle stood fifteen yards away, waving his friend over. Seconds later, all the adventurers huddled together.

"Are you all right?" asked the thief.

Harrison nodded. "We're all still alive."

Pondle gazed beyond the young warrior, thinking of his next move. "Us, too. We rejoined Troy with ten of his men, not counting the three with you."

Harrison felt a little relief. "That'll help."

The thief smiled. "We also found Haren and his men."

The young warrior's eyes widened. "How many of them are there?"

"Twenty."

Harrison, even though the hostile beast flew dangerously close by, sensed a subtle change in the battle. "Get us all together."

Pondle led the men through the burning forest, the smoky smell of scorched vegetation heavy in the air. In less than a minute, the surviving platoon of Troy's soldiers stood together.

Troy came over to greet his brother. "Good job, Harrison! Your diversion allowed us to find everyone."

Harrison noticed his friends and Troy's soldiers, but another vital group remained missing. "Where are Haren, Gunther, and their men?"

Troy motioned with his head in the hidden contingent's direction. "Hunkered down and awaiting our command."

The young warrior gave his brother a wry look. "So, they've decided to listen to us after all?"

"Brushes with death help to change people's minds." The young general grinned.

Harrison nodded in concurrence before asking, "What's the plan?"

The young general scanned the skies, knowing Dracus lurked close by. "We need to force Dracus away from the trees and push him closer to his lair. We can't fight him in the confines of this forest."

The young warrior gave his brother a look of confusion. "Wouldn't it be easier to fight him where he can't see us? We could hide behind tree trunks and hope to trap him under the large branches."

"We thought of that, but if he gets cornered he could torch the forest, leaving us with no other option but to turn and run."

Harrison nodded. "I suppose that's true." A deep roar came from above their heads. The young warrior pointed to the lightening sky. "Dracus!"

The flapping sound of the dragon's enormous wings encompassed the area. Harrison peered up at the impressive beast, this time taking detailed notice of the immense creature that hovered no more than thirty feet above them. Thick, dark red scales covered Dracus's back, while more orange-yellow ones graced his underbelly. The beast's piercing red eyes haunted Harrison the most, eerily reminiscent of those of the minotaurs he had encountered in the sacred Seven Rooms.

The young warrior watched the beast's large head rise atop of its long neck. With at least a twenty-foot wingspan maintaining Dracus's position in the air, the dragon prepared to spew flames once again. Harrison raised his blade toward the creature.

"Hold your ground!" he yelled, before turning toward Troy's men, noticing that they all had shields. "Position your armor to deflect the flames!"

"What about us?" came a frightened voice from behind the young warrior.

Harrison did not have to turn around to know who spoke. "Swinkle, you and the others take cover."

The young cleric started to back away from his friend, not sure of what Harrison had in mind. "What are you going to do?"

"Don't keep asking me that! I don't know!"

Dracus lunged forward, a cone of flames spewing from his mouth. The young warrior, along with his friends, dove from the beast's targeted area. From the corner of his eye, Harrison could see Troy's soldiers hide behind their shields, deflecting the flames in every direction away from themselves.

Just then, someone grabbed Harrison's arm. The young warrior expected to see his brother or perhaps Murdock holding onto him, but instead the sight of Troy's advisor peering down at him caused him to recoil in surprise.

"Follow me!" said the halfling, helping to lift the young warrior to his feet. Seconds later, Harrison found himself sprinting after Teleios, followed by his friends and Troy's soldiers. Lance scooted by, yapping at his master in the process.

Behind the human stampede, the forest burned with newfound fury and, above the trees, hovered the ominous beast. Harrison had no time to look around to gauge his surroundings; instead, he followed the man he believed had the best chance to create a battle plan.

The young warrior, still in full sprint, gazed past Teleios and thought he saw something move in the distance. With each step, he realized his imagination was not playing tricks on him. About thirty yards ahead rested a large fallen tree, and behind that awaited twenty men, their anxious heads peeking over the huge log, anticipating their new commands. Two haggled warriors stood up and waved them over.

"We've been waiting for you," barked Haren. With each word, he gazed with a perilous eye to the sky.

Gunther pointed over to Troy. "His men told us to take cover in the woods and await further orders. Where are they?"

Troy stepped to the forefront, knowing he had very little time for a lengthy explanation. "We must force Dracus into an open area. This forest is already a bit too toasty for my liking."

Haren nodded, then looked over to Harrison. "We need to give him a chance to use that sword in the open."

Harrison grabbed his weapon tighter. "We'll need to get that beast on the ground then."

The old warrior nodded again. "That's the hard part." The unmistakable sound of flapping wings began to draw closer.

Troy glanced back at his men. "I want all of you who have crossbows to get to a position to use them!"

At this command, Murdock stepped forward. "That's a waste of time! Dracus's hide is too thick for these arrows. He won't feel a thing."

Troy grinned. "Precisely. He'll think we're fools, unaware of our 'blunder.' Instead, we'll position Gelderand and Teleios to administer a magical attack."

Murdock smiled, understanding Troy's line of reasoning. "Brilliant! I'll lead the way! Pondle, come with us!"

The ranger and his friend took the lead, followed by the growing comrade of troops. Murdock turned to a young soldier. "Which way to the tree line and how many are coming with us?"

"Five of us have working crossbows, sir. As for the tree line, we need to head uphill."

Speaking to Troy and Harrison, Murdock said, "We're ready. I'll expect something grand from you boys!" Turning to Pondle, he said, "Let's go!"

Pondle waved the men forward and the seven fighters ran away from the others, heading to open ground. Meanwhile, the rest of the men could hear Dracus overhead.

Harrison glanced at Troy. "He's going to torch us again!"

The young general pointed to Gunther, Haren, and their men. "All of you! Follow us! Now!"

Without a moment to spare, the mixed group of thirty soldiers, fighters, a cleric and magician followed Troy just as red-hot flames penetrated the trees and struck the ground.

"Run! Run!" laughed the beast from above. "You will all meet your death before the sun rises today!"

Harrison followed his brother, noticing that the grade of the terrain made a slight pitch upward. He's heading for high ground, thought the young warrior. Though he had not known his brother for long, he admired his quick thinking under pressure. Troy led the band of men toward the tree line, but on a different path than Murdock, Pondle, and the others. If luck were with them, all would meet in the open.

More flames burst through the trees as Dracus tracked the fleeing humans. "Soon you will be mine!"

Troy waved to Teleios, who stopped in his tracks. Harrison briefly paused, only to hear his brother call, "Keep running!"

The young warrior passed Teleios, who nodded once as he ran by. But the halfling stopped Swinkle and Gelderand before they could scamper past.

Teleios grabbed Swinkle's robe. "You two! Come with me!"

Swinkle gazed back at Troy's advisor. "Where are we going?"

"We're going to drop that beast out of the sky."

Murdock and Pondle felt more at ease with each passing step, knowing that Dracus continued to follow their friends.

Pondle pointed in front of them. "Look! There's an opening in the trees!"

A minute later, the seven men stood at the vegetation line. Pondle peered out from the last tree standing before him and the rocky terrain. He took his gaze to the rocky summit, where the dark night sky began to change to a purple hue, signaling the approach of the new day. The area appeared peaceful, though chaos raged two hundred yards away from them.

"I can't see Dracus or our friends," said Pondle. "But I can hear them in the distance."

Murdock took the time to talk to Troy's men. "How proficient are you with your weapons?"

A young man addressed the ranger. "We can hit targets a hundred yards away. Shooting a creature of this size is child's play."

"My thoughts, too." Murdock squinted in the distance, seeing flames erupt in the woods. "I hope those guys know what they're doing."

Harrison dove into the underbrush. Taking his bare hands he patted down the flames that had ignited his clothing. "That was too close!"

Lance scurried to his master, whimpering.

"Take it easy, boy! Just keep close to me, all right?"

The little dog seemed to nod, which Harrison took as a yes. The young warrior could see the outskirts of the trees a short distance in front of him, as well as Haren and his men rampaging forward.

Up ahead, Troy waved his brother onward. "Keep moving! Keep moving!"

Harrison sprinted to the young general's position. "What's the game plan?"

"You'll see! Just have that sword ready!" Troy pointed forward. "We're at the end of the line. Once we expose ourselves, it'll be up to your friends."

The young warrior nodded, hoping Murdock and Pondle knew what he expected of them.

Pondle gazed at the burning forest. "There they are!"

The other men gathered around the thief and watched man after man escape the horrors of the burning woods. Then, from above the treetops, the familiar monster suddenly flew overhead.

Murdock saw the scene unfolding before them. "This is it, boys! Follow me and be ready to fire on my mark!"

The ranger ran as fast as he could, with the others in tow. Fifty yards into their mad dash, Murdock ordered the men to make an abrupt stop.

"Ready your bows!"

Troy's soldiers formed a line, dropped to one knee, and loaded their weapons. Murdock readied his long bow, while saying, "On my mark, shoot at that beast until all of your arrows are gone."

The men watched Dracus circle high above their heads, the beast preparing himself for another attack on the seemingly helpless cadre of soldiers and adventurers.

The ranger waited for the exact moment. The great dragon began his attack run, swooping down toward the men.

"Now!" yelled Murdock.

Arrow after arrow whistled through the air, striking the massive beast on all parts of its body. The projectiles lodged in Dracus's scaly hide, but none seemed to injure the beast.

Acutely aware of the pathetic attack on him, Dracus swung his head in the direction of the archers and began to maneuver toward them.

"It's our turn, Gelderand," said Teleios, upon witnessing Dracus's abrupt move away from the soldiers and its race toward Murdock's position.

"Just what did you have in mind?" asked the mage with concern.

"Anything cold in your arsenal?"

Gelderand nodded. "Well, yes, but nothing that's going to kill him!"

"I didn't ask that of you." Teleios glanced over to the flying beast. "Follow me."

Swinkle was about to ask a question when Troy's advisor interrupted his thought process. "You, too."

The three men made a quick scamper up the slight incline in order to get a better look at the monster. Dracus had almost reached Murdock and Pondle's position. Teleios could feel the apprehension of the other men, even from where he stood.

Troy's advisor pointed a few feet away from his position. "Start your attack from over there. Aim for his underside."

Gelderand heeded the other man's command and moved several feet away from Teleios. Without another moment to spare, the mage began to concentrate and waved his hands in the air. Just as before, three large ice-covered balls hurtled toward Dracus.

At the same time, Teleios retrieved an item from his backpack. Removing a velvet cloth from a metallic, stick-like object, the halfling pointed the wand in the dragon's direction.

Gelderand's projectiles struck the beast under his enormous right wing, knocking the creature off balance in midair. Before he could right himself, Dracus felt the sting of five smaller icy missiles exploding closer to the base of his neck.

Instead of turning to attack, Dracus spent the rest of his energy trying to right himself. The dragon flew higher into the sky, away from Murdock and Pondle's position.

"We got him on the run!" yelled Murdock.

Pondle agreed. "Let's regroup with Harrison and Troy."

With a wave to the soldiers standing next to him, Pondle led the men across the open area and toward the larger group of men.

Harrison and Troy, along with Haren and Gunther, emerged from the burning forest along with the rest of their fighters.

Pointing to the sky, Harrison said, "Dracus is retreating! Teleios and Gelderand must have injured him all right."

A somber expression overtook Troy's face before he could agree with his brother's assessment. "He's coming back and he won't be toying with us anymore."

Harrison turned his eyes skyward and shuddered at the sight. The infuriated creature had flown high overhead, then began his descent toward the men at a blinding rate. Flying like a falcon after its unsuspecting prey, Dracus tucked his wings back and flew like a rocket toward the men running across the open area. The twins could see that their friends had no idea what the great dragon had in store for them.

"They're sitting ducks!" exclaimed Harrison, as he started jumping and waving his hands in the air. "Murdock! Pondle!"

The young warrior's screams drew the attention of the two men, who peered over to see their friend's frantic actions.

Murdock caught sight of the young warrior first, noticing that he pointed up and behind their position. Swiveling his head back, he saw the frightening scene about to unfold around him.

"Everyone get down!"

Murdock threw himself to the ground, with Pondle and the others doing likewise. Everything that happened next felt like a blur. A whooshing sound passed the ranger, then came the backlash of wind from what felt like a missile. In one swift motion, Dracus flew by Murdock with two figures in its talons, followed immediately by a plume of flames.

The ranger rolled onto his stomach, but the blaze had ignited his pants. In no time, his flesh began to burn and searing pain radiated from both legs. Murdock did not hesitate to pat the flames down, but they had started to spread across his body, sneaking under his leather armor.

Before he could scream in pain, someone wrapped him in a blanket, which in turn smothered the small blaze. Looking up, he saw Pondle's face, blackened by the narrow escapes with the fire.

Murdock began to feel the pain sink in. "It hurts."

Pondle nodded. "Let's find Swinkle and get away from here."

The ranger attempted to stand, but just as he raised himself from the ground, he collapsed, wailing in agony. "My legs are charred! I can't stand!"

Before his friend could answer, the sound of distant, horrified screams filled the area. The wails grew louder with every passing second. Pondle looked up to see two figures freefalling from the heavens. Dracus had grabbed both of Troy's soldiers and taken them high into the early morning sky, before mercilessly dropping them from an altitude of five hundred feet.

A moment later came a deafening thud. The twisted bodies lay strewn across the ground a few yards away from Murdock and Pondle. The thief glanced over and quickly looked away. What were once living, breathing humans only moments ago, now lay on the ground as unidentifiable mangled corpses.

Pondle intensified his focus on the ranger. "Get up! We're leaving now!"

Murdock grabbed onto his friend's forearm and raised himself. In one motion, he slung his other arm around Pondle's shoulder, allowing his legs to drag behind him. Every step brought a wince to the ranger's face.

Another person helped lift Murdock onto their shoulders. One of Troy's soldiers had survived the assault, but his other friend had not lived through Dracus's breath attack.

"We'll never make it!" lamented the young man. "Dracus is coming back!"

The three men looked skyward and, sure enough, the dragon had begun his descent once again.

"Now what?" exclaimed Harrison. "We're helpless!"

Troy snapped his head in his brother's direction. "Nonsense! Gather the men into the openness."

"What? We're most vulnerable in that position!"

"Just do it!"

Harrison shook his head, but heeded his brother's command. "Everyone, full steam ahead!"

Troy, Harrison and all the other men ran toward Murdock and Pondle, while Dracus continued his second attack run. Gauging his situation with every passing second, the young general and his men closed the gap between the racing adventurers. To their dismay, Dracus would beat them to the punch.

Troy stopped and turned back to the other men. "Crouch behind your shields if you have them and raise your arms skyward! Whatever you do, hold your position and don't drop your weapon!"

Harrison could see the immense figure of the dragon getting dangerously closer. From his position, some one hundred feet away from his two friends, he yelled, "Get down!"

The three men dropped to the ground, allowing Dracus to fly past them and toward the phalanx of fighters. Those who had shields hid behind them, deflecting the flames that spewed over them. Razor sharp blades pierced the underside of the dragon, cutting the great beast and infuriating him further. Once again, Dracus's sharp talons caught two of Haren's men as he flew up into the sky.

This time, though, instead of flying high into the atmosphere, the winged beast hovered about fifty feet above the group of armed fighters.

"You pathetic fools!" taunted Dracus, as blood dripped from his fresh wounds. "You cannot defeat me!"

As if on cue, in one swift motion the evil dragon reached down with his serpentine neck and seized one of Haren's men with his mouth. The poor man screamed in terror. Dracus silenced the old warrior's shouts of horror by biting down with his muscular jaws, severing the poor soul's head with his sharp teeth. The headless corpse thudded to the ground. Likewise, the wicked beast did the same to the other pathetic soul he had abducted.

Dracus careened his head lower to the men. "Who's next?"

Two icy projectiles from Teleios's wand blindsided the dragon, sending him back. While Dracus tried to right himself, lightning bolts emanating from Gelderand's hands hurtled through the air, striking him and the great creature crashed to the earth with a resounding thud.

Troy watched the events transpire and formed his next plan of attack even before Dracus hit the ground. The young general pointed his long sword at the fallen beast. "Charge him!"

All the men roared as they ran toward the dragon. Dracus, woozy from the surprise attacks, shook his massive head in an attempt to clear his senses, but the small army had already advanced upon him.

Weapons clashed as the human fighters stabbed the unsuspecting beast. Dracus flailed as blow after blow tore his scaly skin. Summoning strength from deep within, the great beast lifted its head and snapped at the closest warrior. Dracus grabbed one of Haren's men with his muscular jaws and crushed him. Jerking his head, the lifeless body flew over the other terrified dragon slayers, landing on the ground several yards away. Dracus then roared, sending a wave of fright through to the very soul of each man.

Harrison could sense a change in the battle. Dracus had forced the men to stop their attack and now it was the beast's turn.

The young warrior grabbed Troy's arm. "Get your men out of here! We need a new plan!"

Troy gazed at the hostile creature, sensing an intense rage burning within the monster. "I think you're right."

Dracus leaned forward, then whipped his tail, sending four men flying in the opposite direction. Next, he reared back and spewed flames over the unsuspecting warriors, setting a few of them ablaze.

Troy yelled, "Everyone, retreat! Retreat!"

Harrison stood with his magical sword in hand, staring at the scene around him. Dracus had started to whip himself into a wild frenzy again. Men ran in all directions — some on fire, some hysterical — while others lay motionless on the ground.

Looking over his shoulder, the young warrior saw Murdock, Pondle, and one of Troy's soldiers fleeing from the area. He could not see Gelderand or Swinkle, and Lance was nowhere to be found. Smart dog, he thought.

A boot-shaking bellow snapped Harrison back to reality. Gazing to his left, he saw Troy out of the corner of his eye, waving him on.

"Run, Harrison! Run!"

The young warrior turned and headed toward his brother. Harrison always understood the rigors of battle, but the look he now saw on Troy's face worried him. Next, he heard a hollow thud behind him. With a quick jerk, Harrison glanced back to see Dracus prepared to strike and lunging forward with his powerful neck.

The young warrior dove to his right, hearing the snap of the massive jaws, as they caught nothing but air. Harrison picked himself up as fast as he could, and with one quick motion sliced Dracus's bottom jaw with his sword. Blood spilled from the open wound as the beast recoiled again.

Harrison tried to get his bearings straight, when he heard a voice call out to him.

"Keep using that sword!" At his side, Harrison glimpsed Troy, who had sprinted to his brother's position. "The creators made the sacred weapon to slay this beast. I'll keep Dracus at bay."

Without waiting for Harrison's response, Troy dashed past his brother and took up an attack position. The young warrior tightened his grip on the two-handed sword. Harrison briefly focused upon the three jewels built into the weapon's hilt before raising the blade to his face. The impressive weapon reflected what little light shone in the early morning sky. Another loud roar broke Harrison from his trance.

Troy stood his ground, waving his long sword at the giant beast. Five of his soldiers advanced upon the dragon in an attempt to help their leader with his daunting task. In addition, a familiar figure appeared to help his friend in his time of need.

"Teleios! Thank the gods you're still alive!" yelled Troy.

Troy's advisor drew his sword, too. "I think we've infuriated the beast, don't you?" The halfling gave his leader an uncharacteristic smile.

The young general nodded. "Indeed!"

Dracus gazed down at the eight inferior foes. "I say again, you will all be dead before the sun rises!"

"Not if I can help it!" Harrison took two steps toward the red dragon, his magical sword poised and ready to strike.

The vile beast stared at the weapon with recognition. "How dare you brandish the blade that was used to take my mother's life!"

Harrison lunged at the monster. "Meet your destiny, Dracus!" A thin frost that emitted a soft mist covered the sword as Harrison approached the dragon. The young warrior swept his blade in the direction of one of the beast's forelimbs. The cold, razor edge sliced through Dracus's scaly hide as easily as a warm knife through butter.

Dracus recoiled in obvious pain. Clenching his enormous jaws, the beast stared at Harrison with its searing red eyes. "Your death will be next!"

The great dragon used amazing quickness to flail at Harrison with his other forelimb. The young warrior dove to the ground, narrowly avoiding a fatal blow. To Harrison's surprise, he heard Dracus bellow in what sounded like pain.

From his vantage point, the young warrior peered over and watched Troy shove his blade deep into the hind leg of the dragon. Harrison could see less than a foot of steel from his brother's weapon — the remaining portion firmly entrenched inside the beast.

Infuriated, Dracus dropped his head in Troy's direction. The young general maneuvered out of the way in the knick of time, feeling the slight breeze made by Dracus's snapping jaws. Without stopping his attack, the dragon positioned himself between Troy and the other men, separating the young general from the rest of his group.

Troy, with his weapon still lodged inside the beast's leg, felt helpless. Making a quick glance around the area, he realized he had no place to hide — he was isolated from his party and completely vulnerable. With another lightning quick move, Dracus used his left clawed forelimb to strike the defenseless human and send him careening in the air. Troy hit the stony ground some thirty feet away and his blood began to spill.

Harrison, amazed at the speed of the great beast, watched in horror. "No!" he yelled, raising from the ground and preparing for another attack.

Dracus took a giant step toward the inferior lifeless body. "Another pathetic death." Before he could attack again, the evil creature felt an intense pain radiating from his right hind leg.

Teleios, witnessing his general's dire predicament, had raced to where Troy's weapon remained lodged in the creature. Grasping hold of the hilt, the halfling pulled down with all of his might, tearing a huge gash in the monster's leg. Likewise, the rest of the men began another attack against the wicked beast.

Dracus, favoring his injury, limped closer to Teleios's position. One of Troy's soldiers struck the dragon near his other leg and with a quick kick back, Dracus sent the poor soul hurtling through the air.

Peering intensely at Teleios, the infuriated beast used his inner strength to muster enough energy to snatch the meddlesome creature with his left forelimb. Teleios, surprised at the amazing quickness of the injured beast, tried to wiggle free, but the dragon tightened his grip.

"You are nothing more than another fool!" Dracus opened his jaws wide, but before he could use them against the frightened halfling, he felt a searing pain in his underbelly.

Harrison used his oversized sword to open up a slice on the preoccupied monster's side. The young warrior caught Dracus's gaze, but before he could inflict another blow, the beast spewed flames at him. Harrison dropped to the ground, his clothing igniting from the searing heat. While the young warrior rolled on the earth in an attempt to put out the flames, Dracus sprung from the ground with Teleios still in his grip.

Harrison managed to extinguish the flames, but not before burns covered his exposed skin. Taking his gaze skyward, he watched as the beast lifted from the ground and flew higher into the air.

Taking advantage of the break in the fighting, the young warrior searched for his brother. A moment later, he found him laying face down and motionless a hundred feet away. Harrison scurried over to his twin's side and knew right away that something was seriously wrong. A pool of blood flowed from Troy's underside and formed a puddle next to his body.

Harrison made a cautious approach to his brother. "Troy? Can you hear me?"

The sound of the young general's name seemed to have come from some far away place. Slowly, though, Troy began to regain his senses. "Is Dracus still alive?"

"Yes, but don't worry about that." Harrison winced in pain as he bent to one knee to better gauge his twin's situation. "You're hurt."

Troy gasped. "He sliced my stomach."

Harrison swallowed nervously. "I need to roll you over; to see the extent of your injuries."

The young warrior waited for a response from his brother, but none came. Taking actions into his own hands, Harrison placed a careful hand near Troy's midsection. After taking a moment, he raised the young general. What he saw shocked him.

"Oh, Troy. It's bad."

His brother agreed. "I know."

Harrison started to roll his sibling on his back in order to make a closer examination of the wound. Troy wailed in pain as the young warrior did his best to flip him over. With the young general finally on his back, Harrison could better see the extent of his injury. Dracus had managed to gouge Troy's midsection, making a deep slice through his belly. The blood flowed unabated.

Harrison knew he had precious little time to save his brother. The young warrior looked up and frantically searched for Swinkle. A little ways away, he could see his friend tending to Murdock's wounds.

"Swinkle!" yelled the young warrior at the top of his lungs. "Gelderand!"

Both Swinkle and Gelderand looked up and saw Harrison on his knees over Troy, waving his hands in a panic. Both men, along with Pondle and Lance, came running over.

Swinkle peered down at Troy and his eyes widened in shock. "We need to stop the bleeding first."

The young cleric hastily rummaged through his pack, searching to find bandages and other medicinal supplies. Then, he laid his hands over the young general's body and, mumbling a prayer, created a soft white glow over the wounded area. Troy's bleeding slowed considerably, almost to the point of stopping.

Swinkle let out a sigh of relief. "That should give us some more time."

Gelderand tapped the young cleric on the shoulder. Whispering, he said, "His injuries are grave. He needs bed rest and prayers."

The young cleric nodded in agreement. Turning to Harrison, he said, "We need to get him out of this environment as fast as we can. I can only pray over him so much."

"And I have only so many magical powers," added Gelderand.

"We still have a big problem." Harrison pointed skyward. "Dracus is still alive."

Troy's advisor watched as the ground drifted further and further away. Teleios felt a chill course through his body. *I must be five hundred feet above the ground!*

Dracus pulled the helpless being closer to his face. "You fought gallantly, but you are no match for me. Back to your friends!"

Teleios felt the dragon's grip relax and he slipped from the beast's hand. An overwhelming feeling of fear overtook the poor halfling as he fell from the sky. Looking for inner strength, Teleios closed his eyes and reflected upon his life. He knew his work as a soldier was impeccable and his loyalty to Troy unwavering. He had helped his leader achieve win after win on the battlefield and earned his undisputed trust. With an air of confidence, he knew deep in his soul that he had achieved everything in his life that he possibly could. After reflecting on his accomplishments, a warm feeling filled his heart. Teleios smiled and opened his eyes. He could see the sun's rays peeking over the horizon and the lush forests in the distance. The cool air felt good against his body and he made peace with himself. Then, all went black.

All the surviving men saw Teleios's body hurtle to the ground, followed by a horrendous thud. Harrison looked over in shock and knew there was no way the poor man could have survived such a long fall. Nevertheless, he raced over with the others to where the fallen fighter lay.

The men looked over the twisted body. The fall had broken Teleios's neck, besides many other bones, and his body lay in a very unnatural position. Swinkle bent to one knee and said a prayer. When he was finished, he closed the dead man's eyes.

A disbelieving voice came from behind Harrison and his friends. "What was that?" The young warrior looked back at Troy with his eyes welling with sadness.

A hollow feeling overtook the young general. Choking back tears, he said again, in a near yell, "What was that?"

Harrison came to Troy's side. "He saved you, Troy. He's a hero."

Troy clenched his teeth. "Don't tell me that was Teleios!" The young general tried to keep his composure, but a tear rolled from his eye.

"I'm sorry, Troy." Harrison hung his head. "I'm so sorry."

The young warrior felt a hand on his shoulder. Turning his head, he saw Pondle staring back at him. "This isn't over yet."

For that brief instance, Harrison had forgotten all about Dracus. Now, he could see the great dragon turning in the sky and heading for the small group of fighters.

The young warrior sprung to his feet and raised his weightless weapon. Before he made another move, he heard Swinkle's voice.

"Harrison, you need to fight Dracus from afar. You can't beat him this way."

Harrison shook his head. "Afar? How?"

"Use your ring the same way you did in the underground caverns. Remember when you defeated the tiger?"

Harrison gazed at the red piece of jewelry on his finger. Images of Meredith ran through his mind as he recalled the night that the First Lady of Concur gave him his special present.

The young warrior then recollected his encounter with the striped beast in the catacombs and how he used his ring to guide his weapon to victory. This situation seemed eerily familiar.

Harrison gripped the two-handed sword and tossed it high into the air. Waving his hand with the ruby-stoned ring, he went into deep concentration and willed it toward the oncoming beast.

Dracus flew faster toward the men, paying the incoming missile little heed. Drawing a deep breath, the great beast readied itself for yet another fire attack. As he advanced closer to the men, Dracus exhaled, sending flames toward the ground. At the same time, the sword penetrated the dragon's skin with ease and found the beast's heart.

The severely wounded dragon shrieked in pain and fell hard toward the earth. With nothing to stop his fall, Dracus dropped out of the sky like a meteor and slammed into the earth, his repercussions forcing the men to the ground likewise.

Harrison lay flat on the rocky terrain, burned, hurt, and exhausted. Peering at the wicked beast that lay mortally wounded some fifty feet away, he could see Dracus's body rise ever so slightly with each ragged breath. The menacing red eyes glared at its assailant without saying a word and with a final breath, Dracus exhaled for the last time, a gray steam coming from his nostrils.

The young warrior knew they needed to collect Dracus's blood, but before that, they had to determine who survived the battle. Harrison gingerly rose from the ground and hobbled over to Troy and the others. His brother still grieved the loss of his trusted advisor, while Swinkle and Gelderand did what they could to help those that lay injured.

Lance, sensing his master's anguish, left his safe haven away from the battlefield and made a cautious approach to Harrison. The small dog rubbed his head against the young warrior's thigh in an act of consolation.

"Am I glad you're safe, boy." Harrison patted the dog on the head. "The worse is yet to come, Lance." The young warrior gazed down at his brother.

"Help me up," said Troy.

Harrison shook his head. "No, you need to rest. You've been through too much."

Troy attempted to lift himself off the ground. "I need to see him."

The young warrior glanced at Swinkle, who assisted Harrison in hoisting Troy up. The young general winced in pain with every step he took on his way to his fallen friend. When they reached Teleios's body, Troy motioned for Swinkle and Harrison to let him go.

The young general carefully dropped to one knee and looked at the lifeless body. Swinkle and Gelderand had done their best to straighten Teleios's twisted corpse, knowing that Troy would want to pay his respects to his faithful companion.

The young general gazed at his friend's face, and holding back tears, asked, "Couldn't you have helped him?"

Swinkle shook his head. "His injuries were too severe. I'm sorry, Troy."

Troy snapped his head in Gelderand's direction. "You're a mage! You can resurrect him!"

The mage interlocked his hands and brought them under his chin, then closed his eyes and slowly shook his head.

At that point, the realization that Teleios was dead hit Troy harder than the force that had driven his friend to the ground.

"No! It's not supposed to end this way for him!" Troy paused and stared at his advisor some more. "He will be laid to rest here, at the site of his final battle. You saved my life, old friend, and you will be given a proper burial."

Swinkle approached Troy and rested a gentle hand on his shoulder. "I would be honored to perform the service."

Troy nodded without looking back. "Has anyone extracted that vile beast's blood?"

All eyes turned to Harrison. "No, we still need to do that."

"Who has the sacred candle?" The young general kept his gaze on Teleios.

Harrison motioned to the young cleric. "Swinkle has it in his backpack."

Troy turned to his brother. "Let's get that blood." While the young cleric searched for the item, Troy asked Harrison, "How many men are left?"

Harrison shook his head. "All of my friends survived, though Murdock's hurt quite badly." The young warrior glanced around the immediate area. "I don't see any of Gunther or Haren's men. I think they fled the scene."

Troy nodded, before asking, "How about my men?"

"Many died, Troy." Harrison knew two soldiers went with Pondle and he found only another five near him. "I count only seven."

Troy looked away with a vacuous stare. "Seven," he said in a somber tone.

At that time, Harrison noticed the sun peek above the horizon, casting orange rays into the dark blue sky. The young warrior then recalled Dracus's bold prophecy that they would all be dead before sunrise.

Taking some solace in proving the great dragon wrong, Harrison said, "It's been a long night. Let's finish our job and get out of this desolate place."

Those around him agreed as they went about the mundane task of determining what possessions they had left and, worse yet, finding out who would not be making the trek home.

C H A P T E R 32

Swinkle retrieved the candle from his backpack and sought out Harrison. The young cleric cradled the gold-colored item in his hands, then brought it to the young warrior. Harrison accepted the sacred gift from his friend and looked it over carefully.

"Thanks, Swinkle."

The young warrior examined the top of the candle and found a long wick protruding out of the top. Furthermore, he could pop the lid off with ease. Holding the cap in his left hand and the base in his right, he said, "I guess we fill this canister with Dracus's blood."

Swinkle agreed. "That is what the book said."

The young warrior noticed an intricate design on either side of the holder. "It looks like an image of a dragon."

"I would have to agree with you. It looks an awful lot like Dracus," said the young cleric.

Harrison glanced over to the dead beast. "There's more than enough blood in that vile creature to fill this canister."

The young warrior then called to Pondle. "Will you come with me?"

The thief nodded and joined the young warrior as they both approached the massive carcass. Harrison looked over the beast, then frowned, "How do we draw the blood?"

Pondle stepped in front of Harrison. "I know what to do." The thief removed his sword from its sheath and started to slice the neck of the dragon.

"His blood hasn't thickened yet. There'll be plenty draining out of this wound." Sure enough, once Pondle hit a main artery, Dracus's blood began to flow.

Harrison placed the base of the candleholder under the trickling stream. "Good work, Pondle."

The red liquid filled the foot-long canister five minutes later. Harrison capped the top, forcing the wick into the thick solution in the process. The young warrior held the candleholder in front of his face. The redness of the blood filled the dragon-like image, creating an uncanny resemblance to the fallen beast that lay before him.

With a heavy sigh, Harrison said, "Our job here is done." Pondle gave the warrior a wry look after hearing his last comment.

Harrison caught his friend's stare. "What is it?"

The thief pursed his lips, not sure of the appropriateness of what he wanted to say. "There's a hoard of treasure in Dracus's lair."

The young warrior pondered the situation, then shook his head. "No, we must leave this place. There are times when treasures and fortunes must be sacrificed for the good of all."

Understanding Harrison's rationale, Pondle pressed his friend nevertheless. "But we're so close."

Harrison gazed at the summit, squinting due to the rising sun. "We know it's there; we'll come back for it another time." Pondle gave a reluctant nod, knowing his friend was right.

The young warrior handed the blood-filled candleholder to Pondle and grasped the hilt of the deadly weapon that remained entrenched in the dead monster's heart.

"We could use a weapon like this in other battles."

Grasping the blade firmly by the base, Harrison pulled the sword out of the carcass. Dracus's remains turned to dust as soon as the weapon's sharp edge exited his body.

Pondle's eyes widened at the sight. "Good thing we extracted the blood from that creature before you went for the sword!"

Harrison nodded, his eyes round with surprise. "You got that right." No sooner had he finished his statement that his sword evaporated into a fine powder, too. Only the three encrusted jewels from the weapon's hilt remained, then fell to the ground, sparkling back at the young warrior.

Harrison took a long look at the ruby, emerald, and diamond that lay on the ground. The young warrior transfixed his stare on the perfect clear stone as something clicked in his brain.

"Our quest is not over." Harrison reached for the gems, but they disappeared before he could grab them. Turning to Pondle, he said, "We need to secure the diamond."

Pondle nodded, recalling what the young general had mentioned before. "Troy said he could help us with that, didn't he?"

Harrison gazed over to his brother, noticing his frail state. "We need to keep him healthy, which means we need to leave now."

Pondle drew a heavy sigh. "I agree."

The two men took their latest prize and walked over to the huddled contingent of men. Harrison looked over the crew — Swinkle, Murdock, Pondle, and Gelderand survived from his group, Troy and seven of his soldiers had cheated death as well, and one fighter from Haren and Gunther's brigade remained.

The young warrior walked past his friends and approached the unknown fighter. After looking the man over, Harrison asked, "What is your name?"

"I'm Luther Harrington." The man cast his dark eyes downward. "I want to apologize for my friends. They're not worthy to be called warriors as you and your men."

"Luther," said Harrison, "we'll need you to escort us back to Dragon's Quarters and to also help us get some medical help."

The thirty-something fighter nodded. "It's the least I can do."

Harrison gave him a look of approval, then set his sights on Troy, who remained lying on the ground. "Troy, we must get you back to the village before we search for the diamond."

Troy winced as he maneuvered to a sitting position. The young general wrapped his arms around his midsection as he spoke. "Leave the diamond to me. I have a score to settle with King Holleris, but we'll secure that jewel first."

The young warrior nodded. "We need to leave."

Troy shook his head. "After we bury Teleios and the rest of my men."

"Of course, Troy." Harrison gazed in Swinkle's direction. "Are you ready?"

During the time Harrison and Pondle collected Dracus's blood, Swinkle had gone about trying to heal as many of the injured men that he could. Troy had appeared better, but upon further examination, the young cleric determined that his wounds were far worse than expected.

Troy's soldiers had also heeded their leader's command and began to dig a grave for their slain comrades, including Teleios. Swinkle and Gelderand had wrapped the fallen halfling in whatever blankets they could gather and had laid him near the makeshift grave.

The young cleric stepped forward. "Yes. Let's all surround the gravesite."

The men created a semi-circle around the two open holes in the ground, one for Teleios and another mass grave for Troy's soldiers, while Swinkle stood before them all. Teleios's body lay next to the smaller, shallow grave. The young cleric removed a holy book from his pack and turned to a page.

"Today, these brave men fought an epic battle, one that cost them their lives. If it was not for their heroics, we would surely be dead along with them." Swinkle sprinkled holy water over the bodies. "Pious watches over you now." The young cleric approached Teleios's grave.

"To those who knew Aidan Hunter, this scene is all too familiar," started Swinkle, recalling that he had to perform a similar service for another fallen friend.

"From the stories we have heard, Teleios was more than a formidable soldier and expert advisor. He was a friend and a —"

Before another word could be said, Troy raised a hand and stepped forward. "I'm sorry, Swinkle, but I need to say something."

The young cleric closed his book and took a step back. "By all means."

Troy took a deep breath before speaking. "Many of us did not understand Teleios, thinking he was different than us. It was no secret that his heritage clashed with our beliefs, but he fought that inner battle every day of his life. Being part Scynthian will do that to you, but he did whatever he could to fit in.

"Because he wasn't accepted as easily as everyone else, Teleios trained harder, studied longer, and did whatever he could to gain our respect. And he did, tenfold. I would never consider going into combat unless I conferred with him, and his battle plans were always impeccable."

Troy glanced at each man surrounding the grave. "Teleios sacrificed himself to save me and I will never forget that. Never."

The young general looked down at his fallen friend. "Teleios, rest here at the sight of your last battle and know that your life's story will be told to generations to come. For when they speak of the day that Dracus died, all will know that you forced the beast airborne, which led to his death. You're the hero and you'll be sorely missed."

Troy appeared as if he wanted to add another thing, but instead stepped back and lowered his head.

Swinkle paused a moment, then opened his holy book again. Flipping to the appropriate page, he began to read. *"All who are forced to fight in the name of peace and diplomacy will rest with me for all eternity, for there is no better person than one who sacrifices himself for the good of others.*

"This passage sums up Teleios's journey, for now we know that Pious will watch over him, since he sacrificed himself for us. May he rest in peace."

Swinkle lowered his head, along with everyone else, in a moment of silence. Then, he took a vial of holy water and sprinkled the liquid over Teleios's body as he mumbled a prayer.

"This concludes my service."

One by one, each of Troy's soldiers approached the open graves, bent to one knee and lowered his head, then rose to leave the area. Harrison and his friends did likewise, leaving Troy and Swinkle alone at the tomb.

"Make sure he receives all the appropriate sacraments," said Troy, staring at his friend wrapped in the makeshift burial dressings.

Swinkle nodded slowly in assurance. "I will. It's time to go."

Troy agreed, then paid his last respects, hobbling away from the gravesite when finished.

Harrison greeted his brother first. "Again, I'm sorry, Troy."

The young warrior's brother accepted the condolences. "We must leave. Does anyone know the way back?"

Harrison pointed to Luther. "This is Luther Harrington, the last of Haren's men. He'll take us to Dragon's Quarters."

The young general smiled at the battered fighter. "Thank you for fighting with us."

Luther accepted Troy's gratitude. "You had asked for our help. I always keep my promises."

The young general fixed his eyes on the fighter. "And you will be remembered, Luther."

Troy's soldiers finished the daunting task of burying their fallen comrades, and Swinkle sprinkled holy water over the site one last time. After completing the final task of his religious duties, the young cleric regrouped with the rest of the men.

Harrison, seeing that everyone was accounted for, spoke. "We need to get Troy to Dragon's Quarters so that we can get him some medical help. Luther will lead the way, along with Pondle and Lance. I suggest the rest of us keep close together. Troy and Murdock can't travel like they did before due to their injuries."

Luther positioned himself at the front of the group, joined a moment later by Pondle. The rest of the men filled in behind the two leaders and the party of battered fighters began their solemn trek back to Dragon's Quarters.

C H A P T E R 33

◘

For three days, Luther led the ragtag group of men through the mountainous terrain. Along the way, Troy's health took a turn for the worse. Swinkle administered as many medicinal herbs as he could, but the young general did not respond to any treatments. Murdock's burns, on the other hand, responded well to the young cleric's repeated healing prayers and he could at least travel without further assistance.

Luther brought a hand to his forehead, shielding his eyes from the midday sun's rays. "Dragon's Quarters, dead ahead."

Pondle could see the buildings appearing out from the woods. "It's about time. We need to see a doctor immediately."

"I just happen to know one quite well," said Luther with a smile. "He's my father."

The fighter guided the group into the village, but before he could get too far, Troy barked, "We go there first!" The young general pointed to The Dead Man's Casket. "I have a score to settle."

Harrison approached his brother. "I don't think that's a good idea. We need to get you healed."

Troy gazed at the young warrior, his blue eyes glassy. "I need to do this."

With great difficulty, Troy limped to the doorway and entered the establishment. The rest of the group followed close behind. Inside, the bar buzzed with old fighters drinking and carrying on, but upon seeing the new party enter, all heads turned to the entrance.

The young general did his best to stand tall, though the slices to his midsection continued to feel like sharp knives piercing his intestines. "Has anyone seen Gunther Slue ... or Haren the Wise?"

The place became still. All activity ceased. The battle-scarred veterans held their stare on the men at the doorway before a voice came from the back.

"We are here." Two men walked through the huddled mass of standing fighters until they stood in front of Troy.

The young general took a step forward, then buckled slightly, holding his midsection. "What kind of men ... run away from a battle?" Troy's words were emphatic. "How can you call yourselves ... warriors?"

Haren gazed upon the sorry physical state of the man before him, then lowered his stare. "We never intended to leave. We thought the battle was hopelessly lost and we tried to save ourselves."

"You never ... leave a comrade during the heat of battle!" Troy coughed and swayed, trying to keep his balance. Harrison came over to prop him up.

"Troy, you need to rest," said his brother with concern.

Troy pointed to a long table. "I'll sit there, but I'm not done yet." The young general took a seat while his friends congregated behind him. Haren, Gunther, and their men took their position across from Troy and the others.

Sweat glistened on Troy's brow. Glaring at Haren, he said, "We destroyed the beast ... if that's what you're wondering."

Haren gave him a look of surprise. "Never in a million years did I think that was possible."

Troy held his stare. "You disgust me," he gasped. "You led us to a battle ... you had no intention in helping us win."

"We fought side by side with you." Haren's voice rose with each word.

"And you left us to die!" Troy coughed and he tasted his own blood. "There's only one person ... I respect from this village ... and that's Luther. He stood by our side ... and fought to the end."

Haren took his gaze to that man, who stared down the older warrior. "You did a brave thing, son." Luther maintained his gaze, but said nothing.

Troy continued. "We saved your village. In return ... we need medical assistance ... and I expect to receive it."

Haren nodded. "It's the least we can do."

"And, when we return ... we will deal with the only person I trust, Luther."

The older warrior looked at the familiar fighter again and a feeling of remorse overtook him. "I understand."

Haren stood up and unsheathed his sword, then slammed his weapon on the table in front of Troy. "You have my respect, General, and that of your men. I'm sorry we failed you."

The battered fighter turned away and returned to the crowd, leaving his weapon behind. Gunther did likewise with his sword, followed by each man who stood on the opposite side of the bench. When the last fighter lowered his blade, Troy slowly rose from the table. The young general caught Haren's eye and nodded, then turned and proceeded out of the tavern. Harrison and the others followed.

"Let's find your father," Troy said to Luther, not bothering to make eye contact.

The ragtag group passed several establishments before entering into a more residential part of the village. Off the road sat a modest home, which their new friend guided the men toward.

"Give me a second." Luther knocked once, then pushed the door open. After a moment of hushed talking, the fighter reappeared and waved the men in.

Troy entered first, followed by Harrison and the rest of the men. An older man stood next to Luther with an exasperated look on his face. "Try to make yourselves comfortable, but I only have so much room."

Harrison peered back at Troy's soldiers. "Why don't you all wait outside? We'll keep you informed about your leader's condition."

The men acknowledged the young warrior's plea and left the cramped building. After the soldiers exited, the rest of the party took a seat wherever they could find one.

Luther's father waited for the adventurers to get comfortable. "My name's Samuel Harrington. My son says that some of you are in need of medical help." The doctor looked right at Troy. "Especially you."

"Let's just say … Dracus caught me off guard." Troy winced.

Samuel came to the young general's side. "Where are your injuries?"

Troy lifted his shirt, exposing his midsection. Three deep diagonal gouges ran across his stomach.

The doctor winced, as if he were the one who had sustained the injury. "You're lucky to be alive."

"Doctor Samuel –"

"Please, just call me Sam."

Troy nodded. "All right, Sam, my friend here … is a cleric and he's prayed over me repeatedly. He saved my life."

Sam gazed over at Swinkle and gave him an appreciative nod. "Your efforts allowed your friend to make it here."

"It's what I'm trained to do."

The doctor moved closer to Troy in order to take a better look at his wounds. Mumbling softly to himself, Sam followed the trail of the claw marks, then held Troy's head in his hands, looking deep into his blue eyes.

"How long ago were you injured?"

Troy shrugged. "Three days."

The doctor nodded and felt under the base of the general's jawbones. "Your glands are swollen and you might have an infection." Sam felt Troy's forehead. "You're also flush and running a slight fever."

"I've felt weak and … have had the sweats."

Sam nodded, then left Troy to go to a cabinet off the kitchen. The doctor returned with two pouches of herbs and a small mixing bowl.

"This mixture should help your fever, but there's not much I can do for your internal injuries." Sam took the crucible and began to grind the dried leaves. After he ground them to the right consistency, he took a mug of warm water and added the mixture to the solution.

Sam handed the cup to Troy. "Drink this."

Troy accepted the container and drank the light blue elixir, making a face in the process. "It's very bitter."

The doctor smiled. "I hear that all the time." Sam's expression changed and he became very serious. "You need rest, at least a week's worth. And I'm talking bed rest. I don't want to see you moving."

"Bed rest for a week?" Troy shook his head. "We don't have … that kind of time."

Sam sighed, knowing all too well the difficulty in telling a soldier to take a break from action. "That's my recommendation. You may stay here with me and my wife so that we can care for you."

Harrison stepped forward, addressing his brother. "Troy, there's no need rushing anywhere until you get stronger. Everything else we're searching for can wait."

Troy frowned, unhappy at his brother's comment but understanding his rationale. "Fine. I'll do what the doctor says."

Sam smiled again. "My wife's at the market now, but she's accustomed to having unannounced guests. Give me some time to set up an area for you."

Harrison looked around and found no extra place for him or his friends. "Where shall we stay?"

"There's an inn a few doors down from The Dead Man's Casket."

"We're familiar with the place." The young warrior gazed at Troy. "Let me get everyone else settled in, then we'll start thinking about our next course of action."

Troy nodded in agreement. "Thank you, Harrison."

The young warrior put a caring hand on his twin's shoulder. "Do you know how many times I wish I could have helped you in the past?"

Troy smiled. "That's why … I want to keep going."

"All in due time, my brother. I'll be back later." Harrison gathered the other men and left Sam's home.

Troy settled back in his chair, allowing the medicine to race through his body. Before he knew it, the young general found himself falling into a deep sleep.

Harrison and his friends found vacancy at The Griffin's Roost and spent the remainder of the day resting and finding something good to eat. Many of the men, including Murdock, nursed their injuries and found the quaintness of the establishment a welcome change from the desolate summit of the mountaintop.

Several hours into the evening, a raucous knock on Harrison and Swinkle's hotel room door woke them and Lance from a sound sleep.

The young warrior jumped out of bed; Lance hopped to his feet. "Who is it?" asked Harrison.

"It's Luther," said the voice in the hallway. "Please, open the door!"

Harrison swung the portal open and found the man gasping for air. With a worrisome look on his face, the young warrior asked, "What's wrong, Luther?"

"It's Troy," the fighter said through ragged breaths. "He's taken a turn for the worse."

The young warrior wasted not a moment. "Let's go, Swinkle."

Swinkle tried to shake the sleep from his body. "What about the others?"

"We don't have time," said Luther. "We must go now."

The three men and little dog left the inn and raced to Samuel's house. Inside they found the doctor wringing out a rag from a bucket of water, then placing it on Troy's forehead.

Harrison stood speechless. His brother lay on a cot, shaking with chills, his clothes soaked with sweat. "Sam, what happened? He was fine a few hours ago."

The doctor shook his head and continued with his task. "His fever has taken a bad turn. I fear he has far worse internal injuries than I suspected."

The young warrior gazed in Swinkle's direction. "Can you pray for him?"

"I can, but my prayers only help open wounds, not infections. Pious might be able to save him, though."

The young cleric approached the sick warrior and mumbled a prayer over his shaking body. "His life is in Pious's hands."

Sam did not share the same thought. "He has to fight this thing himself. I can only administer so much of my solution before it has no additional effects on him."

Just then, Troy raised a quivering hand in Harrison's direction, motioning for his brother to come closer.

Harrison shook his head as he leaned near the sick man. "Save your energy, Troy."

Troy grabbed his brother's shirt near his collar. "We must … leave."

The young warrior could not believe what he heard. "Out of the question! You're too sick."

"You don't understand. Your quest," Troy swallowed, "… will end if I don't survive. The king … will only answer to me and … you'll never find the final … piece to the puzzle."

Harrison allowed Troy's words to sink in. The young warrior never thought of the ramifications of his brother dying before they secured the diamond. A somber feeling overtook him.

"Troy, Dragon's Lair is so far away." Harrison's voice trailed off to almost a whisper.

The young general mustered the strength to continue talking. "A ship … awaits me in Arcadia. We can leave … from there."

"Arcadia!" The young warrior threw an exasperated look in Swinkle's direction. Turning his attention back to Troy, he said, "You won't make it out of Dragon's Quarters in your current condition, let alone Arcadia!"

Troy swallowed. "We … have … no … other … choice." The young general then laid flat on the bed, shaking still.

Sam pulled a blanket up to Troy's shoulders, then waved Harrison and Swinkle away from the small bed.

When they were out of Troy's earshot, the doctor said, "You can't be serious about traveling to Arcadia with him. He'll never make it."

"Sam, is he going to survive?" asked Harrison.

The doctor gazed at the quivering man. "I think Dracus damaged his organs. I'm sure that beast's attack was powerful enough to kill a lesser man. Your brother is lucky to be alive this long."

The young warrior paused, then swallowed, postponing the question he did not want to ask. "How long does he have to live?"

Sam shook his head. "It's hard to say. An infection can kill him within a week, faster if he doesn't respond to any of the medicines. I'm sorry, Harrison."

"He must face his mentor," muttered Harrison.

Swinkle sighed. "He's stubborn, like you. There is no way he'll agree to spending his final days in this house."

Harrison brought his gaze back to the doctor. "Sam, will he be worse if he traveled?"

Sam drew a heavy sigh before frowning. "I'm afraid so. But your friend's right. Troy doesn't seem to be the type of man to stay put, as long as he's conscious and coherent."

The young warrior dropped his chin to his chest, knowing he had to make a decision on behalf of his brother, as well as taking into account how their quest might end.

"We leave in the morning for Arcadia. We'll need as much medicine as you can spare."

Sam nodded and said to Swinkle, "The herbs will keep. I'll show you how much to give him and how to mix them with water."

Harrison addressed Troy one more time. "We'll alert the others of our change in plans and see you back here in the morning." His brother nodded, appearing to understand.

"I'll have him ready," said Sam.

The young warrior placed a hand on the doctor's shoulder. "Thank you again, Sam."

Harrison, Lance, and Swinkle left the doctor's house with heavy hearts. Breaking the silence, Swinkle said, "We have to allow Troy to do what he must do."

The young warrior stared straight ahead. "I know we do, Swinkle, but I can't lose my brother now. I barely even know him and we have so much to learn from each other."

All Swinkle could do was nod in silence, not knowing what more he could say. The trio approached the inn, where they went back to their room to conclude a long, sleepless evening.

CHAPTER 34

ⵔ

The next morning, Harrison informed the contingent of men, which included his friends and Troy's soldiers, of their new course of action. For the troops, they appeared excited to be heading back home, though they felt genuine concern over their leader's failing health.

Pondle and Murdock, along with the seven armed men, collected the horses that the soldiers had left behind before their trek to Dracus's lair. They rounded up thirty steeds, twenty-two more than the number of men that remained alive since Troy took them on their journey from the island of Dragon's Lair.

Harrison watched as the military people gathered their belongings and readied their horses. Murdock and Pondle also loaded their steeds with their things.

"I figured you two would hike alongside the convoy," said the young warrior.

Murdock tightened the reins on his horse. "Normally I would, but my legs are killing me. I'll take the ride this time."

"I'm not too crazy about riding on top of an animal either," said Pondle. Harrison looked past his two friends and saw Gelderand and Swinkle alongside their steeds.

"I don't have any worries about you two, but them," the young warrior jerked his thumb in Gelderand and Swinkle's direction.

Murdock looked at the two men with dumbfounded expressions on their faces. "I'm sure they'll fall off their horses more than once."

The young warrior smiled at the ranger's comment, envisioning the two cloaked members of the group flailing on their steeds. "I'll go talk to them."

Harrison approached his other two friends with Lance sprinting over to greet him. "Will you two survive the trip to Arcadia?"

Gelderand shrugged. "The last time I rode a horse I was chasing after a woman of my fancy." The mage gave the young men a wry smile. "Let's just say I didn't make a good impression on her."

Swinkle appeared a bit more concerned. "I've never ridden a horse. Well, there was this time at the monastery, but that doesn't really count."

Harrison laughed. "You'll do fine, though I'm sure you'll be walking funny by the time we reach our destination."

Swinkle's blank expression turned into an anxious stare. "Why do you say that?"

Before Harrison could answer, he saw Troy next to his mount out of the corner of his eye. "I'll be back." Just as the young warrior started toward his brother, he quickly glanced back and added, "Oh, and Lance will be riding with you, too."

The young warrior came to his brother's side. "Let me help you with that." Harrison took the heavy pack from his twin and secured it to the horse. "Can you ride?"

Troy gave a weak nod. "I'll be fine."

"No, you won't." Harrison noticed Troy's pale face and frail demeanor. "I'll ride with you."

The young general shook his head. "Do you expect me to have my twin brother ride with me? The poor people of Arcadia … will think they're seeing double!" The two men shared a laugh for the first time in days. "Sure, Harrison, you can ride with me."

The young warrior smiled. "I'll get my things. Shall I alert the troops?"

Troy gazed at his soldiers for a few seconds before answering. "Even better … you'll command them on this trip."

"What?"

"I'm too weak … and you're the natural leader, the next in command so to speak. They respect you … just as they respect me."

Harrison swiveled his head from side to side, taking in the armed men, the steeds, and his group of adventurers. "But I've never commandeered a squadron!"

Troy tried to alleviate his brother's apprehension. "You've done a nice job with your friends."

Harrison peered over to his group. "We're all equal, no one leads anyone else."

"If that's what you want to believe," said Troy with a shrug. "I knew you were their leader … the moment I saw you."

Harrison had to gather his thoughts before proceeding. The young warrior never looked upon himself as the leader of the group, but upon further analysis, he did most of the communicating and planning. Maybe I am the de facto leader of the group, he thought.

"I'll lead them only to Arcadia. You'll take over once we head to Dragon's Lair."

The young general nodded. "Fair enough. Now go give them their orders."

Troy watched as Harrison approached his men, gathering them together. The young warrior explained the situation to the fighters, about how they needed to get to Arcadia as fast as possible, that he would ride with Troy, and that he would make all decisions until they embarked for Dragon's Lair. All the men obeyed Harrison's commands and everybody mounted their steeds, readying themselves for their trek to the southern metropolis.

Two soldiers positioned themselves at the front of the convoy, along with two more advanced scouts. The other three brought up the rear, protecting Harrison's group from behind.

Harrison noticed Luther and Sam helping the soldiers with their provisions. Approaching the two, he said, "Luther, might I have a word with you?"

The fighter stopped his menial tasks and moved to the young warrior's side. "Do you need anything else?"

Harrison shook his head. "No, but we cannot tend to these remaining horses." The young warrior motioned with his head to the eighteen riderless steeds. "Keep them as a token of our appreciation."

Luther's eyes widened. "We can't accept these fine animals from you! They're worth too much!"

"It's all right. We want you to have them." The young warrior bent down from his mount and motioned to Luther to come closer. With an odd expression on his face, the man obliged.

In a hushed tone, Harrison said, "Luther, we also want you to go back and reclaim Dracus's treasures from his lair. I trust you and only you. We'll be back some day and we'll seek you out."

The man's face went blank. "Dracus's lair? Treasure?"

Harrison nodded. "Quite a hoard. Bring only the most trusted men you can find, but remember, we'll be back." The young warrior waited a moment to allow his news to sink in. "And you'll be handsomely rewarded."

Luther extended his hand, a wide grin overtaking his face. "You can count on me, sir!"

"It's Harrison," said the young warrior, returning the handshake. "Thank you for all that you and your father have done for us."

Harrison gazed up to the front of the group, catching the lead soldiers' eyes. "Lead us to Arcadia!"

Troy's men saluted, then pulled the reins on their steeds. Two horses raced off ahead of the pack, while everyone else settled into riding formation. With a final nod to Luther and Sam, the long trek to Arcadia had finally commenced.

The journey to the southern city took six long days, over which Troy's health steadily deteriorated. The young general's appearance took a turn for the worse, as well. His face became pale and drawn, and he had trouble keeping down food. Swinkle and Gelderand did everything humanly possible to aid the ailing fighter, as well as administering the medicinal herbs that Sam had given them, but all their efforts had seemed to go for naught.

One of the soldiers from up ahead approached Harrison as the convoy drew near the main trail leading into the metropolis. "Sir, do you wish for us to enter the city?"

Harrison was not sure himself. "Troy, who are we looking for here?"

Troy lifted his heavy head in order to address his soldier. His voice was weak. "Take us to the docks and search for Portheus."

The soldier nodded. "Yes, sir."

Troy answered his brother's obvious question before he could ask. "Portheus is … the captain of the ship we'll be … taking to Dragon's Lair."

Harrison watched the mounted steed head toward the water. "Let's find him quickly."

The group of men traveled through the city, then to the docks by the waterfront. In the distance, Troy noticed a ship with three red flags bearing white crosses waving in the breeze.

"That's it!" He pointed in the direction of the vessel. "*VENTURE 3!*" The sight seemed to energize Troy.

Harrison strained his eyes, trying to read the wording on the ship's hull. Sure enough, the words *VENTURE 3* scrolled across the bow. One of Troy's men walked up the gangplank and a moment later returned with a rather heavy-set man.

"Sir, I have found Portheus for you," said the soldier.

The captain looked at Troy, then Harrison. Shaking his head, he questioned his judgment about finishing off that bottle of rum from the night before. "Troy? Which one are you?"

With his weary eyes, the young general watched the captain move his gaze between Harrison and himself. "Portheus, it is I, Troy."

The captain's face dropped, the poor man's words shattering his silent wish that the healthier man was his leader. "Sir, what has happened to you?"

"Many things, my good man ... but we can talk later. We must set sail immediately." Troy jerked his thumb to the person in front of him. "This is my brother, Harrison." The young warrior nodded in recognition of his name.

Once again, Portheus gazed at Harrison, then back to Troy. "We do have a lot to talk about. Come, sir, let me get you to your quarters." As the captain helped Troy off his steed, he made an important inquiry.

"Where's Teleios?"

Troy kept his head lowered; Harrison answered instead. "He died while fighting gallantly against a brutal beast. He saved Troy's life."

The captain knew how much Troy's advisor meant to him. "I'm very sorry for your loss, sir." Troy nodded in appreciation.

Portheus led the men onto the ship and directed them to their sleeping quarters, while the soldiers loaded the horses and gear. After Troy had settled into his room, the captain took Harrison aside.

"Might I have a word with you?"

The young warrior peered in his brother's room and found him resting comfortably. Satisfied that Troy was all right, Harrison nodded and said, "By all means."

Portheus closed the door to Troy's room and pointed down the narrow hallway. Entering a smaller cabin, he sat down behind a desk, then motioned to a chair. "Have a seat."

Harrison sat down. "What's the matter, captain?"

Portheus interlocked his hands and rested his elbows on the desk. "Troy looks awful. What happened?"

The young warrior sighed before starting his story, the one he knew he would have to recite over and over again. "He sustained near-fatal injuries while trying to slay a dragon. We lost a lot of men, including Teleios."

The captain drew a heavy sigh, looking away. Fixing his gaze on the young warrior, he said pointedly, "Son, he's going to die."

Deep down, Harrison knew Portheus's words were true. "Troy must remain alive in order to face the king. I think he's willed himself to live this long just so that he can make this confrontation."

Portheus nodded. "That sounds like Troy. I've known him since he was a small boy and he's always shown such great resilience." The captain gazed deeper into Harrison's soul. "Where do you fit in this picture? I don't recall Troy having a brother, let alone a twin."

The young warrior nodded, realizing that this also was another story he needed to keep straight. "We must have been separated at birth. The only one who knows for sure is the king, and that's why Troy wishes to stay alive, so he can find out the answers of his existence."

"Then we'll get to the island in double time." Portheus stared at Harrison again. "I still take orders from him."

Harrison lifted his palms toward the captain. "I understand. I need to go check on Troy now."

"And I need to get this ship moving." Portheus rose from his desk and left the cabin, while Harrison went back to his brother's room.

The young warrior knocked and entered the cabin, finding his twin lying on his bed. "Troy, are you awake?"

Harrison's twin pulled himself to a sitting position. "Yes. I was just resting."

Troy's brother found a chair in the corner of the cabin and moved it near the bed before taking a seat. "What's going to happen when we get to the island?"

Troy hung his head for a moment in an effort to gather his thoughts. "I must see the king first ... to let him know I've returned with his prize. Then he'll want," Troy coughed, "... to see you and your men."

Harrison did not understand his brother's rationale. "Why will he want to see us?"

Troy gazed at his likeness. "The king feels the people," the young general paused, "... responsible for uncovering the book must be ... formidable warriors, because only the best fighters ... could handle the rigors of obtaining the scripture."

Harrison huffed. "He's right about that."

"But we must secure the diamond from ... him before anything else. And if he sees you, he'll," Troy winced, "... know something's up."

"You're right. Will you be able to get the jewel without him becoming suspicious?"

Troy smiled and nodded slowly. "I've known the king ... a long time; he's like a father to me. He'd never," the young general gasped, "... expect a turn of events like this."

Harrison shook his head. "You make it sound so simple."

"Trust me, Harrison. He'll," Troy paused, "... cave as soon as he sees you." Troy fidgeted a bit, then lay back down. "I need to ... save my energy."

The young warrior took a blanket from the bottom of Troy's bed and pulled it over his brother. "Portheus is getting the ship ready to depart. We'll be leaving the mainland in a little while." Troy had already fallen asleep and did not hear his brother's last words.

"Sleep, my brother." Harrison quietly left the room and prepared himself for their departure.

A shroud of mist covered the island of Dragon's Lair. Portheus guided his ship to the dock where his sailors secured the anchor and handled the moorings. With the boat tethered to the pier, the ship's captain went to notify Troy that they could disembark.

Harrison had informed his friends about Troy's plan the minute after he left his brother's cabin, a day and a half ago. Though some might have had reservations, everyone trusted Troy and his relationship with the king.

The young general's soldiers gathered the horses and readied them for their trek up the hillside. Wind and a cold rain lashed at the men as they mounted their steeds. Harrison, once again, rode with Troy.

Troy spoke over the sound of the lashing winds. "Once we get to the castle, I'll," the young general coughed, "… have my men bind you and your men's hands."

Harrison shouted into the gale. "As long as the bindings are loose enough to free ourselves at the right time."

"Remember, follow my lead and … everything will fall into place." Troy coughed. "I've been … waiting for this meeting ever since we … spoke that first night."

Harrison felt genuine concern for his twin. "I hope you find what you're looking for."

The young general did not respond to his brother's comment, though he had searched his soul for that very answer. After a moment of private thought, Troy added, "The king can be tricky. We still … must be very careful."

Harrison also asked a question that he had mulled over many times the past several days. "What do you think the king'll do when he sees me?"

Troy did not hold back. "He'll be … shocked and try to discredit you. You'll hear," the young general winced, "… some bad things."

The young warrior encouraged his horse to go forward. "Don't worry, I'm ready, just like you."

The convoy trekked up the rocky terrain, the massive castle looming just ahead of them. As the group approached the gates, two of Troy's soldiers went up ahead to speak with their fellow guardsmen. The large double doors slowly creaked open, allowing the men to enter into the guarded compound. A single sentry rode up the pathway, taking his newfound secret with him.

Harrison watched the sequence of events transpire. Unsure what to do next, he asked, "What's happening?"

Troy spoke in a near whisper. "Part of the plan." Turning as best he could to face his brother, he continued, "It's time to secure your bindings."

Harrison nodded and dismounted, then motioned for his friends to do the same. Murdock and Pondle approached Harrison first, with Gelderand, Swinkle, and Lance following close behind.

The ranger held his hands out to one of the soldiers. Looking in Harrison's direction, he said, "Your brother's plan had better work."

A soldier ran a rope around the young warrior's wrists. "I have faith in Troy," said Harrison.

"What do we do with him?" The soldier pointed to Lance.

"He'll walk behind us." Harrison gazed down at his canine companion. "Follow us, boy, and don't stray." Lance yapped in affirmation.

Troy, hunched a bit and paler than anyone had ever seen before, approached his bound friends. "I'll escort you … inside the castle. Follow me and do," the young general winced, "… as I say."

After Troy led the prisoners into the foyer of the main wing of the castle, the general waved two guards over. "Where's the king?"

The young man snapped to attention. "He's in his chambers, sir. The king is awaiting you."

Troy nodded. "You two come with me." Turning to face the others, he said, "Harrison, I'll call for … my soldiers to bring you up to the king's quarters. They'll also free … you from your bonds."

Harrison nodded. "We understand."

The young general had one more command. "Before I go, I'll need," Troy paused, "… the book."

Harrison motioned to Swinkle, who rummaged through his backpack before finding the sacred manuscript, then handed it to his friend.

Relaying the scripture to his twin, the young warrior said, "Be careful with this."

"Don't worry." Troy stashed the book in his belt, before turning to face his brother a final time. "Wish me luck."

Harrison added a final important thought. "Don't forget about the diamond."

Troy smiled. "All part of the plan, brother."

The young general then turned and headed for a spiral staircase. As he reached the stairs, Troy stopped and took a long look upward. Understanding that the time had come to face his past, he took a deep breath, then started his ascent.

Hobbling as he climbed, Troy reflected on the many years he had served the king. How he raided villages to secure artifacts and treasures, how he bullied lesser people, forcing them to hand over their trinkets, and all for what? To restore an empire to a greedy king who lost everything a thousand years ago? And now, knowing that the king sent his army to abduct him as an infant, then robbed him of his memories of his parents and childhood was too much to bear. All of that servitude would end today.

Troy reached the top of the staircase and took a moment to gaze at the double doors that served as the entrance to the king's royal bedroom. Taking another deep breath, he walked over to the doorway.

The young general did his best to stand straight, knocked, then said, "My king, I have returned with your sacred prize!"

Troy heard shuffling from behind the doors. A muffled voice gave permission, "Enter!"

The young general pushed the doors open, sending them into the room. King Holleris stood before him, dressed in black attire, a look of sheer joy on his face.

"Troy!" The king took a step towards his general-at-arms. "You've returned and so much sooner than I ever expected!"

Troy limped into the room. "The journey was a success, but we ... suffered greatly, my Lord."

The king noticed his general's injured state. "What happened to you?" King Holleris motioned toward a plush-cushioned chair. "Please sit down and tell me all about it."

"I'd rather stand, sir." Bent slightly at his midsection, Troy said, "Our journey took us to all corners … of the land and I'm afraid to say that we ran into some rather … ornery adversaries."

King Holleris showed genuine concern. "Like what? Who could have hurt such as seasoned warrior as yourself?"

The young general flashed a wry smile. "A dragon named Dracus for starters."

A look of shock flashed across the king's face. "A dragon? Did anyone else get injured?"

"Teleios perished in the battle, as did twenty-three of my faithful soldiers." Sadness overtook Troy.

The king took a few steps toward the young general. "That's awful news, Troy. I know how close you and Teleios were. I know there's nothing that I can do to bring him back, but understand that I'm very sorry to hear about this."

Troy heard the older man's kind words and for a second they comforted him, reminding him of times when the king would calm him as a child.

"Thank you, sir." Troy pushed the unsuspecting man's comments out of his mind. Reaching for the article on his belt, the young general pulled the book from its resting place.

"Here's the book … you sent us to recover."

The king's eyes widened upon seeing the scripture. "Are you sure this is the right book?"

Troy removed a knife from his belt and cut into the book's cover. A trail of red blood flowed from the fresh slice.

King Holleris flashed his general a wide, child-like grin. "Good work, Troy! Good work!" The king held out his hand. "Might I see the manuscript?" The young general handed the book to his one-time mentor.

The king took the manuscript into his hands and felt its leathery cover. Then, he leafed through the pages, shaking his head. "I can't believe I've found this scripture at last."

Troy knew the time was right to ask about the final piece to the puzzle. "The men who found," the young general winced, "… this book also had partaken on a quest to find … some elaborate prize. They said they needed … one last piece, a diamond." Troy coughed. "… I believe, and they said you possess it. Is this true?"

King Holleris smiled. "It's true, all right. The jewel sits downstairs in the display case of my royal chamber."

Satisfied with the king's answer, Troy knew the time had come to commence with his plan. Nodding in recognition to the king's last statement, he said, "Would you like to meet," the young general gasped, "… the people who uncovered the sacred artifact?"

"Yes! Bring them to me."

The young general took a few steps toward the entranceway, then called down to his soldiers below. "Escort the adventurers to … the king's room."

King Holleris turned away from Troy, too busy with his new toy to pay his general much attention. Troy, on the other hand, stared at the king from behind, a whirlwind of emotions coursing through his body.

A moment later, a soldier appeared in the doorway and upon seeing his leader, nodded once. Troy nodded back, signaling that the time had come to reveal the party to the king.

"My Lord, might I present … to you the finders of the scripture." King Holleris turned around and faced the entrance.

A ranger hobbled in, his halfling friend helping him. "This is Murdock and Pondle." The king nodded in acknowledgement.

Next, two robed men and a dog entered the room. "And this is," Troy coughed, "… Swinkle, Gelderand, and Lance." King Holleris gave a slight look of surprise at the group escorted before him, not quite sure how such a weak set of characters could find such an elusive prize.

A fierce look of determination flashed across Troy's face as he took a deep breath and announced, "And last, Harrison … Cross."

The young warrior entered the room. The king stared at the armor-clad warrior for a moment before the expression on his face dropped. The rest of Troy's soldiers fanned into the room, blocking the doorway.

Gazing at Troy with a look of shock, the king said to his general, "What's the meaning of this? Is this some kind of illusion?"

Troy faced the king while Harrison and his friends watched. "Harrison's my … twin brother; we confirmed it. I think the question I have," Troy winced, "… of you is, why did you do this to me?"

The king alternated his open-mouthed stare between Troy and Harrison. "This must be some kind of trick! What are you up to, Troy?"

The young general slowly shook his head from side to side. "I have no … agenda, but I do want to know the truth. I've," Troy gasped for air, "… spoken to Harrison at length of a great many things, but now I need to hear … an explanation from you."

A look of anger replaced the king's shocked expression. "I've raised you to be the greatest soldier this land has ever seen! I've given you an army to command and sent you on missions to make you famous."

Troy thrust a finger toward the king. "At what expense? You stole me from my family! You robbed me of my childhood!"

The king spoke through clenched teeth. "I made you the ultimate warrior, did I not?"

The young general did not back down. "Why was I taken?"

King Holleris saw the look of conviction in Troy's eye. Though the king knew that he could argue with Troy for hours on how he made his life better than that of an ordinary peasant, he also knew all conversation would be fruitless with

Harrison standing behind Troy. Instead, the king let out a heavy sigh.

"What is it you want to know?"

Troy's expression changed from anger to one filled with sadness. "Why me?"

King Holleris dropped his chin to his chest, knowing he needed to give his loyal subject an explanation. "I suppose I've always suspected that you'd find out about your past some day." The king, still holding the leather-bound book in his hands, started his tale.

"For a thousand years, a member of the Harkin family served as my general-at-arms. The Harkin lineage produced an uncanny amount of great warriors, you included, and I trusted each and every one of them. But over the course of a millennium, many times a gap occurred between male and female children."

Troy squinted. "A gap? What do you … mean by a gap?"

"I only wanted a male warrior. I had neither a need nor patience to train a girl, and several times during the course of my history, the only offspring born to a Harkin warrior was a female. On some occasions, no child was born at all. At those times, I had to scour the mainland to find a suitable heir to the Harkin lineage."

The king's last statement struck a nerve with Troy. "Please, explain to me how," the young general coughed, "… you went about *finding* a suitable heir."

The king knew he was treading in dangerous waters. "I sent my general-at-arms to select the strongest and healthiest of infant boys and had them brought back to Dragon's Lair for training."

"You *stole* innocent children?"

"No, well, not exactly," started King Holleris in an obvious attempt to backpedal on his previous statement. "I gave firm instructions to bargain for these children, and after six months, I selected only one. I sent the boys who did not adhere to my strict standards back to their parents."

"You're telling me that my —" Troy looked back at Harrison, then turned to face the king again. "Our parents … gave me to your men?"

The king fidgeted. "Not in your case."

"Explain yourself." Troy could feel his blood start to boil.

"The soldiers took you from your parents against their will. We had no idea that you had a brother or we would have taken him, too."

Troy shook his head. "Why? Why would you do that?"

"Look around you, Troy!" The king spread his arms wide as he gazed about the chamber. "I gave you a better life than your parents could have. Even ask your brother." King Holleris pointed to Harrison. "Tell him! Did your parents give you even a fraction of what I've given to Troy?"

Harrison hesitated, but before he could speak, his brother raised a hand in his direction. "Don't answer him, Harrison!" Troy pointed a shaking finger at the king.

"You didn't have the right … to take me or any child away from his parents! You're an … evil man!"

"Troy, don't be a fool." King Holleris glared at his general. "You command a superior army, have all the weapons and riches at your disposal, and never have to worry about the trivialities of life."

"And never will … have a memory of my loving parents." Troy coughed, bending over the stabbing sensation in his abdomen. "The pain you must have … put them through."

The king did not like the way the conversation headed. Using a calmer tone to convey his message, he said, "Troy, what's done is done; neither of us can go back and change the past. But, you and your brother can join me and together we can rule over the land – forever!"

Troy gazed back at Harrison again. The young warrior stared back and shook his head. The king's general then removed his sword from its sheath.

King Holleris saw the blade and took a step back. In a fatherly tone, he scolded, "Troy, put that weapon away before you do something you'll regret!"

Troy took a step toward the royal man. "You should have thought about that before you kidnapped me!" Taking two quick steps toward his mentor, Troy raised his blade and slashed at the older man's neck, severing his head in the process. King Holleris's body slumped to the floor and his head rolled a few feet away.

The king's face appeared expressionless for a moment before his eyes inexplicably opened. "Troy! What have you done?"

Everyone stared in disbelief at the bloody severed head. Troy dropped to one knee and let go of his blade, the weapon clattering on the stone floor.

Harrison rushed to his brother's side. "Are you all right?"

"Yes." Troy looked over to his former leader. "You will remain … immortal on your precious little … island, my Lord."

The king's eyes flitted back and forth in panic. "You can't leave me here like this!"

Troy paid no attention to the wailing head and instead turned to face his brother. "Let's gather the book and leave." The young general approached the headless corpse, took the scripture out of its right hand, and said, "Let's go and get that diamond."

Harrison took hold of his brother's arm, staring into his eyes. "Are you sure?"

"It's time for me to," the young general winced again, "… leave this place." Troy gazed down at the king. "Forever." The young general picked up his sword, sheathed it, then coughed and buckled again.

Harrison helped stand him up and without saying a word escorted Troy to the entranceway with the young warrior's friends following.

After everyone exited the chamber, the king's voice bellowed again. "Troy! You can't do this!"

Troy turned and stared at the head lying harmlessly on the stone flooring. "I can and I did."

The young general grabbed the knobs on the double doors and, as he slammed them shut, an eerie "Noooo!" echoed throughout the royal chamber.

Facing his brother, Troy started to say something when he collapsed. Harrison ran to his side.

"Troy! Troy! Can you hear me?"

Harrison's twin gazed up from his brother's arms. "I need rest, but not until we find the jewel."

"No, you'll rest now." The young warrior looked over to another of his friends. "Swinkle, what can you do for him?"

Before the young cleric could speak, Troy interrupted. "Harrison, I want," the young general swallowed, "… to leave this island for good, and the sooner … the better. I know where the diamond is. Let's get … it now."

Though Harrison knew the best thing for his brother was to rest, he also understood how badly Troy wanted this day to end. Nodding, he said, "I'm going to help you up, then you're going to show us where the gem resides. Understood?"

Troy did not answer; instead, he attempted to get to his feet. Harrison, still holding him, guided his brother to a standing position. "We need to go downstairs," said Troy. "The king's royal display chamber … is on the first floor."

The soldiers descended the stairs first, with Harrison, Troy, and the others following. Taking a right at the base of the staircase, the group proceeded down a corridor before halting in front of another set of wooden double doors.

"The king's royal showroom," said Troy. One of Troy's soldiers opened the doors, revealing a chamber of riches.

Harrison gazed in astonishment at the trove of treasures. "Look at this place."

"The king commanded my … ancestors and me to go to the mainland," Troy paused, "… and bring back everything

… you see here." Troy pointed at the fine tapestries, jewelry, weapons, armor, and assorted artifacts. "Every item in this room … belongs to someone else."

Harrison rested a sympathetic hand on his brother's shoulder. "Don't blame yourself, Troy. The king brainwashed you, and you only obeyed his wishes."

Troy shook his head. "I still should have … known better." The young general started to walk across the room, over to a large glass case at the opposite side of the chamber. "The diamond's over here."

Harrison peered at the showcase in awe. "Are all those jewels real?"

"Every single one of them." Troy pointed to a perfectly cut diamond at the top of the case. "There's what you're … looking for."

The young warrior gazed at the brilliant stone. "Let's take it."

Troy faced his brother. "We're taking everything."

Harrison gave his brother a look of astonishment. "What?"

"Everything this castle offers is ours now. The king's reign of terror … is over."

Harrison thought about what his brother said. "I thought you wanted to leave this island immediately?"

"I do. I'll have my men load the ships." Troy looked at the diamond. "Take it."

Harrison opened the glass cabinet, reached up, and grabbed the jewel. Turning to Swinkle, he said, "Secure this with the other stones we have."

The young cleric took the gem and gently placed it in a sack with the ruby and emerald. "Harrison, this is the last piece to the Talisman of Unification. Should we take a look at the book and see what we do next?"

At that moment, Troy coughed, his knees giving way in the process. Several drops of blood splattered to the floor. Troy gazed up at his twin with sullen eyes. "Harrison, I don't want to die on this island."

"Don't talk like that, Troy!" Turning to his friends, the young warrior said, "We'll leave this island knowing that we succeeded on our quest. But now we have to heed Troy's wishes."

Troy motioned to one of his soldiers. "Tell Portheus ... to ready the ship for an immediate return back to the mainland. Also, inform him ... that we'll need several cargo ships ... to transport all the riches from this island."

The young general pointed to another of his men. "You, gather the army ... and meet us down on the dock." The two soldiers nodded and commenced with their orders.

"Harrison, it's time to ... get to the boat."

The young warrior assisted his brother in getting to the castle exit, while their friends followed. Three of Troy's soldiers gathered five steeds to bring the men back down to the dock.

Harrison again rode with his brother and noticed Troy's deteriorating condition. The young warrior feared that his twin's last outburst with the king might be the final act of his life. Troy's body slumped in Harrison's arms as the wind whipped through the convoy. The young warrior could still feel his brother's shallow breathing, telling him that Troy was still alive – for now.

The men reached the pier fifteen minutes later, and one of Troy's soldiers rushed up the gangplank. After a moment passed, Portheus followed the fighter back down the walkway and greeted the party.

"Let's get Troy to his quarters immediately." Portheus took the young general's body from Harrison's arms and carried him onto the ship. Harrison and his friends followed close behind.

The young warrior watched as the big man took his brother to the cabin and laid him on the bed.

Swinkle could see the concern in Harrison's eyes. "There comes a day when all great men must die, Harrison."

Harrison's eyes welled with tears. "Just not today, Swinkle. There's so much more I need to know about him."

The young cleric nodded in understanding. "You have learned more than you think."

Harrison gazed at his friend. "I'm not ready to let him go just yet."

Portheus emerged from the room. Looking at the young warrior, he said, "He's asking for you. I'm going to get this boat moving."

The captain left to commandeer the vessel, leaving Harrison an open alley to the quarters. The young warrior stepped inside and gazed at his brother, who lay on the bed with a blanket up to his neck, appearing just as he had on their journey to Dragon's Lair.

Harrison approached the bed and knelt by his brother's side. The young warrior tried to read his twin's face, to see if he felt too much pain to continue.

"Troy, I'm here."

The young general opened his eyes, locking his gaze on Harrison. "I've settled … my score."

Harrison nodded and gave Troy a caring smile. "That you have, but now you need rest."

Troy closed his eyes and swallowed. "I'm thirsty."

Harrison looked around the room, noticing a pitcher of water on a table. The young warrior filled a goblet with the refreshing liquid and gave it to his brother.

The young general took a couple of sips. "Thank you."

Harrison placed the mug back on the table. "The captain's getting the ship ready to disembark. We'll be back in Arcadia before you know it."

Troy turned his head to look directly at his brother. "Did you collect … all the pieces to the puzzle you …" He swallowed. "… set out to find?"

Harrison nodded. "The diamond was the last item."

"Good." Troy turned his head and gazed upward. "My soldiers … will listen to you. I want … you to take control of all …" Troy coughed. "… the riches that come on the next ships. Bring … them back to their rightful … owners."

The young warrior furrowed his brow. "Troy, you're sounding like a man making his last wishes."

Troy gazed at Harrison again. "Look at me, brother. My time draws near."

Harrison took a closer look at Troy. He knew that his brother's body was broken beyond repair, his face drawn and pale. Swinkle and Gelderand had done all that they could to help the young general, and Sam's medicinal herbs were only helping so much.

"I need to learn more from you, Troy."

Harrison's twin smiled. "You've learned so ... much already. You'll make a great ..." Troy swallowed. "... general and leader, as long ... as you stay on the course of goodness."

"But I want you by my side."

"I wish for ... that, too." Troy paused. "Make our parents ... proud, Harrison."

The young warrior felt a lump form in his throat. "Mother and Father would have been so proud of you."

Troy closed his eyes again, dreaming of what their parents might have looked like. "Of both of us."

Harrison felt the ship rock and veer away from the dock. "We're leaving the island, Troy. I'm sure we can get more help for you in Arcadia."

Troy smiled. "As long as I don't ... die on Dragon's Lair."

Harrison placed a hand on his brother's shoulder. "You need rest now. I'll check on you later."

Troy nodded and closed his eyes. Harrison waited another moment, then left the cabin. His friends waited for him in the corridor, hoping for some encouraging news.

Harrison approached the small group. "He's still alive."

Swinkle took a step toward the young warrior. "How are you?"

"I'll be fine." Harrison gave a nod toward another room. "Let's go in there."

The group entered the small cabin, with Gelderand, Murdock, and Pondle taking a seat around a small table.

Lance and Rufus huddled in a corner of the room in an effort to stay warm.

Harrison spoke first. "Swinkle, what do you make of Troy's situation?"

The young cleric gave Harrison a hard look. "I can't say that Troy will be all right, but I will pray for him."

"Thank you, Swinkle." Changing the subject, Harrison asked, "What do you make of our predicament?"

The young cleric let out a deep sigh. "A great honor has been bestowed on us. We already possess the Treasure of the Land and we have uncovered the pieces to the Talisman of Unification, completing this mission. Now, Troy has given us so many more riches and an army to go with it."

Harrison nodded, taking in his friend's comments. Sitting tall in his chair, he proclaimed, "We'll sail to Arcadia and find someone who can tend to Troy. From there we'll journey to Tigris." The young warrior caught Gelderand's eye, both acknowledging that they wanted to see Tara once again.

"Once we reach Tigris, we'll assemble the pieces of the Talisman and figure out how it's supposed to work. And after that's done, we'll recover the Treasure of the Land, trek back to Arcadia and pick up Troy, then sail everything to Aegeus where we'll inform the elders of the riches we have found."

Harrison took his gaze to each of his friends who all nodded in concurrence to their new leader's plan.

The young warrior smiled. "Great things are coming our way. I can feel it."

The rest of the men smiled back, sensing the truth in Harrison's comments. With their goal of finding the Talisman of Unification finally behind them, the men took advantage of their time at sea to rest, as the great ship sailed to the awaiting port of Arcadia.

Made in the
USA
Middletown, DE